Maze of Worlds

Brian Lumley
MAZE of WORLDS

TOR®

A Tom Doherty Associates Book

NEW YORK

MAZE OF WORLDS

Copyright © 1998 by Brian Lumley

A Tor Book
Published by Tom Doherty Associates, Inc.
175 Fifth Avenue
New York, NY 10010

Tor Books on the World Wide Web:
http://www.tor.com

Tor® is a registered trademark of Tom Doherty Associates, Inc.

Design by Ann Gold

Library of Congress Cataloging-in-Publication Data
Lumley, Brian.
    Maze of worlds / Brian Lumley. — 1st ed.
        p.   cm.
    "A Tom Doherty Associates book."
    ISBN 0-312-86604-6
    I. Title
PR6062.U45M38 1998
823'.914—dc21   98-11451
                                                               CIP

First Edition: June 1998

Printed in the United States of America

0 9 8 7 6 5 4 3 2 1

This one is for
Keith Grant, Don Craine,
and The Downliners Sect—
"Punks From the Vaults," yeah!

CHAPTER
I

IN SHANTUNG PROVINCE, Ki-no Sung yawned, rolled up his reed bed, and took down from the bamboo walls two big bundles of nets. He carried the first armful out into the dawn light flooding from the east across Hwang Hai, the Yellow Sea, and looked down upon the narrow strip of beach separating the jungle from the ocean. As he put the netting down on the boards of his porch, he could see his small boat lolling there as upon the rim of a vast millpond, calm in the gathering light, with barely a ripple to rock it. Except for when the storms came, it was always like this, a scene that never changed.

Moving quietly so as not to disturb his heavily pregnant wife who was still asleep in a small room of her own, Sung went back inside, put on a wide-brimmed hat, took up the second bundle of nets, and carried it outside—and promptly dropped it!

Down the beach, his small boat seemed to have disappeared, to have been swallowed up. And in its place . . . Ki-no Sung saw a resplendent pagoda! Its uppermost tiers rearing high out of the water, the structure must have been all of a hundred feet tall.

Impossible! He rubbed at his slanted, sleep-filled eyes and looked again. But it was still there. It was real. A wondrous pagoda inlaid with scintillant jade or onyx or both, and the waves of disturbed ocean rolling back against it and foaming ivory-white, as if this—this what, this temple?—had suddenly emerged from the deeps, been thrust up by some earthquake to part the waters. Except the fisherman Ki-no Sung knew that there were no secret deeps here; the waters were shallow and muddy, and this incredible pagoda was clean as if freshly built or sculpted—but by what strange instantaneous builder or sculptor? Because for all that this unbelievable structure was huge, it had neither windows nor doors . . .

Stunned, for long seconds Ki-no Sung stood trembling, his eyes taking in what his brain could scarcely accept. But the wash of newborn waves was in his ears, and the sun's first rays glanced slantingly, blindingly from the pagoda's scrollwork and exotically carven inlays, and in another moment a seabird landed upon a corner scroll of the penultimate tier, where it perched in a flutter of white plumage. So quite obviously this thing was no mirage; it was real, leaving no room for the peasant fisherman to doubt his own senses.

Real, yes, and yet patently the end result of some colossal magic! Except . . .

Magic? Ki-no Sung had no use for it. Not far from Qingdao to the south, he had seen rockets rising from secret launching pads in the jungle, curving out over the Yellow Sea on blossoming stems of white smoke, and falling unerringly, devastatingly on target ships, flimsy test vessels, to destroy them in explosive fire and boiling ocean. How could magic compare with that? And what of the telephone, radio, and television? In the village there were three telephones, several radios, even two television sets, yes! So that Ki-no Sung knew well enough that the outside world was full of magics to rival anything out of ancient times.

Forty years ago, Ki-no Sung's father, a Korean whose real name was Kim (Kim Tsu, the family name coming first), had fought alongside his North Korean countrymen and the Red Chinese army against the South. At the cessation, uprooted, he'd expatriated himself and his family to the Red Chinese mainland, and in Qingdao had told tales of weapons so awesome as to make men's blood run cold.

"We feared that should we fight on," he had told his son, "the American dogs might do to North Korea—and perhaps to China itself—what they had done to Japan. Why, they have a bomb that can destroy a city in a single bright flash of light! What is *that* for an enemy, eh? Your ancestors feared magic. Ah, but this nuclear science is a far more dangerous thing, my son, and it makes cities dangerous places! Now that I have earned Chinese citizenship, the green jungle shall be our protection, and the Yellow Sea our provider."

Following which he had quit Qingdao and moved his family some thirty miles northeast into the coastal forest, settling for the simple life of a fisherman. He and Ki-no Sung's mother had lived out their lives there, and Sung—a man now, remembering his father's words—had kept himself mainly to himself, and to the house on the rim of the sea and the outskirts of the small village where he had grown up to follow in his father's footsteps. Or perhaps in his wake, since he was a fisherman.

He had taken a wife, Chinese, whose name meant Lotus, and she was with child—a boy, Sung prayed, to grow up and learn the secrets of the sea from him. Where now . . .

Where now there was this new secret to be learned.

The pagoda would be visible from the village harbor, but Sung's place was closer by a mile. If he was brave enough, he could even be first to set foot upon the tiers of marble steps leading up to . . . to what? A pagoda with no windows, no doors? He might even—what, lay claim to the place? Hardly that, not if it was something of the scientists' doing, some governmental thing; some secret preparation—like the rockets in their jungle silos—for the protection of the mainland, or maybe for a renewed Chinese assault upon South Korea over the sea one day. But what if it wasn't any of these things? And anyway, whatever it was it occupied Ki-no Sung's patch of ocean, it stood on his watery property. And if he didn't explore it someone else certainly would.

Perhaps sensing something, Lotus sleepily called out, "Kim Sung, did you speak? Is there something?" When they were alone, she reverted to his Korean name, which was much to his liking. She loved him, yes, but her parents did not, not much. They had standing in the village, while Sung had very little. But to be first out into the Yellow Sea, first up onto the strange pagoda . . . that would very definitely bolster his prestige.

Sung made up his mind. And the sight of his boat, suddenly slewing into view on a wave-washed beach reduced to little more than a shingle strip at the edge of the jungle, seemed to validate his decision. "No, nothing," he found his voice and called out, lying in answer to his wife's query— but a white lie, of course. "I'm going fishing. I'm sorry I woke you."

"It's all right," she sighed, and he heard her pallet move a little as she turned over. And: "Catch lots of fishes," Lotus mumbled.

Maybe the biggest you ever imagined, Sung thought, leaving his nets behind and setting off at a lope along the jungle path to his boat . . .

Perhaps the pagoda was something of a mirage after all. The seabird up there on the high ornate scrollwork wasn't able to make up its mind either. It hopped from one webbed foot to the other and seemed quite unable to find its balance. And Ki-no Sung believed he knew why. It was as if the pagoda were only half here. The waters of the Yellow Sea were disturbed around it; they came and went, first sucked in, then repulsed by its presence, which caused shallow, slapping waves about its base. And perhaps the strangest thing of all: from close-up, the pagoda's outline was very definitely . . . blurred? Like a radio wavelength that won't stay tuned in, or a picture on a TV screen that refuses to firm up. During the rainy season, Sung had observed just such atmospheric disturbances. But this thing was three-dimensional, a solid. It displaced water, however erratically. So by definition, how could a "solid" be anything other than firm? The answer seemed simple: it couldn't.

There was only one other possibility: that Ki-no Sung was mad. But driven mad by what? The loneliness of his fisherman's existence, perhaps? Not now that Lotus was here. By her family, then; perhaps they had poisoned him! But no, their dislike of him was hardly so great, while their love of Lotus was. They would not hurt someone for whom she cared so much. And anyway, if he was mad, then so was that hopping seabird up there.

Actually, it *looked* mad, the way it couldn't seem to settle . . .

The waves slapped at his shallow boat and made it difficult for Sung to steer up alongside the pagoda's base. Finally he managed it, and drew his small motor's long-stemmed propeller into the stern of his vessel. But how to anchor? The massive steps swam up from yellowy-green water to form this first level platform . . . the pagoda's ground floor? Well, that was how it looked. Which begged the question: if this was indeed the ground floor, what was down below on the muddy bed five or six meters deep under the surface? The design of the thing was all wrong—or deliberately tricky?—or maybe this wasn't the base and the pagoda's doors were all on the lowest, submerged level.

But where were the windows? And why were there no balconies? Sung lobbed his anchor—more a grapnel—around a fancy curlicue of white stone scrollwork, and used the line for support as he drew himself from his boat onto the first step where it swam in the choppy spray of peculiarly disturbed water. And the water tingled where it washed his hands and soaked through his trousers.

The sensation was like a mild electric shock, so slight indeed that Sung could be mistaken. Or maybe it was the weirdness of his situation: to find himself crouching on something as massive as this, which wasn't here twenty-odd minutes ago. Little wonder it scarcely felt solid at all!

And there yet again was that doubting niggle in the back of Sung's mind, about the pagoda's reality. But Ki-no Sung was real and really here, scrambling up onto the next tier of brand-new steps (the pagoda *was* brand-new, yes) before the eccentric wavelets could suck him back into the sea again. And his craft was there, rocking in the surging water below him, and the pagoda went up and up, gorgeously into the morning light. It went up gleaming—indeed shimmering—and utterly alien.

Shimmering . . .

Maybe that had something to do with the sensation of pent electricity. Maybe the tingling was the ultra-rapid vibration of a mild electrical charge. But alien? Where had that thought come from? Not alien as in a creature or thing from some other world—not necessarily, anyway—but as in inexplicable, or perhaps in its defiance of logic.

A word was on the tip of Ki-no Sung's tongue. And then it slipped out of his mouth: "Imitation!"

A pagoda without windows or doors? Oh, the thing was real, but it wasn't a real pagoda. It was an imitation! And it wasn't yet a perfect imitation.

The blurring was stronger now, the vibrations speeding up. Sung saw every facet of the pagoda shimmering, like the gut of a bow when twanged or the wind chimes when he played his flute too close to them. Then from high overhead there came the sudden hiss and crackle of static electricity, or of some kind of energy, anyway. And just as suddenly, the fisherman Ki-no Sung was deadly afraid.

Shielding his face—he didn't know why or from what—he looked up. From his elevation, where he stood three tall, wide steps up from the agitated water, the shimmering, "unreal" surface of the pagoda climbed a hundred feet. But because each of the levels was set back from the preceding level, pyramidal, he could see all the way to the topmost tier. And staring, he saw blue and white energies snaking and crackling the entire length or height of the now frightening structure. Which was only the start of it.

The steps only a few tiers higher than the level where he stood suddenly rippled—*rippled* as if they were no more substantial than water. And Sung knew in his instantly hammering heart that this was not simply the effect of some strange heat haze—no *earthly* heat haze, anyway. And now the word "alien" must surely take on its other meaning.

Sung had seen science fiction films; the Japanese variety frequently found their way onto the village TV screens. But he had seen horror films, too, and various mixtures of the genres.

The rippling flowed inward and upward, left the steps to climb the broad central stem of the pagoda. And while the base and steps seemed solid again, the first level or platform some eighteen feet higher started to waver and warp like the flimsy canopy of a sun awning in a sudden brisk gust. It lasted only a moment as the effect moved on and continued to "climb" the pagoda, and each level in turn steamed and crackled with snaking energies and went through the metamorphosis from solid to immaterial and back again.

But it was speeding up; the air was beginning to hum like a dynamo; in a matter of seconds the penultimate, then topmost tiers were briefly obscured in steam and blue and white energy traceries, until the wavelike ripple reversed itself and started back down again. And now it was moving really fast, like a wave in a crowd of people such as Sung had seen televised from the Olympics in Seoul ten years ago. But ahead of the wave, in a mad squawking and a bomb burst of bloody red feathers, something else was falling from on high.

The seabird, thudding to the steps only a few paces away from Sung where he crouched. The bird's legs were gone, cut off halfway up its thighs, and its right wing had likewise been severed at the first major hinge. Bloodied and squawking in agony, the maimed creature skittered in a small, hopeless circle. And a horrified glance up at the pagoda told Sung that whatever had crippled the bird was about to do the same thing to him!

The jutting, ornately carved (or otherwise created) landing directly overhead was steaming and writhing, sheathed in unearthly energy discharges, and the broad stem or body of the structure was already beginning to warp out of shape. Then, in a single breathless second as Sung stood there paralyzed, this nightmarish metamorphosis descended to his level and came rushing upon him across the melting steps!

In that same moment, ignorant or perhaps not so ignorant peasant that he was, Sung *knew*; knew that as the pagoda firmed into its final, physical permanency it could only be at the expense of any other reality that happened to be interfacing with it at the time. He knew—albeit without knowing that he knew, in the same way that everyone intuitively knows to avoid oncoming vehicles, stampeding buffaloes, and even other people in a hurry—that no more than one solid object may ever occupy one space at any one time. And it was obvious to him that just like the flopping seabird, he was by far the weaker of the two forces here.

Galvanized, as the *effect* reached to engulf him and flickering energies formed a web to enclose him, he made a headlong dive for the ocean. His left foot was the last part of Sung to leave the "stone" surface of the steps. He felt a terrible attraction, a tugging, as if his sandal were stuck down; but then he was free, flying like a knife through the throbbing air and a moment later plunging down into the choppy water.

Just how he had managed to clear the pagoda's "solid" rim he would never know; a superhuman effort seemed the only explanation, but at an angle of some forty-five degrees he went deep into the hissing sea. And the warping, flowing, metamorphosing *effect* kept pace with him as his dive bore him inches clear of the corners of the submerged tiers of steps, until he shot over the rim of the true base and felt the Yellow Sea open its empty vastness beneath him. Then, in a rush of bubbles, Sung arched his body and outstretched hands to bring himself into a sweeping turn, and looked back.

He was maybe four meters deep and the sea . . . was blurred. But even as he stared the weird distortion went away. And there behind it was the solid—really solid, finally solid—face of the pagoda only a few meters away. But the structure wasn't solid through and through, for as Sung now saw there was indeed an entrance, a door of sorts: an oddly angled aperture receding into the core of the false pagoda. And flanking this orifice, a pair of faceted oval crystals like underwater lights set flush with the stone.

Sung saw it, and at once felt the alien threat of it. This secret, sub-merged, green-lit tunnel, angling back into shifting shadows; this vertical slit of a mouth guarded by crystal eyes. He saw it, and was mortally afraid of it. For the alien pagoda, artifact, lair—or lure?—was fearsome enough on the outside, without him pondering its conjectural interior.

The facets in the oval crystals changed their inclination. It was as if a pair of eyes, real eyes, had blinked and refocused. Focused on Ki-no Sung!

He kicked for the surface—and the Yellow Sea turned red. The crystals glowed red as hellfire, swiveled to catch him in pulsing cross-beams, hauled on him to draw him feet first into the yawning slit of the door. Or the mouth?

And as the shadow of the door fell on him and the crystals dulled and blinked out, Sung felt a different force acting upon him. A terrific suction from within the pagoda, a current that drew him irresistibly into darkness. And he daren't even scream for fear of drowning.

But if he had known where he was going, he might well have screamed and chanced drowning—or gladly drowned—anyway . . .

The men from the village found the strap of one of Ki-no Sung's sandals floating near what was left of his boat. Just the strap, severed as if by a razor in the three places where it had once joined with the sole. As for his boat:

The rear section was discovered sliced end up, bobbing not too far from the pagoda. The boat's aft net-storage compartment had trapped sufficient air to remain afloat, and Sung's grapnel anchor, caught in weeds on the bottom, had prevented the wreckage from running with the current.

When drawn from the sea, the anchor itself was seen to be a blob of fused, blackened metal, with the blunted shape of one tine barely pro-jecting.

And apart from these few things, there was no evidence at all that Ki-no Sung had ever been here . . .

CHAPTER
2

BY THE TIME Spencer Gill left the auditorium where he'd spoken to a doubtful-looking gathering of radio astronomers and astrophysicists, he was himself confused and angry. Confused because he didn't have the vocabulary (no, be honest, because he didn't have the science, the technical know-how) to converse with them on their own level, and angry because he suspected they weren't telling him all there was to know about it—or someone wasn't. "It" being the problem with, or the glitch in, the Jodrell Bank radio telescope. Indeed, the same glitch that appeared to be in all the world's radio telescopes.

Gill's driver—dressed in civilian clothing but wearing a Ministry of Defense lapel tag—was patiently waiting for him in the car park at the wheel of a glittering takes-your-breath-away Peugeot. He had been there for more than two hours but was obviously boredom-proof; from long practice, Gill supposed. The vehicle was equipped with chrome pennant scabbards on its bonnet, chrome star-plates situated centrally over its fenders, and reinforced glass windows that while they were currently inappropriate, nevertheless told a tale of their own: that this was a VIP car, normally used to convey royalty, military top brass, governmental types, diplomats, and foreign dignitaries from place "A" to place "B," wherever.

The place "A" in question was the radio telescope at Macclesfield, and place "B" was to be—or was to have been—the railway station at Crewe. But as Gill made himself comfortable in the wide backseat he noticed that the car had turned out of the car park in the wrong direction. He leaned forward to query the driver, but before he could say anything the man passed him a scribbled note that read, "Convey Mr. Gill to grid reference . . ." Gill didn't bother to read the numbers. In any case he had no map. But his driver did.

"It's a field about a mile north of here." The driver had seen Gill's frown in his mirror and now waved a folded ordnance survey map at him. "A chopper—for you, sir, I would guess. It passed overhead fifteen minutes ago, circled the car park, then headed north. I saw it losing altitude. Then this message from the minister." He nodded his head to indicate the car's radio.

The minister: Gill's sometimes boss in the MOD—but only when there was work of a special nature to be done *for* the MOD. The man who had sent him to have a look at the radio telescope at Jodrell Bank in the first place—which in turn had caused him to believe that he hadn't been told everything, because he couldn't tie Jodrell Bank and the MOD together. The radio telescope was for looking at distant stars; it wasn't some kind of super-computerized radar station on a twenty-four-hour lookout for incoming missiles. It and the MOD just didn't seem to have anything in common, or they hadn't until the glitch or glitches. And suddenly, despite that it was July and the temperature up in the seventies, Gill felt a chill. Knowing what that signified he at once put it from his mind. That was over and done with now, and there wouldn't be any more trouble of that sort. Not from the Thone, at least . . .

"You all right, sir?" It was his driver, of course, drawing Gill's wandering mind back to earth—or to Earth.

Startled, Gill looked back at him in the interior mirror. "Did I do or say something?" he asked, shaking his head lamely. "I mean, do I look . . . odd, or something?"

The other shrugged. "Just for a minute there—well, let's just say you looked pretty serious. Frowning, biting your lip? So, is something up? Something you forgot? Anything I can do?"

Gill's turn to shrug. He couldn't talk about it—wasn't allowed to, not to just any curious party—but in fact several things were "up." And nothing could be done or said to anyone until he was more fully in the picture.

But glancing upward through his window at the clear blue sky, he frowned and began biting his lip again anyway. The sky was clear now, yes, but for two hours on the night before last it hadn't been. Yet from any radio astronomer's point of view it had been extraordinarily clear. More so than ever before in the entire history of Mankind.

A glitch or glitches, apparently.

Or maybe something else? Maybe something else entirely . . .

* * *

The field had a gate and when they got there Gill's "minister," George Arthur Waite (a "junior" in the MOD, but Gill knew that was only a ploy to lend his position a degree of obscurity), was sitting on the gate's top bar with his knees drawn up. Handsome and casually dressed—wearing no tie, and with the loose collar of his yellow silk shirt inside the collar of a light-weight gray summer jacket—Waite looked like a young, rich layabout, like a self-indulgent, done-it-all, know-it-all, precocious kid who never quite grew up. If Gill should half close his eyes, he fancied he might even see a silver spoon dangling from a corner of Waite's oh-so-slightly cynical mouth.

Stretching his long legs to step down easily from the gate, Waite met the car as it drew to a halt. Behind him in the field a helicopter stood waiting, its vanes slowly rotating.

"Spencer." Waite smiled a bland smile, offered his hand as Gill got out of the car. They shook and Gill said:

"George, and still looking like a playboy." The very image, in fact. Nothing conservative about this one. No pin-striped suit or bowler hat, no rolled umbrella or copy of *The Times* anywhere in sight. Just long-legged, smooth-talking, up-and-coming-without-much-going George Arthur Waite. Or sometimes "King" Arthur to his subordinates . . . probably because he had a cutting edge that was easily the equal of Excalibur's. Waite's looks were very deceptive . . .

While Gill had given the minister a quick once-over, he in turn had been checked out by Waite; not only what could be seen of him, but also what Waite knew of him.

At maybe five-eleven, Spencer Gill was perhaps two inches shorter than Waite, but blockier. And at thirty-seven years of age he was also three years Waite's senior. Gill was, however, an "old" thirty-seven and looked forty-something; a rare blood complaint—in remission for four years now and hopefully gone for good—had long since taken its toll. His teeth were evenly white behind slightly crooked but sensitive lips; his nose was straight and narrow. While his complexion overall was generally unblemished, there was a certain pallor residual of his illness. A little overweight at around one hundred and sixty-five pounds, with a high forehead, gray-flecked sandy hair, and unfathomable eyes that were green one moment and gray the next, there was something of an enigmatic look about him. Which was scarcely surprising.

Nineteen years ago as a teenager he'd caused something of a stir; they had recognized him as a new phenomenon, a quantum leap of Nature to keep pace with Science. Gill had "understood" machines. His paternal great-grandfather had been an engineer, which seemed to be Gill's only qualification for any trick his genes might have played on him. In any case it seemed very unlikely that anything his great-grandfather had done could have much in common with Gill's ability.

"In the Age of Computers," a sensational journalist had written, "there will have to be minds that are *like* computers! This young man has that sort of mind." Of course he had had it wrong; Spencer Gill's mind wasn't like that at all. Rather, he understood them, computers and all other types of machines: by touch, taste, smell, sight—by listening to them and feeling for them. But people had first taken note of him when, at the age of eighteen, he had described Heath Robinson's mobiles and mechanisms—those overly ingenious contrivances normally designed *not* to work!—as "soulless Frankenstein monsters." He *hadn't* understood them, because they couldn't understand themselves. "If they were men," he'd said, "they would be complete idiots . . ."

Waite had answered Gill's "playboy" remark with a mainly genuine grin. But now he said, "When I was a young subaltern I was obliged to do a Special Air Service course . . . I failed, naturally. Far too physical! But did you know that SAS officers don't wear badges of rank? And subordinate ranks don't usually salute them? It's true. Can you guess why?"

Gill nodded. "Such formalities would only serve to identify them as priority targets," he answered. "And in their line of work—in hostage situations or as saboteurs behind enemy lines—who needs it? They're targets enough without advertising the fact."

"The diplomatic world is much the same," Waite said, without further comment for the time being. But as he took the gate off its latch and let it swing open, he said:

"Four years ago, while you were being kept busy with that House of Doors thing up in Scotland, I was in Moscow, a 'military attaché'—er, in fact, the Intelligence Corps. Being in the ex-USSR, of course, I was well out of the picture. But alien incursions aren't easy things to keep under wraps . . . let's face it, the whole world knew about it! Anyway, by the time I moved on into the MOD, into our own rather special branch of the Ministry, your very graphic—er, even highly dramatized?—report had become required reading. More recently, even *very* recently, I've been tasked to look at the whole thing again: an in-depth study of the entire case file, in order to be doubly sure that there's nothing more to be gleaned . . . you know?"

Gill felt that chill again, and as they made for the helicopter asked: "How recently? I mean, when were you tasked?"

"Thirty-six hours ago," the other answered, offering Gill a curious or speculative sideways glance. "And only naturally, I suppose, I find myself greatly influenced by my predecessor's role in those earlier events. Er, David Anderson? Or if not in his role, definitely in his subsequent decline."

Gill nodded, tried not to grimace, said: "How's he doing?" But at the same time he wondered why Waite should be concerned about Anderson's "decline." He wasn't the type to worry a deal about anyone's problems except his own.

"Quite well, actually," Waite said with a nod. "Yes, he seems to be over the worst of it . . ." Then he sighed. "He's no longer of any use to the Ministry, of course, so they've pensioned him off. A nice little cottage in Cornwall, I hear . . ."

Gill started biting his lip again. He'd always felt responsible, in a way, for Anderson's eventual breakdown. The fact was, though, that he'd believed the man was stronger than that.

"So," Waite went on, "since any extra information Anderson might have would tend to be—you know, suspect?—that leaves only you. Oh, and Mr. Jack Turnbull, of course. Er, and . . ." He paused and looked at Gill sideways.

"And?" Gill snapped. Waite was getting on his nerves now. Why couldn't the smug little shit just tell him what was going on here? But Gill could play guessing games, too, and so curbed his irritation, waiting for what he knew Waite would say next.

"And Angela," Waite said, offering Gill what was supposed to be a look of surprise. "Angela Denholm, of course. Er, have I touched a nerve or something?"

"*Er,* or something," Gill grunted, and changed the subject. "Where are we going?"

"We're going to a briefing," Waite said. "*I* am going to be briefing you. And the easiest way and place to do it will be in the perfect privacy of this chopper on your way home to Hayling Island. That way we won't be wasting any time, you see?"

"Your Int Corps training?" Gill said abruptly.

"Eh?" This time Waite's surprise was genuine.

"You can't get straight on with it?" Gill said. "You think we might be overheard . . . what, bugged? In this open field in the country miles away from anywhere?" He grinned, however humorlessly. "I think it's time you started talking before I stop walking, George. What's going on here?"

"In the chopper," the other said, cool and unflustered, as he ducked low under the slowly rotating, *whup-whup-whup*ping vanes. "I'll tell you everything in the helicopter. Everything I know, anyway—and I shall expect you to do the same for me." Waite's boyish eyes were very sharp as he mounted the aluminum steps and turned to offer Gill a helping hand, which was promptly rejected. "Oh, and by the way"—Waite shrugged aside Gill's attitude—"if I haven't already mentioned it, you have a crazy friend who wants to be in on this with you!"

"Wants to be in on this . . ." Gill started to say, then saw who was sitting in the aircraft, and finished with an entirely different *"What!?"* from the "what?" he had intended.

For his "crazy friend" was none other than Jack Turnbull. And now the chill was back in earnest . . .

We all got over it in our different ways, I imagine," Turnbull said when they'd taken off. This was in answer to Gill's questions as to how he'd been, what he was doing, et cetera—but it was also his apology for the way he looked, which was rough. "I got over it with booze," he explained with a shrug. "Wrong solution, apparently. I ended up hooked on the booze!"

Gill shook his head. "That doesn't sound like you. I mean, I was mistaken about Anderson—I thought he'd be okay, too—but you're an entirely different kind of animal. Booze? All the stuff you've seen in life, and the House of Doors turned you on to booze?" But in fact Gill could see that it had.

Just on six feet tall, Jack Turnbull was slim in the hips and broad in the shoulders. Shaped like a slender wedge, a real torpedo, he had a bullet head supported by no neck to speak of. His jet-black hair was long; swept back into a mane and held by a silver clasp, he "regulated" it with something that gave it a shine without making it greasy. Not vanity but simply a way of keeping it out of his eyes. Those eyes were heavy-lidded, blue when they flashed a smile or widened in surprise. Such smiles were rare, however, while the creases in his forehead were many and etched deep. He seemed to be always on his guard: his close protection training, Gill rightly supposed. His hands were big, blunt, extremely strong, and very fast and flexible. As for his face:

Turnbull's right eyebrow sat fractionally higher than the other, probably as a result of a long, thin white scar, barely visible along the ridge of the orbit, which tightened the skin there and gave him a perpetually quizzical look. His hard, angular chin was likewise scarred, with tiny white pocks showing through what used to be healthy tanned skin. His skin had *used* to be tanned, yes, but it now looked almost as pale as Gill's. Finally, his nose had suffered somewhat from years of minding (or roughhousing); it cast a crooked shadow on lips that were fleshy over strong, uneven teeth.

So in fact Turnbull *looked* mainly as Gill remembered him. Except . . . there were telltale signs. A certain dullness of eye and spirit, from imbibing too *much* spirit? And maybe his wedge shape was sagging just a little in the middle? And his clothes . . . looked like he'd slept in them. That last wasn't too unusual for a minder. But the stubble on Turnbull's jowls and chin was. Unkempt was the only word for him.

Meanwhile he'd absorbed Gill's comment about the House of Doors getting to him. "Who are you kidding, Spencer?" he grunted. "We all of us saw stuff in there enough to turn our hair white!"

"I came through it okay," Gill answered, but he still felt guilty about it. He knew that his survival was down to the fact that he was the only one who had understood what was happening. Which was true even now, mainly. "And so did Angela . . ." he added, letting it trail off.

"And Anderson?" Turnbull lifted that querying eyebrow. But when Gill went to answer him: "Don't bother," he said. "George here has already told me about Anderson. And hey, stop blaming yourself, Spencer! Me, I never blamed anyone but myself for my problems—or my mistakes. Anyway, as of right now I'm off the booze. Let's face it, who would put his faith in a drunken minder, eh?" And he grinned lopsidedly.

Gill grunted, tried to smile, and failed. Until he had seen Turnbull sitting there, he hadn't known he needed a minder. But now it was obvious that Waite's "in-depth study" story had been so much bullshit, only a small detail of the entire scenario.

"So tell me about Angela," Turnbull went on. "You and she are still together?" But seeing a certain look on Gill's face, he misinterpreted it. "It didn't work out?"

Gill glanced once out of the corner of his eye, at Waite, who happened to be looking the other way. Turnbull got the message. The "Machine Man"—as he had always thought of Gill—wasn't going to talk about Angela in front of the man from the Ministry. And so Turnbull quickly continued, "And the Frog—I mean, Jean-Pierre Varre? What of him? And that American, Clayborne? Is he still with SCOPE: the Society for the, er . . ."

"For the Correlation of Paranormal Experiences," Gill helped him out, and this time looked at Waite deliberately. "I haven't kept track of anyone—well, except Angela. Maybe the minister can bring us both up-to-date? I mean, on everything?" For Gill knew beyond a doubt now that this was all connected.

"Very well," Waite said with a nod, "let's get down to it. But if you don't mind I'll leave the personalities until later. Spencer, you were sent to Jodrell Bank to have a look at the radio telescope. With your superior knowledge of machines—"

"My machine empathy," Gill corrected him. "I couldn't build a television set or jet engine to save my life. I haven't the foggiest notion what makes a complicated machine work—or perhaps *only* the foggiest notion—but when I'm close to a sick one I can usually tell what's wrong with it. And yes, I do have a knack when it comes to operating them."

"A sick machine?" Turnbull frowned. He wasn't thick by any means, but he'd had similar conversations with Gill before. And he hadn't been able to make much of them then either.

"Sick, inefficient, stressed, broken," Gill said. "Didn't you ever get into your car and when she complained about starting up you called her sick? Or when you had her running, you heard something you didn't like and headed straight for the garage? If it were someone else's car, perhaps you wouldn't notice it, but your car . . . you *know* when she's sick. Well, that's the way it is with me. Except, it's not just cars but everything—everything mechanical, anyway. Let it go at that. It's much too complicated to explain in detail."

"I know." Turnbull shook his head. "You've tried before!"

"Can we get on?" Waite wasn't as patient or secretive now. "We do have some things to go over." And after Gill nodded his agreement:

"Two reasons for sending you to Jodrell Bank," Waite continued. "One: to see if there was in fact a glitch in the radio telescope. So, was there?"

Gill shrugged. "A couple of nights ago, yes, apparently—but . . ."

"Save the buts for later," Waite cut him short, "and tell me how this 'apparent' glitch manifested itself?"

"Four areas of space, each with a radius of about a hundred miles, stopped transmitting," Gill said. "They went dead."

"Ah, no!" Waite jumped on him at once. "That's *your* interpretation, right, Spencer? We're not asking what went wrong with space, however, but what went wrong with the radio telescope. What *you've* just said is that there's nothing wrong with Jodrell Bank—"

"There isn't, not right now," Gill cut in.

"—But that in fact," Waite quickly went on, not wanting to lose his grip on it, "that in fact there *is* something wrong . . . with space?"

"Was," Gill answered. "Yes. Two nights ago . . ." But now he knew exactly where all of this was leading, and: "My turn with the questions," he snapped. "First question: what is it that's proving so very hard to talk about? Second question: what *precisely* has happened? Third and last question: in the event you don't know the answers to the first two questions, tell me who does because in that case I'll be through speaking to you."

"*Huh!*" said Waite dismissively, and sat back in his seat.

"I mean it, George," Gill told him. "In the last fifteen minutes you've pissed me off a whole year's worth! Now listen, it's obvious you need me, so let's lose all of this cloak-and-dagger stuff and just do some straight talking. Starting with me asking you, for the very last time—what's going on?"

Waite narrowed his deceptively boyish eyes, looked at Gill, and saw that he was serious. Knowing that he couldn't afford to alienate him further, he took a deep breath, let it out slowly, said, "Those spatial anomalies two nights ago . . . they weren't natural, didn't result from sunspots, magnetic field fluctuations, meteor showers, or 'glitches.' At least we don't think so. And you've just confirmed it. Actually, we already had confirmation. Jodrell Bank is only one radio telescope, after all . . ."

As Waite paused, Turnbull said, "Anomalies? Spatial anomalies? Hey, I said I wouldn't mind *minding* for Gill. I said that if he needed looking after, I was your man. But this is beginning to sound like . . . hell, like it's something like the last time!"

Gill nodded grimly. "It *is* like the last time, Jack. These holes in space are only the beginning, but George here is going to tell us the rest of it. Right, George?"

"Holes in space?" Turnbull repeated, before the minister could say anything further.

"Holes, negative zones . . . call them what you will, Jack," Gill answered. "But you can think of them as grid references—or maybe targeting devices?" Then turning more fully to Waite, "Cards on the table, George. Where is it? Where has it landed, or materialized, this time? Where *is* the House of Doors?"

But Waite, grim-faced now, and no longer so young-looking, slowly shook his head. Suddenly husky, he said, "Not house, but *houses*, Spencer! Try Houses of Doors. And you've just confirmed something else: that you are the right man—and probably the only man—for the job . . ."

CHAPTER
3

THERE WEREN'T JUST four 'anomalies' but eight," Waite continued. "Four over the northern hemisphere, and four more over the southern. They held their positions, turning and orbiting with the Earth. And much as you have pointed out, Spencer, they were like targeting devices that have locked-on, forming the corners of a perfect cube with the Earth hanging in the middle. Jodrell Bank, the big dish in Puerto Rico, and others in various locations—including the VLA, or Very Large Array, in New Mexico—all of them recorded the same, well, interference."

"Spaceships?" Turnbull's lined forehead showed his shock, his alarm. Experience is the best teacher. But:

"No." Gill shook his head. "These were holes, Jack—but rather special holes. Radio telescopes 'see' radio waves from outside the Earth's atmosphere. Here's an analogy: imagine you are sitting in a swivel chair in the center of a large, square room. Looking up, you can see all four corners of the ceiling. Then, suddenly, you can't. There's just emptiness there. Light isn't reaching you from those regions. That's what happened to the radio telescopes. They couldn't see the radio waves coming from those areas of space. Something—or several somethings, invisible forces—were in the way, interfering. And they were in the way for two hours."

"Targeting devices," Turnbull said, still frowning as he repeated words from an earlier part of the conversation, words which had registered, stuck, and continued to echo in his mind. And he slowly nodded his understanding. "Like when a fighter's weapon systems lock on to an enemy plane, just before it fires its missiles . . ."

"Right," said Gill. "Then, with a bit of luck, the target aircraft picks up the lock-on signal and takes evasive action. And with even more luck it survives."

"*If* it's lucky." Turnbull glanced at the minister, and at Gill, then back to Waite. "Is that it? Someone's got us in his sights?"

"Worse than that," Waite answered. "He's already squeezed the trigger, delivered his payload. The radio holes—for want of a better description— were evident for two hours, but they were followed by other manifestations before they vanished."

"Other manifestations?" Gill stared at him.

"Radio telescopes aren't the only kind." Waite could only shrug. "UV, X-ray, infrared—the Hubble has them all. And all of them affected. Especially infrared. When those holes linked up to fire their shots, there were massive heat emissions and God only knows what else. At CERN and the Fermilab, months and even years worth of experimentation was lost when these—hell—these *glitches* got into the works. There was some damage but nothing that can't be recovered or duplicated in time. It was as if someone had waved a gigantic magnet over the doughnuts."

"Doughnuts?" Turnbull was lost again.

"Rings half a mile across," Gill told him. "Conduits for proton acceleration. CERN near Geneva, and the Fermilab forty miles west of Chicago. But these weren't the targets. Any damage to the instrumentation was simply an effect of the firing, similar to the electrical chaos near the ground-zero of a nuclear bomb burst."

"Right again." Waite nodded. "But there are instruments, and there are instruments. We don't only point things up into space but down from it. And the West's listening stations are far and away our most powerful early warning tools. Though in this case—well, patently we're not much concerned with our own 'alien' nations."

And Gill said, "So then, we do know where they've materialized. The other manifestations you mentioned, right? So *how* do we know? Aerial photography—spy satellites? That can only mean the ex-USSR, China, Iran, Iraq, Libya . . . maybe a handful of other nations of similar inclinations."

"Oh, really?" said Waite. "But it could also mean America. The USA isn't much known for volunteering this sort of information either, you know."

"No more guessing games!" Gill snapped. "Even stuck in a fucking helicopter it's still a waste of time! So how many are there, and where are they?"

Waite's face reddened up a little. "Spencer, I would like to remind you that—"

"Don't," Gill told him, sharply. "Instead, let me remind you. It's no boast when I say there's only one of me. But if I have to work through a minister, I know they'll always be able to find another you. You see, I don't give a twopenny toss for your career, George. If everything you've said so far is true, everybody's career, from Her Majesty on down, isn't only on the line but could very easily be at the *end* of the line . . . !"

Waite gritted his teeth and seemed about to go on the defensive, until Turnbull said, "George, I haven't agreed to work for you yet. If I do I'll call you 'sir,' maybe. What it boils down to is a matter of attitude. Gill and me, we've been there. We know what it's like when people get in the way. Which means that until we can all start getting along, you're just part of the problem. And in that case . . . well, instead of calling you 'sir' I'll call your bluff and stand with Spencer."

Waite swallowed his pride. It wasn't his show and he knew it. Without Spencer Gill he didn't *have* a show to speak of! "I . . . I suppose I'm being overly cautious," he said. "Overly anxious. But for thirty-six hours now my nerves have been on edge. I believe I'm the Ministry's bloody scapegoat! I mean, this job isn't like anything anyone ever had before. It's been dumped on me because no one else wants it. Upstairs, oh, they're all playing it down—but you'd better believe the hotlines are buzzing from London to Washington, Washington to Moscow, Moscow to Beijing and back again! Frankly, I didn't *expect* to be able to recruit either one of you. Which is why I chose to break it gently, let you get used to the idea slowly. And that's why we sent you to Jodrell Bank first, Spencer, so that the rest of it wouldn't come down on you like a bombshell. But you're right: I need you—*we* need you—your expertise, your advice, whatever you can do for us. The whole world needs you!"

Gill heard him out and nodded, just a nod, and again said, "How many, and where? But without the histrionics, okay?"

"There are three of them," Waite said. "Three that we know of, anyway. One is more or less straightforward, one isn't, and the other's as weird as hell! The easy one's a pyramid. You can guess where . . . okay, okay." He held up a placating hand. "It's in Egypt. Easy because we're on speaking terms with the Egyptians. The second one's a pagoda—in China, the Shandong Peninsula—yes, yes, you were right. And the third . . ."

"Well?" Gill said.

"Is an iceberg." Waite flapped his hands, helplessly. "No-man's-land, in the middle of the fucking ocean!"

Gill tilted his head back, considered what he'd been told. "The first two seem typical," he eventually said. "Pyramid and pagoda. In Egypt and China, of course. Both equate to a castle in Scotland. But the iceberg . . . puzzles me. As for the reason why: that puzzles me even more, and worries me more yet."

"Why what?" Waite was all attention now, hanging on Gill's every word. "And what worries you more yet?"

"Why this second visit?" Gill murmured, still deeply wrapped in his own thoughts. "I mean, we were—what, cleared? We were accepted, we *proved* ourselves—the first time around. Huh!" He gave a self-derisory snort. "The Thone gave me their word . . ."

Turnbull leaned toward Gill, took his arm, caused him to look him in the eyes. "I don't follow," he said. "I thought it *was* all over, definitely. Hell, we proved our point!"

"Cleared? Proved your point?" Waite repeated. "Do you mean our right to exist? That's what it was all about, correct? Up in Scotland? That's what your report said, anyway."

"Yes," said Gill. "That's what it was all about." And very quickly, he summarized the scenario:

"The Thone are an alien species spreading through the universe and seeking suitable habitable worlds. Not all life-forms are deemed worthy—damn few, in fact! So if the Thone had got here sixty million years ago, the dinosaurs would have been eradicated. Or if not wiped out they would have had to move aside, make way. As for Man: he would never have existed. Again, if we had been visited five thousand years ago . . . we might just have squeezed in. Two thousand years, we'd have been on fairly safe ground. But four years ago, it's like Jack said: that's when we proved our point. Or at least, I thought we had."

"So how come you had so much trouble?" Waite was puzzled. "From space it must be obvious that we're an advanced race. We have cities, planes in the sky, ships on the sea. We communicate by radio, television, satellite, and we've sent probes out into and beyond the Solar system. Our scientists, too, are looking at the stars, looking for intelligent extraterrestrial life or any kind of life. So who could possibly doubt but that we're fit to exist?"

"The Thone have their own standards," Gill told him. "Okay, we're a couple of steps up from the amoeba, but we're also aggressive—very! There hasn't been a single day, not a day, in Man's entire history when someone somewhere hasn't been killed as a result of warfare or just for the hell of it. Why, according to the Bible, even the first men who were *born* and not made men couldn't live in peace! There were two of them—and sure enough one killed the other. Worse still, they were brothers!"

"But as a race—" Waite began to protest.

"Species," Gill stopped him. "Think of us more in terms of a species. The human race has many 'races,' but we're only one species. And—what did you say—we have cities? But so do termites. We fly through the sky? So do birds, insects, and even the seeds of plants. We communicate? Possibly the weakest evidence of all. Whales communicate, over hundreds of miles of ocean! And they don't have radio and television. So we've sent probes into space? So what? For all we know there may be creatures out there that actually *inhabit* space! There's a hell of a lot of it, after all. Why, before the Thone we couldn't even be sure but that we were on our own, and million-year-old fossil microbes in Martian rocks to the contrary."

Through almost all of this Waite had sat shaking his head dismissively, but Turnbull was more thoughtful as he said, "An alien might have a different way of looking at intelligence or worthiness. Is that what you mean, Spencer?"

"That's exactly what I mean," said Gill. "We simply might not fit the picture. And that's if the alien was playing by the rules according to Hoyle. On the other hand, he probably never heard of Hoyle. And if he *wasn't* playing by the rules—or no rules to mention . . ." He paused, looked at Waite, and said:

"You asked why the original House of Doors gave us so much trouble. Well that's why, or maybe you didn't read my report as closely as you say? You see, the Thone have their own rules of acquisition. Never by conquest, for that would be to admit that they had opposition, which in turn would be acknowledgment of a degree of their opponents' worthiness. Let's face it, you have to respect someone who's willing to stand up and fight you even when you're a far mightier foe, right? So their scales are balanced differently.

"When the Thone find that a world they would like to live on already contains a sophisticated species, they let that species define or determine its own right to existence. In our case—in an alien maze of worlds, the original House of Doors—we were up against our own worst fears, our worst nightmares made real, and we could either face up to them . . . or not. That was bad enough in itself, because we had no idea what was going on. No one had explained the rules. Of course they hadn't, for that would have been to give the game away! But far worse, the Thone gamesmaster, Sith, wasn't playing by the rules. He'd built himself into the game, to ensure that even if we won out over our own evils we wouldn't triumph over his."

"But you did win," Waite said, nodding, "and this—this 'rogue controller,' Sith?—was brought to book by his own kind, his superiors. But it was *you*, Spencer, who brought Sith's game to their attention. Which is where your report leaves a lot to be desired. Or maybe a lot to the imagination? I mean, just exactly *how* did you turn the tables on this alien? There's no real explanation in your report."

Gill shrugged; not out of indifference or in defeat, more out of impatience, and with himself as much as with Waite. "The House of Doors was a machine," he said. "It was *the* machine . . . or one of them, as it now seems. When I was drawn inside along with the others, I was a spanner thrown into the works. Not immediately, for the thing was alien to my mind, my way of thinking. But as you know I have this knack, my empathy with mechanical things. And gradually I came to understand what was going on. But explain it to you or to anyone else for that matter? I can't even 'explain' it to myself! But I did get into the system; I leveled the playing field and stopped Sith from moving the goalposts. And then, with Turnbull and Angela on the team, we won. Sith got his comeuppance, and the Thone promised they wouldn't be back. It was over . . ."

"Except it isn't," Waite said.

"Apparently not," Gill answered.

"And you're puzzled, and worried?"

Gill shrugged again, tiredly now. "Yes, of course I am," he said. "Who wouldn't be . . . who isn't? That's why we're here, right?" He sighed, let his head fall back against the headrest, and closed his eyes. And they all took a break from talking—but not from thinking.

Feeling eyes on him, Gill squinted sideways at Turnbull. The minder was looking at him from under that scarred eyebrow of his, with an expression on his face that Gill knew only too well. It was the one that said: *Spencer, you're not telling us all you know, are you?*

Gill pursed his lips and narrowed cautionary eyes at his big friend. Then he chanced glancing the other way—at Waite where he sat fingering his chin, staring into space—before turning his cautionary look on Turnbull again. It was as good as saying, *Later, Jack. We'll talk later, you and I—in private.* And later it would be.

And like a giant dragonfly, the helicopter whirred south under throbbing, near-invisible wings . . .

Why were you so interested in Anderson?" Gill said, suddenly sitting up straighter, frowning at Waite. "You said you were—how did you have it?—influenced by your predecessor's 'role' in the House of Doors thing? But what role? Just like the rest of us, he was taken prisoner. No 'role' as such but a trick of fate, a coincidence. He just happened to be in the wrong place at the wrong time. He made up the numbers Sith needed to start playing his game. After that, if he had any role at all it was to be a nuisance. As Jack here pointed out, he got in the way, became part of the problem. That's all there is to it. So what is it that really interests you?"

"I also said I was interested in his subsequent decline," Waite pointed out. "But perhaps I'm more interested in a certain—I don't know—anomaly?"

"More anomalies?" Turnbull deliberately yawned.

"Again plural, yes." Waite nodded, turning again to Gill. "For it applies to you, too, Spencer."

"What does?" Gill asked defensively, believing he already knew.

"Medical records . . ." said Waite, pausing as he saw Gill's reaction—the way he drew back, almost visibly pulling in his horns. And sure of his ground now, Waite quickly went on:

"Anderson had a problem with cysts. In the softer, membranous areas of his body: his testicles, throat, et cetera. Also with nasal polyps, rodent ulcers in the back of his neck, and so forth. Every two to three years he'd have to be snipped and gouged in as many as half a dozen places at a time. These were usually minor operations, you understand; he wasn't about to keel over and die. He was due for a visit when the House of Doors took him. A specialist had already seen him and selected the matter for excision. But after you had all returned safely from your—well, your abduction, I suppose—when Anderson went for a premed checkup . . ."

Waite's pause came at a well-chosen juncture and was very deliberate. Since he was looking pointedly at Gill, it invited comment.

And Gill obliged. "They discovered that he was okay," he said. "All of Anderson's little disabilities had disappeared. Yes, and my *big* disability, too. The Thone have an aversion to disease. Not only in themselves but all species. Whatever Anderson's system lacked—which caused him to be prone to these cysts and polyps and such—they fixed it. Just being there in the House of Doors fixed it. And as for me, it turned my water into wine."

"It did what?" Turnbull hadn't been privy to this. No one had, except Spencer Gill in his first and last telepathic conversation with the Grand Thone.

"My blood," Gill answered. "After the time I spent in the House of Doors, it was pure as a baby's! Not only that, but my immune system started working like anyone else's, and my body's natural defenses went into high gear to block toxins, or neutralize them if they got in. But that was then and this is now. Now I'm just as prone to a dose of illness as anyone else.

But my doctor assures me that currently I'm quite well." He looked again at Waite.

"Is that what's been worrying you and the people upstairs, George? What do they think, that the Thone did a deal with me, and four years later they've come back to collect the interest? Is that why I—why we—have been watched so closely all this time? Because you didn't know whether to trust us or not?"

It was Waite's turn to be caught off guard. "I . . . really don't know what you're—"

"Of course you do!" Gill cut him short. And to Turnbull: "Jack, where did they pick you up?"

"Where did they pick me . . . ?" Turnbull stared hard at him, then at Waite, and back again. "You know something, Spencer, I never even thought to ask?"

"To ask what?" Waite blustered, trying to bluff it out.

"To ask how your goons knew where to find me," the other growled. "All of this going down in just thirty-six hours, and after only twenty-four of them your people just happen to bump into me in a bar in Charlottenberg, Berlin? Shit!"

Gill grinned a tight grin. "Four years," he said. "Didn't you ever get the feeling you were being watched, Jack? Dear, oh, dear! And you a minder and all . . ."

Turnbull gritted his teeth, said, "Yes I fucking did! But I thought it was the booze!"

Waite laughed, albeit shrilly. "I don't believe this!" he said. "Your attitude in this. Jesus Christ, men go into space, to the moon, and when they come home again they go into quarantine. People work in the nuclear power industry, and in biological research, and every day after work they're checked out for . . . for their own good! Not a one of them sees it as some kind of conspiracy! Yet you people . . . you're kidnapped by an alien machine, kept for days in an alien environment, and when we get you back you expect—"

"To be told what's going on!" Gill snapped. "We expect some privacy, some understanding. Hell's teeth, you'd think *we* were the aliens! I mean . . ." But here he stopped dead and looked at Turnbull—who was looking at him the same way, with his jaw hanging slack. And then they *both* looked at Waite.

"It was before my time!" he protested. "You can't blame me for that. You can't blame anyone! Or if you have to, then blame yourselves. It was you who gave that finger to Anderson . . ."

"Finger?" Gill repeated, before he remembered and understood. The finger that a lucky shot from Turnbull had blasted from the hand of an alien—but an alien who had looked like a man. Exactly like a man.

"It had blood that wasn't *quite* blood," the minister said. "And its skin was almost but not *quite* skin. But close? Only an expert with a microscope would have been able to tell for sure. It was synthetic, a near-perfect counterfeit. And of course the 'person' it came from was a forgery, too."

Gill closed his mouth and said, "We knew that. But all of this time—four years—you've been checking us out, making sure that we . . . that we aren't synthetic, too?"

"A little over two years, actually," Waite said. "It took two years of covert testing before the boffins were completely satisfied that you—*what in the . . . ?*"

For Jack Turnbull had come out of his seat and was crouching over him, bunching Waite's casually smart jacket in a huge fist, and showing his teeth in an utterly convincing snarl. And shaking Waite like a baby's rattle, the enraged minder growled: "Fuck the boffins! What about you, George? Are *you* 'completely satisfied'?" But:

"Let it be, Jack," said Gill, with his hand on Turnbull's arm. "George is only the asshole end of the affair. The brains are far removed. As for being satisfied that we're only human: of course he is. Can you really see him getting in this plane with us if he wasn't?"

Turnbull was reluctant to release his hold, and as he did so Waite glared at both of them. Human? Well, he was satisfied about Gill, anyway. But as for Turnbull—maybe not an alien, but some kind of animal for sure . . .

CHAPTER
4

S O WHAT'S NEXT?" Gill asked, watching as the minister shrugged himself back into shape and flattened down his crumpled lapels. "Where do we go from here—I mean, after I've packed my toothbrush?"

"Can I take it I've recruited you?" Waite answered with a question of his own, while continuing to scowl at Turnbull. "If so, then it's your choice. No problem with the Egyptian authorities; they'll welcome us with open arms. China . . . may be less welcoming, but they won't turn us away. They're nervous as hell and looking for answers—which we would dearly love to deliver before they decide to take things into their own hands! What do I mean? Well, for one thing I mean they're a nuclear power, and for another they're obviously suspicious that this pagoda thing is some sort of joint military experiment—maybe a bridgehead on the Chinese main-land?—that the Americans and South Koreans are fooling with. Do I need to enlarge upon that scenario? No, I didn't think so. And finally there's the iceberg which—since it doesn't belong to anyone—might well be your best starting place. It's adrift in the North Atlantic some six hundred miles southeast of Cape Farewell. Except 'adrift' is maybe the wrong word, for in fact it isn't going anywhere. It's stationary, big and flat, and we believe we could land a plane on it. Also . . ."

"*Whoa!*" said Gill. "Slow down, can't you? I mean, now that you've got up steam you're really going flat out! So let's take it easy, step by step. To start with, you ask if I'm in. But we both know I have to be because this isn't just a visit. I mean, whoever these people are—let's call them 'people' for now—they have a reason for being here. If it's an entirely friendly reason . . . well at least they might have knocked, or dropped us a line. But they didn't. And right off you want to land a plane on one of their probes?"

"Probes?" The minister stared at him. "But what would they have to probe? They've been here once, done their recce run, and looked us over. They know us—know *you* personally—and also what makes us tick. We passed their bloody IQ test or whatever! Yet to hear you talk now, it sounds almost like you're not sure that these are the same . . . that maybe they're *not* the same . . . 'people'?" Waite's eyes were very wide again. "So how about it, Spencer? Is that it? You think they're not the same bunch?"

Gill shook his head, but it was neither a yes nor a no. "I don't know," he said. "How can I know anything from what little you've told me? But whoever they are, their methods seem pretty much the same."

"Methods?"

"The Thone put a castle up in Scotland. Of course we were going to notice it, but at first we'd consider it a curiosity, or maybe an enormous hoax. We wouldn't see it as a threat, not immediately. We certainly wouldn't consider it an alien invasion. Which gave them time to study us . . ."

And Turnbull put in, "But surely the study period is long since over? Spencer, you've got me as baffled as George here!"

"And myself," Gill told him, frowning. "I'm just trying to think it through, that's all. Why in hell would they want to do it again? Why the pointless—what, subterfuge?—of another House of Doors? Why *three* Houses of Doors, when one was sufficient the first time?" Again he looked at Waite. "A question: do they or don't they?"

"Eh?"

"Do they have doors? Does the pagoda—or the pyramid for that matter—does either one of them have anything that resembles a door or an entrance?"

"Would you expect a door in a pyramid?" Waite answered.

"I would in a pagoda," Gill told him.

The minister took out a slim manila envelope from his inside jacket pocket, shook out photographs, and passed them over. Gill studied them, gave them to Turnbull. But after looking at them the big minder said, "Photographed from all sides. But no doors, or windows. And the iceberg . . . Jesus, it's huge!"

"I need to get close to one," said Gill. He was very quiet now. "No, I don't intend to land on one just yet, thanks, but I do need to get close. And sooner rather than later."

"What is it that you see, Spencer?" Waite leaned toward him, stared at the pictures as Gill accepted them from Turnbull, and again pored over them.

"My talent, do you mean?" Gill shook his head. "It doesn't work that way, George. I can't see or feel anything, not from a photograph. But it strikes me you're right. Assuming this to be the Thone, I can't see any reason why they'd want to come back. And I *definitely* can't see a reason for three probes. So, maybe it isn't the Thone. Which in turn means . . ."

And Turnbull finished it for him: "That the sooner we discover just exactly what's going down here, the better we'll all feel about it, right?" But then, looking at them from face to face, he added, "Or maybe we won't . . ."

Hayling Island, which Spencer Gill had never considered a real island but more a promontory, was bathed in yellow early evening sunshine as the helicopter sliced the sky over Petersfield, crossed the hills, and swooped down over Sussex, rapidly losing altitude. A big green jewel, bordered in gold and set on a turquoise sea, that's how the "island" looked. Saddling a curving horizon, it was a very pretty sight. But Gill couldn't appreciate it.

Angela wasn't expecting him home until later tonight. So how in hell was he going to explain this—his arrival by helicopter, and the fact that his ex-minder, Turnbull, was with him again—*and* George Waite, whom she'd met two or three times and didn't much care for? Hell, if he knew Angela she wouldn't even give him time to explain! She'd know just looking at him. Gill hadn't as yet considered the possibility that she might *already* know, that having been a captive in her own right, Angela, too, was reckoned to be an "expert" on the House of Doors.

Gill's place—their place—was a modern bungalow sprawling in one and a half acres of fields. The entire property was hedged around, set well back from the roads, and secluded despite its size. There was a copse fenced with fallen branches, a fairly large vegetable garden that Angela somehow found time to look after, a once-orchard running wild with brambles where she and Gill collected blackberries in season, and apples and pears mainly to give away, and a small rose garden with rustic seats and crazy-paved paths. She had hinted that she would also like to have a small stable one day and a couple of ponies, just so that she could take care of them.

For his part, Gill had designed a swimming pool and marked off an area close to the bungalow where he would soon start to dig. "Soon," yes. But all such planning had been four years ago, in the dawn flush of living together, when they had first bought the place. Since then . . . projects had taken a lot longer to actually get under way.

It wasn't that there'd been any kind of emotional climb-down; their love for each other hadn't failed or even faltered. No, it was more like they had been waiting. But for what? Gill hadn't known . . . until now. And Angela had seemed even more uncertain. She'd wanted children, or a child at least, but hadn't wanted marriage. So . . . it had been the late 1990s after all. But to Gill's surprise he'd discovered himself the old-fashioned sort. Despite the millennium, he had *wanted* to get married. "Who will explain to the kid?"—that sort of thing. Or perhaps all such problems, every objection, had been excuses. And on both sides.

When Gill had thought about it, which he had often enough, he hadn't really wanted children. It was because of his machine empathy (or so he had tried to convince himself). If it was in the genes—if something like that could be in the genes—did he really want to lumber his offspring with it? He had actually used those words, and Angela had chastised him for them:

"Lumber? You or your children could be Man's next evolutionary leap forward, and you call your machine empathy a . . . a *lumber*? An encumbrance? Like some kind of deficiency or deformity? Well let me remind you, Spencer Gill, that without your little encumbrance we'd all be in a sorry mess right now—if we were in anything at all!"

And he had been forced to admit that indeed a great deal had balanced on the scales of his rapport with the machine that had been—that *was*— the original House of Doors. Namely, the fate of an entire world. His argument was simply an excuse disguising the uncertainty in his mind. Not about Angela but about the future in general. Or specifically.

And now that specific future was here . . .

This was to have been my pool one day," Gill said as the helicopter settled to earth and the declining whine of its engine became a booming throb. "Right here."

"Splash!" said Turnbull. And a moment later: "What do you mean, 'was' to have been?"

Gill shrugged. "Haven't got around to it," he said.

As they swung the door open and lowered the steps, Angela came running from the house—with two men running after her!

Gill and Turnbull looked at the men pursuing Angela: well-built, grim-faced, determined-looking types. Then they looked at each other, mere glances that said a whole lot. And clambering down the steps, they went ducking under the *whupping*, viciously slicing vanes toward the house.

Synchronicity; both Gill and his minder had remembered the same thing at the same time: a cold night in Killin under the Grampians, when a man who wasn't a man had come looking for Gill to kill him. Then there had been only one House of Doors. Now there were three. So who, or *what*, were these men?

Angela was close to the shimmering arc of the rotors; she paused to duck low as the pair caught up with her. One of them grabbed her arm, brought her to an abrupt, skidding halt; the other caught her up bodily and hauled her away from the whirling danger. But by then, barely aware of Waite's frantic shouting over the *whup-whup-whup* of the helicopter's fan, Gill and Turnbull were on them in a fury.

Gill's man went down, seemingly amazed at being punched on the nose. Turnbull's target crumpled sideways as the big minder delivered a kidney punch; before he could hit the ground, Turnbull grabbed his ponytail, yanked him upright, hauled back his fist to hit him again. But:

"For Christ's *sake!*" Waite was yelling. "Jesus, they were only looking after her!"

"Yes," Angela gasped, "they were, in their fashion. But I refuse to be a prisoner in my own home even if it's for my own supposed good!" She flew into Gill's arms.

Gill's man had fallen to one knee. Lifting an arm to protect himself as Gill stepped close, he sputtered, "Jesus! Hold your fire, will you?" He was bleeding profusely from his nose. As for the other MOD policeman, he gave a groan, held his side, flopped to the ground as Turnbull released him.

Gill turned to Waite. "You should have said," he shouted through the rapidly decreasing blast from the chopper's fan.

"I didn't know until I saw them," Waite answered, leading the way out of the danger zone. And to the two astonished men: "Wait for me in the helicopter."

At the house, Angela wouldn't invite the minister in. And in the conservatory that doubled as a porch, she turned on him and snapped, "You say you didn't know about this?"

"About them, no." Waite shook his head. "But at the same time I'm hardly surprised. The MOD will want to . . . well, *protect* anyone who had anything to do with the first contact."

"It is true, then?" Angela pressed. "They're back?" Anxiously she scanned Gill's face. But when she looked at Turnbull and for the first time actually recognized him . . . then it was as Gill had expected it would be: she knew for sure. Nodding, and tight-lipped, she said, "And they've called you in on it."

Waite held up his hands. "You have things to talk about," he said.

"And I have to get back to London. Spencer, give me a ring later tonight. Let me know what you've decided, anything you'll need. And, Jack"—unconsciously he straightened his lapels again as he looked at the minder—"it seems you've elected to be in on this, too. So for the moment I'll leave you all to it. But, Spencer, time is of the essence. We'd expect to be mobile by early tomorrow morning. Our destination . . ." He shrugged. "That's for you to decide." He nodded, turned, and ran back to the helicopter. And looking back: "I'll call off the close-protection people," he yelled. And again to the minder, "It's all yours now, Jack. But if you do happen to come across any more furtive-looking types, do try to remember they might be on our side."

"Tell those blokes we're sorry about the mistake!" Turnbull shouted after him.

Under her breath, Angela said, "You speak for yourself. From where I was standing they seemed like a couple of rough diamonds to me, if not roughnecks! Silent, surly sons of—"

"Policemen!" Gill said, ushering her inside the house. And Turnbull followed on behind . . .

Shortly Gill wanted to know, "Did they really give you such a hard time? If so they deserved what they got, and more!"

"No, not really." She shook her pretty head. She was in control again, no longer angry, resigned if anything and maybe just a little resentful. "As they kept trying to tell me, they had their orders. And as I kept telling them, to hell with your orders! I wanted to go into the village just to shop, but they told me I was confined to the house. Then, after I'd seen those first fumbled reports on TV this morning—from Egypt, and that Norwegian icebreaker—well I sort of connected things up. And when I pressed them for information . . . they told me what they knew, which wasn't much. But they said that when you were home you would have a lot more information. Do you?"

Gill shook his head, told her, "No, not a lot. Norwegian icebreaker? It seems you might know more than me! I would have been on the train, or talking to the people up at Jodrell Bank, when they showed that stuff. We can always catch the repeat on one of the news stations. Until then—I can only tell you what Waite told us." He did, then showed Angela the photographs. And while she pored over them, he sat there admiring her as so many times before. For it still thrilled him, indeed it thrilled him more than ever, that she was his.

She was small, no more than five feet four or five, long-legged, slender, and oh-so-pretty. With elfin ears half-hidden in tight black ringlets, a not-quite-perfect mouth, pert nose, and slightly tilted, deep, dark eyes, she looked almost Eurasian and was often taken for it. But in fact she was as English as they come. Or British, anyway, since her father was a Scot. But she had inherited her mother's face and slim figure, and a lot of her independence, too. So much so that on occasion Gill found himself puzzled that she'd ever given it up for him, and that they'd become "an item" and lived together. He could only put it down to the fact that she must really love him. And God-only-knew he loved her.

Jack Turnbull had meanwhile picked up the remote to switch on the TV. "Maybe I can get a news station," he said.

Angela and Gill were seated on a couch while Turnbull had an easy chair; they all faced the TV set on its stand in a corner of the living area. Pictures flashed on the screen, interpreted by some American newsreader's nasal commentary like white noise in the background. Turnbull turned down the sound to concentrate on the pictures, which told the usual depressing tale of worldwide unrest: political tension in Korea, Bosnia, Turkey, and Greece; cross-border warfare in the former Soviet Union; civil disobedience and riots in several big American cities as a new designer drug took its toll. But there was good news, too. Good results from the new AIDS immunization program; a declaration of cooperation between Great Britain and Argentina as a result of oil and natural gas finds around the Falklands, and a Czech-based international paedophile ring broken up, its ringleaders killed in a shoot-out in Prague.

But when the screen showed a massive ice floe, pictured from the air, then Turnbull quickly brought the sound back in time to catch the commentary midsentence:

". . . in the North Atlantic, thought to be a result of the thinning ozone layer and global warming. Currently the iceberg seems trapped in the gigantic swirl of the Labrador and Irminger currents and doesn't appear to be drifting anywhere at any great rate. Also, in this part of the Atlantic, the warm currents of the Gulf Stream should soon begin to reduce even this giant's bulk. But with its massive diameter and unknown thickness, 'soon' won't be soon enough for the fishermen and other vessels on the northernmost routes between the UK and USA. And if the berg should drift southward, it will block many of the major Atlantic cargo and passenger routes.

"With this in mind, shipping agencies have contracted the *Olso Star,* a Norwegian icebreaker returning to base from Arctic waters, to check the big floe out and report on her true dimensions. It's also possible that if the vast iceberg should prove to be too great a menace, then she could be broken up with air strikes, the theory being that smaller segments would melt more quickly.

"Just three hours ago we helicoptered a team aboard the *Oslo Star,* and in a little while we'll try to bring you a report and pictures direct from the icebreaker itself where she's maneuvering just a few feet away from this King Kong of icebergs, the largest free-floating mass of ice in the world."

The screen switched to a studio shot of the smiling newscaster at his desk, shuffling his reports. "Time now to switch from Arctic cold to Mediterranean heat," he said. "Cairo, where Egyptian authorities have reported one of the strangest mysteries since the *original* pyramids, as weird a thing as we've ever heard of. An enormous hoax? A mirage? Images from four thousand years ago caught in the bowels of the planet and only now projected to the surface by seismic convulsions deep within Earth's crust? *Phew!* What am I talking about? Well, a picture is worth a thousand words, or so I'm told, so I'll show you some earlier Egyptian TV footage and let you make up your own minds . . .

"This is Dan Laduca, switching you now to scenes shot yesterday morning on the Nile . . ."

Laduca's face shrank into a box that transferred to a corner of the screen, where he did a double take at something offscreen, then frowned and shrugged his apology as a picture that wasn't the one he'd promised appeared in the vacated space. And a little shakily, his commentary continued:

"Sorry, folks! This is just one of those technical things that sometimes happen. But since it does connect with our story we just may—and indeed we *are*—staying with it for a moment. You're looking at, er, Professor Harry Zorn, geological adviser at the New Mohole Project in the, er, Qattara Depression . . . ?"

Through this ad lib introduction, Professor Zorn had stood mouthing soundlessly into some unknown presenter's microphone. Behind the pair, a huge derrick silently drilled a hole into a sun-drenched, calcined, deeply riven surface, against an oasislike backdrop of palms, tethered camels, sweating workers, canvas tents, and near-distant dunes. But as Laduca's face blinked out, so on-site audio cut in and Zorn said:

". . . how it could possibly be as a result of our drillin' here. Indeed ah'd go a whole lot further and say it's out o' the question. Ah mean, this damn hellhole—the Qattara Depression—this mohole site where we're a-standin' right now, is all of a hundred and eighty miles from the Nile Delta site o' this so-called 'pyramid phenomenon' o' yourn! Why, you might as easily blame it on the great Ethiopian depression, right?" While speaking, Zorn had taken off his khaki shirt, wrung the sweat out of it, and thrown it across his deeply tanned shoulders. Now, pushing a wilting Stetson to the back of his head, he sluiced sweat from his face and spat into the sand.

"Well yes I suppose we might," the correspondent answered, reasonably enough. "Except no one happens to be drilling there! Professor Zorn, are you sure you couldn't have shaken up, well, *something*, from the Earth's core?"

"Hell," said Zorn, in an accent that was pure Texas, "the Earth's core is four thousand miles down! And we're not through the crust yet! That's what the Mohole Project is about: just to get through the crust. So you can believe me, son, your pyramid mirage in Cairo ain't got any damn thing to do with what we're a-doin' here. No sir." And he spat again.

Turnbull grunted, "Well many thanks, Professor Zorn!" But Gill put a cautionary finger to his lips, then pointed it briefly at the screen. Laduca was back in his box but the main picture had changed to a shot of a pyramid, albeit a pyramid with a difference, a pyramid of sorts. And:

"The iceberg is one thing," Gill husked. "A gigantic near-featureless block of ice. Also, if we can judge by those aerial shots, the iceberg has firmed-up; it has real mass; it's a very now thing. But this pyramid footage was taken yesterday, in its early stages, before it assumed concretion around its node. Now, maybe you'll recall, the castle on Ben Lawers went through just such a phase before it solidified. So now look at this picture, will you, Jack?" He nodded at the screen, his face pale, cheeks a little sunken.

And in a lowered tone, the minder said, "No question about it, right?"

Gill nodded. "I had hoped there might be some mistake, but the guessing games are over. This *is* very definitely a House of Doors. Which probably means that the others are, too. The problem is that I just can't imagine what it—or they—are doing here."

But after a moment's pause he added, "Or rather, the problem is I can . . ."

CHAPTER
5

THE PYRAMID ON the screen was blurred. But it wasn't that the camera was badly focused, for the background detail was sharp in every respect: the Nile Delta, sunlight sparking glints off the water, a felucca tacking with the morning breeze under triangular lateen sails.

Dan Laduca's commentary continued. "The replay I promised you," he said, after a glance offstage from his box in the top right corner of the screen. "Just another Egyptian pyramid, apparently"—for all the world as if there were dozens of them littering the landscape—"but this one is different. Because according to the local people, it wasn't here the night before these pictures were taken! I'm sorry about the picture quality; heat haze or some such—or maybe its those 'disturbed subterranean forces' that you heard Professor Zorn discounting just a few moments ago? Whichever, there's one more thing about this pyramid that's worthy of mention."

"Only *one* more thing?" said Gill.

There followed a jittery aerial shot, obviously taken from a badly piloted helicopter circling overhead. And now the size of the thing was more properly appreciated. For the vast structure was as large . . . as a pyramid! *Big as the real thing,* Gill thought, his attention riveted to the screen. While out loud he quietly said: "Heat haze? Have you ever heard such mumbo-jumbo? And as for 'projections from the magma'—utter rubbish!"

"It has only three sides," Angela said, in a small voice, her timing perfect as Dan Laduca made the same observation. But when the presenter stopped right there, Angela went on: "And it isn't weathered. It's like . . . like a very poor imitation."

And Turnbull added, "Which covers at least two more things that Dan Laduca seems to have missed."

"Or else he is only saying what he's allowed to say," said Gill. "That is, what he's been told to say."

"You think so?" Turnbull glanced at him.

Gill nodded. "This 'happy-talk' style of newsreader crap went out of fashion years ago. Oh, this stuff is news and they have to tell it, but they're keeping it lighthearted. Someone has remembered the panic caused by that old Orson Welles 'Martian invasion' thing. And don't forget the scale of the cover-up following our little adventure up in Scotland. Just think back, Jack . . . do you remember? They were going to *nuke* the original House of Doors!"

"Afterward, they said it was a military exercise." Turnbull rubbed his chin. "A nuclear war scenario; evacuation on a massive scale; the wilds of Scotland rather than a major city. They compensated the local populace with a little hard cash—which of course will turn the trick every time— and that was that. Do I remember? Oh, I remember! Hell, I was the fool out there on the side of that mountain, yelling like a madman into their viewers until they stopped the countdown!"

"But of course the government knew the truth of it," Gill said, nodding. "Just about every government worldwide knew the truth of it, and they all hid it. They're good at that: hiding stuff that isn't good for us to know. Panic, mass hysteria: all such complications were avoided. The rest of the world forgot about it, and we got the big once-over—or twice-over. And now that I come to think of it, there hasn't been a day since that I've felt entirely on my own. Always a pair of eyes somewhere, just looking me over."

Angela gasped. "Is that what it was?" she said. "Spencer, have we been under surveillance all this time?"

He shrugged. "Put yourself in their shoes. We'd been inside the House of Doors. We were the only people who *had* been there. And we were there for quite some little time. Kidnapped by aliens—or an alien. Angela, when soldiers get taken by a foreign power, what's the first thing you do when you get them back? Let me tell you: you check that they haven't been brainwashed, gone over to the other side. But the Thone aren't just a for- eign power, they are a superpower, an *alien* power. Certainly we've been watched, and closely. Our initial debrief . . . well, that's all it was. But all those interminable months of checking us out were just the beginning. And according to that . . . that MOD tea-boy, Waite, it's only just recently that they finally stamped us 'safe' and cut us loose—that's if we can *believe* him!"

"And now out of the blue, this new stuff," Turnbull grunted. "Stuff that casts a whole different light on things. 'Who ya gonna call?*Bug-busters!*' "

Gill was very grim-faced now. "You'll note that the news agencies haven't as yet connected up the castle to all of this stuff? Or maybe they have but they've been shut up, censored? Whether it's the Bermuda Triangle, little green men in the suburbs of Moscow, a squadron of fighters gone missing, or flying saucers in New Mexico, it's always the same old story. As then, so now—keep it quiet. Tell the people as little as possible, or better still say nothing at all. Not until you've called in the experts and got their opinions. And if you don't much care for expert opinions, continue to say nothing."

"And now?" Angela said (and the men could sense pent fury in her voice). "Are we supposed to—what?—answer the call? Sign on for another dose of God-only-knows what and go through all of that again?"

"We're supposed to be heroes again, yes," said Gill. And then he frowned. "Except . . . well, I don't recall saying anything about *we*. I mean, what's all this *we* stuff? Jack and me, that's one thing, it's our job. But—"

"But nothing!" Angela cut him short. "When it comes to the House of Doors, Spencer Gill—or even *Houses* of Doors—you're not doing anything or going anywhere without me!"

"Hold your fire," Turnbull told them curtly. "Take a look at this."

The picture had changed again, and Dan Laduca was saying, "Well, it seems we finally made it. For here we are aboard the *Oslo Star,* and I'm about to hand you over to our European correspondent, Steve Richards. Steve, can you hear me? We've got you there, so what have you got for us?"

"We hear you, Dan," a tall, heavily muffled man in a headset answered, from where he stood with his legs spread for balance in front of a satellite communications dish. "As for what we've got *for* you, well, you'll have to make what you can of it. I've got the first mate of the *Oslo Star* here with me, so while we have good connections it might be best if I talk to him. Is that okay with you?"

"Sure," Laduca told him. "Back in a moment, folks." And he and his box peeled back from the screen and were gone.

"Thanks, Dan," Steve Richards's London accent took over. He held lightly to the ship's rail with one hand, beckoned someone offscreen to join him. But before that someone could reach his side he went on: "Well, as you are all about to see, this isn't what you were expecting. Oh, the iceberg will be"—the camera swung away from him, through ninety degrees or more, to take in the port side of the vessel and, maybe eighty yards to stern, a rearing blue wedge of scalloped ice cliff that dwindled into an Arctic-seeming distance—"but the sea definitely won't be." And now the camera inclined downward, lighting on what should be the ocean's surface . . . but wasn't.

And: "It's weed!" Steve Richards said. "Seaweed. But seaweed like we never saw before. A giant raft of the stuff which we find almost as fascinating as the iceberg itself. And right now we have the *Oslo Star*'s first mate, Mr. Harold Kristian, to tell us what he makes of it. How about it, Harold?"

The weed was dense to say the least. So dense it was difficult to detect anything of the ocean on which it floated. It looked like a cross between giant kelp and bladderwrack, grown huge out of all proportion. When Gill was a boy he had used to "pop" the latter species on seaside holidays; those flat brown paddles with their fringes of bulging, squelchy bladders. *They* had had bladders Gill could trap between his thumb and finger, but with this species he would need to stamp on them with both feet! Moreover, this stuff was mobile; it moved with an undulating current all its own; blindly exploratory tendrils banged against the side of the ship, bounced off, and sank down to be replaced by others.

Of course, this was simply an effect of the sea's motion beneath the weed, which wasn't in any way sentient on its own but merely—or weirdly?—full of life. So Gill told himself, while simultaneously likening the fantastic raft to the canopy of some tossing, ocean-going jungle. Or maybe an alien jungle?

"Never mind what the mate makes of it," Turnbull grunted, obviously fascinated. "What do you make of it, Spencer?"

Mystified, unwilling as yet to speculate, Gill could only shake his head. "Let's hold on a minute for Mr. Kristian's opinion—that's assuming he hasn't mutinied yet." His attempt at humor was lost on the others as the camera lingered for a moment more on the weed, before swinging back again to the deck of the *Oslo Star*. And there stood the man himself, Harold Kristian, the very epitome of a cartoon Norwegian sailor, full-rigged for foul weather and full-bearded to boot. Steve Richards had fixed a tiny mike to the throat strap of the first mate's sou'wester, and now stood dwarfed by the huge man looming over him.

But the caricature didn't stop there. For despite that he spoke in a rough-and-ready English, still Kristian's voice was full of the lilt of his homeland fired with the verve and spirit of seafaring Viking ancestors. And like his face, his voice was as craggy and direct as a fjord.

"Is weed," he grunted. "Stinking weed. We see before, but not like this.

Is like Sargasso, you know? But Sargasso is legend and lies to south, in warm seas between Azores and Western Isles."

"The Sargasso?" Richards looked up into Kristian's darkly weathered face. "The sea of weed? You think that maybe part of the Sargasso broke away and drifted north? Is that what you're saying?"

"*Hah!*" The other gave a snort and laughed. But his laughter sounded pretty strained to Gill. "No, by God, I didn't say that. Sargasso is legend, but this scummy stuff is real. Can't say where it comes from. Might be an Arctic species that broke away with berg, growing like crazy as berg drifts through warmer waters. But *Oslo Star* is icebreaker. Can't do nothing with weed. We getting home now."

"And the iceberg?" Richards persisted. "Have you measured it? Do we know how big it is?"

"Oh, is big!" Kristian grinned. "But *Oslo Star* is breaker—not kamikaze ship!"

"Come again?"

"We designed to cut through ice inches, even feet thick," Kristian explained. "But this berg is twenty, twenty-five feet above water, and maybe one hundred twenty feet below! Now jus' you think. You can drive car over ice inch and half thick, eh? Also, I hear talk about bombing. By God, but that be some bomb if you be try sink this one! Anyway, we think she sits still. Leave alone, she melts."

"And the weed goes, too?"

But here Kristian frowned. "The stinking weed . . . I think she swims— er, she *drifts*—south. And we sit here too long. The weed piles up, is too deep, fouls the prop. Is like the . . . is like flypaper, right? And *Oslo Star* is icebreaker, not fly. So, we go home." Something caught his attention offscreen. He waved, shouted an order in Norwegian, made off before Richards could question him further.

"Which appears to be it from the *Oslo Star.*" The correspondent shrugged apologetically as Dan Laduca's box returned to its corner of the screen. "Obviously the crew have much to do, a lot on their minds . . ."

"Thanks, Steve," Laduca said. "We know that you and your team will be staying aboard until you can be lifted off. Maybe we'll be in touch later. But for now, we'll love you and leave you on a last shot of the iceberg, okay?"

As Richards waved good-bye, the camera obligingly returned to the enigmatic ice cliffs rising sheer as a blue plateau from the blanket of heaving weed, and panned along the scalloped rim mile after mile into a slightly misted, uncertain distance. But it seemed that the cameraman, too, was a lot more interested in the weed. He chose a parting shot to stern, where a narrow lane was being churned through the greeny-brown raft. But where normally there would be a foaming white channel, now the surface had the texture of boiling mud. And the weed, with its strange semblance of sentience, was closing in on the wake almost immediately. Only forty to fifty yards behind the *Oslo Star,* there was no evidence that the surface had been disturbed at all . . .

Then Dan Laduca and the newsroom filled the screen again, but as the rest of the news rolled on it was obvious that Gill had been right: the "happy talk" was absent now. And shortly:

"Well?" said Turnbull.

"Stranger and stranger." Gill shook his head thoughtfully.

"Your machine awareness?" Turnbull pressed him. "Did you get anything at all?"

But Angela said, "It doesn't work that way, Jack. Spencer doesn't feel anything from pictures, not even 'live' pictures. And anyway, don't we already know that these things are Houses of Doors?"

"I was simply wondering if Spencer had formed *any* kind of opinion yet, that's all," Turnbull told her. "Like, since this has to be the Thone, why they've come back?"

Gill's face was grimmer than ever as he stared at both of them, but especially at Angela. Then, as he and she came to an unspoken agreement, they both looked at Turnbull. "Jack," Gill said at last, "there's something you weren't in on. While you were out on the slopes of that mountain trying to convince the military not to blow us all to hell—"

"You two had an audience with the Grand Thone, I know that," Turnbull said with a nod. "He told you okay, you'd won your case, Sith would get his, and we, and our world, would be left alone."

"Left alone by the Thone," Gill said, with emphasis on the last three words. "But he also told us some stuff that we never reported."

"That you never . . . ?" Turnbull frowned. "And that you never told me?"

"For the same reason that world governments never released all the facts about the House of Doors," Gill answered. "It was—I don't know—a worrying, anxious-making, need-to-know sort of thing. We'd already been through enough. You, me, all of us. If it was up to me I wouldn't even have wanted Angela in on it, without that I should put any extra burden on your shoulders."

Turnbull looked from face to face. "So you kept something back, you and Angela? Something that the Grand Thone told you?" And now he remembered what Gill had said, and repeated it: "He told you that in future we'd be left alone . . . by the Thone!"

"Except—" Gill started to say.

"Except," the big minder again beat him to it, "except they aren't the only ones out there, right?"

Angela took Turnbull's hand and said, "The Ggyddn, Jack. They're out there, too."

"The . . . what? G'giddin?" He got the pronunciation right first time.

"A space-traveling race, people, species," she continued, "who don't have the ethics of the Thone. Which is about all we know about them."

"Not quite," said Gill. "We also know that the Thone find them disgusting and maybe fear them."

"Ethics?" Turnbull snorted. "The Thone? The hell you say! On the other hand maybe they do have their own brand of ethics, else we wouldn't be sitting here now. But on the *other* hand I'm damn sure Sith/Bannerman didn't!"

"And neither do the Ggyddn," said Gill. "Not according to the Grand Thone and his council. Whenever the Ggyddn were mentioned, all the council members to a—well, to a 'man'—they all took an attack of the shudders. And as for what the Grand Thone actually said about them, he said: 'Let's hope you never come across the Ggyddn, and that they never find you.' "

Angela nodded and said, "He also reminded us that space is a big place. Which we took to be the optimistic approach."

The minder had long since turned down the TV. Now, switching it off entirely, he said, "Space is a big place, yes—but maybe not big enough?" And as the screen's flicker and insect sounds faded away, he went on, "Is that it, Spencer? You think that maybe this is the Ggyddn?"

Gill stood up and began pacing the floor. "I think I wish you'd give me a break, Jack!" He tried not to snap at the minder, found it hard. "I won't know a damn thing until I can get up close to one of these manifestations— maybe not even then. But if their science, their machines, are different, then I'll know it. If this is the Thone, I'm pretty sure I'll recognize that fact; I'll know their machinery. But if these things are, well, *alien* to me, to anything that's gone before—"

"Then they'll be Ggyddn," Turnbull said with a nod. "Yes, but it still seems to me that whoever they are they're playing by the Thone rulebook. First the House of Doors, Houses in this case, and then the game. So if they are the Ggyddn, and even if they don't have ethics, they *must* have rules. Some kind of rules."

Gill chuckled wryly and said, "I don't know if I ever mentioned it before, but sometimes I think—"

"That I'm not as dumb as I look?" Turnbull was as quick on the uptake as usual.

"I wasn't going to put it quite like that," said Gill. But Angela was frowning as she commented:

"Didn't you ever hear about the Romans, you two? They had games, too, you know. They called them games, anyway. But they weren't so fussy about rules."

"Oh, sure," Turnbull said gruffly. "Those good old Roman games. Heads I win, tales you lose games. And the winners were always the ones on the *outside* of the arena!"

"And why not this game, too?" Angela said, with a terrible logic. "I mean, didn't the Romans *prepare* their arenas, before all the bloodshed?"

The big minder thought about it. "You're saying that setting up these Houses of Doors could be just part of the scenario? Like setting a stage before Act One, or building a scaffold before a hanging? Or like, 'Hey, you! This is no subterfuge but simply a warning. We'd just like to watch you running around in circles awhile before we turn the lions loose.' "

"Let's think about that," said Gill. "First you set up the arena, then you bring on the gladiators, or the Christians, and next—"

"You open the cages," said Angela.

"But the Christians couldn't fight back," said Gill. "They had no weapons. We do, and some pretty heavy stuff at that. And whoever these people are they must know that. I mean, you don't have their kind of technology without taking into account something as basic as that: the fact that we might hit back. These people *know* that we have nuclear weapons."

"And it doesn't faze them," Turnbull pointed out.

"Apparently not. But if that's the case—and if they're bandits, bad guys—why not simply come in shooting? Why give us any advance warning at all?"

"Because it *is* some kind of cruel game," Angela insisted. "They want to see us knocking ourselves out first—running in circles like Jack said—fleeing from the as yet unseen lions, even before they turn them loose! That is, before they show us their strength, start making demands, turn their weapons on us if or when we fail to comply."

"But before we could . . . well, comply, or otherwise, we'd need to know what their terms were." Gill chewed his lip, turned things over in his mind. "We'd need someone up front, negotiating."

"And we have someone," Turnbull told him. "You."

"Our people up top will have worked all of this out before us," Gill said. "Of course they have—it's why they've brought us together again."

"Because we, or you, turned the trick last time," Turnbull said, nodding. "We're the ones, the only ones, with the experience. At the same time, though, I'll bet the bomb bays are already being loaded—just in case we don't have *enough* experience."

"Anyway," Angela put in, "we're not the only ones with experience. Varre, Clayborne, and Anderson survived it, too."

"Anderson is out of it," Gill said. "As for the other two: if they were to be part of the team I wouldn't want anything to do with it. It's my opinion that their team spirit was a couple of degrees below zero. Anyway, I kept tabs on them for a while. Clayborne went pseudo-religious, became the high priest of some kind of cult or coven in the Nevada desert. And Varre . . . well, he disappeared along with ESP, the European Space Project. Some kind of cold fish, that one. Do you remember, he had claustrophobia? God, that phobia of his cost us some gray hairs! But I fancy that will have cleared up by now, killed off by proximity to the original House of Doors: Thone loathing of all diseases, physical or mental. Still, I wouldn't be any too happy knowing that our safety depended on Varre."

"Which leaves us," said Turnbull, standing up as Gill sat down, and pacing the floor in his turn. Until suddenly he said, "Angela, I'm dry. Any chance of a drink?" But then, looking at Gill, "Or maybe I shouldn't?"

Gill shrugged. "It's your life, Jack," he said, and waited for the other to respond.

Turnbull licked his lips, looked suddenly haggard, bleary-eyed. But then, the minder frequently looked that way. He glanced at Angela, also waiting for his decision, then stopped pacing and squared up to it. "The hell with it," he said. "I hear what you say about Varre, and I agree with you. I wouldn't want you thinking you can't depend on me either. But I have to tell you, this doesn't feel like a good time to go on the wagon!"

"Funny, isn't it," Gill said. "We all had problems when we entered the House of Doors, and we were cured. But what do you know, we're no sooner over one thing than hooked on another."

"Eh?" Turnbull stared at him; Angela, too.

"Anderson was as sane as they come. A bit power crazy, but most politicians are," Gill started to explain. "Now—he's as mad as a hatter. Oh, harmless mad, but mad all the same. Varre liked to be in the limelight: he's disappeared, gone into hiding. Clayborne, president of SCOPE, was a long-time devotee of the They-Walk-Among-Us set. Now *he's* the one walking among us. Well, among those idiots in the Nevada desert anyway. And then there's you, Jack?"

Turnbull shrugged. "I . . . I had my hangups, too," he said. "I had a couple of rough times out in Afghanistan. All my life they stayed with me. Now they've gone, but I'm a drunk—or I was . . ." He looked at Gill and Angela where they sat together. "So you two are the only ones who came out unscathed."

Gill shook his head. "I was dying," he said. "Doing a good job of it, too. The House of Doors fixed that, yes, but it gave me something else."

"Likewise," said Angela. "My only 'fixation' was Rod Denholm, my husband. I was scared to death of him, with damn good reason. Now he's gone, but I'm afraid anyway."

"Angela's right," said Gill. "That's what it is: fear. You see, ever since the House of Doors we've been stalled, not daring to make too many plans, wanting but not daring to start our family or look too far ahead. To know that there are such creatures as the Ggyddn—or even the Thone for that matter—is to admit that the future is one hell of a vast uncertainty. And we admitted it, and we were right to."

The minder nodded. "But we did come through it," he said. "And for my money we'll still make one hell of a team. Oh, I'm not looking forward to it, don't get me wrong. But if I have to be in on this with anyone, I'm glad that it's you two . . ."

A car's tires crunched gravel on the drive. An engine cut, and a moment later there came a ring at the door. Gill answered it. Two men delivered a crate to the doorstep . . . but the crate had airholes, and it whined a little.

One of the deliverymen got Gill to sign for the crate and handed him a note. It was from George Arthur Waite.

Spencer—

By the time you get this, you will know what's going on. In that regard: this old boy's master died a couple of weeks ago—since then he's been living in a pound sweating on a major decision. In your report, you gave him a lot of credit. With that in mind, we thought you might find him useful . . .

Angela had come to the door by the time Gill had got his thoughts together and was opening the gate on the crate. "What on earth . . . ?" She began to say, until a dog—a black and white mongrel with a frantically vibrating stump of a tail—bounced out of the crate right into Gill's arms, toppling him from his crouch and causing him to sit down with a bump on the gravel. Then she burst out laughing and said, "Barney?"

"Yes." Gill couldn't avoid that wet nose and tongue. "The one and only Barney. And you're dead right: 'what on Earth'—and off it!"

"Looks like the team's complete," said Turnbull, from behind Angela. "At least *this* member has no hang-ups!"

"That's right," said Gill, still fighting the frantic dog off. "None at all— well, except rabbits. And six-legged rabbits, at that!"

CHAPTER
6

IN THE HEART of the pyramid node, Sith, no longer of the Thone, made ready to converse with Gys U Kalk of the Ggyddn. Audience with the Kalk had taken more than a little time to achieve, had eaten deep into Sith's less than plentiful reserves of patience. This was evident in his mental agitation, was emphasized by the sharp "tone" of his telepathic voice as finally the Kalk turned from the node's flowing, liquid-motion screens and made himself available.

"I've kept my side of the bargain," Sith said without preamble. "I informed you of this world, detailed its suitability, within certain parameters, and gave you its coordinates. Now I expect you to attend to your side of things."

Had there been a human observer in the node's operational area, it is doubtful if he or she would have recognized Sith or Gys U Kalk as sentient creatures, or even the control room as a "room" as such. With wraparound liquid screens aflow in kaleidoscopic color, and a ceiling that was indiscernible through a haze of bright white mist—with a floor that was "soft," offering only thirty percent the resistance or traction of a solid floor—and its alien occupants a pair of barely opaque, luminous, forty-inch, tendril-dangling jellyfish as insubstantial as will-o'-the-wisps, nothing was designed to interface with human sensory systems. Or rather, everything would interface violently, certainly at first contact. Yet just as well-balanced minds will adjust to a maze of mirrors, strobe lighting, or the deprivation of one or more senses, so they would adjust and get used to

this, and in time come to accept the superabundance of sensory information, the impact of an alien environment.

"Has there been some indication that I would not hold to our agreement?" Gys U Kalk was coldly aloof; his reply rang in Sith's mind as sharp
as the splintering of vital tissues in the ice chamber of an executioner. In
the ninety-plus degrees temperature of the control room, the Kalk's
thoughts would seem especially frigid. Or perhaps not; for despite their
body heat the Ggyddn were notoriously cold in all their affairs and dealings. It had much to do with their status: Thone outcasts—knowing that
they had been found wanting, unworthy—they were bitter and resentful.
They were Ggyddn, which meant literally "without warmth, deviant,
unethical, un-Thone." So why should the Kalk care whether he kept his
side of the bargain or not?

Sith might have guarded his thoughts more closely, for the Kalk had
"overheard" that last. "There is honor even among the dishonored," he
said. "Without it we'd be scattered throughout space, forgotten on whichever blighted rocks the Thone chose to abandon us. We are deviants, true,
but we are *all* deviants. You, too, Sith. So stop thinking like the Thone.
Now you are Ggyddn. I would have lifted you from your prison anyway,
because we are few and the Thone are many. *You* are the one who set the
conditions, not I. But I did accept them. And indeed, you were right: this
world is ripe for Ggyddn colonization. But I must tell you that personally
I find your feud a petty thing. What, you would pit yourself against these
men—or this man? Revenge? But what is this for revenge? You are
Ggyddn, like a great shark in the seas of space, while he is like a small fish
hiding in his hole on this reef of a planet."

"But this fish has a stinger!" Sith snapped. "He bested me not because
he was better, but because I underestimated him. He was different; he understood our machinery, got into the synthesizer, turned the House of
Doors against me. I could have been the Grand Thone; but for him and
his I might even have ascended the crystal pedestal!" In the middle of his
outburst, sensing the Kalk's cold amusement, Sith paused. "What? Do you
find me an object of derision?"

"No," said the Kalk. "But you *are* Ggyddn. And never have I seen one
more qualified. When finally you've destroyed this man and quelled your
passion, then you'll be a force to be reckoned with. And always remember:
you might *yet* ascend the crystal pedestal, or have one of your own, when
the Thone worlds are under the control of the Ggyddn! Revenge? Oh, yes,
I understand the need for it. But my sights are set higher than a single,
cold-blooded bipedal life-form on this one small planet. Higher than the
planet itself or even a hundred such. My sights are set on the Thone!"

"Mine, too," Sith agreed. "Especially the so-called 'Grand Thone'—in the right place and at the right time. But for now I'll settle for Spencer Gill."

"But he is doomed anyway," the Kalk said irritably. "Him, his race, even his world in its current form."

"Yes, but I want him to know who did it to him."

"That . . . is deviant, if not devious," the Kalk observed, an observation as pointed as narrowed eyes or a slow, thoughtful nod.

"Deviant *and* Ggyddn," Sith answered, with the mental equivalent of a broad, humorless grin.

"You'll search him out?" The Kalk seemed about to accommodate Sith in his vendetta. "If so you'll need to synthesize an environment suit."

"Not yet," Sith answered. "Oh, I could find him. Except I won't have to. Spencer Gill will come to me. And I'll know him just as the node will know him. The instrumentation will react to him even as he reacts to it. And so you see I don't need to seek him out. Meanwhile—"

"Meanwhile," Gys U Kalk cut in, "it isn't my intention to wait. If these creatures divine our purpose they might well try to stop us. And nuclear radiation is as harmful to us as it is to them—*and* to their world! Or our world, as it will be. So, whether you go after Spencer Gill or he comes to you makes no great difference: the work goes on. Our schedule supersedes yours."

"Understood," said Sith. "But he will come, be sure. However, I will accept your good advice and synthesize an environment construct, just in case. For I would hate for Gill or his world to die without knowing that I was at least partly responsible. Do I require your permission to use the transmat? Mobility is important, for I can't be certain which of the nodes he will visit first. Instrumentation at each node will tell me if he is or has been in that vicinity."

"Use the transmat by all means." The Kalk offered his version of a shrug. "Only remember, the Ggyddn controllers of the individual nodes are their own authorities. As I am in control here—indeed, as I am the sole presence here, with the exception of yourself—so they are in control there. As a newcomer, you will apply to them for permission for any extranodal activity in their areas; though should you encounter any difficulty you may always refer back to me. For the understanding is that within our limited society—within the bounds of this synthesizer—I hold the position of Grand Ggyddn."

"I scarcely need reminding," said Sith archly.

"Ah, but I think you do!" Gys U Kalk replied. "As a Thone invigilator you broke the rules, risked your all and lost. What assurance do the Ggyddn have that your ambitious, 'deviant' nature has in any way changed through four years of isolation upon that barely adequate rock of an inner moon where the Thone left you? Not that we would want it to have changed, you understand. Certainly your need to settle with this man, this Spencer Gill, remains a constant. Thus I require you to think on this:

"Where the Thone are known for their mercy—where they calculate the so-called 'worthiness' of the denizens of worlds, and on that basis generally tend to leniency in allowing inferior races to exist and decide their own fates—we are Ggyddn. The Ggyddn accept no such degrees of worthiness; inferior is inferior, and might is the only right. And where Thone leniency may be stretched even so far as to merely banish such a traitor as yourself, Ggyddn justice is far more decisive. I have aboard this synthesizer a containment chamber that I can cool to within a half degree of absolute zero. And I can do it . . . slowly."

The Kalk had delivered this item of information, this warning, with an icy detachment worthy of his chamber itself. Sith "shivered" as he pictured his heat energy long since exhausted, his molecular motion slowed to immobility, his matter devolving to essential gases so reduced in volume as to be . . . nothing.

"Precisely," said the Kalk.

And Sith quietly excused himself . . .

Gill hadn't slept well and thought when he crept out of bed at 6:00 A.M. that he'd be up on his own. But Jack Turnbull was already in the kitchen, cradling a mug of coffee and looking like hell.

"Breakfast?" Gill poured himself a mug from the pot Turnbull had made.

"It'll do, thanks!" the other snapped. "Anything else—I'd probably throw it up."

Gill wasn't about to suffer any of Turnbull's withdrawal tantrums. "Just as well," he answered sharply. "In any case, there's only cold turkey in the fridge."

Turnbull got the message and crumpled down more yet into himself.

"Will you be able to handle it?" Gill didn't feel at all sympathetic, or he wasn't going to show it. "I mean, I thought we had this out last night. Or do I have to start marking the levels on the bottles in my drinks cabinet?"

Turnbull looked at him half miserably, half inquiringly, all sullenly. "What's all this hard-man shit, Spencer? I mean, do you like pulling the legs off spiders, too?"

"Jack," Gill said, "I've been awake most of the night puzzling this one out. And I've got nowhere. Nowhere good, anyway. I think it's possible we'll have to do it all again, like last time, which means we'll need to be pretty damn tight. Frankly, right now you look about as tight as a whore's crotch." He got up, went into the living area, returned with a bottle of whiskey, and set it down on the kitchen table right under Turnbull's nose. The minder looked at the bottle, then looked red-eyed at Gill.

"So it's your choice," Gill told him. "But you'll have to make it now. I can call you a taxi and you can take the bottle with you, and be back in that bar in Berlin by tonight or whenever you're capable. Or . . . you can leave the bottle alone and forget it for the duration. What do you say, Jack?"

The other looked away, lit a cigarette that trembled visibly between his lips, and opened a corner of his mouth perhaps to say something that neither man really wanted to hear—

And Angela appeared from nowhere in an angry swirl of dressing gown, saying, "Bacon and eggs: I'm going to cook them and you'll *both* eat them! You—" she snapped at the minder, "can stop feeling sorry for yourself. And you"—this time at Gill—"can quit the bullying. We were a *team*, for God's sake, and a good one! We helped each other; we didn't run each other down, spit in each other's faces!" She snatched up the bottle, whirled it away, came back in a moment still angry as hell, and yanked open the fridge door. But now her bottom lip was trembling. "So since we're all feeling so . . . so good and *full* of the old team spirit, isn't anyone going to tell me . . . tell me where the fourth *bloody* member has got to?"

"Eh?" said Gill, thrown right off track, and blinking as if he'd been slapped.

But Jack Turnbull had been well and truly woken up—and in more ways than one. For after all, this could well prove to be his one and only way back from the brink. It could be, yes, and he had almost thrown it away. "Barney . . . er, seemed about to pee himself," he said lamely. "So I let him out."

As Angela went to the door the big minder looked at Gill, shrugged apologetically, and said, "Hey, you two. It's . . . it's going to be all right now, I promise you. I'll make sure it is. And, Spencer, Angela is right. We're a team, or we can be. Just like before."

Gill had heard all of that already; he nodded, said nothing. And Barney came in and went through his ritual skittering, wagging, and licking, until Angela got him something from the fridge. Cold turkey, just as Gill had said, which in Barney's case went down just fine . . .

* * *

The sun had cleared the sea, and Gill had just finished outlining stage one of his plan when the telephone rang. "Waite," he told the others, sourly, picking up the handset. "I'll give you odds it's him. Nice of him to leave us alone for so long!"

"Spencer," said Waite urgently. And without waiting for an answer: "Are you watching the morning news?"

"Should we be?" Feeling the tension in the other's voice, Gill tried not to get caught up in it. But he looked pointedly at Turnbull, twitching his head to indicate the TV set. And as the minder switched it on: "What's up, George?"

"See for yourself, then get back to me. Right now, I want to watch, too; make sure they're not reporting what they're not supposed to." And the phone went dead.

Meanwhile, the television screen had snapped into life; it showed the BBC One studio in London, with a blown-up picture of the Houses of Parliament as the backdrop to an unusually cluttered news desk. The newscaster was in full swing, midway through a sentence:

". . . believed to be similar to the algae that infested the Ligurian Riviera and some stretches of the west coast of Italy three years ago, and the freshwater variety that blocked northern reaches of Lake Tanganyika in '94. The current outbreaks are thought to be mainly due to unusual weather patterns, though blame has been laid as widely afield as several recent volcanic eruptions, the ongoing depletion of the ozone layer, Saddam Hussein's attack on Kuwait and the pollution of the Persian Gulf by oil, and the atmospheric damage caused by the firing of Kuwait's oil fields. British scientists who studied the 'Japanese Weed' epidemic of the early nineties, which blighted southern coasts of England, are of the opinion that the spread is likely to increase until the autumn, when declining weather conditions should cause the weed to 'suffocate.'

"The weed masses were first reported by local people, and then picked up by weather satellites as their bulk became visible from space. There is not thought to be any connection with the raft of weed brought down from the Arctic by Iceberg Irma, named for the Irminger current that keeps the giant floe 'tethered' in the Atlantic, nor to the geological formation of limestone crystals in the shape of a pyramid in the Nile Delta, despite that a lesser weed infestation would appear to have accompanied this latest freak of nature, too.

"We are sorry to have no additional pictures at this time, but hope to show close-ups of the weed belts in later newscasts.

"And now to the state of the economy:

"While Germany continues to press for an early introduction of the Eurodollar and fiscal union in general . . ."

Gill had gone to stand beside the TV. "Balls to the Eurodollar!" he grunted, and switched the thing off. "And congratulations to George and his minions—or maybe to someone above him?—who had the common sense to put a lid on the media."

"You think it's right that people shouldn't know?" Angela looked uncertain.

"The military knows," said Gill. "George Waite *is* the military. He's MOD . . . and so am I, right now. I signed papers with them long ago—a contract, if you like—when I thought I didn't have much time. Stuff like that didn't seem to matter much. Oh, I like to pretend I have the upper hand, and it's true that if push came to shove they'd get rid of Waite before me, but in fact I'm in their pocket. The only good thing about that is . . ."

"That so far they've done all the right things, right?" This from Turnbull.

And Gill nodded. "However close they came, they did manage to get it right up in Scotland that time. It looks like they're following a similar game plan now: keeping it cool, not letting panic set in. Plenty of time for that, we hope—and for retaliation—if or when our visitors start something nasty."

"But haven't they already?" Angela said. "What about this weed, Spencer? What on earth is it?"

"On Earth?" He looked at her. "Well it is now, yes. Let's wait until I've spoken to Waite."

But as he reached for the phone it rang again, and it was the man himself. "You didn't get back to me."

"We were thinking it over, what we heard."

"Well?"

"Enlighten me," said Gill. "This weed: where is it? And is it the same stuff we've seen around the iceberg? Is that one of the things you didn't want reported?"

"Yes, of course it is—to both questions! As for *where* it is: it's in the Nile, heading east through the waterways of the Nile Delta toward the Suez Canal. In fact, it's probably there by now—and then south into the Gulf of Suez, and north to the Med. That's *one* or *some* of the places where it is. Ah, but it's also twenty miles out from Irma on all sides, and the belt gets wider hour by hour! Where is it? It's *every*-fucking-where, Spencer! And there are more than just three sites of origin. Pagoda, pyramid, iceberg . . . islands, rocks, and *houses*! A 'mansion'—a House of Doors, yes, but of course without doors or windows—in the Newport Estuary on the Isle of

Wight. Christ only knows how we missed *that* one! Or maybe it's recent. And a 'villa' in Jamaica on the Cuban side of the island. But it's also in Honolulu and Tasmania, in Lake Superior and the Gulf of Mexico, in the Bay of Bengal, the Falklands, and the Shetlands. Everywhere, or if not everywhere, then soon to be. It spreads like wildfire. We calculate that each source—what did you call them, nodes?—is putting out this stuff at a fast walking pace. For example: this bloody mansion on the Isle of Wight was reported to us just last night. And this morning the weed's out past Cowes and filling the Solent!"

Gill made mental calculations for several long seconds and said, "Picture a model of, say, twenty-four nodes, and let's say that six of them are spread out evenly around the equator. Four thousand miles between each node. But the spread is in both directions, which cuts the distances in half. At an average of, say, five miles an hour, how long will it take to link up? Five into two thousand goes four hundred. Four hundred hours is maybe two and a half weeks before . . ."

"Before we're fucked!" Waite finished it for him. "No river, canal, lake, or ocean transport. No shipping at all. And God only knows what it's doing to the fish—or how many ships will be stranded—or how drinking water will be affected. And what of our hydroelectric power systems? This stuff can block the world's dams, clog the reservoirs, change the entire climate. Spencer, we not only live by water, we're made of it! So what is this shit? A symptom, an infection, or . . . a weapon?"

It's a weapon, Gill thought, but said nothing out loud. *Or perhaps not a weapon but . . . the very opposite? Like a hoe or a plow, a tool for preparing the soil? Or maybe an insecticide, for getting rid of the pests? Or perhaps it's a greenhouse, to warm things up a little. What was that Waite had said: "It will change the climate?"*

Damn right it would, but *some* like it hot!

"Spencer, what is it?" Angela tugged at his elbow, causing him to start. "Your face . . ."

He held a finger to his lips, said into the phone: "There are things we'll need."

"Name them," Waite told him.

"A helicopter, a pilot, and unlimited access to refueling across the board."

"No problem. Anything else?"

"Yes, you can advise your boss to keep a tight rein on the media. He's doing okay so far, but he mustn't let it slip."

"My boss?" Waite was playing dumb, innocent, but the catch in his voice gave him away.

"Who are you trying to kid, George?" Gill said quietly. "I mean, we both know you're way out of your depth. All of this is too big for any one man. I said your boss, but there's probably a whole team of them."

And in a little while, "No," Waite said, "to my knowledge there's just the one. Or if there is a team, it's a step higher up again. As for your message: my 'boss' wants to meet you, so you can pass it on yourself when we deliver the chopper in . . . say an hour and a half?"

"Talk in miles," said Gill. "Say, seven and a half *miles* and you might start thinking a little faster."

Waite got the point, said, "I'll get right on it. Maybe an hour?"

"Good," said Gill. "You can tell the pilot our first stop will be the Isle of Wight. I said I wanted to get close to one of these things, and here one of them's got close to me! A look at this mansion of yours can't hurt—or it might, but I don't intend to let it. Oh, and one other thing: on your way down you might like to give a little thought to something else I need."

"Oh?" said Waite.

"Do you know of a deserted little island I can use? A private place no one ever visits? A rock in the sea just a mile or so offshore? A couple of acres, maybe? Thing is, I need the use of some ground for . . . well, for a sort of building development I've been planning."

"A what? A building development? Spencer, what are you—?"

"I'm going to build a house of my own there," Gill cut him short. "A very special house. A House of Doors . . ."

CHAPTER
7

I N FACT, IT was more like sixty-five minutes, but still barely sufficient time for Gill and Co. to eat and get themselves together, before the helicopter came whirring from the mainland east of Hayling and settled toward the rambling garden.

Gill and Angela had done a little rambling themselves in their four years together, and climbing, too; it was a fitness thing they'd brought back with them from their House of Doors experience, when their physical limitations had been made all too obvious. Thus they'd dressed themselves in the tough gear—the boots and camouflaged combat-styled clothing—of outdoorsmen and survivalists, while Turnbull was stuck with what he'd been wearing throughout: his somewhat disheveled suit of casual clothing. He'd made a mental note, however, to get himself suitably kitted-out at his earliest opportunity. And Angela had stuffed a strong, lightweight sausage bag with useful items . . . most important of which seemed to be toilet tissues!

As the three ran out under the fan of the helicopter, Gill joshed her: "What, were you a Girl Guide or something?"

"Or something," she yelled back over the blast. "I was the half-naked prisoner of an alien castle whose rooms went on forever! Your memory may be failing, Spencer Gill, but mine is as sharp as ever. I remember times when I would have given almost anything just for a square of paper."

"Anything?" This was Gill being flippant, which he recognized as a mistake the moment the word slipped out. For Angela had barely avoided giving her all, which in the terrifying circumstances she'd faced in the House of Doors would quite literally have been a fate worse than death, though certainly death would have been a part of it. The last part.

But choosing to read it the way he'd intended, she merely turned her nose up and haughtily repeated, *"Almost!"* . . . Then, with a grin, "Well, depending on who was trading."

He frowned. "Funny, but I don't remember it that way. The way I remember it, we didn't have to go."

"True," she answered, "but I'm a woman. And I *felt* that I should go anyway."

Barney ran with them and was up onto the step first and in through the sliding door at Gill's urging. Amazingly, it was as if time had never separated them; Barney had remembered Gill instantly and accepted him as his new master. For Gill's part, he had been surprised to find the dog still alive and kicking, and indeed active beyond his years; he was by no means a young dog. But then again, Barney, too, had been a captive of the House of Doors. Had he also been rejuvenated, Gill wondered, or at least given a new "leash" on life?

He grinned at his own cleverness, a grin that quickly disappeared as he and the others took sidelong seats and came face-to-face with the chopper's occupants. Waite was one, of course, but the other . . .

"Miranda Marsh," she introduced herself as Turnbull signaled to the pilot that he'd locked the door in position, and Gill reached over to accept the slim, cool hand that he'd been offered. "And before you ask," she continued, "there is a committee I take advice from and answer to, yes, but I'm the coordinator and—"

"Your new boss," Waite cut in, barely able to contain a smirk and the kind of knowing look that said: *And if you think that* I'm *a double-dyed bastard* . . .

"*And* I'm your boss," she told him with a sideways glance. "And I feel sure that Mr. Gill won't be nearly as difficult to work with as you seem to have found him."

"Oh?" Gill said, raising an eyebrow. "Tales out of school, George?" But:

"Miranda," said Waite, sighing, then thought better of it, whatever "it" was, bit his lip, and went on to make the rest of the necessary introductions. While this was going on, Gill took the opportunity to study "his new boss" a little more closely, albeit covertly.

Miranda Marsh was something. She was lovely, leggy, and, to be descriptive without all the words, "built." This would probably be Turnbull's description, anyway, Gill thought. Her smart gray trouser suit was well cut, the rolled lapels of the jacket made feminine by the frills of a white blouse that softened the edges without accentuating the inner curves, which in any case didn't need it. Standing, she'd be tall—maybe five-eight or-nine— and her high heels would make her taller still. Advantageous if you want to look down on people. Doubtless Gill was going to find out about that.

Executive features: she *was* the boss lady from any one of a handful of American TV shows, but without their unconvincing glitz. Oh, it was there—she knew about makeup—but also how to wear it without looking like it was wearing her. She would be maybe twenty-nine or thirty, but as yet no lines were showing through. High cheekbones, penetrating gray eyes under long, natural lashes, as blond as they come and very lightly tanned. Holidays in the south of France, Gill imagined. But with a boyfriend (or girlfriend?) or on her own? Somehow he couldn't picture this one going short of loving company. Maybe her affairs were short-lived; she wore no rings on her well-manicured fingers, and there was that about her that felt somehow . . . what, predatory? Gill had sensed it before in unmarried women, something he termed "the hunting instinct." And not always in the single ones, either.

Even suspecting that his appraisal was cynical and as yet unjustified, Gill continued with it as Miranda spoke to Angela. And from the look on Angela's face he guessed she was thinking much the same things. Oh, she hid it well but Gill knew her . . . that wide-eyed innocence of hers, as the mind behind the fluttering eyelashes probed, analyzed, and sought to define. But what was she looking at? Miranda Marsh's firm, immaculately painted lips, her jet oval earrings set in silver, the fine lines of a sculpted jaw and neck, and the gleam of her almost too-perfect teeth? Or was she perhaps gauging the other's obvious intelligence, or maybe wondering about her impact on Gill?

"Oh, my hand!" said Angela, aware that Miranda was looking curiously at her own hand. "My hands are so rough! Did I graze you? It's the gardening. I mean, I like to garden . . ." And Gill knew that Angela was suddenly aware of her combat suit, embarrassingly aware of her own makeup—the fact that they'd left the house in something of a hurry—and over and above everything aware that by comparison Miranda was, well, immaculate!

But: "Oh, I'm *so* sorry!" said the woman from the ministry. "But, Mrs. Gill, you're such a pretty little thing, and your hand felt so . . ."

"Rough, yes," said Gill, before Angela could say anything herself. But he knew she wouldn't much care for Miranda's "pretty little thing" compliment (or was it?). And as for that very deliberate "Mrs." . . .

"We're not married," he continued, knowing instinctively that she already knew. "And Angela's hands *are* a little rough, yes. She's far happier with a spade, doing something constructive, than pushing a pen, er, 'Mrs.' Marsh?"

"It's Miss," she told him. "Or better still Miranda. And I really am *so* sorry for my gaffe. You must think I'm so gauche! But you're such an obvious couple that . . . oh, it just slipped out."

And Waite sitting there trying not to smile; and Gill not daring to look at Angela, knowing the picture she'd now have in her head: of herself with a piece of straw in the corner of her mouth shoveling shit in the garden—as seen through *his* eyes! No wonder she'd fallen so utterly silent now, while *Miss* Marsh spoke to Turnbull:

"And I certainly need no background notes on you, Jack, if I may call you by your first name? David Anderson, my predecessor, had nothing but the highest praise for you. Except . . ." and she frowned, causing the shallow "S"s of her eyebrows to straighten out a little, "well, I hear you've been having something of a difficult time of it recently. Nothing permanent I hope?"

Turnbull could be quick on the uptake, too. Indeed, and as Gill had long ago discovered, his frequently heavy-lidded, dull-eyed Robert Mitchum-like looks concealed a mind sharp as a tack. Not in every respect but in most. To get to the top as a minder he had had to be sharp. Now he said, "Don't you worry about me, sweetheart." And glancing at his watch, "Why, I haven't fallen down drunk in . . . oh, a couple of hours now!"

She looked at him very pointedly for a long moment—then burst out laughing. And it seemed to Gill a throaty, even sexy, very genuine laugh. "So as you can see," she was finally able to speak, "I like my men with a strong sense of humor . . ." And then, more soberly:

"But now let's get on. This morning, George gave you what new information we have; he told you about these new phenomena, these additional 'nodes' if you like. We can't be sure how many there are because they don't form any recognizable pattern. Our guesstimate is maybe twenty to twenty-four. Several of them are so out of the way that we—and by we I mean friendly and cooperative world authorities—haven't yet had time to fly over or visit them. For example a small 'island,' more properly a rock, has appeared way out in the middle of the Pacific. We know that it isn't merely some volcanic upheaval because of its attendant raft of this sargasso weed. But if the Americans hadn't reprogrammed their spy and weather satellites, we still wouldn't know it was there at all! And there's a good chance there are others still to come to light.

"Now, this Pacific node could be especially important. For as I've said it's out of the way, right on the edge of the Pacific-Antarctic Ridge. And in the event that you can't, er, talk to our visitors, Spencer?"—she looked at him for his approval of first-name terms—"or that contact, if we're able to establish such, should break down . . ."

"That's where we—or the French, presumably?—would try to nuke them." Gill smiled a hard smile, one that was open to misinterpretation, and nodded. "Several thousand miles from any sizable human habitation. Yes, a good choice . . . but a very bad idea." He dropped the smile.

"Oh?" Miranda's eyes were bright and sharp now. "And what makes you say that?" Gill got that hunted feeling again; at the very least he sensed himself in the *presence* of a hunter, or if not a hunter as such, then an unscrupulous woman with a severe ego problem—which might equate to very much the same thing.

"I have my reasons," Gill answered, "which, if they should come to nothing, I'll tell you about in plenty of time."

She half smiled, said, "I'd very much prefer that you told me now. For if not, then how can I possibly pass on your recommendations? What, on the strength of a hunch?"

"My hunches were pretty good last time." He tried to smile back at her but found himself distracted, frowning.

She only sighed, and commenced to say, "Spencer, I—"

"Wait." He held up a hand and cut her off. "Speaking of hunches, right now there's something far more important." Something that had been bothering him for some little time, indeed ever since climbing aboard this helicopter. Undoing his safety belt and standing, he swayed up the narrow aisle and slid open the hatch to the pilot. Sticking his head into the cockpit, he spoke briefly to the man, then returned to his seat. His fellow passengers couldn't help but notice how his face had taken on a pale, slightly strained look.

"What is it, Spencer?" Concerned, Angela took his arm.

And Miranda asked, "Are you feeling ill? And do you think that what-ever your problem is, it's really more important than what we were just talking about?" Her look was suspicious now, her tone harsh. And Gill wondered, *Does she think I'm avoiding the issue?* Well of course he had been, but his subsequent actions hadn't been part of any deliberate or planned subterfuge.

"Yes I do feel a little out of sorts," he answered, tight-lipped. "And yes, it is more important than what we were talking about just now. Far and away more important—that is, if you want to go *on* talking, continue being the boss, and generally carry on coordinating. You see it's not me that's ill but this damn machine, this bloody whirlybird! However, since it's only a minute or so to our destination, we should make it safely enough before anything awful happens. And between times, if it's all right with you, well I'd rather not talk about anything very much. Instead *I* would prefer to simply sit here and worry—okay, boss?"

And the unnoticeable vibration (except to Gill) in one of the rapidly rotating vanes continued to bother him all the way down to a perfect but nevertheless welcome landing . . .

Waite introduced Gill and the others to the pilot. "Ex-navy, a squadron leader, Falklands vet, and a really *big* chopper pilot. This one is a baby by comparison. Fred Stannersly and his bird have buzzed a good many extremely important people around, and no complaints to date." Waite displayed his dubious knowledge of flying jargon while F-for-Freddie Stannersly stood with his tawny head cocked a little on one side, looking at Waite quizzically and feeling more than somewhat embarrassed for him.

"And is this your 'bird'?" Gill asked him, when Waite was through. He looked askance at the now motionless helicopter in a corner of a field overlooking the water, or what used to be the water. Where it would once have been standing at high tide and full of boats, now everything was green, brown, and alive.

"No." Stannersly shook his head of tawny hair. "This is a 'Ministry' chopper, whatever that means—MOD, I gather. I was offered this rush job, lots of money, a little danger, and all the avgas I could use free of charge. My own, er, 'bird' "—he glanced uncomfortably at Waite who had his back turned and was talking to Miranda and a party of senior policemen and officials—"is in the hangar having a regulatory once-over. But they wanted me for the job and so offered me this French-built model in her place. It's a bit flashy but usually a very reliable machine. Then again, they're all reliable these days. I'm just unhappy I wasn't able to check her out, that's all. I was sort of pushed for time to pick up this ministerial asshole and the woman."

Stannersly was five-nine or-ten, heavily built, thirty-nine or maybe forty years old. He had long since lost the military look, though Gill had noticed the faded shadows of wings and other patches on his worn flying jacket, revenant of ancient insignia. Old habits die hard, Gill supposed. But with his square jaw, shrewd green eyes, and generally willing attitude, already Stannersly had made a favorable impression. Though he might be a little slow-moving on the ground, his main requirement was to be capable in the air. A pilot is a pilot, and an ex-Falklands flyer was good enough for Gill.

"Well, is there a problem with you checking her over now, right here?" Gill asked him. "We may well be putting her to a lot of use. For the moment, though, I have some stuff to talk over with my colleagues here, so there's no great hurry. And I can fill you in on what we're doing—what's going on—later. Then, too, we'll have time for proper introductions, okay?" He reached out and they shook hands.

"Sure, that sounds fine." But Stannersly was frowning now. "Er, some problem with the rotor, you said? One of the blades, maybe? Am I to take it you have some experience of these machines?"

"Of machines . . . yes," Gill told him, nodding. "Why don't you check it out and see what you find? Then if I'm wrong I'll buy you a drink."

The other shrugged and said, "Fair enough, I'll get right on it. And if you're right I'll buy *you* a whole bottle! See, I never yet met anyone with a better ear for a dodgy engine than me . . ."

Gill and the others walked down to the water, or rather to the weed. Inland, Newport was visible in the south. But in the next field, at the edge of the weed and the high-tide mark, a sprawling building obscured most of the view.

"A mansion." Angela shivered and held tight to Gill's arm. "A House of Doors." It was sunny and hot, and with a breeze out of the west might even have been described as balmy, but Angela shivered anyway. And the stench from the weed was indescribable despite that it was downwind.

Along the water's rim men were at work in both directions as far as the eye could see, except near the mansion that had been isolated and cordoned off with posts and police NO ENTRY tape. They wore face masks and were spraying the weed with something toxic.

"There goes the neighborhood," said Turnbull. "More pollution for the fish to deal with—if there are any fish under that lot—*if* there's any water!"

Outside the taped-off mansion, police cars and other official or semi-official vehicles were lined up nose to tail like a wagon train under attack from redskins; tents were being erected, various vans with blacked-out windows and curious antennae stood in clusters, and uniformed policemen and wary-eyed civilian security men were everywhere.

"Sort of reminds you of a certain scene on a certain Scottish mountainside, doesn't it?" Gill said to Angela.

"Yes," she answered, "it does. Knowing what this 'mansion' is, I find it just as ominous. Not knowing what the weed is . . . I find *it* frightening."

Miranda Marsh overheard that last and stepped closer. "An American botanist working for NASA has come up with the theory that in fact the weed is a nonintelligent alien life-form and the nodes are simply its spores. He thinks that's how life may have come down from space to Earth in the first place."

"Really?" Angela answered. "And this nonintelligent life-form's spores imitate Earth buildings and monuments, do they?"

"Evolution," the woman from the Ministry said with a shrug. "There are flowers that look like insects, and insects that look like flowers."

"And," Gill put in, "there are *highly* intelligent aliens, called the Thone, who look just like jellyfish. Obviously your NASA man hasn't read our reports."

"Oh, I'm with you, Spencer," Miranda told him. "But as for your reports—you must know they were Top Secret, Cosmic? Only a handful of people have *ever* read them! I was simply reporting what I know, that's all. I just wish that I could get you to do the same."

"When it's time, appropriate, or necessary," Gill answered. "Meanwhile, are there any other theories?"

If she was ruffled it didn't show. "Well, there is someone else who thinks that the weed is a contagion, something carried by these nodes like wood lice in a clod of earth, spreading and contaminating whatever they touch."

"Contaminating?" He raised an eyebrow.

"The weed is poisonous," she said. "As deadly as the most toxic mushrooms. Not one test animal has survived. Fortunately for us, when the weed dies the poison dissipates entirely."

Angela shivered again. "This stuff is life in death."

"Would be," said Miranda, "if we were willing to sit still for it."

"But does the poison *itself* spread?" Gill wanted to know. "Apart from the weed, I mean? Or is it contained *by* the weed? Does it actually contaminate water, making it undrinkable?"

"Too early to say for sure. So far it has remained a part of the weed. But so what? The weed itself clogs up the works!"

"And does it kill fish?"

"Only if they eat it."

"I.e., we're not supposed to touch it." Gill nodded. "It's not designed to invite interference. I have only one more question: what does it live on?"

"The weed?" Miranda shook her head. "We don't know."

"But it is life," said Turnbull, "and it can be destroyed. Look there—"

They had moved up the water's edge toward the mansion. A great patch of weed was lying inert, dead, turning black where it had been sprayed. A group of workers in face masks were prodding the stuff, talking excitedly to each other.

"Oh, I don't doubt we can kill it," said Gill. "But can't you see? Long before we could destroy all of the weed we'd have killed off the planet, too! This stuff's set to fill the oceans of the whole damn world—like a vast Sargasso Sea!"

The senior policemen were still with their party. As Gill lifted the NO ENTRY tape to stoop under it, one of them stepped forward and said, "Sir? Are you authorized to—"

But George Waite was quick off the mark. "Yes, we are." He came forward. "Indeed, this man is Spencer Gill, our top expert in this field."

Then they were under the tape and the mansion or House of Doors loomed close.

And Gill could feel it sitting there—or curled up and lying there—like a sleeping cat, this blight on his machine awareness, this technology from the stars. Alien? It was that all right. But to Gill machines were analogous to mathematics, and this was an equation he'd worked on before. Maybe not exactly the same, but close enough. And:

Thone! he thought. *Or so similar as to make little or no difference.*

Which meant that if he could get close to the node's synthesizer, he could probably learn how to control it. Of course, before he could do that he must first enter the House of Doors, an idea he wasn't at all happy with. For it seemed obvious that the Thone had broken their promise, and if that were really the case . . . was it likely they'd let a mere man stand between them and an entire world?

What would the life of a single man be worth compared to a world? he wondered. And who could say who or what else might or might not get broken along with the promise?

Distracted by his own thought processes, he had been edging forward. Now Angela warned, "Spencer, aren't we getting a little too close?" She looked anxious.

"Yes," he answered. "I need to, but you don't. All of you stay where you are while I go just a little closer. At the moment I can't sense any real danger, but still I won't be taking any unnecessary chances."

He paced forward, one, two paces—and stopped abruptly. Because at that precise moment he'd felt the alien machine put itself in gear. The sleeping cat was awake; it had blinked its eyes and seen him. And it had *known* him! Then—

Several things, all happening in unison . . .

CHAPTER
8

S OMETHING ABOUT THE mansion—other than the fact of its nature, that
it was an alien edifice, a House of Doors—had been bothering Gill for
quite some time. Of course the thing had no doors or windows, but it did
have the outlines of such, it did have them in bas-relief, as it were. Win-
dowsills, lintels, pillared porticos and such, all were there, but the door or
window spaces that they framed were empty, or rather solid. Solid, and
very small. Way too small. And that was what had been bothering Gill.

Now that he was closer, though, the fact of the matter became obvious.
A door is seven feet high, or in a rich dwelling, in a mansion like this one,
nine or more; and windows are likewise spacious. The reason Gill now
found himself so close, even uncomfortably close to this thing, was simply
a matter of perspective. He had in a way been "lured" to his current proximity; distance had been distorted by dimension. The mansion's door and
window spaces were a third too small. The entire mansion was a third too
small!

This sudden dawning of the obvious—along with the fact that this was
one of the most recent nodes—plus the knowledge that it was a synthetic
structure whose size before permanent concretion could be adjusted and
corrected at the whim of its controller, to bring it to an Earth-proper
norm—was what had brought Gill up short in the moment before his machine empathy had "switched on" to the node's awareness of him.

That was the first thing that had happened.

The second, taking far *less* than a second, was when Gill had dug his heels in and leaned backward away from the perceived danger. The third was to hear his name, fired in a warning shout from Angela's terrified, convulsing throat, ringing like a gunshot in his ears. And the rest of it was a kaleidoscopic, multilayered jumble of frantic activity and distorted impressions as, flailing his arms, Gill tried to turn and run *and* understand what was happening, all at the same time.

The House of Doors, shimmering threateningly, its walls expanding, warping out of focus, and rushing headlong upon him. Angela—God bless her!—still shouting, and grabbing at him from the rear. Her arm around his neck, hauling as if to rip his head off, trying to drag him to safety. And from somewhere down on the water, or the weed, screams of terror; a jarring, fleeting visual impression, as Gill fell onto his side, of something terrible *erupting* from the dead, blackened weed patch, grabbing with crablike pincers at the men in the face masks, and dragging two of them away and under the rotting mat of weed. And George Waite—of all people—hurling himself headlong to Gill's and Angela's rescue!

But whereas Angela, and now Jack Turnbull, too, had taken up positions *behind* Gill—hauling on him bodily and trying to draw him to his feet—Waite actually ran *past* him, and threw himself full tilt at the mansion as if to attack it!

And . . . the House of Doors ate him! He simply disappeared into the blurring shimmer of the onrushing wall; was there one minute, gone the next.

Meanwhile Gill was back on his feet, fleeing for the security tape with Angela and the minder, and grabbing up Miranda Marsh on the way. And a half-dozen policemen running forward, two of them in flak jackets with machine pistols at the ready. And the House of Doors still shimmering, expanding, and eating up the earth right behind Gill and Co.; he could *feel* it hot on their heels.

Then the two parties—Gill's and the police squad—came together, clashed, and merged into a small, milling crowd, and the switch in Gill's brain that governed his machine mentality slid back into neutral . . .

As quickly as that it was over, the House of Doors quiescent once more. And when Gill looked back . . . not six feet away, there that monstrous cat lay sleeping: the mansion, standing as solid as the synthetic material in which it was carved, or from which it had been conjured. And its facsimile, bas-relief doors and windows were all the right size. But—

Was it really over?

No, not yet. Gill felt it again, that surging in his head, like the pulsing of alien hydraulics. And: "It's not finished!" he tried to cry his warning, but his bone-dry throat could only manage a croak as the wall of the mansion only a few feet away *rippled* like the surface of a pool, and George Waite's figure, and then Waite himself, was outlined spread-eagled or crucified upon its surface.

Waite . . . *emerged* about eighteen inches above the ground. It was as if he came floating to the surface of a vertical wall of opaque liquid. The wall parted around his figure to eject or maybe to *re*ject it, re-forming behind it. And when he was wholly visible, then the wall became rigid and Waite fell from it and crumpled to earth.

The police started forward, grabbed him, dragged him out of there. And Gill let them. He had come too close and knew it. The House of Doors had wanted him, not Waite. So why hadn't it taken him? Then he saw the snouts of those police machine pistols pointing at the mansion as Waite was dragged clear of the place, and believed he knew why.

The Thone (if this was the work of the Thone) were fragile creatures even in their own environment. If Gill had been snatched, it was possible that some of these policemen—and their weapons—would have been taken, too; and doubtless they would have been dealt with. But not before they'd done a little dealing of their own. And with that thought Gill resolved to avail himself of a gun at his earliest convenience. Or if not a gun, a weapon certainly.

"Jesus! Jesus *Christ!*" Turnbull shook his fists in fury. "It *is* going to be just like the last time—or worse!"

As for Angela, for the moment she was only interested in Gill's welfare. "Spencer, are you all right?"

"I'm okay, yes," he answered as Miranda Marsh caught at his arm. And turning to the woman from the Ministry, he said: "What the hell was George trying to do?"

"I don't know," she answered, badly shaken for the first time in a long time, her eyes wide in a face that was pale and drawn. "I . . . I'm not sure. Or maybe I am." And then, angrily: "But was that an example of how you *communicate* with these . . . these bloody things? Did you see what happened to those men at the water's edge?"

Before he could answer her, Turnbull's raised voice came to them from where he'd pushed his way in through the group attending to Waite. "George is alive! He's breathing . . . he has a pulse . . . he's coming out of it, maybe." Angela went to see if she could help.

"Did you hear that?" Gill took Miranda's elbows, held her still. "Those 'bloody things' could have killed him—but they didn't. Which tells me there's a good chance they want to talk. They wanted me, not him. And giving him back could be their way of telling us that. All well and good, and I will talk to them if I can, yes—"

"When it's time, appropriate, or necessary?" She looked at him in something akin to scorn.

"Right," Gill told her. "And hopefully on my terms, when I'm good and ready. But I've been here before, boss lady, and no way I'm going to make the same mistakes. Not if I can help it." He released her.

"But they *have* killed those poor men who were taken under the weed," Miranda said. "Where's the justification for that?"

Gill shook his head. "I don't know how there can be one," he said. "But I didn't trigger it, and neither did the node's controller. It was that construct."

"Construct? What, that crab-thing? That creature from the weed? Are you telling me *that* was a machine, a kind of robot?"

"So maybe you think I talk and write science fiction, eh?" Gill said harshly. "Didn't I say that the weed isn't there for us to interfere with? The beings controlling these nodes create constructs for all kinds of purposes. That one, probably one of a great many, was there to protect the weed. But it's all in my report, Miranda. Are you sure you've read it?"

"Your bloody report!" she snapped, and tossed her head to set her blonde hair flying. "Are you never bloody wrong?"

"About machines? Rarely," he answered, but with little of pride and maybe even wryly.

At which moment Fred Stannersly came hurrying from outside the cordon of police vehicles, with Barney trotting eagerly behind. "Spencer," the pilot called ahead excitedly, unaware that anything had happened here. "Spencer Gill?" Then, seeing Miranda and Gill together, he approached and took Gill's arm. "Spencer, I don't know how you do it, but . . . damn, I owe you a bottle! A locating pin had come loose on the rotor head. The bolt was so badly worn it could have sheared through at any time. I fitted a new one. But how . . . ?" He let it trail off, shook his head, and waved his hands in defeat.

"It's something I do," Gill said. "In fact, it's the only useful thing that I do." And with a sideways glance at Miranda, "Which perhaps explains why I'm so bloody good at it . . ."

Waite was to be taken to the hospital in Newport for a medical report. Gill and Angela, Miranda and Turnbull, would follow on behind in a police car, and Barney would remain with Fred Stannersly at the helicopter while the pilot awaited instructions.

As the ambulance and police vehicle moved out and climbed to a slightly higher elevation, Gill looked back and shook his head. And his face was very grim.

Turnbull noticed and looked back, too. There were no workmen at the water's edge now, and the "U" of vehicles around the House of Doors was foreshortening itself, pulling back from the high-water mark. It was a bright summer day, but somehow looked a lot darker, despite that it wasn't yet noon. And the big minder quietly inquired, "Is there something, Spencer?"

Well obviously there was something, but Gill knew what he meant. He nodded, said, "Things are starting to come together, yes. But there are a couple of ambiguities here, things I just can't figure out."

And Miranda Marsh said, "Whatever happened to that silly old notion that two heads are better than one, eh? Perhaps if we were both trying to figure out your ambiguities—*if* I knew what they were—the answers would come that much easier. What about it, Spencer? You show me yours and I'll show you mine?"

Gill grinned but there wasn't much humor in it. "That's a game I haven't played in a long time," he said.

And Angela put in, "Not since last night, anyway." Except she wasn't grinning. And yet more seriously: "Miranda could be right, Spencer. Is it cards on the table time?"

"She probably is right," he admitted. "But it's also possible she's wrong. On the wrong side, I mean."

That interested Turnbull. "Come again?"

Gill shook his head, to clear it if anything, explaining, "Not as in opposed but wrong as in wrongheaded. The wrong attitude—and again not toward us, nothing personal, but toward this whole scenario. Let's put it in perspective. The Ministry of Defense, a branch or subsidiary of government, has been instructed to prepare a feasibility report, or a plan of action, toot sweet. Miranda here has been told to explore the options and present that report. Am I right so far?"

Miranda nodded, however warily. "I thought that was understood," she said.

"Okay," said Gill. "Now this is a for and against kind of thing, pros and cons. From our point of view the pro will be if they allow us to handle things our way. But the clock's ticking away, time is narrowing down, and there's the weed. Pretty soon it's going to be hard to keep a lid on all this. A lot of people may be deaf and dumb but they're not blind. It won't be long before the weed is everywhere. So once again from our point of view, the con side of it is that Miranda's going to advise pulling the plug on our alien visitors and flushing them away. She will advise nuclear strikes, 'tactical' of course—at first."

"You're saying that's the *con* side of it?" Miranda's face mirrored her disbelief, and it was plain she found Gill's attitude a suspicious thing in itself. "Do you mean you don't *want* me to flush them away?"

"I'm not even sure you can," he answered. "But I'm pretty damn sure you can ruin the world trying! And I think that they are, too, and that's the last thing they want."

"Well of course they don't want us to destroy them," she snorted.

"I'll say it again," said Gill. "I'm not sure you can destroy them. What I meant was that they don't want us to destroy or damage our world, or theirs as it might be."

"Explain."

"The reason for these nodes in their current form," said Gill, "is to arouse our curiosity, nothing more than that. But in locations where we're not likely to be curious, well why go to the trouble? Hence the iceberg, and the appearance of these new islands or rocks in the sea that you've told us about. But in populated places, where men are *likely* to be curious, there they've provided something to be curious about. A weird pagoda, a mansion, a pyramid, et cetera. They know we'll examine such things. From a distance, maybe, but we won't simply attack on sight."

"Which we might," said Turnbull, "if they looked nasty. If they were obviously alien artifacts. Or ugly, powerful weapons. Or damn great spaceships bristling with ray guns."

"Right," said Gill. "The castle on Ben Lawers was exactly the same sort of thing: a curiosity. We didn't destroy it, but we did examine it."

"And eventually it examined us," Angela said.

"So"—Miranda set her jaw, and Gill could see that she was being convinced but in the wrong direction—"what you're saying is that these things are just so many Trojan horses. When we've accepted their presence, that's when the troops will leap out."

"No," said Gill. "The first one—the castle—was like a mousetrap set to catch specimen mice and examine them. Which is one of the ambiguities. For *this* time, while our visitors seem to be using the same game plan, I don't think they're much interested in catching anyone. Well, perhaps with the exception of myself."

"Wait!" Miranda held up a hand, frowning. "I can't take it in as fast as you're dishing it out. So go back a bit. You said you're not sure we can destroy them. What, not even with 'tactical' nuclear weapons?"

"And if tacticals didn't work, what then?" said Gill. "The really big stuff? And how *many* strikes, eh? What, only two dozen? And one of them right here, the mansion, the Isle of Wight? Oh, they'd all be coordinated, of course. Hit them all at once, right?" His sarcasm dripped, until he said, "Christ *Almighty!*" and lapsed into silence.

"A grim scenario," she said in a while. "But no worse than losing our world to these invaders. And you still haven't answered my question: what makes you think we can't kill them?"

"Two reasons," said Gill. "One, because the invaders *themselves* don't think so. If they did they wouldn't be here. Hell, they're an advanced intelligence! They know we have nukes! And two . . . is harder to explain."

"Try." Miranda felt she was getting the better of him; she thought she could feel him giving way, giving in to the inevitability of her argument.

Gill nodded. "I'm no nuclear physicist," he said. "I never claimed to be. But what we can do with science these people can do in spades. Inside that node, that mansion or House of Doors, they can create whole worlds. We know, because we've seen something of them, lived in them, survived in them. Matter is crazy putty to these aliens. Yesterday there was no mansion. Today, a couple of thousand tons of stone which could as easily be steel or some metal we never even heard of. Miranda, I've seen a machine world with a metal sun and ball-bearing stars! These things I've seen were *inside* a House of Doors! If you don't believe me then ask Jack and Angela. I'll tell you what will happen if you try to nuke these things: you'll wreck the country around, risk a nuclear winter, and achieve absolutely nothing. The nodes will still be here, or if not they'll be replaced, and our . . . our *invaders* will be pissed off something cruel!"

"You nearly said 'the Thone' just then"—Miranda's frown was back again—"but you stopped. In fact, I've noticed how you haven't called them by name for some time. All right, Spencer. I've done my bit, admitted or agreed to some of the things you're concerned about, and now it's your turn. I haven't seen yours, yet."

Gill looked at Angela and Turnbull and shrugged. "Well, it has to come out sooner or later," he said. "Okay, Miranda, but you're not going to like it. I haven't mentioned the Thone, you say. Answer: no, because I can't be sure this is the Thone. You see, they aren't alone out there. There are these others called the Ggyddn. And compared to the Ggyddn, the Thone are among the nicest people on Earth. Or off it!"

Following which he had a lot more explaining to do . . .

George is getting the works," Jack Turnbull reported back to the others in the otherwise empty private ward where they were waiting on the results of Waite's examination. "A to Z, a thorough going over." And:

"My turn," Miranda sighed. "Since you'll soon find out all about poor George anyway, I don't suppose he'd mind my telling you. Spencer, you wondered why George did what he did back at the mansion. It was totally out of character, I agree. Well, I think I know. And when I tell you, you'll know why I was given this job over him. You see, we did read your reports after all . . . and especially your medical reports. The original House of Doors was a cure-all, a universal panacea, and these Thone creatures weren't quite as nasty as they might have been. Not all of them, anyway. So, perhaps George was hoping it would be the same thing all over again. You see, he has a brain tumor . . ."

When that had sunk in, finally Gill said, "George wasn't trying to rescue me back there?"

"I don't think so," she answered. "It's just that wherever you were going, he was going with you. Oh, he's well enough for now, but he has only three or four months to live. So whichever way you look at it, he had nothing to lose. Not really."

"That explains his interest in David Anderson," Gill said. "George hid it well but he was pumping me for information. Now I can see why it was so important to him. Well"—he shrugged helplessly—"and so it would be. The poor bastard."

"While he might have appeared to be working against you," Miranda said, "he was actually with you all the way. He *intended* to be with you all the way, and I do mean *all* the way! The top people at the Ministry thought that might be the case—"

"Which is why you were put over him," Gill said, nodding. "He couldn't be trusted to make an unbiased decision."

"And we couldn't be sure how long . . . well, how long he'd last out." Miranda looked away. Gill saw her bite her lip, and he also saw her as human for the first time. But then, tossing her hair, she looked up again and said, "There. Is the playing field level now?"

"Not quite," Gill said. "Has George said anything to you about my wanting the use of a deserted island somewhere, maybe off Scotland?"

"No," she said . . . then snapped her fingers. "But on the way to your place on Hayling Island he did spend a little time fiddling with a map. Something you'd mentioned to him, apparently. Could that be it, d'you think? I have his briefcase right here." She opened it, thumbed through Waite's papers, and—

"There!" She took out the folded map, pointed at a location ringed in ballpoint, and handed the map to Gill.

"A lighthouse," he said excitedly. "Off Cornwall. Probably no longer in use. A couple of acres of nowhere, which is just about exactly what I had in mind. Okay, now we can level the playing field." And reaching into an inside pocket of his combat suit, he took something out and handed it to Miranda.

She looked at it, turned it in her hands, and her look of surprise became one of delight. "A model castle!" she said. "A perfect likeness. But don't I know this thing? Isn't it—"

"The castle on Ben Lawers?" Angela spoke up. "Yes, it is. The original House of Doors."

"Damn clever little carving, isn't it?" Turnbull put in, winking at Gill.

But Gill couldn't carry the joke any further. "Something else that wasn't in my report," he said. "This isn't a model or a carving, Miranda. It's the real thing. And when I reenergize it on that lighthouse rock it could be poor Waite's panacea. What's more, it might even be the saving of a world . . ."

CHAPTER
9

HUGGING HERSELF AGAINST a breeze that played with her hair and kept a handful of gulls soaring on high, Angela looked out from their vantage point on the outer platform of the old lighthouse across an empty ocean, and down through almost one hundred feet of empty air to the barren salt-bleached rock below. The height didn't bother her; she felt oddly at ease leaning on the tubing of the three-bar safety rail. Despite that the place was totally unfamiliar, she felt at peace here. Or if not at peace, comfortable. The calm before the storm, maybe.

"Spencer," she said, glancing back over her shoulder, "what is it, do you suppose, that I like about this place? What is it that makes a place I never saw before—a barren, inhospitable place like this—feel so comfortable? Can you tell me that?"

"Yes," Gill said with a nod, "perhaps I can." For he'd been dwelling on much the same question. "It's that for however brief a time this is our escape, a sanctuary. In a normal world, this is the sort of place we'd want to be off. It's too sterile and scarred and dead. But in the last couple of days our world has stopped being normal or natural. While out here . . . well, you can't get any closer to nature than this. I mean to *our* nature, the old natural world. So what we're feeling probably isn't so much genius loci, the spirit of this place, as anticipation of the *loss* of place. Of our place, our world. Or maybe anticipation is the wrong word. Foreboding might be better." Following which he wished his assessment of the situation hadn't sounded so gloomy. But on the other hand he saw no point in disguising the truth, and Angela would know it if he'd tried.

"All that out there," she said, with a sweep of her head that indicated the sea, the great width of its curve from horizon to horizon. "It's hard to imagine something, or anything, that can be capable of changing all that."

"I know," Gill answered. "Even knowing what we know, having seen what we've seen, still it's hard to imagine. But it's real for all that. In just two weeks time the view . . . will be different. Green and brown, and probably burning, or steaming. And there'll be fires on the horizon near and far, where ugly, drifting poisoned mushrooms climb two or three miles into the sky. That's if we—and I mean us personally—can't or don't do anything about it."

"But we will?"

"Our damndest, yes. There's no other way."

"And do you think they really understood what you said to them this morning?" She meant George Waite, Miranda Marsh, and Fred Stannersly. Of course Jack Turnbull had understood almost every word of it. But then, he'd had firsthand experience.

"I think so," Gill answered. "Anyway, a picture's worth a thousand words. And have we got some pictures to show them! But, sweetheart, come away from that rail. It's very rusty, probably dangerous. No one has been out here—or up here—for a long time."

And as she came and sat down, and snuggled to him where he sat with his back against the wall of the lighthouse's observation deck, Gill did a mental reprise of the talk he'd delivered just an hour ago, down in the damp, deserted living quarters as had been . . .

Time, as they say, is of the essence," he'd told them. "The world is going to hell fast, and there'll be worse than hell to pay if we can't stop it. And, as Miranda here is proof, there's more than just these alien nodes, these Houses of Doors to worry about. It's true that they're like blemishes, cancers on the face of the Earth, but the only possible cure's a military one, which looks about as bad as the disease. But there again, there are other military powers in this world who are a lot less tolerant than our people, and they're quite capable of jumping the gun and setting things going before we can achieve anything. Or rather, *if* we can achieve anything. So even if I have to leave a lot out, I'll try to keep this short and sweet.

"Now I won't kid you I know everything. I could be wrong about some or even most of this, but this is how I see things. The Thone warned me about the Ggyddn. Fine, except they didn't go into detail, didn't tell me a hell of a lot. The impression I got was that they abhorred the Ggyddn, feared or even dreaded them. And the really bad news is that I think our new visitors *are* the Ggyddn. But don't ask me about them; I don't know about them, not even what they look like. I can tell you this, though: the thing that dragged those men under the weed wasn't one of them. It was one of their machines. I, we—Jack Turnbull, Angela, and myself—have had business with such before.

"Now about the weed. Something I've heard has stuck in my head; it may have been about Earth species of weed and algaes, how they spring into being with climatic changes, usually when it's hot. In most recorded cases, abrupt or unusual changes in the weather—heat waves, long hot summers, etc—have been responsible for bringing this stuff into being. Well I think this alien weed is meant to work the other way around.

"Anyone familiar with science fiction themes will know the word terraforming: the systematic restructuring of alien environments to accommodate Earth species, primarily Man. The way I see it, this weed is the Ggyddn equivalent: the first stage in a program that will alter our world to accommodate . . . them. If I'm right, it won't be too long before the planet's climate starts suffering. In that respect:

"I've said I don't know anything about the Ggyddn, but I do know about the Thone. They like it hot. Assuming the Ggyddn are similar—and I know that their technologies are similar—this would seem to fit the picture. One thing that doesn't fit, though, is us, humanity. What I'm saying is, our visitors seem to be putting the cart before the horse. The first thing Angela did when she was clearing out our old greenhouse to grow tomatoes, she got rid of the wasps, ants, fungus, et cetera. What I would like to know is why the aliens haven't make provision for us—for getting rid of us, I mean—right from square one? Or have they . . . ?

"Anyway, back to the weed. We have to ask where it comes from and what it lives on. Well, obviously it comes from these nodes. But in my opinion—and it's only mine—it isn't 'growing' out of them. Nothing I know of can grow at that speed. So it's being made. The nodes are spinning that stuff out just as fast as they can manufacture it. You find that too fantastic? But Angela, Jack, and myself, we've seen and existed—however briefly, thank goodness—on entire worlds that had been 'remembered,' stored, and synthetically reproduced. So it is possible, yes.

"As for what the weed eats: water and sunlight I suppose. So maybe that's how we're scheduled to make our exit: by sacrificing life's little necessities to that stuff. But that only highlights yet another ambiguity. Long before we reached such a low—but certainly *as* we reached it—even the doves would accept that the military solution was the only answer. Now the aliens aren't stupid; they know that, too. So it's my bet that *their* ultimate solution—that is, their answer to the problem that *we* pose, our in-festation of this world—will come somewhere between the total suffocation of our oceans and the time when our patience runs out. What that solution will be . . . who can say? But I'm not planning on sitting around, doing nothing for two weeks, just waiting for it to happen.

"But I don't believe we can fight this with Earth science or weapons, and certainly not with nukes, where even if we win we lose. No, instead we've got to fight fire with fire. I have to get inside one of these alien machines, find out more about how it works, and maybe use it in our defense. And that could be the other reason the mansion tried to snatch me, got George instead, and spat him back out. The controller of the original House of Doors sensed my machine empathy and it got to him, it worried him. So maybe I worry this new batch, too. Now I don't like to sound all me, me, me, but that's how I see it: if they got hold of me, there'd be no more opposition. They'd throw me in the brig or kill me, and that's that. Ergo, breaking into a Ggyddn synthesizer is out. But how about a Thone node?

"That's why we're here. You see, there's this secret I've kept for four years, ever since Jack and Angela and I survived our—well, call it an 'ex-perience'—in the original House of Doors up in Scotland. Now, you can argue that I shouldn't have kept it to myself, that I should have given it to the responsible authorities, let them take charge and perhaps prepare for what's happening now. I have no answer to that except to say I wasn't about to hand over that kind of technology—technology that even I didn't, don't, understand—to our kind of 'responsible' authorities! What, to the politicians? To the West, the East, the military powers? To everyone?

"Oh, sure! But do you remember something called nonproliferation? That was in connection with nukes, right? And now *this* stuff . . . ?

"See, I've known once before what it's like to feel that my race—in-cluding myself and the ones I love—was about to become extinct. And I couldn't help but ask myself this question: if human beings had that kind of power, would they be any different from the Thone or the Ggyddn?

"Oh, it wouldn't happen in my lifetime. In fact I'd take bets it wouldn't happen in fifty or more years. But sooner or later someone would find his way around the House of Doors"—at which point Gill had produced the "model" castle, weighed it in his hand, and showed it to them—"*this* House of Doors, yes. And that same someone—someone pretty much like me, maybe even a child of mine—he'd get something of an understanding of its technology. After that . . . look out Thone, Ggyddn, and anybody else out there. The bloody Earthmen are coming!

"So then, did I take too much on my own shoulders? Maybe Miranda will say that it wasn't my responsibility in the first place? And she could be right. But didn't Albert Einstein once say that he wished he'd never struck upon that famous equation of his, $E = mc^2$? So, Miranda, let me say this: while I was the only one who knew about it, I did see it as my responsibility, yes. But now . . . well now you know about it, too. All of you. So now it's also your responsibility."

Basically, that had been that. Leaving the others to think it over, Gill had climbed up here with Angela to be alone. And in the lighthouse's old kitchen Jack Turnbull had set about cooking breakfast on a camping stove he'd bought in Newport, while Barney sat up on his back legs and begged for scraps.

To the dog, if only to him, everything seemed just fine. For now, at least . . .

Behind the lighthouse the rock was flat, shaped by storms into a horizontal lava flow of striated granite. There were several small outcrops or stacks sticking up here and there, but then, Ben Lawers in Scotland had had its boulders, too.

"I don't think the terrain matters a lot," Gill told the others. "A mountainside, lake, or jungle, the nodes make automatic compensation. When they materialize, they conform to the locale."

"And that thing"—Miranda pointed at the castle where he had placed it on a flat surface—"is just such a node, a House of Doors? And you'll . . . make it bigger? But it only weighs a few ounces, Spencer, half a pound at most! Entire worlds, you said. How can whole worlds exist inside such a tiny space? How can they be made to materialize?" She wanted to believe; she'd seen certified evidence, MOD film, of the Ben Lawers manifestation, and with her own eyes the restructuring of the Isle of Wight mansion. But still she found it hard to accept. It went against logic.

"How do you get all that sound—entire bands, orchestras—on a CD that weighs only a few grams?" Gill countered. "Or all that information on a floppy disk? How do a couple of microscopic twists of DNA determine the characteristics of a man? We're just beginning to scratch the surface of such stuff. But the aliens have gone way past that. By comparison, our science is primitive."

"But matter out of nothing?" She shook her head.

"Not nothing," Angela explained as Gill touched the castle, stared at it, and tried to throw that switch in his mind that would put him on the same wavelength. And Angela went on: "The machine at the core of each node uses a world's energy—whichever world it happens to be—to bring its outer facade into being. They're like . . . I don't know, parasites, sucking up the energy of the host world. Spencer says they're entropy engines: for each day of a synthesized world's existence, the real world pays a like amount of time; its life is shortened to the same degree. We do the same thing when we extract coal, oil, and minerals, or burn up fuel, or cut down trees, or even breathe. But with us it's natural, our part in Nature's plan. It's just the natural aging of the world, and in turn the universe. It's a winding down. Entropy."

Gill looked up. "It's nothing to worry about," he said. "Even if I have to create worlds of our own, we can afford it out of the billions of years the Earth's got left. Or you can simply measure it against all the years that *we* won't have if we do nothing." And then, in frustration: "*Damn!* Look, I hate to sound patronizing, but you're distracting me. I mean, this isn't like riding a bicycle: like once you've cracked it it's forever. It's more like recalling a name that's right on the tip of your tongue and won't come. Except it's a whole string of names and they're in the wrong order, and each one of them is part of a combination. Or not like that, but just as difficult. So why don't you all go back to the lighthouse and if I can do this thing . . . well, you'll know soon enough."

"If?" Miranda said with a sharp little laugh, as if her location—the entire situation—had suddenly dawned on her and she found it farcical and even ridiculous. "*If* you can do it? Do you mean there's some doubt? Listen, Spencer, my people don't know where I am; I haven't found time to tell them yet. And of all the places I *could* be, and all the useful things I could be doing, I'm—"

"We're going," said Angela, taking her elbow. And Jack Turnbull said:

"Miranda, we've seen this before. Well, maybe not exactly this, but something like it. Personally I find you distracting in more ways than one, and so I can see Spencer's point. So be sensible now and come with us. All your questions can keep until later, right?"

"What?" She stared at him in amazement—and at Angela's hand on her arm—and her jaw fell open. "Be . . . *sensible*, did you say?" But then she snapped out of it and hissed, "Listen, *Mr.* Turnbull! Aren't you forget-ting something? Like, who you're working for and what—"

"What we're trying to help Gill to do?" he cut her off. "The fact that we've got perhaps two weeks to live? No, I don't think I'm forgetting any-thing." And then the big minder smiled, however tightly, and added, "So what's it to be? Will you walk now, or do I have to carry you? I'd quite enjoy that."

Miranda whirled to look at Gill, who was no longer interested in any-thing but the miniature castle. She glared at Angela, and again at Turnbull.

She turned to George Waite, but he was pale, withdrawn; he seemed shrunken as if by some terrible tragedy, a very different man from the one she'd known. And as for Fred Stannersly: the pilot was forty yards away, seeing to his helicopter. So there was only one thing to do, and Miranda did it. She walked, or stamped, all the way back to the lighthouse.

Only Barney stayed behind with Gill. Seated beside him, he stared at the castle almost as intently as his new master. But for once his tail wasn't wagging . . .

Barney," Gill said, without losing a jot of concentration, because in fact he was talking to himself, "would you believe me if I said that once upon a time I was on top of this thing? Of course you would, because you were there. Hey, you're not stupid! So, was it just beginner's luck, do you think?" Gill knew that it hadn't been, that he really had been on top of it. But that was then and this was now. Then he'd held a couple of ace cards, or "keys," to the castle's conjectural doors.

One such had been the alien weapon he'd acquired when Sith of the Thone had come after him, before he'd actually entered, or been snatched, by the House of Doors. That weapon had given him his first clue to the way these things worked. Another had come when he'd first contacted the crab-cum-scorpion construct that had pursued the unfortunate Alec Haggie to his death. But the real breakthrough had been to actually live inside the awesome House of Doors; with the bulk of that great machine surrounding him on all sides, the switch in his mind had been like a compass needle drawn to point him in the wrong (or as it had worked out, the right) direction. But now:

Gill no longer possessed the Thone weapon. Deeming it too dangerous an item in the wrong hands—or in any hands—he'd left it behind when he deactivated the castle. But in any case it would only have worked until its charge was used up. And no way that Earthly science might ever recharge it.

As for getting close to a construct a second time around:

The only construct encountered so far had been that murderous thing that protected the weed. Unprogrammed for specific individuals, it seemed to be indiscriminately targeted on anyone seen interfering with the weed. And it was doubtless only one of a great many similar constructs. No way Gill was going to get close to *that* kind of thing!

Which left him only one avenue to explore: he must somehow find a way to pick up "vibes" from a node—this node, this uninhabited House of Doors—of which he had prior knowledge. But that was a Catch 22 situation. To talk to, "communicate," with this thing he must first activate it, and to activate it he had to talk to it. Currently, it wasn't talking because he'd deactivated it!

So how to get it up and running again?

Well, there was a chance. But everything hung on a play of words: whether or not "deactivated" and "deenergized" were synonymous in this respect. If they were—then all of this was a pointless exercise.

For at the end of that affair up in Scotland, Gill hadn't done precisely what the Grand Thone required of him. He hadn't deenergized but simply *deactivated* the castle; hadn't redirected its stolen energy to the Earth, not all of it, but reduced it to an absolute minimum. So now the House of Doors, this synthesized "model" castle, was leeching only the infinitesimally small energy of a rock as compared to that of a world. And the fact that it hadn't disappeared entirely was what gave Spencer Gill hope that he might yet recall, reactivate it.

But if it worked on the same principle as Thone weaponry . . . just how long did their energy storage cells last? Or had its batteries long since run dry? Was it running, maintaining its existence, on a few last sparks, as it were? Like an electric clock that ticks to the last, then suddenly stops? If so it might explain why Gill was no longer on top of things. To get light from a kerosene lamp you first need kerosine. Which set him to thinking further along the same lines.

Where do you get the kerosine? From a hardware store, of course. And if you need *alien* power—or a means of supplying an *alien* system with allegedly unusable or untappable entropy energy—?

Gill's thoughts wound four years back in time to a scene as vivid as yesterday. A scene from a nightmare world of weird woodlands, poisonous fruits and insects, tree-dwelling spiders that made a noise like rattlesnakes and spun webs like rigging, bat-winged carnivores, and rubbery black troll-apes that howled in the night through mouths like razor-lined tunnels. So that all in all Gill's and Turnbull's discovery of a Thone hunting construct in difficulty had seemed the most trivial thing. And in fact it had been, for the alien machine wasn't hunting them but a criminal called Alec Haggie. Unlike Gill and the others, who had been snared, Haggie had somehow blundered his way into the House of Doors and from there into its synthesized worlds. And the construct had been tasked to find and . . . remove him.

The pictures came clearer still in Gill's mind's eye:

It was daylight, and he and Turnbull were seeking Angela, held captive by the unscrupulous Haggie. Crossing a dried-out river they discovered the giant, scorpionlike Thone construct—a machine that imitated life—stuck in a crack in the desiccated riverbed. As big as a medium-

sized car, the thing had damaged several legs when the side of the crack had caved in.

At first they were relieved and thought to leave the construct to its fate. But then Gill reconsidered, realizing that even if he wasn't able to find Haggie and Angela, the scorpion probably would.

So they set about to free it. They tumbled boulders into the fissure close to the lodged machine. And finally gaining a foothold, the thing clambered out.

And that was when it happened . . .

Gill sensed something strange. Suddenly his machine consciousness was aware of a weird, invisible influence. It was like a tingle on the surface of your skin, or the crawling motion of your hair and scalp close to a powerful electric source. Except with Gill it wasn't physical but mental; it was in his mind, in the mutant region of his brain that recognized and responded to machine activity.

And its nearest source was in his pocket! It was the weapon taken from Sith of the Thone in their first encounter. That metallic, tubular "knife" made of a substance unknown on Earth, and shaped by a science from the stars. For just as the damaged construct was drawing on some external power source, recharging itself and repairing its "injuries," so the weapon was leeching on the same beamed energy . . .

Gill snapped out of it, jumped to his feet. He felt like shouting "Eureka!"— but that would be premature. Thone and Ggyddn technology might not be compatible. Only one way to find out.

And as he picked up the castle and ran back to the lighthouse with Barney at his heels, Gill called ahead, "Fred! Fred Stannersly! We have to go back to Newport, to the Mansion." For now when he thought of that House of Doors, it was with a capital "M." Much like the Castle had been capitalized once upon a time.

And as it would be again, with a bit of luck . . .

CHAPTER
10

H E WAS MET by Miranda where she stood with her arms crossed on her chest, tapping an impatient foot at the base of the lighthouse. She'd heard what Gill was shouting, and was in complete accord. "That's the first 'sensible' thing I've heard since we got here," she said. "For frankly, Mr. Gill, I've had more than enough. The one thing on which we agree is to disagree! Or, if there's a meeting of minds at all, it's only when we arrive at the same and obvious conclusion: that there are only two weeks left in which to organize and initiate a preemptive task force. After that, any retaliatory strike will be too late. Two weeks, yes, or from my point of view two hours."

"Two hours?" Gill repeated, wondering what had happened to the "Spencer" part of his name.

She nodded. "About as long as it will take to fly back to Newport with you and contact my people in the MOD."

"Right," he said with a nod, and knew where the "Spencer" had gone. Her other protests had been like warning shots but now she was done simply shooting across his bows. Since she couldn't agree with him, sway him, or cow him, he was now her enemy. The ultimate egotist's ultimate weapon: to ignore any other opinion. But then, Gill could hardly blame her. Wasn't he built of much the same stuff? Yes he was, as Miranda was about to find out.

Angela and the others came out of the door from the lighthouse's living quarters. "Fred," Gill said, "we're flying back to Newport. And, Jack, I want you to come with us."

"Me, too," said Miranda. But Gill shook his head.

"No, you'll stay here with George, Angela, and Barney. I'm sorry, Miranda, but I think I'm onto something and have to give it a shot."

She set her jaw. "You're insane if you think you can make me stay here."

"I'm not making you do anything," he answered. "I'm just not taking you with me, that's all. Do you want me to explain, or will that be a waste of time?"

She was furious now, but controlled it well. "Oh, you had *better* explain!" she said. "That way the others will be witnesses as to why I'm going to have you arrested—eventually. As I would right now, if there was a phone on this bloody rock!"

He ignored the threat, held up the miniature castle. "Very well, so listen in. This thing is flat, like a battery about to give up the ghost. And if it does, we might as well do the same thing. But I think I can recharge it using a construct, one of those weed-crawlers."

"Oh," she sneered, "and how will you manage that? You'll just call one up out of the weed, will you?"

"Something like that, yes." Gill nodded. But he could see that he wasn't going to get anywhere with Miranda Marsh. "Okay, Fred, Jack—can we go now?" And to Angela, "You'll be okay?"

"How long will you be?" she said anxiously.

"As long as it takes," he could only shrug and hold her to him, but briefly. Then, to George and Miranda:

"Anything . . . awkward happens to me and Jack"—and with a glance at Angela—"it's not going to, you understand, but *if* it does—Fred's first job will be to come straight back here for you three. And there's no way I'll put him in danger."

"How thoughtful of you!" Miranda sneered again. Angela at once turned on her.

"Why don't you shut the fuck up?" she snapped. "You're not the only one who's afraid. In fact you're in good company. Most of us have been here before, and that was *real* fear!" With her woman's intuition, she'd hit exactly the right spot. And Miranda's mouth opened and closed with nothing more said. But in the next moment:

"Spencer," said George Waite, his voice thin as paper yet carrying unexpected authority and a lot of respect. "Don't concern yourself about us. Just get on with it, and good luck."

Gill was taken aback. If his plan failed, what difference would that make to George, who was going to die anyway? On the other hand, maybe he shouldn't be surprised; Waite had obviously decided he wanted to live, and he was going to stick to it.

But Miranda wasn't finished. "Mr. Stannersly," she snapped. "There's a radio in your airplane. I need to contact the mainland, tell my people I'm coming and where to meet me. Then I'm ordering you to take me with you. You're still working for the MOD, and I'm it! I'm far more your employer than is Mr. Gill."

Stannersly nodded and said, "Yes, I know you are. And are you going to pay me, too? What, two whole weeks from now? When the world's gone up in smoke, and money and life aren't worth a shit?" And without waiting for an answer, turning to Gill:

"What you plan, it's part of your machine thing, right? I mean, it's this thing you do?"

"Like flying is to you, this is to me," said Gill. "Or you can make it double or quits. I can always use another bottle of the good stuff."

"Too true!" said Turnbull, quickly averting his eyes when Angela frowned at him disapprovingly.

"In that case, you're on." The pilot nodded and forced an uncertain grin. "Let's go."

And they did . . .

Making a brief detour, they landed at Exeter to refuel and pick up some emergency avgas, canned aviation fuel. And then, without further pause, they followed the coastline east for the Isle of Wight.

For half an hour everything looked normal; down below, the sea was blue where whitecap after languorous whitecap rolled to shore, frothing and sparkling in the noonday sun. But all three men shared the same foreboding, indeed the same knowledge: that it wasn't going to last.

Using his radio to get a weather report, Stannersly got a "weed report" instead and relayed the news back to his passengers. "Southampton Water's completely choked, likewise The Solent. And the mid-south coast is blocked from Bournemouth to—*Jesus!*—Selsey bill? One hundred and fifty *miles* as the crow flies? The Isle of Wight is blockaded on three sides; only the Channel coast from Shanklin to Ventnor and St. Lawrence remains clear. And there are reports of . . . *things*, 'creatures' in the weed—your constructs, Spencer?—and of people being dragged under if they try to fight the stuff. And . . . and . . . more weed has appeared off Weymouth and points east. The government is still trying to play it cool, but the people aren't having any. They know this is wrong. They can see it for themselves."

Following which his hoarse voice fell silent. For by then they, too, could see it for themselves . . .

Crossing the Isle of Wight at low altitude—and keeping well clear of the Mansion, because Gill feared it might be able to detect his presence—Stannersly got into hovering mode over the river Medina midway between Newport and Cowes. Visibility was brilliantly clear, too clear by far. And:

"Christ Almighty!" Turnbull husked, shaking his head in disbelief. "Spencer, will you look at that? The weed is alive and well and living . . . well, just about every-fucking-where!"

But for now Gill was speechless where he too stared from a window on the incredible scene. From Newport to Cowes and as far across the Solent as was visible, the Medina and its creeks and harbors formed an eerily mobile green swamp! And where the land was especially low-lying, the weed had even crept some way ashore. The entire landscape of the ex-waterway was now like a surrealist's nightmare; just a mass of creeping, growing green, shot through with brown veins and leprous splotches; as if some cosmic artist had taken up a muddy brush, dipped it in a loathsome green, and with giant strokes removed everything that was remotely blue from the canvas.

"Alive!" Stannersly shouted back to his passengers, as if repeating what Turnbull had said, but in fact he was doing his own thinking. Whey-faced, he wanted to know: "Spencer, how can that possibly be? You said it was synthetic, manufactured. But I mean, isn't that God's province? We can't *make* life!"

"No," Gill answered, "but they can, our visitors or invaders, whatever. Life of sorts." And seeing how shaken Stannersly looked: "Try to hang on to things, Fred. Put her down a hundred yards from the bank, then keep her ticking over. You know what to do if . . . well, if."

Stannersly did as instructed. By the time they landed, and with the engine *whup-whup-whupping* less noisily, he was more his old self. "Take it easy, you two," he shouted down to Gill and Turnbull as they moved out from under the rotating vanes, each of them carrying a can of avgas. "I mean, be careful."

They waved up at him and headed for the riverbank, and as they went Turnbull said, "It's nice that you have faith in me."

"In what way?" Gill wanted to know.

"In that you believe I can do serious harm to one of those things with my little pop gun." And Turnbull showed off his 9mm Browning in its underarm holster.

"Well you can, can't you?" Gill frowned.

"I've been a marksman with this baby for more than twenty-five years," the minder answered. "Not that I've had much practice just lately, you understand. But at close range I usually hit what I'm shooting at, yes."

"The joints are what you'll be firing at," Gill told him. "Where the legs join with the carapace, that'll be your target area." And frowning again: "What, are you still shaky?"

"Hell, no," said Turnbull. "I'm steady as a rock. But for God's sake don't blow on me too hard!" And grinning, he added: "Hey, I'm joking. I always joke when my asshole starts twitching."

"Nothing like a sense of humor," said Gill . . .

They had found themselves a vantage point on a shallow, grassy bank, where Turnbull was pouring a careful measure of avgas on the weed, when the distant sound of a revving engine and harshly clashing gears attracted their attention. Half a mile to the west, a black van whipped up dust where it came snaking along a bone-dry track.

"Oh?" said Gill wonderingly. Then they heard the rising/dying, two-note *dee-daa, dee-daa* wail of the siren.

"The law," said Turnbull, finishing pouring. "There, that should be enough for starters." Straightening, he unzipped his combat-suit jacket and eased the gun in its holster.

"So what's your problem?" Gill asked him as the van sped closer, left the track, and came bumping across the field. "We have our IDs, and that's all the authority we need."

"Oh, yes," the minder answered with a growl. "But it's my experience that in uncertain times—times when everything is going to hell—IDs don't carry too much weight. In fact, they can be a downright handicap. As for 'authority': well all too frequently that goes to whoever's holding the biggest gun. So before these people get here we'd better get things underway. Do you think we should maybe step back a couple of paces?" He took matches from a pocket, struck one and let it catch, then sent it curving out and down over the bank.

Gill had already picked up his can and started to retreat. Turnbull joined him as the black van skidded sideways and came to a halt on the crushed grass maybe fifty feet away. Then, as the pair turned to face the newcomers, a small explosion—the sudden *whoof* of ignition—sounded from behind and flames shot up from the weed. Moving farther from the bank, they looked at the newcomers. Three uniformed officers had come piling out of the van; one of them carried an ugly-looking automatic weapon slung over his shoulder. And they weren't policemen.

Feeling the heat of the blaze at his back, now Gill recognized the insignia on the side of the black Maria: the letters HMP forming a small red semicircle over the center of the word—or rather the name—"Parkhurst," with the word "staff" completing the circle below. And:

"Whoops!" said Turnbull as the men approached. "They're prison staff from Parkhurst. And again, in my experience, your average screw is far and away more obnoxious than any common or garden-variety copper! The prison is only a few miles away. The island must be running out of regular police and these lads have obviously been recruited."

"To do what?" Gill asked without thinking, and more than a little anxiously. The weed was well alight behind them, sending clouds of stinking black smoke up to the sky; and now there was this to deal with.

The warders were close now; they could probably hear every word. Still Turnbull grinned tightly as he answered, "I suppose they've been tasked to keep people away from the weed."

"That's right, my old son," said the senior of the three. "And who, might I arsk, are you?" He was squat, bald, and ugly, and had very little neck. Without even trying to, he bristled. The others were younger, crewcut, and looked too nervous to be entirely in control of themselves. Especially the one with the machine pistol.

Meanwhile Gill had got it together; he knew that if these people saw fit to interfere they might ruin everything. Trying to keep one eye on the blazing weed and the other on the warders, he said, "My name is Spencer Gill and my colleague here is Jack Turnbull, MOD." Slapping uselessly at his pockets, he wondered where he'd put his ID. "Anyway, we're authorized to examine one of these weed creatures. Right now we're, er, trying to attract their attention . . . ?" The moment he finished he knew how lame it sounded.

It must have sounded lame to Turnbull, too; the big minder snorted his derision, then quick as thought kicked his jerrican over onto its side. He still had the cap in his hand, and black avgas smoked where it glugged from the spout of the jerrican to go slopping toward the lip of the bank. Immediately backing off Turnbull said, "Er, let's get away from here, should we? We can sort this out a little closer to your van if you like." Crouching down into themselves, he and Gill ran for the black Maria.

"Eh, wot?" the senior warder snarled, and reached for the jerrican to set it upright again. "Wot 'ave we 'ere then? Kero, is it?"

"Oh, it's better than that," Turnbull shouted back. "Aviation fuel, 'my old son,' and if the fire backtracks it's going to blow your arse off!" By then the three had smelled the reek of the high octane fuel and were backing, turning, and finally running away from the burning bank. As they came, the youngest member—the one with the machine pistol—was unslinging his weapon from his shoulder.

With his back to the van, Turnbull drew his gun. And Gill said, "Oh, *Christ!*" But it wasn't only the idea of a gunfight that concerned him. It was something else. For in the last few seconds his machine awareness had come to life; it was picking up a deal of furious activity from the river, but nothing that felt remotely familiar. Or only remotely.

The young warder had freed his weapon; now he was trying to cock it while still running. "No time for standoffs," Turnbull yelled, taking careful aim with his Browning. "I'll have to try to wing him!" But fortunately he didn't have to.

The fire backtracked to the jerrican. Almost empty, still it went off like a bomb! The warders were picked up and hurled forward, facedown and arms outstretched, their eyes starting out and their mouths forming huge round "O"s. And the machine pistol landed right at Turnbull's feet.

The big minder gave his Browning to Gill, stooped to pick up the far more lethal weapon. Jerrican shrapnel and clumps of grass were still raining down; the men on the ground were hugging their heads; Stannersly came hurrying from the helicopter.

"What's up?" the pilot called out anxiously as Gill tried to wave him back. By which time the bull warder had managed to prop himself up on one shaky knee, croaking:

"You blokes are in real bovver now!"

"Bovver?" Turnbull repeated, grimly. "The world's got enough bovver, bruvver. You can't frighten the totally terrified. Spencer?"

They helped the men to their feet and Gill said, "What we told you is true. But we've no time for long explanations. This man"—he indicated Stannersly—"is our pilot. He'll verify what we said. And if he can't convince you, well, that's too bad. But right now we have to concentrate on—"

Which was as far as he got before his concentration, or rather his machine awareness, put itself in top gear.

Something was emerging, erupting from beneath the burning weed, coming up right out of the fire and levering itself onto the bank. Avgas blazed harmlessly on its grotesque insect/crustacean/arachnid body, while it squatted there like some monstrous tick, its four crystal "eyes" swiveling to and fro.

Then through the smoke and flames the alien construct detected the men where they stood in a frozen cluster close to the black Maria. Sensors at once locked on, its eyes stopped swiveling, and without pause it headed straight for them!

As well as seeing all of this, Gill felt or sensed it—he knew what would happen even as it happened—for his weird ability was way ahead of his eyes. But paradoxically, and despite the situation, as well as terror he felt like clenching his fists in triumph and shouting, *"Yes!"* For finally he recognized this thing—or if not the construct itself, its "mechanics"—and his machine empathy was telling him, *Yes, you have compatibility.* Telling him that indeed this might easily be the Thone all over again, the technology was that similar. Which in turn meant that this Ggyddn construct was precisely what he needed, except he needed it far less active.

Jack Turnbull knew that, too, and action was his speciality. Slamming back the cocking lever on the machine pistol, he lined up the waddling, flat-bodied construct in his sights and let go with a stammering stream of steel-tipped bullets. Sparks flew as the rounds ricocheted, bouncing off the thing's chitin-plated forward appendages where they joined with its body. That was his designated target area, all right, but the legs were as thick as tree trunks and had the dull sheen of blued steel.

Meanwhile, eager to get away, the warders were making hard work of boarding the black Maria. Battling with the doors, they skidded about on the crushed grass yelping like whipped puppies. Gill could only suppose that they'd seen it all before. "Get in the van, mate!" the older man shouted, reaching out a hand from the side door. "You can't stop that ugly bugger. It'll nip your head off and drag you under. Get in the bloody van!" Obviously he was now satisfied with their credentials.

Gill's thoughts were mainly for Angela and the others at the lighthouse. He shook the warder off, looked for Fred Stannersly. But the pilot was already halfway back to his airplane. So maybe Fred and the senior warder had the right idea: simply to put as much distance as possible between. But then:

"Got you, you weird-looking fuck!" Jack Turnbull growled, and Gill turned to see what was happening.

Low to the ground, like a crab, the construct had waddled forward to a position between the weed and the van. Some forty-odd feet away, straddling Gill's forsaken jerrican—his *full* jerrican—the thing uncoiled whip-like feelers to examine or push aside what must seem a suspect object. And that was when Turnbull yelled, *"Down!"* And taking careful aim, gritting his teeth, the big minder squeezed the trigger.

He and Gill hit the deck together, and the warders in the van shrank down behind its reinforced paneling, as everything turned blinding white flecked with yellow. Then the concussion hit, and the van's windows shattered in a mighty bomb burst of heat and senses-numbing blast . . .

And it was over. The glare receded, leaving a substantial crater smoking in the earth, the grass still rippling, and the black Maria rocking on its springs. But the explosion had extinguished the fire, and now a column of thick black smoke went up to the sky.

Then for long seconds Gill lay absolutely still and wondered how he felt. He was shaking from head to toe—Turnbull, too—but they both seemed okay.

"For Jesus Christ's sake!" The fat warder was out of the van again, shaking powdered glass from his head and shoulders. But by now he looked almost friendly. "Are you two all right, then?"

Gill and Turnbull stood up and shakily dusted themselves down. "Probably," the big minder answered. "But he . . . isn't."

Gill's and the warder's gaze followed Turnbull's to where the construct lay on its back twenty feet away from where last seen. Three of its eight legs were dangling from their sockets, scrabbling uselessly at the smoky air; its carapace oozed gray goo from a jagged crack, and one of several flat, glassy blisters on its back had shattered against a rock.

"Look and learn," said Turnbull. "Now you know how to incapacitate these bastards."

"Oh, really?" said the fat warder. And: "Where've you been 'iding, you two? Fact is we've incapacitated quite a few of the buggers . . . but they don't *stay* that way." Grim-faced, he indicated fresh activity in the construct. "Just look wot's 'appening now—or better still, don't. We can't do a fing ter stop it and I guarantee there'll be more of these weird bleeders on the scene before too long. Best if we get on our way, and that means you, too. *And* I'd very much like you ter give my man 'is gun back." He scowled at Turnbull.

But Gill had already seen—already sensed—what was happening to the construct, and now he was making his way eagerly toward it. "This is what we came for!" he said excitedly. And to Turnbull: "Jack, cover me."

For in his machine-conscious mind Gill sensed the regenerative power flowing from the south, from the Mansion some miles away, and in his hand he held the miniature castle like a flat battery just waiting to be charged . . .

CHAPTER

II

THE CONSTRUCT'S BODY was oval in plan, turreted like a limpet, and armored with fused chitin plates. Toward the center, the turret housed two eyes. Two more were seated in bulging sockets on the thing's flanks, each had a one-hundred-eighty-degree scanning capacity. There were four stubby crawling or waddling legs in front, supporting a projecting anemonelike group of sinisterly mobile feelers, probably some kind of exotic sensor array. At the rear, the other four legs were thinner; they were equipped with spade-shaped paddles like the swim blades on the back legs of free-floating green crabs. The blisters encircling the turret's outer disk were probably flotation chambers.

So Jack Turnbull reckoned. And now that the thing was on its back, he could also see that its stomach cavity was packed with an arsenal of stabbers, claws, pincers, and whiplike metallic tendrils, all of which had been spastically clattering and clashing in the aftermath of the explosion. But during the few seconds it had taken the minder to check the construct out, all such activity had died away as the thing became quiescent.

And now:

"Sarcoptes scabiei," said a young warder through the shattered wreckage of the black Maria's front window. *"God . . . !"*

Pausing a moment before following on behind Gill, Turnbull felt the shudder running through the warder's voice. Half turning, he asked: "Eh? What's that?"

"The scabies bug," said the other. "That's what these bastards look like but a zillion times bigger. I've seen 'em under the microscope." And he further explained: "I occasionally do a stint in MedCen at the prison. Some of our inmates are infected with scabies when they come in. The bug, a fucking insect, gets under the skin just like these bastards get under the weed. And they look just like 'em, too! Except scabies: well they die, no trouble. But *these* fuckers . . . Christ, you can hurt 'em all you want, they simply fix themselves up again!"

Or maybe not so simply.

Following on three or four paces behind Gill and a little to one side—keeping on the construct's side, and thus giving himself a clear arc of fire—the minder found himself agreeing that the thing was a monster; far more terrible than the scorpion creature in the forest world. But its capacity for healing itself—or rather its dependency on regenerative energy beamed to it from a node, this time the Mansion—seemed much the same. And as Turnbull watched the thing "repairing" itself, then just like Gill but without his machine empathy or intuition, he too marveled at the similarity in the two alien technologies.

The construct had stopped twitching its damaged legs; its eyes were no longer swiveling; it lay there like a dead thing, like a limpet prised from its rock when the tide's out, or maybe a hedgehog sideswiped by a car. And it seemed to be leaking gobs of a thick gray liquid, but Turnbull knew it wasn't blood. It was glue, some kind of fluid mechanics. And while this goo was spurting from its damaged joints and cracked carapace, the construct lay still and soaked up alien energy, letting itself mend.

Fascinated, the big minder couldn't help thinking: *Now if only they built cars like that. Or better still if I was built like that!* In his profession it would help, certainly.

And meanwhile, as Gill stood there with his right hand extended, holding out the miniature castle to leech the invisible energy, more of the thick fluid was being ejaculated from the construct's torn sockets. So that now it could plainly be seen that this was no ordinary glue. The stuff flowed outward, even *up*ward, completely sheathing each crippled appendage in a rapidly solidifying yet amazingly elastic coating. And the big minder knew that not only was the goo repairing or "bandaging" the construct's external "bones," the injured parts of its metallic chitin exoskeleton, but replacing them with functional substitutes.

And in a while, like nets drawn in, the sheaths of living liquid retracted, drawing the damaged hard parts back into the carapace and sealing them in position in their sockets. Following which the surplus goo flowed *backward*, with a mind of its own, disappearing into the construct's body. As it went it filled in and hardened over the last few cracks and "raw" exposed areas.

Twenty or thirty seconds maximum and the incredible process was complete. Repaired or restructured however temporarily—recharged almost to capacity—now the crab-thing could recommence its deadly animation. Which it did with a vengeance!

"Spencer, be careful!" Turnbull cautioned as the sensory array of stubby tentacles in the snout emerged and began vibrating in Gill's direction, and three of the conjectural "tools" housed in the thing's belly cavity unfolded and extended themselves toward him. "He's back in business!"

"So are we," Gill answered huskily, "I think. Don't concern yourself, Jack, I'm watching what I'm doing. But damn it, I know that the closer I get to this bloke while he's still sucking on Mamma Mansion's nipple, the more power I can leech."

"Well then, let me try to get you closer," Turnbull said. And moving two paces farther aside from Gill, he took careful aim and put a bullet smack into one of the flanking eyes. Crystal shards went flying, and the construct's turret eyes immediately turned themselves on Turnbull. Then the feelers whipped in his direction, and a pair of blue-gray retractable grapples like scaled-down mechanical diggers cranked themselves forward and snapped at him. He danced backward out of the way, shouting, "There you go!"

And there Gill went, moving closer still to the construct and holding out the miniature castle as if it were an offering to some otherworldly god. But that was the last thing it was. Or at best a poisoned chalice. Then . . .

Under the bank, twin eruptions in the weed signaled the arrival of two more crabs. Crystal blisters pushed rags of green aside as a pair of chitin turrets rose into view—which was more than enough for the warders. Their black Maria revved into life, its tires flinging up grass and dirt as the vehicle reversed away from danger.

Gill and Turnbull, too. They turned and ran for the helicopter, which came hovering down the field toward them just a few feet clear of the fluttering grass. And having hauled themselves to safety, as Stannersly took her up and up, they looked down on the scene at the once-riverside, where the crab newcomers had clambered up out of the water and gone to work turning their colleague right side up.

The scene at the riverside, yes:

A morass stretching as far as the eyes could see in both directions, a column of thick smoke still rising from a blackened patch of dead or dying weed, and three nightmarish, alien machines tilting themselves backward to look up at the dragonfly chopper through emotionless crystal eyes.

It was scarcely the world they'd known. And early days as yet, this thing just beginning.

As they passed over the black Maria where it had come to a halt on a dirt track at the edge of the field, Turnbull grabbed hold of a safety strap, stood framed in the open door, and waved the machine pistol at the warders. There was maybe half a magazine, some forty rounds of ammo left. "I'm going to hang on to this for now!" the big minder yelled. "Sorry, boys!"

Over the throbbing repetitive thunder of the rotors it was highly unlikely they would hear him. But there again, he didn't much care whether they heard him or not . . .

An hour or so earlier, noon at the old lighthouse, and Miranda Marsh had gone up onto the observation deck enclosing the long-dimmed lamp. Apart from Barney, she felt she hadn't a friend in the world. But of course that had always been the lot of people in positions of power. Something the little people like Spencer Gill, Jack Turnbull, George Waite, Stannersly, and Angela would never be able to understand, but something she felt weighing on her, especially in this place, as never before. She had responsibilities, to herself and to the world. Except her world was a very small and isolated place now; no bigger, indeed, than this bloody rock! And even Barney wasn't a true friend, just a curious dog following at heel because he had nothing better to do. And at times a nuisance, too.

"What on earth is *wrong* with you!" Miranda snapped at him as he whined and worried at the stylish, slightly belled cuffs of her trouser legs. It was the third or fourth time he'd gone running off around the curve of the platform, only to return in a minute or two to tug again at her expensive clothing. "Is it Spencer Gill you're waiting for? Your master? Well *yours,* maybe, but no way mine, not ever! Anyway, you stupid dog, he'll be coming back from this direction, not from over there!" She had been looking north and a little east, at a flat, distant wedge on the horizon that she knew was the mainland. And Barney . . . ?

What, was it something out in the Channel that had caught the dog's attention? Listlessly, she followed him this time as he headed yet again for the far side of the deck. But now Barney was really excited, barking, urging her to greater effort.

And there he stood, poised like a gun dog, his head stuck out over the lower bar of the safety rail, tail pointing stiffly to the rear. It was as if he were saying, *Look, for goodness' sake, look!*

She did, and maybe he wasn't so stupid after all . . .

*   *   *

George Waite and Angela were down in the living quarters. She would have talked—she had offered to tell the troubled minister anything he wanted to know about Spencer, Jack, herself, during their previous alien encounter; things they hadn't reported because Gill had reckoned them better left out. In other words, their adventures in detail—but George seemed to have lost all interest in things. In almost everything. It was only on the odd occasion when he would stroke the back of his neck, his head, that he showed any emotion at all. The wrong kind of emotion: a tightening of his lips, a deep-etched frown and momentary squeezing shut of his eyes. Pain, Angela suspected. And then she would think to feel something of the pressure herself: that inoperable lump of malignant flesh in Waite's brain, growing bigger moment by moment. She had never much cared for him, and now she hated herself for it.

"There were times," she suddenly said—for no particular reason except maybe to solicit a response and take Waite's mind off things, perhaps give him hope—"when I thought it was all over for us, all done, finished. It must have been the same for the others, too. But we saw it through and survived. Come what may we'll see it through again. Spencer *will* be back, and . . ."

Waite looked up from where he sat at a table, his sunken eyes seeming to lighten a little. He wasn't looking at Angela, however, but the base of the spiraling staircase. He'd heard the echoing clatter of Miranda Marsh's heels, her shouting, and Barney's frantic barking. And: "Can that be Gill back now, do you think?" he breathlessly, anxiously inquired.

But it wasn't. Angela stepped into the center of the spiral, looked up. Overhead, Miranda paused to lean out across the handrail, panting, "Angela, there's someone in the sea, by the old pier! Someone adrift on a raft . . . or wreckage . . . I'm not sure . . ."

"What?" Angela gasped in the moment before Miranda's message sank in. But then it did and she was heading for the door. Waite followed behind, animated now, but the dog beat them all to it. Bounding past Angela where she went slipping and skittering on the pebble path to the crumbling concrete jetty, in a moment he was in the water and paddling furiously for the raft of wreckage.

Basically the raft was a tangle of rigging with some timbers and shattered planking shoved through the netting. A life belt and an armful of cork floats and plastic bottles supplied the finishing touches, but the whole thing seemed very fragile. Indeed it was coming to pieces even as the dog closed his jaws on the end of a rope, turned, and made laboriously for shore.

Mercifully it was summer, and the sea calm as a millpond. Angela was a good swimmer but this was no kind of place to find yourself fighting the tide. She waded out up to her waist, then went completely out of her depth as the rocks suddenly vanished from under her feet. Just a stroke or two to the disintegrating jumble, and in another moment she was aiding Barney in floating the raft and its ragged passenger to shore.

And as her feet found bottom again, the castaway or survivor, whatever, lifted a mop of wet black hair from the tangle to look at her through dazed, bleary, and probably disbelieving brown eyes. Then, as his head lolled back into the slop, George Waite was in the water between Angela and Barney, helping them to get the rescue done with . . .

With an ex-army pullover looking huge on him, hot coffee, and a bite or two from a bacon sandwich inside him, the man from the raft hadn't looked too much the worse for wear. He'd slept for an hour in front of a roaring fire that burned the last of the lighthouse's coal, and come out of it like a man waking from a nightmare. Which in all probability he was. And now he was telling them his story.

And at last George Waite was interested in something. Angela believed she knew why. This little man was a *real* survivor, and Waite was hoping some of it might rub off on him.

"What was your ship?" Waite asked him, pouring more coffee into an old mug.

"Eh?" The man, of oriental origin, hugged Jack Turnbull's heavy pullover closer to his thin body, accepted the coffee, and warmed his hands on the mug. "Ship? Ah, he call *Hambug*."

"The *Hamburg*? A German ship?"

"Is right. German freighter. Me deckhand. A kid, me stowaway. Been on ships twenny years."

Angela went back to the main subject. "There was weed, you say?"

"Damn right! Plenny weed. In the night . . ." The little man shivered. "Hey, nobody watch too much time! Open sea, men watch for ship, not weed. Then we hit. Slow down. Stop. The . . . paddles?—the props?— the . . ."

"Screws?" said Waite. "The propellers? They got fouled?"

The man grimaced and made a tangled, hand-jive motion with his forearms. "Ship stop!" he said. "He stop dead. But okay, is calm. Three men go down, cut weed." A shrug. "No come back."

Waite and the two women glanced at each other, and back at the man they'd saved. And Angela said, "And then?"

Another shrug. "The weed alive—it move, grow, make pile at side of ship. So, we try burn. Fuel oil."

"His use of English gets better moment by moment," Miranda commented.

And his understanding, too. He had heard her; he looked at her, said, "Me speak German five years. No English. Now it come back."

"So you tried to burn the weed," Waite prompted him, impatiently. "And?"

The man shook his head, looked down, spoke to the mug. "Is hard," he said. "Me see what happen, but . . . no understand. One hour, two, day-time, middle of morning . . . they come."

"What come?" said Angela.

"Out of weed. Come up. Crabs, but *big* . . . big like . . ." He held out his arms, shook his head again. "Is hard. The ship, he gone. Gone down in weed. Crabs punch holes, water come in, ship go down. Is hard, but . . . you believe?" He looked up again.

"Oh, yes," Miranda told him. "We believe." And to the others, "And will *you* believe that Spencer bloody Gill is stopping me from doing what's necessary here, what *must* be done?"

George Waite looked at her, and his eyes were alive again, but she didn't like where they lived. And he said to the man, "How many survivors? Men in the water, with you?"

"Me find net, timbers, bottles, floats. Then night. Water clear, weed gone. Then day. This day, me guess. Men in water?" He shook his head yet again, and his eyes were bleak. "Me." He thumbed his chest . . .

But Barney was barking again, and this time he was truly frantic where he came breakneck down the spiral stairway. They all knew what it meant and broke for the door. Coming from the east, that at first distant *whup-whup-whup* of rotors, but rapidly growing louder. And a speck in the sky expanding, losing altitude, falling toward the lighthouse.

Gill was eager to get on with it, couldn't wait. The tiny castle was like a hum in his mind: the hum of a dynamo or a power station with all its leashed energy, and the grid just waiting to be brought on-line.

He knelt in the middle of a group formed of his "volunteers," Angela, Turnbull, and Barney, and one who for now must be a passenger: George Waite. Only Miranda, Stannersly, and the sole survivor of the wreck of *The Hamburg* held back, standing well away from the group. But as everyone fell silent and Gill concentrated on what he was trying to do—establish some kind of contact with the node and bring it to life, unleash its potential—Fred Stannersly called out:

"Spencer, wait!" The pilot came forward, looked at all of their faces looking at him, said, "What's the point of me staying here? I mean, if I can't take Miranda back to the mainland, what's the point? So I'm waiting for you lot to get back from . . . wherever. But what if you don't? In the end I'd be tempted—no, I'd be obliged to take her back—if only to see for myself how far things had gone. I mean, I'd have to give her one last shot at it, right? Especially if she was the last bullet in the gun."

"She won't be," Gill said. "A couple of days—a week at most—they'll have written her off. Someone else will be doing her job. And we're only the little old British Isles, remember? You can bet that the rest of the world won't be sitting still on this. Plans are being made right now, and units, even armies, are mobilizing. I'll tell you the truth: I don't think we can stop all of it even if we succeed. Fingers are hovering over buttons this very minute, Fred, and sooner or later someone is bound to press one."

Stannersly nodded, considered it, said, "Okay, let me put it this way: I want to come."

"And so do I," Miranda Marsh said, from where she stood a few paces away, having made a quiet approach. "That is, *if* you can go anywhere, do anything. Because you're right, Spencer. I can be—will be—replaced. And my work will be done. But if I'm with you at least I can keep tabs on you. So I'll come . . . on one condition. If we're going into places such as you described in your reports, I want a weapon. For my protection, yes, and for Angela's."

"I can look after myself," Angela said.

But Gill said, "If we leave Miranda here she's as good as marooned, like our shipwrecked friend over there. If she comes with us . . . I can see no reason why she and Angela can't share a gun—maybe your 9mm Browning, Jack? You'll still have the machine pistol, which is a much more deadly weapon. Let's face it, you can only handle one at a time."

Turnbull nodded his agreement, but: "What about the Chinaman, or whatever he is?" he said. "He'll be on his own."

"We'll leave him as much food as we can spare," Gill said. "He'll be okay for five, six days. Then he can live off the sea until we get back. And if we don't get back . . . well it probably won't matter anyway. At least he's better off now than a few hours ago."

"All very logical." Miranda gave a humorless laugh, shook her head disapprovingly. "And you think *I'm* a cold fish!" Then, to Turnbull: "May I have my gun now?"

"Uh-uh." Gill shook his head. "When we're inside, then you can have it. But you may not have to use it. I mean, I hope you never have occasion to use it. This, well, venture is meant to be entirely exploratory. I don't intend for us to go wandering off into any synthesized alien worlds. I just want a better understanding of Ggyddn technology. If this were a motor car—or for that matter a helicopter—I'd be wanting to see if it was feasible to drop a spanner or two in the works, or maybe a bomb in the gas tank."

"Talk all you want." Miranda tossed her head. "The fact is you don't trust me."

"Oh, I do," Gill appeared to contradict her. "Even as far as you trust me. But right now, out here, on this rock, I don't see any danger. So what do you want with a gun? Maybe to order Fred here back to the chopper? So be patient. In there—if I can make an 'in there' and get us inside—it's possible there could be danger. Then you get your gun."

And then he got back down to business . . .

Something less than two hours later, well toward evening, Gill was about ready to give it up. That word on the tip of his tongue just wouldn't come. A glance at the weary faces around told him that the others felt much the same: disappointment was etched deep in every line. Except perhaps for Miranda, who told herself that she hadn't expected a lot in the first place. Angela, however, had kept faith; she knew what was in Gill, or at least what was possible in him.

"The power's here," he said, breaking with his concentration and snatching up the miniature castle. "It's *here!* I have a car and its tank is full, but I've lost the bloody key!" He tightened his fist on the castle, as if to crush it—

And felt it give in his hand, felt its surface *sliding*, mobile under the pressure of his fingers! Simultaneously, as if from a thousand miles away, he heard the big minder asking, "So why don't you hot-wire it?"

And maybe that was the answer. With the Thone, and presumably the Ggyddn, mentalism was everything. Physically fragile, they operated their mechanisms through mind alone. And in that respect—if only as a result of usage, practice—they were far and away superior. Inhabiting the bodies of jellyfish, the advantage of mental superiority was their only ace card. Without it, they'd never have advanced, never have developed their synthetic machine technology.

But human bodies aren't like that. They're not fragile at all. Not a bit of it. They're flesh and blood and bone. And if Gill didn't have the *mental* key to this thing, or if he'd simply forgotten it, still he might have the physical equivalent. Or maybe—what?—a combination of the two?

Hot-wire it? Well why not? Hadn't he "hot-wired" the silver-cylinder weapon that time, in the mad machine world of his worst nightmares? Now how had he gone about it? He had touched a fingertip to the metal, which had at once indented like mercury. But despite responding like some weird liquid, it hadn't run or flowed. And when he'd flicked it with his fingernail it had been hard as steel. Just like this miniature castle was as hard as rock. But rock that could be molded, made massive.

No nuts and bolts here to be coaxed or forced, no screws to be unscrewed; to know how was the whole trick. And to understand was to master . . .

Gill had partial understanding, which came from his machine empathy. But that was a feeling for Earthly machines, Man's machines, and this was something else entirely. It had been one thing to shut the castle down, sever its link with the world's accelerated forces of entropy and give them back to Nature, but it was quite another to plug it in again.

The castle was still malleable in Gill's hand, and however briefly a spark of that transient knowledge returned. Picturing the castle as it had been on the slopes of Ben Lawers, suddenly he felt the incredible expansion, the *shifting*. And at the same time, through a distorted swirl of vision—as if the world had turned to a painting on water and was being sucked down the funnel of a whirlpool—he saw the shipwrecked oriental making his way across the sea-scarred lighthouse rock toward him and his group. But the Chinaman wasn't supposed to be part of this. He could only be a hindrance. And:

"Get back!" Gill tried to yell. "You, damn it! What's-your-name? Go back!"

But it was too late. And too late Angela's startled answer to his question, as the Castle—but "Castle" now, with a capital "C"—rushed to enclose them. "His name?" she said, feeling the impossible whirling but continuing anyway, as she, and her voice, too, were sucked into the spiral. "Why, his name is Ki-no Sung! Sung! Sung! But Spencer? . . . Spencer? . . . Spencer? Is something wrong? . . . wrong? . . . wrong?"

I just may be able to tell you shortly, he thought as he was grabbed up into the swirl of things. *Well, with any luck!*

For the fact of it was that he couldn't be sure even now that what was happening was entirely of his doing . . .

CHAPTER
12

S ITH, ONCE-OF-THE-THONE, now Ggyddn, had achieved the first of several objectives: to get Spencer Gill and his party (especially Gill, but also the female and that mass of murderous reflex action and destructive energy called Jack Turnbull) into a synthesizer, or in their terminology a House of Doors. Better yet, it was a Thone House of Doors; for if they'd been taken by the Ggyddn . . .

But the Ggyddn didn't "take" creatures, only their worlds. The inhabitants of those worlds, where there were inhabitants, had no say in the matter. They were simply . . . removed. A process that was even now well under way. But it would be a clean, in the main nonviolent process—that is, unless it provoked violence—the first stage in the metamorphosis of a planet: the weed.

A few days, that was all, perhaps a dozen planetary rotations, and the weed would have spread into almost every ocean, lake, river in the world. Seven-tenths of the planet's surface would be weed. And then, with nowhere left to spread, its task completed, the weed would die. And at the last Earth's peoples would discover the weed's real secret. Too late they would see the great green bladders swelling, turning black and bursting, releasing their deadly poisons into the doomed atmosphere.

Oh, the Ggyddn could exist in Earth's oxygen-laden air for a while, but they would much prefer their own atmosphere—and they would certainly prefer it radiation-free. Only get through the first stage without triggering a nuclear response, the rest would be easy. Even a warrior species such as

Man would quickly see the futility in attempting to destroy that which was indestructible. Let them evaporate a node—such as the unoccupied "island" in the Pacific, which was there specifically for that purpose—and the Ggyddn would instantly replace or resynthesize it. In any case, even if it were possible, what race would deliberately, permanently pollute *one hundred and forty million* square miles of their own homeworld? Which was what they would have to do if they wanted to be rid of the weed. A bomb or two, yes, perhaps, but when they saw it was to no avail . . .

Then the poison, swift and painless, as the weed completed its cycle. And a species, and all the lesser species that supported it, gone forever to make way for the Ggyddn; for one or two of the Ggyddn, anyway, because in the main they were solitary creatures.

After that, plenty of time for the rest of the metamorphosis. The weed-gas would take care of the ozone; the sun's rays would blaze through; the polar caps melt into warm oceans. The black hole gravitor at Earth's core would be leeched, its power reversed and utilized in the reduction of gravity in and around the crystal palaces of the new owner or owners—owners of the planet, that is. And around these wondrous manses, geo-gravitic forces would build volcanoes, furnishing controlled lava flows from the core to provide the required landscaping and temperature. Finally, a few finishing touches: fungus jungles, reeking swamplands . . .

To the Ggyddn, paradise. And to the people of this world, hell. Except they wouldn't be here to see it. And that was the one facet of this jewel of a project that grieved Sith once-of-the-Thone as he had never believed possible, not even when his transgressions had caused his own kind to maroon him on a barren rock of a moon barely capable of supporting life. Sith, who might even have been Grand Thone, and his seat the crystal pedestal itself!

Ah, but all such dreams were swept away, all thanks to Spencer Gill and his party. Gill, because out of five point six billion human minds his had been the one that found some kind of resonance with the synthesizer. A mutant intelligence, he understood something of machines. But his understanding wasn't that of the draftsman, engineer, or operator. No, it went far deeper than that: "machine empathy," as if machines were living things that Gill could feel for.

Well, and maybe Gill wasn't alone at that. Perhaps, somewhere out there in those five point six billion incredibly cold bodies, there were other minds like his. But he was the one who by his presence, his deliberate interference, had made himself available the first time around. And out of curiosity on Sith's part if for no other reason, Gill had been chosen as one of the group to undergo examination. Spencer Gill, and the female Angela

Denholm, and Jack Turnbull, a modern man of primitive warrior skills and a basic if not animal instinct for survival.

It should have been simple: the group was to be tested in various synthesized worlds under conditions best calculated to gauge their worthiness. In the event they survived the rigors of these (to them) alien worlds—that is, if they weren't driven to madness or suicide—their species must then be judged worthy. Worthy not only of mastery of their planet, but literally of existence. The Thone would then back off, leaving them to evolution in an environment relinquished to their control.

It *should* have been that simple. For despite that during Sith's term of preparatory observation he had found the species rude, despicable, and unbelievably destructive, still he'd been fairly sure that they would overcome.

But then—coming just when he was ready to initiate the test program . . .

Word had been received that the Grand Thone was preparing a statement of abdication; it was generally understood that he would retire to well-deserved isolation and uttermost insularity in a world on the outermost rim. And Sith was named as one of several aspirants to the crystal pedestal . . . the very pinnacle of Thone authority!

Then (for all that it was unorthodox and very definitely un-Thone, a crime in itself), Sith had found himself, as in a fever, wondering, *How might I distinguish myself, advance myself, put myself ahead of the game?* And the answer had seemed obvious. Worlds were seldom ideal as this one, with a warm sun, a hot core, and—despite the requirement for entropy enhancement—at least four billion years of lifetime ahead of it. If Sith could deliver this world to the Thone . . . then the stairway to the crystal pedestal would seem assured. And so he had rigged the game, the tests, the synthesizer itself. And to be absolutely certain, he'd inserted himself into the process of examination—or rather elimination. For from then on there wasn't even a remote chance that the test group would survive that process.

And yet . . . they *had* survived.

For much as Sith had feared, Gill's machine empathy was a weapon in its own right. Using it, he had gradually discovered the first principle of Thone technology; shortly he'd been able to communicate with the synthesizer itself. From then on things had gone more and more against Sith, until he'd decided enough was enough and the game must end.

Alas that it had ended in Gill's favor when Sith, having fallen foul of one of his own devices, floundered to a halt in a world of high gravity, snow, ice, and pain. A whole world of pain. He had been fortunate to survive . . . or perhaps not. The Thone had been watching him, and Sith was condemned by his own base actions. They declared him un-Thone.

Since he was no longer Thone he was Ggyddn, outlawed. Banished to a rock of a world, Sith had believed that this was the end, albeit a slow, miserable end. But by a miracle of fate the free Ggyddn had found him. Their aim was expansion—to eat up every un-Thone world, and eventually the Thone's worlds, too—and they didn't care how they went about it. Thus Sith was rescued to swell their ranks . . . also because he knew the coordinates of a planet ripe for conquest. Or rather—since conquest was guaranteed—for colonization.

And through all of this—especially Sith's spell in exile on an inhospitable planetoid—a burning hatred building inside him, and terrible dreams of a yet more terrible revenge against one man, his friends and entire race. But no way to bring those dreams to fruition, no way now to pit himself, his intelligence, a second time against Spencer Gill's. No, not ever . . .

Oh, really? But that had been then, and this was now. And Sith was free, Ggyddn! The last time . . . who could say? Perhaps he had been tied (well, however loosely) by Thone "ethics." But it wouldn't be like that this time. Oh, Sith was a deviant and un-Thone, no question. But right now he was glad. Thone? No, he was *definitely* Ggyddn!

With Gys U Kalk's permission, Sith had used the Pyramid's transmat to visit those nodes most likely to attract Gill's attention. The first and most obvious of these was the House of Doors, or the Mansion, on the Isle of Wight. Since Gill was a native of this small island group, the odds were in favor of his being there. But the instrumentation failed to indicate any external interference; there was no "static" record indicative of Gill's peculiar machine rapport; he hadn't been there, not yet. But Sith had no doubt that he would be, given time.

After that, in short order, Sith checked the instrumentation of several nearby nodes, including the North Atlantic iceberg. Nothing.

Transmatting farther afield, eastward, he visited the Pagoda, a "manned" node where Assu Lan, Ggyddn, was in control. There at least there had been some activity, albeit minor. Assu Lan showed him a captive, kept alive awhile as a curiosity, while Lan decided whether to thrust him back out into the world or otherwise dispose of him.

Trapped within a containment cell, the small man was a pitiful sight; or he would have been if the Ggyddn knew pity. Groveling at the foot of a wall of flowing colors, Ki-no Sung cried out to his ancestors for a merciful release. And his slanted eyes bugged as the apparently endless walls melted and convulsed, kaleidoscoping all around him.

"You took him?" Sith was puzzled.

"More by accident than design," Assu Lan was defensive. "The node was in flux, yet he came on. I observed, wondering at his bravery. Or perhaps his stupidity? But in any case, I had no desire to precipitate warlike activity in the populace while the node was in flux, and myself as yet unacquainted with the planet, this region, or its inhabitants. As it was, the node very nearly caught him in its final flux, before stabilization. Better that he simply disappear than that his severed trunk be discovered floating out to sea! And so I took him."

Sith's telepathic mind registered the equivalent of a superior smile. "You feared retaliation? From such as him?"

"As I recall," Assu Lan's mental voice stiffened, "we discovered you in a leaky node on a stony moon whose energy was barely sufficient to sustain your prison habitat! That situation resulted directly from your dealings with . . . with such as him! Furthermore, I was not wrong to fear retaliation. Perhaps you are not fully acquainted with our methods, Sith? We desire clean worlds, intact worlds, and worlds free of nuclear radiation and other contaminates. Or have you forgotten? These creatures do indeed have weapons of enormous destructive potential. Until I was better informed, that was a fact I could not fail to take into consideration."

At which Sith offered the equivalent of a sniff or a dismissive shrug, before answering: "Well, they don't seem to have bombed you yet."

"You are flippant," the other told him coldly. "Very definitely un-Thone—but if I were you I would take care not to become un-Ggyddn, too!" And before Sith could think to compose a response: "No, they haven't bombed me yet—but instrumentation shows that they *have* given it some thought!"

"Oh?"

"Air transports have passed overhead, carrying crude nuclear devices. On the eastern peninsula, missile projectors are in place. Their warheads are primitive: that is to say, chemical explosives. To the west—within physical sensor range—other batteries have a mix of what are referred to as conventional and 'tactical nuclear' devices. 'Tactical nuclear'? Need I add that in circumstances such as mine I tend to spend a lot of my time here, close to the transmat?"

Sith was studying the information on a viewscreen. To human eyes it would convey nothing at all; Sith saw the outside world in all directions, to a distance of some miles. "There is some activity on the shore there beyond the weed, in the jungle fringes," he agreed.

"Every day they tend their surveillance devices," Lan told him. "Probes, vision aids, crude radio and other radiation detectors, and so forth. It would seem there is enmity between those on the mainland and those on the peninsula. Each believes the node to be some sort of weapon placed here by the other!"

"Well, so it is a weapon," Sith answered. "And except that it was placed here by us, they are right."

"Mine is not an enviable situation," Lan complained.

"Others are in similar straits," Sith replied. "I myself, upon a time, experienced just such discomfort. Worse for me, for I was a Thone invigilator! I knew that in the event of any harm befalling me, the guilty creatures were not likely to be punished. For in Thone perceptions they were worthy!"

"*Huh!*" A thought like a snort from the other.

"I agree entirely," Sith answered. "But in the event of a worst-case scenario, you do have the transmat. And now I must be on my way via that very device."

But pausing before taking his departure, and a deal more politely, Sith requested: "Lan . . . oblige me, if you will. Do not dispose of that small yellow man just yet. I may find a use for him."

"As you will," the other answered with a shrug, returning to his instrumentation. And Sith returned to the Isle of Wight and the node known as the Mansion . . .

. . . **B**arely in time to reacquaint himself with the node's controller, Yarth Phin, and to commence scanning recent recordings, before the instrumentation "flickered" from some infinitesimally small exterior interference.

"Probably their sensors," Yarth Phin shrugged it off. "You'd scarcely credit the variety of primitive detection devices they've set up out there!" His situation was fairly stable; thus far he hadn't experienced any of Assu Lan's problems. Sith, however, was far more suspicious.

"But this is exactly the kind of interference I'm looking for," he answered, adjusting the external scanners.

And sure enough it was Gill! It was Spencer Gill *thinking!* And the instrumentation reacted to his—to this human being's—thoughts! Oh, the merest flicker, but to Sith it was like hearing a dolphin speak . . . or more properly, as if he observed a gorilla sharpening an ax!

A moment more to convince Yarth Phin, and however reluctantly the node's master temporarily relinquished control of the instrumentation to Sith.

Then:

Gill's group coming closer across the field—and Spencer Gill himself closest of all, deliberately trying to communicate with the Mansion! Sith felt, sensed it in the instrumentation: that rough contact, so faint, but oh-so-real! A mentality, a *human* mentality, groping in places where only Thone thoughts (no, Ggyddn thoughts now) should ever reach! Fantastic!

It had been the same in the Castle in Scotland, the reason Sith had taken Gill in the first place; but his reason was entirely different now—*if* he reasoned at all! Indeed his loathing on merely sighting Gill seemed to spark an *un*reasoning madness in him, so that without pausing to consider the consequences he expanded the Mansion . . . !

Then one of Gill's group running forward, apparently sacrificing himself, to be sucked in by the flux. And the policemen with their crude but dangerous weapons, and the rest of Gill's party, including the woman Angela Denholm—*and* that viciously efficient Jack Turnbull—trying to drag Gill out of danger.

No, Sith wouldn't have it! He even considered—he was on the verge of—expanding the Mansion again . . .

When Yarth Phin cried out a warning in his mind and snatched back the instrumentation. And:

"What? What?" Phin raged. "Are you a mad creature? This node is stone. Expand it without substance control, it would be pumice. Too far and it would be sand, insubstantial! And if you had succeeded, what then? Would you have taken those law enforcers, too? *And* their weapons? The node's walls are our protection. Within these walls, and without survival suits, we'd have no chance against creatures such as these!"

But Sith wasn't listening. "A locator, a bug!" he insisted. "Insert a bug . . . in this one . . . *now!*"

"What?"

"A bug, in his skull, under a tooth. Do it now. Believe me, this is of *immeasurable* importance! And we don't have time for explanations. But these creatures have teeth. When their teeth decay they have them filled with a metal, this time with a Ggyddn metal! So that I shall know where *he* is, where *Gill* is, at all times!"

And Phin had done it. The work of seconds: to scan the unfortunate Waite and instruct the synthesizer to cap the surface of an existing filling in a tooth at the back of his lower jaw with a coating of "intelligent" Ggyddn metal. While the cap was a "machine" of sorts in its own right, inactive it would be too small for detection by Gill's machine empathy. But from now on Sith would be able to detect Gill at a moment's notice.

That had been that. George Waite had been thrust from the Mansion's wall and returned to the world, and in a little while Gill and his party departed. But no matter where they went, Sith knew that he could always track them . . .

*   *   *

And Sith had tracked them—to an island and a lighthouse off the Cornish coast. Following which he returned to the Pagoda and Assu Lan . . . and Ki-no Sung.

For there were bugs and there were bugs. Even by Earth's primitive technological standards—even in this world—the range in spying devices was vast. Ki-no Sung's bug would be a complicated thing, with synthetic flesh connecting it directly to his central cortex. And if Sith's scheme worked, Sung would be his eyes and ears on Gill's movements and his group's activities, and if need be even his mouth in their conversations.

That would mean inserting the yellow man into the group's activities, obviously, and Sith must find a convincing way to do that, too. But here his years on Earth as a Thone invigilator—the fact that he had regularly gone among them—stood him in good stead.

But all of this to be achieved with dispatch if Sith were to enjoy his revenge as planned. For Gill was more than just a target; he was still the ultimate irritation: the very *idea* of a human being with the mind of a giant! A mind compatible not alone with Ggyddn or Thone technology but *all* technology, all machinery.

And more than just an idea, but an indisputable fact. For Sith's "excitement" as Gill had approached the Mansion wasn't merely because it was him, his enemy, but what he brought with him. And when Sith had exhorted Yarth Phin to action with his promise that this was of "immeasurable" importance, he hadn't simply been playing with words.

For there had been more than just a "flicker" or "glitch" in the instrumentation; indeed as Gill approached, the sensors had registered a deal of interference, "static" that increased commensurate with his proximity—as if a pair of magnets had been placed within each other's fluence. Or a pair of nodes . . .

And Sith had known what that signified:

That Spencer Gill was in possession of a deactivated node, which could only be the original House of Doors!

CHAPTER
13

"SPENCER!" ANGELA'S ANXIOUS gasp—an exhalation, an exclamation formed of Gill's whispered name and a hiss of air, forced out through the elongated "O" of her mouth as everything turned inside out and upside down—was a tortured, echoing rasp trapped in the flux of the expanding Castle. "Spencer . . . Spencerrr . . . *Spencerrrr!*"

He heard it and tried to answer: "Angela . . . Aaangela . . . *Aaaangela!*" Only to hear his own voice—the single word that was her name—distorted and echoing as in the awesome configurations of some alien cavern complex. But then out of nowhere, out of a whirlpool of meaningless color and kaleidoscopic retinal images that *might* have been the molten debris of blue sky, black rock, rearing white-walled lighthouse and gray-green sea, suddenly her groping hand found his as together—and together with the others—they were absorbed by the Castle.

For a moment darkness fell as a heavy yet liquid something enveloped them, passed over and around them like a leaden wave, left them weighted yet tumbling in its backwash. But amazingly when the wave had moved on—despite the churning and spinning of their psyches—they sensed that they were still standing, albeit frozen like statues, in their original positions . . .

Standing for a moment, that is, until disorientation struck home like a hammer blow. Then with normal, no longer distorted cries of shock, astonishment, and terror, they staggered, stumbled, and without exception thumped down on their backsides or crumpled to their knees, or simply collapsed down into themselves as if their legs had been deboned.

All of them had closed their eyes. The visual assault of a melting world had been too much for them, too fearful: like the sudden stab of a white-hot poker too close to the eyes, or some runaway locomotive bearing down on them. But now that they were . . . *here*, almost in unison, Gill, Turnbull, and Angela squinted, then opened their eyes. And:

"We're in!" Gill husked.

And Jack Turnbull gulped, "And sober at that. But if I had a bottle right now—you and the SAS both couldn't stop me from sinking it!"

"In," Angela echoed Gill however shakily. "But in where? I mean, are we where you want us to be?"

"Let me feel my way," Gill answered. "But first of all let me feel anything!"

The three of them were up on their feet first, too, offering helping hands to the others and trying to calm them. Miranda Marsh was almost speechless for once; she could only gasp as Turnbull lifted her to her feet and steadied her. George Waite, on the other hand, had seemed to come to life.

"In?" He grabbed Gill by the arm. "Are we really? Did you do it, Spencer? Is this it, the inside of that little . . . that little castle?" But then, looking around, he shrank back as he recognized the fact that that was the only place this could be. For the "walls" were a mass of crawling, nauseous colors, and the floor was spongy, and the ceiling was hidden in a luminous white mist. As for distance or geometry or perspective: it was impossible to tell. The only constant or continuation from the outside world seemed to be that of gravity: up was still up and down was still down. But as for directions . . .

Seeing the sick look on Waite's face, and understanding it only too well, Angela told him, "The walls are the worst of it. You can walk right through some of them."

"Which is an excellent way to go missing," said Gill. "And this place is a veritable maze. So for the time being let's all stick close together."

At which Barney yipped a couple of times, ran off, and was gone from sight in a moment. "See what I mean?" said Gill, who wasn't about to start worrying over the dog. Time was when Barney had known his way around this place—not to mention a few other places—better than anyone else in the world.

Fred Stannersly seemed worst affected. He hugged the spongy "ground," tried to dig his fingers in, didn't look like he'd ever try to get up. But as Gill got down on one knee beside him and put a hand on his shoulder:

"It . . . it's okay," the pilot mumbled. "Just give me a second. It's a spatial thing—I think. I'm a flyer, and I suppose all of my senses are tuned to it—tuned to three dimensions, I mean. But in this place . . ." He offered a helpless shrug.

"You don't know the tune, right?" said Turnbull. And Gill said:

"I wish I could tell you you'll get used to it."

"Head count," said Miranda curtly and ominously. She'd got her breath back, and something of her orientation and composure, too; from her tone of voice it was obvious that something other than the drastic change in their surroundings was bothering her. The others knew what it was immediately.

"Ki-no Sung!" said Angela.

"He was coming toward us when . . . when it happened," Miranda said. And turning to Gill, "Couldn't you have stopped it?"

He shook his head. "Hey, I was trying to *do* it, remember?"

And Turnbull said, "Spencer, you don't look any too comfortable. So what do you think happened to Ki-no Sung? What is it that's bothering you?"

"I don't like to think what's happened to him." Gill shook his head again, frowned, looked puzzled. "As for what's bothering me . . . I don't know. One minute I thought I had everything under control, and the next it went wild. It was like I was—what, steering a car?—something like that. But lightly, using only my fingertips. Then, suddenly, it was like I hit a rock or a ramp; the wheel was wrenched out of my hands! As for the China-man—Ki-no Sung?—I tried to wave him back. But he ignored me. It all depends how close he was when the Castle firmed up."

"He could have made it inside but somewhere else, in some other 'room,' " said Angela.

"Or he could be outside." Turnbull chewed his lip.

"Or . . . in between." Gill's face was drawn now, his cheeks hollow.

"In between?" Miranda looked at him, at Turnbull, at Angela. From one face to the next, all three of them.

"In the walls," Gill told her. "He could be trapped in the solid exterior walls. Locked in, crushed, suffocated, dead. The Castle doesn't discriminate. It's a machine. Animate and inanimate are all one to the Castle. It's insensitive as a bulldozer. It grows up out of, or around, its surroundings."

"My God!" she burst out. "Are you always this . . . dispassionate?"

Her outburst took him aback. He blinked and said, "No, I'm truthful, that's all. In here, we don't have time for anything but the truth."

"But . . . what about *us*?" she went on. "Why weren't *we* simply brushed aside, or flattened, when you activated the thing? Why did we survive? Why are we here? Why did this indiscriminate Castle 'discriminate' in our case?"

"Because we—or I—activated the thing," Gill told her. "Because we're at the center, or should be, and because we're the users. If you put yourself in front of a train you'll get run down, but the passengers will be perfectly safe."

Miranda shook her head, a little wildly Gill thought, and blurted, "God, I don't know enough about what we're doing, why I'm here!"

"But it was your choice, remember?" Angela snapped, putting herself between them. "You didn't believe Spencer could do it. Worse, you hoped he couldn't—because you have your own pigheaded ideas on how things should be handled. But now that he *has* done it you're scared again, and when you're scared you go on the offensive, right? It's the only move you've got: to put the blame, where you think there is blame, on someone else. Oh, I think I've got your number, Miranda Marsh!"

And she was right, Miranda was afraid. Afraid and furious. "Why, you little—!"

"Little nothing!" Angela cut her off, her dark eyes sparking fire. "In here—in the Castle, the House of Doors—we're all the same size. *Human* size, that is. Anyone who thinks she's bigger could soon find herself cut down to nothing."

Miranda's face went white. "You dare threaten me?"

"Oh, kiss my . . ." Angela was barely able to stop herself in time. Whirling on Gill she said, "Why did we have to bring her? Spencer, can't you put her back outside again? We won't get anywhere with mouth almighty Miranda along to f-f-*foul* things up!" And again she only just managed to curb the curse word.

"Cool it, everybody!" Turnbull's booming voice hit like a fist, knocking some sense into them. "So okay, it looks like we made a bad start and lost somebody. But no one is to blame, and in fact we don't know that we have lost Ki-no Sung for sure. So let's hope Angela is right, that he's in here somewhere, scared witless, no doubt, and wondering where *we* all went to and where the hell *he* is."

"If that's so, then I can sympathize with him," said Gill quietly. Which was his way of telling them something.

Knowing him, Angela caught on at once. "Spencer, does that mean what I think it means? That we're not where we're supposed to be?"

"It means I have a problem," he answered.

And Turnbull said, "Which in turn means that we all have a problem, right? So don't keep us in suspenders, Spencer. What's up?" The minder's tone was deliberately light, but there was an edge to his voice.

"This should be the synthesizer's control room," Gill said, moving toward one of the mobile, three-dimensional walls. "And these wall-sized screens should be full of information. They're—I don't know—like files in a computer? Or like pages on the screen of a word processor. Or they should be. But now it looks like, or rather it *feels* like, to this sixth sense of mine, you understand . . . like maybe someone's downloaded or erased them?" He wasn't too sure himself just exactly what he meant.

"Done what?" said Miranda nervously. She had no knowledge of computers. That stuff was for lesser persons, civil servants, paper-pushers, office types.

But Fred Stannersly was a user. "The files have been emptied," he reiterated. "Is that what you're saying, Spencer? But surely it was all alien stuff anyway. Doesn't that mean you can start afresh, build up your own database?"

"I don't know, maybe." Gill shrugged. "But in fact it was the alien stuff I wanted to get into. And the hell of it is I'm probably to blame." He put out a hand, touched a wall—except his hand didn't stop but went right on through up to his wrist. Shaking his head, and quickly withdrawing his hand, Gill turned to the pilot. "Tell me, Fred: what happens if you yank the plug on a computer in the middle of work in progress?"

"I can tell you that," Angela said. "At least where a word processor's concerned. I've done it once or twice myself, tripped on the cable, broke the connection, lost what I was working on. That is, until I learned to save it as I went along."

"But I didn't save it," Gill said ruefully. "When I deactivated the Castle, I simply pulled the plug . . ."

"We're doing nothing!" Miranda Marsh said, her voice high-pitched and perhaps a little hysterical. "How long are we going to just stand here talking, doing nothing? What were you thinking of, bringing us in here, Spencer? Surely you have a plan? I mean, why the hell are we here?"

Before Gill could answer, if he would, Angela said, "Well, two of us are here because we wanted to be. Because we wouldn't let Spencer do it on his own. And Fred came along for the same reason, I think. He didn't want to be left out, left on his own on that rock waiting for us to get done. As for George—"

"I'm here because it's my one chance," Waite said simply. "If this place is a cure-all, then maybe I'll come out of it with a future. I'm sorry now that I lied to Spencer and the others in the first place, about my real interest in the House of Doors, that is. I know now that it was my job taught me how to be a liar, just as yours is teaching you, Miranda. Too much responsibility can do that. The trouble is it gets so easy you don't even realize you're doing it. You're so involved guiding others along your predetermined route that you don't give any thought that it might be the wrong route. And then, instead of guiding them you end up pushing, probably in the wrong direction. Of course, that's when you start lying—even to yourself. Because you so desperately want to be right."

"Too much responsibility?" Miranda glared at him. "And I'm a liar, am I? Well I'm not lying when I tell you that right now we're *all* responsible, and for the entire world! A world that's going to hell while we're stuck in here, or stuck on that lighthouse rock in the middle of the bloody sea, doing nothing!" She faced up to the rest of them, glaring and clenching her fists.

Waite shook his head, looked at her almost pityingly. And: "No," he told her. "You'd only be responsible if Gill were stupid enough to put you back outside, where if you were given the chance it's entirely likely you'd cause the world to go to hell that much faster."

Meanwhile Gill had been trying to concentrate, trying to get his thoughts together, bring his machine empathy into play. But the rest of them were making it very difficult . . . and that now included Barney, where he reappeared with a worried yip and a stiff-legged, sideways sort of lurch back through the flowing wall that Gill had shoved his hand into. But Barney didn't come back alone.

"Christ!" Jack Turnbull yelped as a figure stumbled, then fell into view through the wall right behind the skittering dog. A human figure, yellow-skinned, but now red with blood! It was Sung, his mouth silently working and slanted eyes bugging, glazing even as he fell. And Gill, the closest, barely able to slow his fall and gentle him to the floor.

Then the others were down beside him, willing hands reaching but not knowing where to touch, what to do to help. And the Chinaman staring up at them where he lay on his back, his mouth and eyes like black holes in his pale yellow face. Or yellow on the right side. But the left side was red. His left cheek, from the high cheekbone to his chin and back as far as his ear, had been skinned, and the whorl of his ear looked as if it had been finely sandpapered down to the cartilage. Or it would do if the blood wasn't running and dripping, spattering everywhere.

And it wasn't only his face. Until he had gone down, Ki-no Sung had held his left hand bundled up in the green wool of his outsize ex-army pullover. The garment seemed stuck to him, and at the wrist was heavy, matted with his blood. As Angela speedily but carefully unwrapped his lower arm, the Chinaman passed out. Which was something of a relief. And seeing that he could no longer feel anything, Angela got on with it that much faster. Until his lower arm came into view.

Then she clapped a bloody hand to her mouth, flopped back away from him, and sent herself sprawling. For Ki-no Sung had no left hand. He'd been holding a raw stump, sliced through at the knuckled, hinged section of the wrist. And arterial blood still spurting in time to the beat of his heart.

Jack Turnbull knew something about first aid. In just a moment or two he had Gill squeezing the pressure point in the Chinaman's armpit, while he tore the bloody pullover away from the shoulder and ripped it down the seam. "It'll make a sling," he panted, working hard and fast. By which time Angela had got herself together again, producing bandages and the makings for a tourniquet from her sausage bag.

"We have to cauterize it!" Miranda cried, her hands fluttering about her face.

And George Waite said, "Well you're hot stuff, Miranda. So why don't you do it?"

But surprisingly Fred Stannersly said, "For God's sake let her be! Can't you see she's in shock?" Waite made no answer but stripped off his combat jacket, his pullover, and tore the silk shirt right off his own body.

"It's not real silk," he muttered. "Some kind of nylon. I had an accident once, dropped a cigarette on one just like it. The stuff melts like plastic; it burns into your skin, forms a seal." He got down, pulled Angela gently aside, and wrapped the torn shirt around Ki-no Sung's stump. The tourniquet had stopped a lot of the spurting, and before Waite's shirt could soak up too much blood he turned up his cigarette lighter and applied the hissing blue flame. With the exception of a damp black blood-soaked circle on the flat of the stump, the shirt immediately melted down and formed a plastic cup like a ferrule.

As Angela went to pad the stump and bandage it, Turnbull said, "Wait," and took a small hip flask from an inside pocket of his combat jacket. He poured half of the liquor on to Ki-no Sung's forearm, glanced at Gill, shrugged, and poured the rest. "Medicinal purposes, as you see. Er, protection against infection?" The minder grimaced, and under his breath said, *"Shit!"*

Despite the situation, Gill might have grinned but didn't have the time. He was busy sorting bandages for Sung's flayed face . . .

So what happened to this poor bloke?" Fred Stannersly was nervous, which was only understandable—they were all nervous.

Gill looked at Angela and Turnbull. "We can only hazard a guess," he said. And Turnbull took it up:

"It was the same that time in Scotland. When the House of Doors firmed up, it cut a sheep in half. There was a witness, a local gillie or gamekeeper . . ."

And as he trailed off Angela was left to finish it. "This time," she said, "well obviously this poor man was inside, but only just inside. He must have seen the Castle expanding toward him and tried to draw back. Maybe he was leaning backward with his left hand extended, turning his face from something he didn't understand. Then, as the outer wall firmed up, it took his hand and the skin off his face, and flattened his ear."

They had made Ki-no Sung comfortable, laid him down with his back and shoulders against one of the walls—a solid wall. Miranda had placed a sausage bag behind him as a backrest. But even this minimum of activity had made her perspire. They were all perspiring.

"Well," she said, lifting her chin to dab at her long neck when she was through patting the bag into position, "there's at least one thing to be said in favor of this awful place."

"Oh?" said Gill.

"The temperature," she answered. "We definitely won't die of exposure in here. But on the other hand, we could certainly dehydrate!"

"The Thone like it hot," Gill reminded her. "They *liked* it hot, anyway. That's why we're carrying plenty of water . . ." And as he fell silent:

"What now?" Turnbull wanted to know. "I mean, obviously we have to look after our oriental friend here, but meanwhile time's a-wasting."

"I know," Gill answered. "But there are too many distractions. I can't do anything here, with everyone around me. I know that must make me sound like some kind of prima donna, but I've got to be able to . . . well, to *listen* to this thing, this House of Doors. I need to be alone. So I'm going to take the dog with me and go off a little way. Then, even if I get lost, I'm sure Barney will know the way back."

"Be careful," Angela said as he made to move off.

"Oh, I'll be back for you, sweetheart." He hugged her however briefly, not wanting to suggest that there was any kind of permanency in this good-bye. "Come hell or high water, you know that."

And she did know it . . .

CHAPTER
14

GILL HADN'T VOICED all of his fears to the others. He couldn't because he didn't know what they were. But one thing for sure, things weren't "right" here. The temperature, for one. Miranda had brought that to his attention, and now he puzzled over it. When he'd deactivated the Castle, had he really wiped it clean? Oh, the hardware—the Castle itself—was still here, but what about the software? Wiped? But wouldn't that mean he'd voided the temperature, too? Or did the synthesizer automatically assume that there would be a Thone controller? And if it did "assume," didn't that mean that the basic program was still there waiting to be brought back to life? So why couldn't he feel it? Why couldn't he sense it?

Gill didn't know about computers, didn't "know" about the workings of anything but the most basic machinery. The thing he had wasn't in any way comparable with an engineer's or fitter's understanding of mechanics. It was, rather, a machine psychometry, literally an empathy: a feeling and more than a feeling of oneness with functioning devices. Thus if machines had minds of their own—*all* machines, from safety pins to spacecraft— then Gill might be said to be a psychologist. More even than that, a telepath.

They "spoke" to him—well, figuratively at least—and the machines of Earth spoke in a "tongue" he could understand, that he'd been brought up with. But the synthesizer, this House of Doors, was an alien machine; its technology, psychology, and language were very different. That time in Scotland, he had thought he had it, believed that he'd crossed the language barrier. But apparently he'd been wrong. Or if not, then the current situation was wrong.

So maybe he should spend some time talking to Fred Stannersly about computers, get a better understanding of their physical workings. Or then again maybe not. Alien was the key word. Just because Thone and Ggyddn technologies were compatible—at least to the extent that they drew on identical energy sources—that didn't mean they were remotely similar to Earthly engineering.

And in fact Gill knew they weren't. Liquid parts (*not* oil, no), "intelligent" hydraulics, and entropy engines that speeded up devolution to feed on the energy of the future were about as far removed as you can get from human technology! And now Gill kicked himself that he hadn't attempted to study the miniature castle—hadn't explored it, tried to stay "in touch" with it, hadn't slept with the fucking thing—since the day he deactivated it. Maybe that was the real problem: familiarity. Or lack of it. For after all it hadn't been like riding a bike or swimming, or any normal human activity. It wasn't something you did once and then remembered forever.

Which was why he'd found it necessary to get away from the others: so that he could concentrate on this thing, get back in touch with it, get his mental fingers back on the keyboard.

And Barney the dog was Gill's only companion now, as he walked and wondered through flowing corridors of bilious color, like a maze in a madman's nightmares . . .

Barney?" Gill queried. "Aren't you getting tired walking on a bloody conveyor belt that doesn't go anywhere sane?" Which was a fairly accurate description, really. Not only of their physical progress but also of his thoughts. For the endlessly mobile walls and spongy floor made it feel like the motorized walkways in an airport, except there were no exit signs, gates, or other passengers. Likewise his mind, which couldn't find the way out. And that was the other big physical difference, too: no doors.

Which was when it hit him: that this was a House of Doors without doors! The last time the Castle was active it had been as a trap, a terrible game, with Sith of the Thone in the role of gamesmaster and Gill and his colleagues as captive players. In playing the game—by going through the doors and learning the rules—Gill had come to understand how the thing worked. But this time around there were no doors, no rules, no gamesmaster . . . obviously no game. The synthesizer hadn't been programmed. It was *waiting* to be programmed!

At which point Barney gave a *yip!* and came to a stiff-legged halt with his tail wagging furiously and his nose pointing at a blank-seeming wall.

Or rather, a wall full of meaningless colored swirl. But Barney seemed to know exactly where he was, and Gill reckoned he was probably right.

"Through you go, then," he said. And the dog looked at him in a curious manner, cocked his head a little on one side, finally forged right on through the "wall," with Gill immediately behind him.

Dog and man, they were both right: Angela, Jack Turnbull, and the rest of them were there just where Gill had left them. And there was something else there that he hadn't seen before. But he had seen its like.

A door! An ornate, massive oak door, banded with iron and studded through the leaves of its great hinges with bolts that were easily two inches across the heads. A door from some medieval castle out of legend, arched and Gothic and forbidding as the entrance to a dungeon or torture chamber. A door without a wall, just standing there, waiting, draped in luminous ceiling mist that for some ominous, unknown reason had thickened and was descending in writhing tendrils.

Gill's colleagues were backed off from it. Alert, anxious, afraid, they had Ki-no Sung on his feet; the Chinaman was moaning but conscious. And the whole group seemed ready to run. But where to? It was obvious that they'd been waiting for Gill, for his leadership. And as they saw him, so Gill noticed the door's centerpiece: a huge iron knocker in the form of a question mark eighteen inches high and nine across. The hinge was in the center of the top curve and the actual knocker was the lower punctuation mark or period: a ball of iron like a child's clenched fist.

"Gill!" Miranda gasped. "Is this your doing?"

And he could see how she might think it was. And indeed he himself wondered if it was!

"Spencer it . . . it's a door," said Angela, unnecessarily.

And Turnbull, burdened with Ki-no Sung, as was Fred Stannersly, asked, "What do you reckon, Spencer?"

Gill joined them, shook his head. "See that knocker? That's as much as I can tell you. I'm baffled, too."

"What?" Miranda gave a harsh laugh. "You leave us alone in your damned House of Doors, go off with a dog, and while you're away this appears, and then you tell us you're baffled? What's going on here, Spencer Gill?"

"I have an idea, that's all," Gill answered, hearing Angela's hiss of anger and grabbing her arm to keep her still. And he very quickly went on: "Just a moment ago I came to the conclusion that the main thing that's different about this place is that it has no doors, that it's waiting to be programmed. So it could be that I am 'in tune' with it after all. See, there's no keyboard, no buttons to press here. It's all in the mind—in *my* mind, that is. So maybe the thought itself was enough. Simply thinking about programming it set it off. The same as inserting a disk, if you see what I mean."

"And this door's the result?" Fred Stannersly kept one eye on Gill, the other on the door. "You mean like a new file waiting to be opened?"

"That might explain the question-mark knocker," said Turnbull.

"As if it's asking you what you want to do," Angela added.

"And it might not," said Gill hurriedly. "I mean, I'm only hazarding a guess here. As yet, everything I've said amounts to little more than a notion, an idea."

But looking from face to face in seeming amazement or outrage, Miranda Marsh said, "I don't know which one of you is the more crazy! Spencer, are you saying you might have created this out of your mind? What, like you think you're God or something? If so, then you really are out of your mind!"

"He made the Castle, didn't he?" Angela defended Gill. And George Waite said scathingly:

"Oh, no, Miranda. Good Lord, we all *know* that there's only one god-like being here . . . or goddess!"

Jack Turnbull cut right to it. "It's your call, Spencer," he said. "Whatever you decide I'm with you. But just in case no one has noticed, this mist is getting thicker. And the floor is—I don't know—a mite wet?"

He was right; the spongy feeling was now a soggy feeling. The ceiling vapor had settled—was still settling—into a ground mist that lapped at their ankles, and below its surface the floor squelched underfoot. The light, too, had dimmed, and the walls had receded—*were* receding, finally disappearing—into swirls of dull color lost in the distant night.

Night! And overhead a night sky, and alien stars beginning to wink into life in alien constellations. And the Gothic door, standing there all unsupported, its base obscured by the ground mist, its question-mark knocker gleaming wetly in the luminous glow of the mist and the dim light of vapor-dulled stars.

It was all happening so quickly that there wasn't time to keep up, scarcely time to think. Ki-no Sung stood, or was supported, between Turnbull and Stannersly; Miranda Marsh leaned on George Waite's arm, who allowed this sudden familiarity if only for the sake of mutual comfort and human companionship; Angela clung to Gill. And in the near distance the swamp (a swamp now, yes, with gnarled, leaning trees, spiked grasses, and other rank vegetation) made threatening belching and gurgling noises, and something, not necessarily a bird, hooted in a way that suggested demonic derision.

"If it's really as you suspect," Fred Stannersly whispered, then realized he was whispering, gulped, and went on more normally, "then I might know what this is."

"Go on," said Gill, trying to remain calm as he noted that the dimly outlined horizon was now alive with humped, strangely mobile shapes.

"It could be," the pilot continued, "that this is a file or program with restricted access—owner-user only. Having deployed it, called it into being, you either know how to use it or it becomes useless. Except in this case the file doesn't simply deny access, it self-destructs. But, well, maybe that's not right, either. From where I'm standing, this disk doesn't just wipe itself . . ."

"It wipes us?" This from Jack Turnbull.

Stannersly nodded. "The ultimate fail-safe. Make any unauthorized attempt at entry, and the fucking thing kills you!"

"Or you're invited to carry on regardless, enter of your own free will," said Angela. "And then if you don't know what you're doing, the program will kill you anyway!"

"Or maybe you do know what you're doing," said Gill. "In which case you just might survive."

"Yeah, but *do* you know what you're doing?" Turnbull felt something moving in the deepening sludge underfoot, and though he was hampered by Ki-no Sung, he began to edge away from that spot. Then, after a moment: "Fred!" He muttered a low warning, releasing the dazed Chinaman into Stannersly's care so that he could cock the weapon slung over his shoulder. And the cocking lever made a reassuring metallic ch-*ching!* as the minder armed the machine pistol and stood grim-faced, in full militant mode, with the muzzle of his weapon sweeping the quaking muck.

"Truthfully?" said Gill in answer to his question. "No, I don't know what I'm doing. Or I'm not sure. But that's nothing new."

"What?" Miranda screeched. "Is this the right time to tell us that? And in any case, what are you talking about, Spencer? Listen to you, and I mean all of you. You're carrying on as if this door might actually lead somewhere. But it's obvious that there's swamp on both sides!"

"Are you *sure* you read our reports, Miranda?" Angela said. But the sharp edge went out of her voice as she anxiously followed up with: "Spencer, there are . . . *things.* In the swamp."

"I know," he told her, looking around. "Go and get Jack's Browning."

"I thought I was to have it?" Miranda let go of Waite and went stumbling toward Turnbull through ooze that was now calf-deep, but Angela got there first.

"You thought wrong," she said as the big minder reached inside his jacket, took out the automatic, and handed it to her. A moment later and another ch-*ching!* sounded. At which a near-distant, querying snort was heard, and several answering cries or calls from the opposite direction.

"What are they?" George Waite nervously scanned the lumbering, mist-wreathed shapes, which now appeared to have turned as one in the direction of the group of humans and were poised in an attitude suggesting that they listened. Barney also scanned them; his muzzle curled back from his jaws as a low rumble sounded in the back of his throat. He was stiff-legged again, forward-leaning. But in as little time as it had taken him to indicate the threat, his growl became a whine as his stump of a tail went down between his legs.

Unless the poor light made distance deceptive, the things were elephantine in size. But they were also snail-shaped, and in profile appeared equipped with long, swaying horns. Before anyone could hazard a guess at their true nature, however, the muck less than sixty feet away erupted as a humped back reared into view, extending a groping, corrugated blue-gray "foot" or mantle from beneath its thick coiled shell. Hissing and snorting, tossing filth, the thing came gliding in their direction.

"Warning shots!" cried Turnbull, and let rip with a stitch of five or six bullets. The rounds *spanged!* on contact, and hot sparks lit up the creature's body armor. It looked and sounded like blued-steel plate.

At which point the "ground" between them and the gliding thing tilted and burst open almost underfoot, sending them slithering in waves of mud and slimy debris away from the emerging dome of a second coiled shell toward the enigmatic door. And now they could see that the swamp-dwellers not only looked like but were snails—of a type. And that they were apparently voracious.

"No leaf-eaters, these!" Stannersly gasped as the thing's tongue flickered forth, its rasplike rim blurring, buzz-sawing through the bole of a sick-looking tree that was in its way. As the tree was leveled, the snail came on. Its "horns" were eyestalks; their faceted eyes had luminous green pupils that were centered on Gill and party. And, as if in anticipation, a thick blue saliva was dripping, forming a curtain of goo that dangled from the lower rim of its mouth aperture.

As for the creature's rubbery, elastic mantle: it steamed where it sucked at the mud, and the rising stench of its vapor was a hard acid reek.

"Gill, do something!" Miranda cried, and Gill thought:

At least she's ready to admit now that I might be able to do something. But of course there was only one thing he could do.

Jack Turnbull was already reaching for the heavy knocker; Gill beat him to it by a split second, said: "My idea, Jack. So it'll be my fault if this goes wrong." With which he lifted the blob of metal at the foot of the question mark, and let it fall clangingly onto the sounding plate.

And with a *crack!* like a great boulder splitting, the door separated down the middle and slammed open "inward," away from them, its vacuum seeming to suck them in . . .

It was also night where the great door deposited them, slammed shut behind them, and left them in a tumbled, bruised, and gasping heap. But a night that was very, very different. And almost before Gill smelled the steel, felt the flaking rust under his scrabbling fingers, and sensed the senseless—and to him morbid—near-distant machine activity all around, he knew where they were.

Likewise Angela, Turnbull, and Barney. For they'd all been here before.

"Your machine world?" Angela found herself sprawled beside Gill. She pressed close to him, staring wide-eyed at a face familiar in silhouette, made strange and gaunt in the intermittent, varicolored shadow play of a mechanical aurora flowing into the metal cave from outside.

Gill freed a trapped hand to touch the bruises on his left arm, his numb shoulder and thigh where he'd come down hard. And as he sucked blood from a gash at the base of his thumb, he supposed that Angela would be hurting, too. And what of the rest? "Is everyone okay?" he called, spitting out flakes of rust that had come off his hand. "I mean, I know you're not okay. But are you all in one piece?" Angela nodded where she continued to hug him; he sighed his relief, moaned a faint protest as she hugged him harder still.

Then Barney whined, stuck a paw in Gill's ribs, and licked his face, and Gill jerked his head back—but not too far back. For he remembered only too well. If they *were* in that junkyard cave on the mad machine world, rapid reaction could be extremely dangerous. Even landing here could be dangerous. And maybe it had been, for as yet there'd been no response from the rest of the group—

Until Jack Turnbull groaned, and said, "I came down on my face on a girder, I think. When things stop spinning, then I'll be able to tell you if I'm okay—maybe."

And almost in unison Miranda and George Waite said, "Where the hell are we anyway?" And Miranda followed up with: "I'm all right, I think. But I landed on something soft . . ."

"You landed on me," George told her. "And I think you just might have broken one of my ribs—*uh!*—or maybe a couple."

"Oh, my God!" she said. "And what about Fred? And the little Chinaman, Ki-no Sung? How did they make out?"

"I'm okay," Fred Stannersly's voice from the darkest shadows. "But Ki-no Sung . . . he's out of it. He's breathing though, so probably just knocked himself silly. Or he's passed out from his original injuries. I can't tell."

As they talked, Gill left Angela and crawled carefully on hands and knees to the mouth of the metal "cave." Their refuge, if that word applied, wasn't a true cave but a space left empty in what was in every other respect a jumble, a mountain, a city of mainly defunct mechanical parts—mainly. And the parts that weren't defunct made no sense anyway, so that Gill was tempted to exclude them entirely from his reasoning. Except he daren't, because alien though they were they might well prove to be his one contact with the synthesizer. Which was how it had been the first time around.

And as Gill reached the "mouth" of the cave—a gap looking out through the tangled debris of useless machine parts on an unbelievable outside world—and as he stopped crawling, he saw that indeed this was the same place. There could be no mistaking it.

Angela tried not to sob as she drew up alongside him, murmuring, "Oh, Spencer! All that again?"

He nodded. "I'm afraid so, sweetheart. But before we do anything else, there's someone I want to see this. And I want her to see it now." And turning his head he called out, "Miranda!"

She came. And lying between Gill and Angela, she saw. She saw what Gill had seen the first time he'd spent a night—or a nightmare—in this weird mechanical universe:

Against an indigo-turning-black horizon, the chaotic jumble of the sky-line—a tangle of leaning, rust-scabbed piston towers, drill-tip spires, and crumbling scaffolding—was like a jacket painting from a forties book of fantastic fiction. Off to one side, the incredible scene was lit by red and orange pulsing fires, like a row of coke ovens or blast furnaces roaring in the darkness. Their fiery voices were bellows blasts reaching out across a mile or more of derelict canyon streets lined with sagging, skeletal structures, most of them in darkness or only part-illumined.

Closer at hand but deep down in the bowels of the city, a great hammer gonged dully like a subterranean pile driver: ker-*thump!* Ker-*thump!* Ker-*thump!* These dull vibrations, transmitted through the metallic debris, the rust and rubble of other long extinct engines, felt like the pounding of blood in an ear compressed against a pillow on a soundless night. And:

"Look over there," said Gill. And Miranda looked.

In the direction he'd indicated, the dead or dying machine city's sil-houette had a scattering of lights, white and yellow, red and green. And there, set central in a great swath of inky darkness, something gigantic nodded twin, gleaming hammerheads monotonously over a revolving yellow light. Chains rattled and clanked rustily, chinked into silence, rattled again—and so on. Some strange, spindly wheeled thing on a shuddering gantry wheezed like a ruptured bellows, puffing smoke and steam as it trundled to and fro, with lights fore and aft that changed color with each change of direction.

And in the sky . . .

The stars were like bright silver ball bearings, all the same size, radiating their light in faint auroral waves.

"The stars . . . !" Miranda gasped, then stopped because she didn't know what else to say.

"I haven't seen the moon, if there is a moon," Gill told her, quietly. "But *if* there is I'll bet it's octagonal, like a nut, and its craters will be perfectly circular, as if drilled there by some cosmic machinist. And the swarf will be piled up in the form of silver mountains. Pretty imaginative stuff, eh? But wait until tomorrow, when you've seen the sun . . ."

Then she found her voice. "The machine world," she said, "from your debrief report."

"Exactly," said Gill. "So make yourself as comfortable as you can, for we're not going anywhere tonight. Not tonight, no. And certainly not out there."

And: "Spencer," she said, brokenly. "For what it's worth, I owe you an apology. I . . . well, I've had my doubts. And I've been foolish."

"Save it," he told her. "Believe me, you're not the only one who's doubtful." And to himself: *And I've a feeling you're not the only one who's been foolish, either.*

As for the proof of that last, well, he could only wait and see . . .

CHAPTER
15

MORNING. IT CAME with light, and it came with Barney's bone-dry probing nose and the none-too-damp ministrations of his tongue. Gill
felt the mongrel's tongue trying to lift the skin from his face, woke up,
and pushed him away. From all around Gill, groans of bewilderment and
complaint began sounding as the rest of the party woke up to each
other's stirrings praying that it was all a nightmare and discovering that it
wasn't.

Gill felt like he had dents all over his body. And in fact he *had* dents
all over his body, from where he'd been lying. But Angela was more fortunate; she'd slept on the gentle inner curvature of a sheet of die-cut metal
that looked like the discarded hood of a car. Its rim had left a groove in
Gill's forearm where he'd thrown his arm across her during the night.

But the rest of them were in various stages of discomfort, their flesh
and clothing red with rust and gouged by metal projections. Little wonder,
for now they could see what their cave was really made of.

"A junkyard," Fred Stannersly muttered. "Like some failed inventor's
worst-case scenario."

"Mine, in fact," said Gill. "For you're right: this is the land of nightmares come true. In this case, my nightmares. Look around and you'll soon
see what I mean."

And now that it was safe to move, they did look around the inside of
the junk-metal cave.

For Angela and Turnbull it was literally déjà vu, paramnesia; they'd been here once before, but that visit had retreated now into the limbo of all bad memories. So that this was almost something new, and something they fought against accepting. But merely glancing about the cave brought it back in full.

The light—a hazy, dusty shaft of daylight—entered the cave through its gaping oval "mouth," and also in smoking beams through holes in the compacted ceiling. But this wasn't a "ceiling" in the common usage, and the walls weren't walls. The cave was in fact simply a hole that hadn't yet given in to the massive compression of metal parts. When it did, then it would simply crumple up like an old automobile in a crusher.

Suddenly aware of that fact, the seven (for Ki-no Sung was conscious again and looking all the better for a night's sleep) grew silent and cautious where they clambered over the obstructions in the crushed metal floor to examine their surroundings. And indeed the place was a junkyard.

There were pipes and cables, and broken plastic and metal conduits hanging everywhere, like twentieth century stalactites, and the floor was littered with rusting levers, nuts and bolts, pistons and jacks and metallic scrap of every kind, size, and description. Every mechanical principle was represented: the lever, universal joint, camshaft, belt drive, worm gears, ratchets and pawls, toggle joints and ball bearings and cogwheels galore. An Aladdin's cave of junk. Amazing to most members of Gill's party . . . but appalling to Gill himself.

For if the others were to look closer they would see what he had seen, what he'd known from the start: that none of this stuff had ever worked. Oiled ball bearings spilling from shattered races were ever-so-slightly pear-shaped; the cog assemblies didn't match up, wouldn't mesh; the ratchets didn't ratch. If these parts were people, they'd each and every one be a Thalidomide victim, circus freak, or poor gibbering retard. So that where ordinary machines "talked" to Gill, these things shrieked at him—or they would if he would let them. Which was why he busied himself with other things. Like the provisions.

"When we came through," Gill's voice cut into the others' thoughts as they scanned about, "what happened to the luggage?"

Angela, Turnbull, and Waite had carried sausage bags containing items of spare clothing, some dressings (though probably not enough, as recent events now made it seem likely), a little fresh fruit, some canned meats, military-style condensed chocolate, and bottled water. Not a very comprehensive list in any case, but the water was Gill's main concern.

Angela patted her sausage bag, said, "I don't know how but somehow I managed to hang on to this."

Jack Turnbull was still "wearing" his; he had put his arms through the straps so that it sat high on his back like an army pack. His training, Gill correctly supposed.

But George Waite glanced at Miranda, who looked bewildered for a moment, then said, "George's sausage bag was . . . well, it was what I used to make Ki-no Sung comfortable after we'd dealt with his horrific injuries. The last time I saw it was just before that door appeared."

"My fault, I suppose," Waite said. "I was so busy looking after myself, that—"

"No one's fault," Gill cut him short. "I don't even have a pack, just a few items in my pockets, that's all. It's so I can be unhampered, get on with what I do best—or worst, as it now appears."

"You didn't want to come here?" Stannersly said.

"No"—Gill shook his head—"I didn't. Anyway, the reason I thought to ask about the provisions is because Barney's thirsty. We have to spare a little water for him."

"I'll see to it," said Angela.

"But just a little," Gill told her. "And please dampen his nose. That's a hell of an important nose he's got there."

"The dog?" said Ki-no Sung, sibilantly. The others looked at him in surprise, especially Gill. Gill knew the little man's story, but he hadn't had much of an opportunity to talk to him.

"Yes, the dog," Gill answered him. And indicating himself, the big minder, and Angela, he explained, "Some of us have been here before. And Barney, too. He probably knows his way around these worlds better than any of us. That makes him special and we have to look after him."

At which the Chinaman thought to ask, "These . . . worlds?" The way he said it indicated surprise.

And Turnbull frowned and said, "You mean you haven't noticed anything strange? Like, we're not on Earth?" In fact they were, but it scarcely felt like it.

"He's been out of it, mainly," Miranda said. "And he's not too sure of our language, either."

Gill shrugged it off. "Anyway," he said, "how are you feeling?"

Sung lowered his head, looked at his bandaged stump. "How I feel? Hand . . . gone," he said. "Face, skinned, wrapped up in cloth. I thank you." He bowed slightly. "But . . . how I feel? I feel hurt, and hungry."

"Stupid question," said Gill. "What I meant is do you feel okay to move on? We'll help you all the way, of course."

Another slight bow. "I be okay. Not problem."

"His English improves all the time," Miranda noted. "Back on that lighthouse rock he referred to himself first person as 'me,' and now it's 'I.' "

Sung lifted his eyes to look at her, however briefly. And maybe there was something in the way those eyes glittered.

"Damned clever, the Chinese," said Turnbull. And to Gill: "Before we move on, can we talk, you and I? Like, in private?" He moved toward the mouth of the cave.

Gill had seen that look on the minder's face before. He began to follow him, thought again, turned back, and explained to the others: "Er, logistics. Don't worry about it. Get something to eat while we talk." And to Angela: "Sweetheart, save a bite for me, please, to eat along the way."

And outside the cave, high over the decaying machine city, clinging to the rail of a gantry of sorts in a perilously blustery wind, Gill said, "So what's bothering you?"

"If you don't know, then maybe it's nothing," the big minder answered.

"I'd like to know anyway."

"It's the Chink," Turnbull said at once. He had never in his life considered political correctness to be anything more than an obstruction to plain language.

"What about him?" said Gill.

"Three things," the minder answered. "One: Miranda Marsh is right—his English improves by leaps and bounds. But she's also wrong; I think he understands pretty much everything. Two: he should be in a hospital bed, preferably intensive care. Yet here he is, badly fucked yet ready to move on. And three: he's a complete outsider."

"An outsider?"

"He isn't one of our original group. Don't you remember how it was up in Scotland that time? *Huh!*—now it's me who's asking stupid questions—of course you remember. The outsider then was Bannerman, who wasn't what he made himself out to be. Or more than he made himself out to be. Or other."

Gill nodded, frowned, and said: "I'm beginning to see what you mean. And come to think of it, there are other comparisons you can make. Bannerman got himself separated from us, too, and the next time we saw him he also had terrible injuries. In fact we thought he was blind! All of which was cover, camouflage for the fact that he was other than human. We were so sorry for him that we didn't look too close."

"So shouldn't we look a little closer at Sung?" Turnbull's logic was disturbing. "I mean, let's face it, from now on we're going to be taking care of him. Shouldn't we first make sure he isn't planning to take care of us? What about your machine empathy? Doesn't that have anything to say about him?"

Gill frowned again, and shook his head. "Maybe we're being paranoid," he said. "I mean, this little bloke was washed in on the tide, for God's sake! And that was *before* there was a House of Doors, before we got back from the Isle of Wight. Just supposing he is an alien—a thing in a human suit, that is—how would he know about us? Also, if the Ggyddn are mobile, if they are able to move among us like that, why didn't he just do away with the rest of the team before we got back? These beings have mastered a superior technology after all. So you see it doesn't add up." Gill paused for a moment, then went on:

"As for my machine awareness—you couldn't have picked a worse place to put too much faith in that. What, surrounded by crazy machine activity in a mechanical graveyard, a rust world orbiting an atomic sun? Why, I scarcely dare switch on to it!"

"But you will? You'll check him out?"

"When I get a chance, yes."

The minder nodded, said: "Something else."

"Oh?"

"When we bandaged his face," Turnbull went on, "I noticed a small scar high up at the back of his neck. It was healed up, but it looked recent."

"How recent?"

"What, do I look like a doctor?" The minder scowled. "Anyway, weren't you talking about high tech just a moment ago? Like they couldn't heal scars more quickly than us?"

"A scar doesn't make him an alien," Gill argued. "And anyway, that poor bloke's all set to have scars galore! Hey, don't *you* have scars?"

Turnbull fell silent, scratched his jaw, and gave an irritated shrug. But in another moment he said, "I don't know, maybe I am a bit paranoid after all. But, Spencer, how come we're back here? What in God's name are we doing here? The way I see it, this is your nightmare world, right? So are we back on that old program again? Isn't this simply a replay of an old tape? And what the hell are you aiming for anyway? I mean, even our being here is beginning to seem pointless."

Gill glanced sideways at the other, shrugged, and wondered how best to explain. He might even have started to explain, but then he blinked and looked again, stared at the minder where he stood scratching his jaw.

Finally Gill drew a sharp breath, reached up, and fingered his own face. And his brow lined over as his puzzled expression changed to one of surprise and then of understanding—or half understanding—or an attempt at understanding, at least.

Turnbull began to look like he found Gill's intense stare offensive. "What in hell? Did I blink a third eye or something? What's going on? Christ, are you checking *me* out, Spencer?"

But Gill shook his head, reached out, and touched the minder's face, wonderingly. "Uh-uh," he murmured. "Not me. You're the one who's paranoid, remember?"

"Then what—?"

"When did you last shave?" Gill cut him off.

Turnbull felt his chin. "Er, yesterday morning? Do I look that bad? And what has that got to do with anything anyway?"

"It might have a lot to do with anything," Gill told him. And before the minder could answer: "Tell me, are you thirsty, Jack? Hungry? Do your cuts and bruises still hurt? Do you have a headache? Could you use a good stiff drink?"

"The answer is yes, to everything," Turnbull said.

"Me, too." Gill nodded. "And that's wrong."

"Wrong? But what could be more natural?" The minder looked mystified. And Gill went on:

"My turn to ask you, Jack. Don't *you* remember how it was up in Scotland that time? I mean, after we entered those synthesized worlds?"

"Do I remem . . . ?" Turnbull's jaw fell open. "We didn't need to shave," he said, in sudden realization. "We didn't even need to eat, and those who did eat threw up in short order. Our injuries healed quickly . . . amazingly quickly! Our stamina was way above the normal human average. You know, I can't even remember answering a call of nature? Didn't need to, because . . ."

"Because it wasn't you," said Gill. "Still hard to believe, right? Because you *experienced* it. But you know it's the truth. You, we—all of us, except Haggie and Bannerman—were replicas, Thone constructs, with our minds, habits, fears, passions. But they weren't us. They were clones, synthetic reproductions. *We*, our bodies, were in storage, in stasis, while Sith was scaring the shit out of our minds, putting them through his synthesized hoops while he stood off and laughed at us."

Turnbull closed his mouth. "Of course I remember," he said. "But you're right: it was very real at the time. It *did* happen, if not to 'us,' or if not to our bodies. And this time—?"

"This time we *are* us," Gill told him. "You, me, Angela, and the rest of them, we're all real. Real cuts and bruises, hurts, hunger, thirst. And real beards." He looked at Turnbull's stubble one more time, just to be certain, then showed the big minder the gash in his thumb. "In those other worlds—or in that other body—this would have healed by now. And your face would be as smooth as a baby's backside. As would mine."

"Of course," said the other. "Because that first time Sith was playing a game with us. But this time there is no Sith. *You* programmed the synthesizer this time. And because you're new at it, you programmed 'your' world, this mechanical madhouse."

"Something like that, yes," Gill murmured, but very quietly. And giving him a speculative glance, the minder saw that he was gaunter than ever. Truth to tell, Gill didn't know for sure that he'd actually programmed anything.

"So what else is wrong?" Turnbull asked. "Are you thinking that maybe we're stuck here?"

Gill shook his head. "No, I think I know how to get out of here, but . . ."

"But?"

"Some of those other worlds were poisonous, and their creatures were deadly. We only lived through it because we weren't real. It was a test, to see how much we could take. But here we are real, and we're human. We can't take that much."

Turnbull slowly nodded. "Got you," he said. "In the event we move on, which we must, you don't know for sure where you'll be taking us . . ." And, after a moment's pause, "Are you going to tell the others?"

"No," Gill said. "Why would I want to give them more problems than they've got right now?"

Again Turnbull's nod. "And is that it? All done?"

"No, there's more," said Gill. "From the first moment the House of Doors firmed up on the lighthouse rock, I've had this feeling that I wasn't in control. For example, the temperature in what should have been but wasn't the control room. I didn't do that. Okay, maybe the temperature inside a node is a constant, but I don't know that for sure. And then, as you yourself just pointed out, why did we end up here, why this place? Damn it, I mean this was the *last* place I was thinking of! And then there's the . . . I don't know, the *feel* of everything."

"Its feel?" Turnbull looked all around, shook his head.

"To my machine awareness," Gill tried to explain, and got it wrong. "No, not that. Just to me! Listen, did you ever play a tape mono when you were used to hearing the music in stereo? All of a sudden this well-known tune is wrong. The various instruments are all sounding from the wrong directions—or from the same direction. Know what I mean?" But he didn't think the minder would know what he meant. He wasn't sure himself.

"Like, this isn't the original?" said Turnbull. "Or like it's a—what, a photocopy?" The minder's level of comprehension was frequently much higher than Gill gave him credit for. "But couldn't that be because this time it's us? Our real bodies? Okay, maybe I'm wrong, but aren't we bound to feel things differently from a bunch of robots?"

Gill blinked, took a firm grip on the catwalk's handrail, perhaps to ground himself, and said, "You could be right." And the other was glad to note that much of the tension had disappeared out of his friend's face. At which he drew a deep breath, exhaled, and said:

"So, what's the next move?"

"The next move . . . is up to Barney," Gill said, his voice that much steadier. "That old dog knows the way out of here. Or he did the last time we were here, anyway." Then, straightening up and stretching his aching back, "Come on," he said. "They'll be wondering where we've got to. And it's time we were all moving on . . ."

If the interior of the cave was a madly cluttered junkyard, the exterior was a junk world. Gill, Turnbull, Angela, and Barney the dog, they'd seen it all before; to the others it came almost as an electric shock, and by no means a mild one. They were startled, visibly shaken, when for the first time they gazed out and down on the decaying machine city.

Gill supposed it would affect them much as it had affected him the first time around, and so gave them time to adjust. And as the strangeness of it sank in where they stood on the higher ramparts of that ramshackle mountain of rust and ruined metals, so he let his memory drift back to his own initial reaction:

A machine world, but ninety-nine point nine percent broken down. Or perhaps—as with the pseudo-mechanical clutter in the cave—most of it had never worked in the first place. Anyway, there it was. A world filled to brimming with the debris of defunct devices, with nothing of grass or trees or anything so healthy as stone; no hills except hills of metal rubble, and no streets except giant iron catwalks and tottering skyscraper gantries that spanned pile to pile, like bridges to the end of the world . . .

But as Turnbull took the lead and began searching for an easy route down, so Gill forced his wandering mind home again.

Though the party's vantage point was high above the bridged-over, often debris-obliterated tracked canyon causeways of the city bottoms, still the horizon seemed a long way off. Yet for as far as their eyes could see there was only metallic litter, a little plastic, and a lot of dead machinery. Or rarely, machinery that wasn't quite dead—though in Gill's opinion it might as well be.

The crane-thing (if it could be called a crane) was still there on its spindly tracks at the very rim of the chasm, just as it had been the first time around. But then again, it would be. For this was a synthesized world, and all of this a repeat performance. And though there might be some uncertainty about calling the pointless monstrosity a crane, it could very definitely be designated a "thing!" For as well as a crane it might also be a steam shovel or maybe a giant mechanical woodpecker, or a thing for clutching and folding other . . . things. But in any case it was horrific to Gill, as was so much of this junk. To watch it performing its crazed "function"—trundling along its track, pausing, whirling, bending and nodding, grasping at thin air, pecking, hammering, and doing sweet fuck-all!—was dizzying to the point of nauseating. To be surrounded by machines or their parts, and not understand the workings or principles or purpose of a single one of the bloody things.

And whatever else he might do, Gill knew that he daren't commune with any of them, mustn't let them into his mind. For their designs were diseased, and that way lay madness . . .

CHAPTER 16

Everything seemed exactly the same except, as Gill had pointed out, the "feel" of things. But since the others didn't seem to notice, he supposed it was only him: his machine empathy, held on a short leash. For of course while he kept his talent under rigid control—while it wasn't allowed to work for him—he couldn't possibly feel the same.

It was his sixth sense, after all. Gill supposed he would feel much the same if he'd lost one of the other five (a lesser sense, that is, say taste or smell, which would be much less of a trauma than hearing or sight), and made an effort to put this small, niggling concern to the back of his mind during the partial descent of the treacherous metal mountain.

As for Jack Turnbull: he found it easier going this time. For one thing he knew the way, and for another he wasn't "lumbered" with caring for an alleged blind man. Ki-no Sung was far less a problem than Jon Bannerman had been, and anyway Miranda Marsh and George Waite had taken charge of the Chinaman . . .

The early morning wind had died down; the dawn had turned to daylight or close enough; all that remained was for the sun to rise more fully from a littered skyline between the fantastic latticework of a pair of distant skeletal spires. Turnbull and Angela would accept that sunrise readily enough, of course, if not the four newcomers. Gill had decided to say nothing more about it to them, give them no further advance warnings. He was interested to observe their reactions to that weird alien sun. Especially Ki-no Sung's, who hadn't read the debrief reports . . .

As on their previous visit, Turnbull, Angela, and Gill led the way where they climbed down toward the nearest "roadway," a giant catwalk all of ninety feet wide and . . . and they still didn't know how long! It stretched away below them in both directions out of sight. The climb wasn't difficult, not even for Sung; this boosted Gill's hopes that the synthesizer's healing properties continued to operate with their previous efficiency. Indeed, Barney was the only member of the team who experienced any real difficulties. Gill kept a firm grip on the dog's collar through the most perilous, vertical stages.

But overall the going was fairly easy. There were metal ladders, dangling cables, pipes and pylons everywhere. It was as if the core of this world (was it a world? Or was it just a vast ball of junk all the way through?) were a giant robot factory that had been running amok for centuries, churning out mad machines and machine parts until it had buried itself. Maybe it was still down there, its frantic production lines unceasingly manufacturing meaningless machinery.

The spaces between fantastic engines as big as city blocks were bridged by gantries where spiderlike "repairmen" abounded. Stiff and immobile (no longer attendant to their giant engines, if they ever had been, *if* they'd ever functioned at all), these robot arachnids clung to the fragile gantries as to cobwebs, or lay where they'd fallen in tangled heaps under collapsed or sagging sections of the skeletal frameworks. TV screens, or viewscreens of sorts, but as big as small cinema screens, were protected behind electrified grilles not all of which were dead.

Coming across just such a screen and remembering his first visit, Jack Turnbull repeated an old experiment. Choosing a big iron bolt from a heap of debris, he hurled it at the screen. It hit the grille, resulting in a bright coruscation of electrical energy as the bolt was part vaporized and incandescent blobs of metal sizzled down onto iron surfaces, skittering about like so much solder. And:

"Well, things seem pretty much the same to me!" the minder commented, turning to Gill. And Gill said:

"Was that the same screen you got mad with the last time?"

"I think so, yes."

"Then we'd better hold it right here," said Gill, looking around for Barney. But that, too, was the same as last time. On the level from which they had just descended, say eight or nine steps higher up a stout iron ladder, Barney stood looking down at them, his head cocked on one side and his stumpy tail wagging furiously.

Gill nodded his satisfaction. "Looks like I'm right," he said. And to Angela: "Do you remember the first time? You said he looked like he wanted us to follow him? Well he did, but we ignored him. We went down, vertically, while Barney went somewhere else, horizontally. The point is, there's more than just one door in these places. While we took our crazy, nightmarish train ride into the rust desert—to the hives of those rust-worms, which, incidentally, might easily have done for us—I think it's highly likely that old Barney there was off hunting funny rabbits in some comparatively pleasant forest world. And me, I'm not about to make the same mistake twice."

He started back up the ladder—

At which point Fred Stannersly felt the warmth on his back, sensed unaccustomed light, turned and saw the sun standing well above the ho-rizon, where it now emerged from behind a spindly, gravity-defying spire's rotting steel framework. More than a third of its great bulk was still ob-scured, causing the spire's tangled scaffolding rim to burn rust red and old gold where it was pierced through by slowly fanning shafts of radiant light. But enough of the disk was already visible to cause awe and astonishment among its observers.

"Jesus!" Stannersly said as his jaw fell open. A moment later and Mir-anda's gasp was her acknowledgment of a wonder; and likewise Waite's barely articulate:

"Oh, my God!"

What they saw was this: a "sun" maybe three times as big as Earth's sun, like a giant, silver ball bearing more than a million miles across, pep-pered with crater blowholes that issued spokes of fire, light, and radiation in a never-ending series of nuclear chain reactions. A *machine* sun stand-ing central in what could only be a machine system of worlds, in a mighty machine universe.

Gill, however, had seen it all before; he didn't anticipate spending too much time here, and wasn't greatly interested in the sun's reactions, nu-clear or otherwise. But he was interested in Ki-no Sung's.

The others gaped . . . but Ki-no Sung took one look, and at once fell to his knees and bowed his head in supplication. For where George Waite had merely called out "Oh, my God," the little Chinaman had apparently *seen* Him; seen God Himself, or His Equivalent, in that monstrous me-chanical orb. And Spencer Gill couldn't say whether he felt relieved or disappointed. But in either case, he was satisfied that Sung had passed the first, and possibly the last, test . . .

"Barney!" Angela gasped.

"Eh?" Gill glanced down at her, followed her gaze, and saw Barney heading off along the higher catwalk where he was about to turn a near-distant corner. "Barney, come back!" he called after the dog, who paused just for a moment to look back, then carried on around the corner. "Damn it to hell!" Gill groaned. And to Angela: "I have to catch him."

So that by the time she'd helped the others back up onto the catwalk, Gill too had already disappeared . . .

Sith, once of the Thone, looked back on his progress so far:

First, implanting Ki-no Sung and using Thone healing techniques to disguise the small wound at the back of his neck, he had checked instrumentation's contact with his guileless human probe until satisfied he could take a measure of control whenever he pleased. But only a measure.

That is, he could use the Chinaman's eyes and ears to spy on Gill and his colleagues—and even his voice to join in and perhaps guide their conversations—but that was the extent of it. Unless Sith were willing to burden himself with total control of the little man for the duration of the party's ordeal, this was as far as it could go. Anything more would have required a far bigger implant, in which case it would have been as well to synthesize an entire duplicate and fit it with a computer mind. But with Spencer Gill's much-vaunted awareness, his "machine mindedness," that could have proved a dangerous route to follow. No, it had been far safer to employ Sung in a small role than give him a leading part and have the subterfuge discovered.

Then the easy part: to deliver Sung via transmat into the ocean close to the lighthouse, where in a post-hypnotic dream-state—*believing* himself to be dreaming, despite that he had been shocked physically awake by immersion—Sung had set out to swim for the looming land mass. And finally a stroke of good fortune when through Sung's eyes Sith had seen a raft of flotsam bobbing on the ocean's swell. Thus the background tragedy that he had prepared for the Chinaman found instantaneous corroboration; Sung had been so typically "shipwrecked" that the people in the lighthouse must surely accept him without question. And they had . . .

Then, waiting for Gill to return—knowing that his hated enemy possessed a Thone synthesizer, the deactivated node from a Scottish mountainside—Sith had felt obliged to reconsider his plan. In its initial form it had been a very simple thing: the entrapment of Gill, the female, and that brute of a creature, Jack Turnbull, too, was to have been the first phase; and torture and a hideous, lingering death for all of them the middle and the end. Ah, but to attempt these things in the *original* House of Doors, that was something else! For half of Gill's team had experience of some of the Castle's worlds, and it had all depended upon how much this infuriating man had learned in the intervening years. If he'd learned anything at all.

But then, having seen his adversary's desperate, fumbled attempts to reactivate the Castle, Sith's confidence had returned. For it appeared that Gill knew nothing, or so little as to make no difference, and that everything he did was by trial and error. And so, while Gill had continued his struggle to realign his mind with Thone technology, Sith had synthesized himself an environmental survival suit. For what Gill wasn't able to do on his own (namely, find a way to materialize the Castle, and then enter into it) Sith must now do for him.

Nothing elaborate, Sith's survival suit was a lightweight cylinder of super-flexible plastic protecting that midsection of his "person" enclosing his three vital organs: brain, primary motor system, and the spongy, siphon-cum-nerve chain that linked them, which corresponded in Earth-type creatures to the spinal column. But as well as protecting Sith's essential organs, the suit served one other very important purpose; powered by microconverters, its gravitic deflectors reduced gravity by seventy percent, and so reduced his weight to a bearable Thone standard. Lacking the suit's support, a low-grav mainly liquid creature such as Sith would be little more than a stain on the sea-sculpted landscape of the lighthouse rock . . .

Which was where he had caused the transmat to deposit him just as Gill was reaching the end of his tether, in the moment when he'd snatched up the miniature castle as if to crush it in his fist.

Having scanned the lighthouse rock through Ki-no Sung's eyes, Sith had known precisely where to materialize: behind a clump of massive, rounded boulders some forty yards away from the closest of Gill's party where they'd stationed themselves close to Gill and the deactivated node. In doing so, in transmatting himself, Sith had taken a not inconsiderable personal risk: to isolate himself "outside" in order to engage in what Gill's people might call EVH or Extra Vehicular Activity. The transmat could be used in this way, certainly, but Sith would require access to another transmat to move back inside, lacking which he'd be obliged to call for the assistance of other Ggyddn.

But Sith was used to EVH; during his years as an invigilator he had spent a lot of time in the guise of a human being, enabling him to go among them. And in any case he intended to reactivate Gill's node, which would furnish him not only with access to a fully functional synthesizer and all the information currently lying inert within its hyperspatial "memory," but also to a transmat, the one being an integral part of the other.

The trick of it would be to let Gill believe that *he* had activated the node, and more importantly to ensure that he and his party didn't emerge from the flux inside the control room. For in normal circumstances that would be the case: the procedure itself would "identify" the operator, who would then find himself instantly and automatically inducted into the synthesizer's control room. Of course, in Gill's case the odds were a billion to one against that happening—

Except it almost *had* happened! Sith's worst moment had come when Gill actually achieved contact with the node, mental rapport, when for a second that felt like an hour it had fully appeared that he would assume command of the synthesizer.

Only Sith's immediate response, his countermanding of "erroneous authorization," had saved the day; the synthesizer had recognized him as the true authority—if by a hairbreadth—and he had emerged from the flux within the control room while Gill and the others were inducted and isolated in blank space. But the episode had only served to confirm Sith's worst suspicions, that indeed Gill was a dangerous man.

Well, and all the better. And despite, or perhaps because of, Gys U Kalk's assertion that Gill was no more than a "cold-blooded bipedal lifeform," a two-legged worm, totally unworthy of any sort of vendetta, still Sith took pride—even the malicious pride of a deviant—in his determination to challenge Gill's upstart skills a second time. To challenge, defeat, and destroy him, yes. And all of his colleagues with him.

And the means were now immediately to hand.

Holding his captives in isolation, Sith had accessed his old files and synthesized a construct out of the past. A construct in human form, an EVA system, and a weapon all in one. So that when Spencer Gill saw him, he would know at once what and who he was up against. He would know some of it, anyway.

But for a prelude . . . why not give the newcomers, Gill's latest acolytes, a taste of things to come? For as yet George Waite, Fred Stannersly, and the female Miranda Marsh had seen nothing of the legion of terrors hidden in the spaces between the spaces, in the hyperspace heart of the House of Doors.

Yes, and simultaneous with their initiation Spencer Gill would be made to understand that he wasn't and never would be in charge . . .

Barney wasn't hanging about. Now that Gill was following him, the dog seemed intent on getting somewhere. It was up to Gill to keep him in sight. As for the others: they kept up as best they could. Angela and Jack Turnbull were the intermediaries; knowing the importance of sticking together—of not allowing their group to get separated—they formed major links in the human chain: Gill up front, close on Barney's heels (or pads), the big minder maybe fifty yards behind, Angela another fifty behind him, and the rest well back but always in sight. That was the trick, to keep them in sight.

Gill didn't entirely recognize the terrain or route that Barney was following. But in any case he wasn't too enthuiastic about orientating himself in an environment so much in conflict with his mundane machine conceptions, and couldn't even be sure that "terrain" was the right word—nor "landscape," for that matter. Machinography? Well, maybe. Metalscape? But nothing that even hinted at Earthly topography, never!

Nevertheless, as time passed and ground—no, *metal*—was covered, he did begin to note this or that landmark structure that struck a chord in his memory. Back there and one machine level higher, that lidded refuse skip for instance. (More lunacy; what use a skip in an entire world of metal rubbish?) It could have been the galvanized steel bucket where he and Barney had slept on the night of his second visit to this place.

On that occasion Gill had been alone—or he and the dog had been alone—and it had been a visit of great importance, when he'd first learned how to commune or interface with Thone technology; learned something of it anyway. So why couldn't he do it now? Mainly, he supposed, because this was a synthesized world, unreal, the world of his own worst nightmares. In a nutshell, there was nothing here to communicate with.

That other time, he had been able to fathom the workings of a Thone weapon brought with him from a real world, his own world. But now, in this place—this *un*real place—the technology was all wrong.

Take for example that pile of rusty six-inch screws immediately ahead. They would be just like the rest of the junk in this crazy place, totally useless. He snatched one up in passing, let his eyes and his mind play on it for a moment, tossed it away in disgust. A left-hand thread for half of its length, right-hand from there to the head, and no groove for a screwdriver. Senseless . . .

For just a moment or two Gill's attention had been diverted, precisely what he'd been trying to avoid.

Barney!

Now where the hell was Barney?

And up ahead, that towering, purposeless heap of haphazardly piled scaffolding, leaning dangerously toward the outer chasm. Gill wondered: did he recognize it? If so, then he was right. He knew where Barney was going. And again his thoughts flew back to the last time he was here:

He had been of the opinion then, and still was, that Barney wasn't just any old hound dog. He had been a gamekeeper's work dog—a gillie's closest friend, companion, and watchdog—and by the time he'd made contact with Gill and the first test group of human beings kidnapped by Sith of the Thone and taken into the Castle, he had already survived for two long years on his own in the many worlds of the House of Doors.

So that Gill had often wondered: what secrets were locked in Barney's brain? And how he had wished that he could talk to him. But speech wasn't the only means of communication. Hamish Grieve, Barney's old master, must have used several: a mixture of whistles, signals, and shouted commands. And, since the old man had been a gamekeeper, Barney might well be a bird dog, or a tracker—any number of things that Gill knew nothing about. But there was one thing at least of which he had felt certain: that the dog's intelligence was way above average.

And in that he'd been right.

Through the higher levels of the rusting, rotting machine city or factory they'd made their way to a place Barney knew of old. The dog had led the way; even if Gill hadn't followed him, he would have continued on his own. He'd had to, because unlike Gill he had needed to eat. He'd been here in error, and Sith of the Thone had not caused him to be processed, altered. In short he was all dog, a real dog, and dogs get hungry. And in some of the synthesizer's reconstructed worlds, he knew that there were good things to eat.

Finally, they had reached the dog's objective: one of the giant TV screens. It had seemed no different from the rest, but it was. Its screen had been full of alien "static" in the form of colors all muddled together in a vast swirl, like a strange "Galaxy" by some surrealist painter. And protecting the screen from accidental damage . . . an electrified grille, of course.

Tail down and hair bristling, Barney had inched carefully through the lethal squares of the grille, to pause in front of the great screen in a typical bird-dog pose. There he'd stood, rigid from tip to tail, as if fascinated by the slow, monotonous distortion of muddy colors in meaningless motion, causing Gill to reconsider: maybe it wasn't meaningless after all.

Periodically, the screen would display a moment or two of brilliant flashes of white light, like real static, and Barney would lean forward as if drawn to it, as if he were hypnotized by it. But he wasn't hypnotized, merely waiting. Waiting, Gill had later supposed, for the right sequence of flashes. And finally, when that sequence came, he had pounced straight forward—directly into the screen—and vanished!

Later . . . the dog had come back from whichever world he'd visited; returned with a six-legged rabbit freshly dead in his mouth, just as he

*would have returned with his kill to his old master, because he couldn't
know that Gill didn't need to eat. But food had been the last thing on
Gill's mind. Far more importantly, he'd been shown the way out of this
place.*

*Now . . . well that way was still here, and once again this good old
dog had sniffed it out . . .*

Squeezing through a bottleneck where the walkway had been crushed
by a buckled girder, Gill saw Barney up ahead, and saw that he stood
waiting and whining before the very screen. That good old dog!

"Barney, stay!" he called out, then turned and yelled for Turnbull to
slow down, wait for Angela and the others. Shortly, Angela drew level with
the big minder, and Gill could see that the rest of the party weren't far
behind. Then he beckoned the two on and together they joined Barney in
front of the screen.

"This is it," Gill told them breathlessly as they in turn rested and caught
their breath. "It's our way out. The dog remembered it from the last time.
I couldn't have done it without him. I've no sense of direction here. All
this useless machine clutter, it throws me right off track. Dumping me here
is like waving a magnet in front of a compass: everything gets knocked out
of kilter." And he paused for breath.

"And from here?" Angela was eager for them to be on their way, naturally.

"Well the last time," Gill answered, "I managed to conjure some pictures up onto this screen. Do you recall? I saw you and the others on
Clayborne's 'supernatural' world—that terrible place made up of a super-
stitious fool's worst nightmares—and of course I followed you there."

"Er, but not this time, right?" Jack Turnbull had paled a very little, a
rare sight to see.

"God, no!" said Gill. "At least I hope not. I'm just praying I haven't
lost the knack and I can still get this thing to talk to me. Then with any
luck I'll be able to get us into the synthesizer's control room, try to repro-
gram the entire system."

"So the plan is still on track?" said Angela, her spirits lifting. "First to
discover the secrets of the House of Doors, and then to use them against
the Ggyddn?"

"Something like that," said Gill, frowning. Angela's brief assessment
of the situation had returned him to earth, causing him to remember that
as yet—however desperate things seemed—their plight was still only a
small part of a very much bigger problem. "But"—and he shook his head—
"I don't know, I still have this feeling that something is somehow different,
and very wrong."

At which Barney suddenly stiffened and growled low in his throat, in the moment before a voice from *behind* them—a deep, bass, amplified voice from the screen—said, "Wrong? No, not wrong, Mr. Gill. Why, from my point of view it's exactly right! But different I will allow. For you see, it's a different program, my friend. And it's *my* program!"

And with a thrill of utter horror and disbelief, Gill recognized the voice . . .

CHAPTER
17

GILL, ANGELA, TURNBULL, all three of them had started violently, snapping their heads around as one to gape at the screen; then almost falling into each other's arms—even the big minder—as they saw what it displayed. For the swirling colors had formed a picture, a giant face in larger than life detail. And:

"Jesus!" Turnbull croaked, and at once spat out the words, or name, "Sith Bannerman . . . that's his face!"

"Correct, Mr. Turnbull, Mr. Jack Turnbull," said the booming voice from the screen as the corners of the giant mouth turned up in an inhuman grin. "I am Sith—Sith of the Ggyddn—yes. And as you are well aware this is my . . . well, shall we say my 'assumed' face?" The great eyes narrowed, swiveled to look at Gill. "As for your current situation, Mr. Gill—your predicament?—*that* is my program! You may think that you recognize it, but you don't."

"Not a door," Gill mumbled, backing off and hugging Angela close. "Not anymore. It's a viewscreen now."

"A door, a viewscreen, whatever I choose," Sith told him with a shrug. "But you're wasting time in stating the obvious, Mr. Gill. Clearly you and I are opponents again. Or rather, you and your friends are pawns in the game. So, can I perhaps interest you in the rules?"

With a massive effort, Gill got a grip on himself. Rules? Sith's rules? He suspected he already knew them, and knew that the alien jellyfish disguised as the robotic "Bannerman" could break them just as easily as he made them. Written as clear as day on the sardonic face on the screen, the rules were a death certificate. Gill's and everyone else's. But at least he could play along for now. Play for time, for space—for room to get this straight in his head—and maybe for an edge, an advantage.

"It seems you've . . . caught us out," he said, straightening from his half crouch and releasing Angela, putting her away from him. "I—er, that is we—didn't expect to see you again. Your being here is a shock, to say the least. But here you are, telling us that there's some kind of game and that we're involved. It's hardly surprising we need time to adjust . . ." In fact, Gill needed time to get inside this new program, Sith's program, as it now appeared.

Meanwhile, Miranda Marsh—along with Stannersly and Waite, who between them assisted Ki-no Sung—had arrived on the scene. Approaching obliquely, and noting the attitude of Gill's party, how they seemed to cower before the great screen, they came on more cautiously. And:

"What is it?" Miranda called out, anxiously.

Frowning, Sith Bannerman swiveled his eyes this way and that. He was obviously trying to locate the source of Miranda's voice. She and the others were offscreen, beyond the periphery of his vision. But after a moment or two, smiling again in that humorless way of his, Sith returned his gaze to Gill and said, "Ah, but of course! Your three new traveling companions. I was wondering where they had got to."

And: *Good!* thought Gill. *So you can't follow everything we do. You don't know where we are all of the time. If we were to split up, you'd find it difficult to keep tabs on us.*

Gill was a rare man in more senses than one, the kind of man who always works best under pressure. Finding himself in a tight spot, now his mind was alert, racing. And Sith Bannerman was so sure of himself that already he'd made several mistakes. Or if not errors as such, he'd given away some important clues. Now Gill must try to prod him into giving away a lot more. And suddenly the thought struck him:

This is what I've been waiting for! I've even been expecting it! It's what was hanging over me all this time. I should have known; the Castle felt wrong right from the start; I lost control from the moment I reactivated the damn thing. But how?

"The game is waiting, Mr. Gill," Sith Bannerman boomed impatiently. "I'm eager to get on with it, as you see. And so to the rules. You can hear me out or ignore me; it rather depends on how eager you are to die! Oh, I'm not going to lie to you: your death *is* the ultimate object of the game. Yours, and your woman's and all your friends'. You'll play in order to delay it as long as possible, while yet knowing that you can't possibly endure forever. So, how is that for a game?"

"The last time," Gill began to formulate a wild guess—anything to engage Sith's mind while he tried to get *his* mind in sync with the synthesizer, the power behind Sith's power—"you must have seen what was coming, reprogrammed the Castle in advance of your defeat. Coward that you are, you weren't taking any chances. And now *you,* the you on the screen there, are simply a synthesized version of Sith of the Thone."

And: *Damn!* Gill thought. *For all I know I could be right!*

The vast face swelled so as to fill the screen almost entirely, and the huge eyebrows arched in amusement—and perhaps a degree of appreciation? "But what a clever idea, Mr. Gill! In fact, I almost wish I'd thought of it myself! But alas, you are quite wrong. For I really am . . . myself!"

But suddenly Sith's eyes narrowed again as he drew back a little, and his amused look turned to one of suspicion.

"What?" he said. "A tweak? Is that you tweaking, Mr. Gill? Could that be your feeble mind I feel attempting to infiltrate my program?" He tut-tutted. "Well much as I admire your temerity, I'm afraid it's against the rules, a foul. And there are penalties for fouls." With which the giant face looked off to one side, and Sith's shoulder, barely visible at the bottom of the screen, moved, presumably to extend his arm and hand.

Maybe he had touched or adjusted some mechanism. But certainly he'd caused something to happen . . .

For Gill staggered, reeled, clutched at his head, and cried, *"Christ!"* And still stumbling, windmilling his arms, he came dangerously close to the edge of the chasm, reeling there on the brink with five or six hundred feet of tangled girders, scaffolding, scrap metal, and thin air beneath him. If he fell, his body would make fatal contact with plenty of solid objects before he hit the steel-tracked bed of the machine gorge.

But Angela was already beside him, pulling him away from danger as he went to his knees and tried to control his whirling senses. "Spencer!" she gasped, wide-eyed. "What happened?"

For a moment he couldn't answer, and Sith Bannerman took the opportunity to explain, "Rule number one: the penalty for cheating as Mr. Gill tried to cheat is instantaneous. Pain and disorientation—even death in certain circumstances. But of course, I'm not going to tell you which circumstances."

"You alien slime!" Angela raged, shaking a small, impotent fist at the screen.

"As for the rest of the rules," Sith continued as if she hadn't even spoken. "I'll make them up as we go along. But to give you a clue: you people have a child's game called Snakes and Ladders? My game is similar. I have programmed the synthesizer to simulate a game of Snakes and Ladders. Throw a good number, you climb a ladder. Throw a poor one and slide down a snake. And I know I don't need to remind you how many snakes there are in the House of Doors." Once again the face on the screen smiled its sardonic smile, and said, "There, all done. The game can begin."

But now Turnbull spoke up. "Your game doesn't work," he called out. "You can't possibly make it work." Like Gill, the big minder was a specialist of sorts. He specialized in survival and close protection, in which *self*-protection plays the most important role. He'd had dealings with terrorists before, and to his way of thinking that's all Sith was: an alien terrorist.

Now Sith raised a sarcastic eyebrow. "Ah, the abominable Mr. Turnbull! The iron man, fighter to the last, and throwback to the cave. So tell me, what flaw do you think you have discovered in my game?"

"A game needs players," Turnbull said. "What if we don't play? What if we simply find us a nice quiet spot to sit this one out? Also, you mentioned death—ours, that is. But we all know it's not like that—you only *appear* to die in a House of Doors. I mean, the system's at work right now, curing ailments we might have even if we don't know we have them. In fact it's beneficial, right?"

And Gill saw what Turnbull was doing—in fact what Gill himself had been doing—trying to draw Sith out. For if you don't talk to a terrorist, then it's also impossible to talk him down, find a way to overcome him. And:

"Astonishing!" said Sith. "So, there is a mind in there after all, however deluded. Well then, now let *me* explain the faults—not in my game but in your reasoning, Mr. Turnbull.

"Let's start with your assertion that simply being here, adventuring in the House of Doors, is curative. Well, so it is, because that is the nature of the synthesizer. The Thone abhor illness, even in lesser creatures—or in your case, the very least of creatures. Much as I disagree with the principle, it cannot be changed. But again in your case, wouldn't you agree that it's very similar to fattening a turkey for Christmas? As for merely *appearing* to die . . . that would be true if you were replicas, not the real specimens. But you are as real as I am; only witness the growth of your facial hair, and all the other functions of your odious bodies. An injury will heal more rapidly in this maze of worlds, it's true, but a mangled, burned, drowned, devoured, or otherwise dead body will *stay* dead in any and all worlds. Oh, believe me, you can die—and you will.

"And finally, you wonder what will happen if you decline my invitation to play. But isn't it clear that you're obliged to play, and then to move on? I should think it would be obvious even to a primitive that you can't remain indefinitely in Mr. Gill's machine world. What will you eat? Each other? A fascinating thought, and if circumstances were different I might even be interested to see the outcome. But no, you *will* play, and you will move on."

And under his breath, Gill told the minder, "It's pretty much as we thought. The same synthesized worlds, but this time we aren't synthesized people."

Sith heard him anyway and laughed. "Oh, Mr. Gill! I'm sure that you'll never cease to amaze me. Well, not until you *cease* . . . permanently. But so clever, and already hard at work on the problem. Which in turn means that like it or not you're already playing my game! Ah, but I want you to play it with a deal more enthusiasm, more spirit. Just like the first time . . ."

Sith's "jovial" mood changed on the instant; likewise the look on his face as he said:

"Do you remember Haggie? Well, I'm sure your small, sweet lady remembers him, eh?" His eyes slewed, flickered over Angela in a manner that, in a man, would be considered lewd, and almost reluctantly returned to Gill.

"Haggie's gone," Gill told him bluntly. "He paid for his crimes many times over—paid for them in all the hells that you created for him. There's no bringing him back." But to himself he said, *At least, I hope there isn't.*

"Really?" said Sith, raising an eyebrow. And as he lowered it again: "Really . . . ?" And now the eyes in that great face glittered speculatively, if only for a moment, until he agreed, "Well, perhaps not, not Haggie himself. But I'm sure you remember the creature that *pursued* him?"

Gill started, couldn't help himself—and Sith Bannerman laughed again. "I see that you do remember! And here's Mr. Turnbull asking what if you simply find a nice quiet spot to sit it out." And now the face on the screen grew dark with rage. "This is *my* House of Doors, and for you there is no nice quiet place. No, for I shall keep you moving. *He* . . . shall keep you moving!"

Sith's face transferred to a smaller box at the top right of the screen, and the rest of the picture dissolved back into a crazy swirl of muddy color. But it only lasted for a second or two. Then . . .

The colors separated out, and the swirl shaped itself into a very different picture; but definitely the last picture in the world that Gill and his friends wanted to see. By which time Miranda Marsh and the rest of the group had edged closer, so that they, too, saw what was portrayed—and *more* than portrayed—on the screen!

For as Sith Bannerman boomed, "Let the game begin!" so the *thing* in the main picture suddenly came jerking, scrabbling forward. And humming, vibrating with electrical energy, the screen seemed to erupt in spastically convulsing skeins of white light as the air began to reek of ozone. Another moment and Gill felt his hair standing on end, writhing over his head and giving off sparks in the highly charged field.

Then, as the screen itself *parted,* and something began to come through, Gill yelled: "Run for it! Get away from here! Go back the way we came!" Which might work well enough for Miranda and the latecomers; they were still far enough away, hadn't been blinded by the glare of the display. But as for Angela:

Holding up her hands before her face, she came stumbling into Gill's arms. But he, too, had been temporarily blinded by the screen's coruscations and couldn't see a thing. On the rim of the scrap metal gorge like this, he didn't dare risk moving. Not with Angela in his arms, and certainly not hurriedly. They might as well be in the middle of a battle zone—a minefield lit by incendiary flares—where one wrong step could be their last. Worse than that, for out of the glare of battle an enemy tank was advancing upon them. Except it wasn't a tank.

Gill knew what he had seen on the screen, and so did Angela and Turnbull. In any case Sith had given them advance warning by mentioning Alec Haggie and the "creature" that pursued him. Except it wasn't a true creature as such but a construct, a mechanism created by the synthesizer. On that previous occasion the thing had only been interested in Haggie, who hadn't been a part of the game and so must be removed. It was like a groundsman, tending the field of play. Or it had been. Now it was integral *to* the game, neither an umpire nor a scorer but a player in its own right.

And as in a fevered dream, Gill remembered his very first impressions of Sith's "creature":

It was like . . . an elongated crab—a rearing scorpion or mantis—a nightmare given form and substance and grown to monstrous proportions. Nine feet long, five wide, four high, with stalked eyes, incredibly articulate claws, antennae, a stinger arced over its segmented back, and other appendages whose functions were entirely conjectural. It was blue-gleaming chitin, ivory mandibles, feathery, flickering feelers . . . all of these things and now, something more:

It was a hunter-killer, but it could also be a sniper, or an ambusher lying in wait at the tail end of a snake. And that, Gill thought, was how it felt right now: like someone had made a very bad throw of the dice. For the screen was still parting, and the thing's eye stalks and a pincer were coming through!

And everything—all such events, thoughts, and actions—occurring in the space of seconds, until:

"Down!" Turnbull's bull voice, roaring over the crackle of static and the hum and sputter of electrical discharge from the screen. "Hit the deck!"

Shit! Gill thought untypically, because he knew instinctively that it was about to hit the fan. And sure enough, as he grabbed Angela and pulled her down with him, it did. First the angry snarl of the big minder's machine pistol—just a short burst of half a dozen rounds, at least one of which was vaporized by the screen's grille—but in the next moment it was as if Turnbull had fired a bazooka!

There came a sound like a cross between shattering glass and torn sheet metal, and the screen went out with a bang like a clap of thunder. A blast of hot air warmed Gill's scalp where he sprawled across Angela, and arcs of electrical fire and blobs of molten metal went sputtering overhead. Then it was over. The screen was a smoking, gaping black hole in a buckled frame, and in front of it lay the hinge and upper section of a plated pincer and a steaming eye stalk whose eye had already glazed over. These were the only parts of the hunter-scorpion that had made it across the threshold before Turnbull "slammed" the door.

And: *"Whoa!"* said the minder, rubbing watering eyes where he stood braced against a stanchion, his combat jacket smoking where hot metal had spattered it. "But this is some kind of ammunition!"

"You took one hell of a chance then, Jack," Gill told him as he got shakily to his feet and helped Angela up. "A *hell* of a chance—thank God!"

"You should thank Him it was daylight," Turnbull grunted. "Else you really would have been blinded, and me, too. And if I had been, that would have been that." He wasn't boasting; that wasn't Turnbull's way. He was just stating a fact. "Christ, it was like looking into the sun!"

And Gill asked him: "What was? What exactly did you do?"

"Like I said," the other answered, still shaking his head and rubbing at his streaming eyes. "I looked directly into it, right into the middle of the glare. And that's where I put my shots. It was Sith who gave me the idea when he said—"

" 'A door, a viewscreen, whatever I choose.' " Gill nodded. "And you figured if he could send something through—"

"Then I could send something the other way," Turnbull answered. "Namely a couple of rounds of hot lead! But I wasn't aiming at that." He indicated the smoking parts. "I aimed high and a little to one side, dead center of the screen. You see, in a conventional TV set, that's where the tube is."

"Jack, you're one dangerous son of a . . ." said Gill, shaking his head. And once again: "Thank God!"

Angela was first to fully recover. "Shouldn't we get away from here?" she said. "Sith knows where we are. Though he can't harm us right now, he isn't going to stop trying."

"You're right," Gill answered. "And in any case this door . . . well, it isn't. Not anymore. So we have to find another."

Still shaky, he led the way back along the catwalk toward Miranda and the others. And he sighed his relief on noting that Barney had joined them, and that he was unharmed.

"Another door?" Turnbull sounded dubious. "Another screen, you mean? *Huh!* Another entrance for Sith's damned bloodhound!"

"Maybe," said Gill, "and maybe not. First off, before Sith tried to send that hunter-killer through, he was using the last screen literally as a viewer. Well, there are a number of these screens about, viewers or doors, whichever he likes. But surely he can't be watching all of them at once?"

"Why not?" said Angela. "Even in our technology we're capable of that."

Gill thought about it, rubbed his chin ruefully. "Wishful thinking," he said. "But of course you're right."

And Turnbull said, "I shouldn't think the bastard will be watching any of them for a while. The way that thing detonated back there, I reckon I hit his console."

"It's all guesswork," said Gill, shaking his head in frustration. "We don't know what he's capable of. I mean, think of it. This is a synthesized world, totally unreal. Hell, it's an entire planetary system, built around *my* worst nightmares! And Sith can tap into it like changing channels! But how can he do that? Is he plugged into my head? Is the synthesizer telepathic? Does it know what I know? If so, we don't have a chance."

"We didn't have a chance last time either." As usual, Angela was defiant. "But we still came out on top . . ."

They had closed with the other members of the group where they waited, and Miranda Marsh had heard Angela's last remark. "What?" she said. "We don't have a chance?" She grasped Gill's arm. "What does she mean, Spencer? And who was that back there on that screen?" Her eyes were wide with fear.

"When we're well away from here, then we'll take a break and I'll tell you," Gill answered. "But in fact the main question isn't who he is but how he is. We thought that we'd seen the last of Sith."

"Sith?" she pressed. "Was it Sith of the Thone, the invigilator from your report?"

"Sith of the Ggyddn now," said Gill, picking up speed as they retraced their steps. "Which might tell us a great deal, or nothing at all. But either way it spells trouble."

Miranda had more questions, a lot of them, but before she could ask them: "Oh, Good Lord!" said George Waite, holding his jaw. And his cultured voice was full of pain.

"What?" Gill looked at him in concern. "Did something hit you back there when that screen blew?"

"No." Waite shook his head and clutched at his jaw again, his face screwed up in agony. "God, how stupid! What a ridiculous time for this to happen!"

"So what is it?" Turnbull asked him, frowning.

"Forget it," said Waite. "You have enough on your minds. And I have a lot more than this to worry about. It's just that . . . I don't know. It seems to be getting worse, damn it!"

"What does?" Miranda insisted. "If it's something that's going to affect us, we all should know. There have been several occasions when I've noticed you holding your head. Back at the lighthouse, for instance." But suddenly her voice was that much softer. "George, it isn't . . . is it? I mean, it couldn't possibly be your . . . ?"

"My tumor?" He gave a small brittle laugh, and held his jaw tighter still. "God, no! I've a cap on a tooth at the back here, that's all. It must have come loose or something. But so what? We've more to worry about, like I said."

As they moved on Angela commiserated, "There's nothing as bad as a toothache, no matter what the circumstances."

But Gill and the minder, falling back a little, exchanged worried glances. And Turnbull grunted: "I thought the synthesizer was supposed to fix small ailments like that?"

Gill nodded, and under his breath answered, "Let's keep an eye on things. And maybe we'll learn something as we go . . ."

CHAPTER
18

B UT YOU'VE SIMPLY accepted it!" It was an accusation, emphasizing the look of disbelief on Miranda's face where the hollows of her eyes and mouth were like holes punched in the dusty sun haze. "It's as if you were expecting some such to happen—and yet you saw fit to let us walk right on into it!"

And the trouble is, Gill thought, *I can't deny it.*

The disparate group had found themselves a resting place, a location safely distant from any viewscreen so far noted, set back from the vertiginous chasm of the machine gulf in what appeared to be the hinged "jaw" of the biggest mechanical scoop or digger of all time. Upturned, this detached, rusting dinosaur-skull of a bucket let in daylight through the four-foot prongs of its teeth while keeping the heat and possibly the radiation of the atomic sun out.

A cool draft found its way up through the tangle of scrap metal below, wafting like a sweet breath of life into the scoop through the tightly meshed iron grid that formed the floor. And there the group sat, using the seven-sided heads of giant bolts as seats, their backs against the curving teeth, with shafts of blinding sunlight to separate each member from the next. And:

"Miranda," Gill said, having silently considered her words awhile. "You know I didn't want you along. Not simply because our viewpoints were so different, but mainly because I couldn't say for sure how dangerous things might get to be. Yes, I understand your concerns; I know what you're

saying and I won't deny it. Since the moment I reactivated the House of
Doors I've been expecting . . . well, *something;* because I sensed that
everything was wrong. And I was right, but the Castle was activated and it
was too late to do anything about it. As for accepting our situation: tell me,
what else can I do? I have no choice in this. Putting it simply, the situation
exists. It is."

"And that—that creature, Sith?—he and his constructs are trying to
kill us?" She still seemed half in shock. Angela, on the other hand, was
about ready to boil over. But realizing that she and Miranda were directly
opposed—that their characters were literally opposites—she worked hard
to see things from the other's point of view. It seemed the only way to keep
things cool.

"Miranda," she said, "it seems you've forgotten why we're here. The
Ggyddn aren't just trying to kill us; *we* are nothing but a game to Sith, his
chance for revenge. We're here because they're killing our whole world!
Once you've got that fixed in your head you'll be okay. We're here
because . . . because we've got to be. And anyway, if we weren't we'd probably die all the more surely."

Fred Stannersly said, "That's it in a nutshell. It really puts it all in
perspective. See, I've been sitting here thinking pretty much the same kind
of thing: like, what the hell am I doing here?" He looked at Angela, nodded
his head in appreciation and total agreement. "Well, now I know."

For once Miranda had been listening, taking it all in. Finally, falter-
ingly, she said, "We'd die all the more surely, you say? Well, maybe
we would—maybe we will—but not necessarily as slowly. That's what
he threatened, isn't it? To give us all the hell we can endure before end-
ing it?"

"Something like that," Gill told her. "But in a place like this we can
endure a lot. If we get hurt—cut, bruised, poisoned—we'll heal, and very
quickly. It's only when our hurts become too much, too shattering,
that . . ." He let it taper off, cursing himself that he wasn't more diplomatic.

"That we'll die?" she continued his train of thoughts, and sat shivering
even though it wasn't cold. "I never expected it to end like this, that's all,"
she said. "I don't think that I've ever really seen myself as dying."

"Intimations of mortality," Jack Turnbull said from where he sprawled
against the vast steel tooth adjacent to Miranda's. Then, reaching across
the gap, he took her hand. "Me, I've seen myself dying all too often—but
it hasn't happened yet. I was just born lucky I suppose." And with a grin
he didn't much feel like, for her sake if not his own, he continued, "Stick
with me, kid, and who knows? Maybe it'll rub off on you, too. This could
be the beginning of a beautiful friendship." His Bogart impersonation was

atrocious, but Miranda went with it, managing something of a smile at least. Turnbull caught her grateful glance, saw a brief flash of white teeth through the blaze of unnatural sunlight.

They had eaten a bite, sipped a little water. Ki-no Sung was asleep, nodding where he sat between George Waite and Miranda. Under his facial dressings, new baby skin was forming at an astonishing rate. The dressings would probably be redundant before dark. The injury to his left arm was something else; no one was eager to look at that too closely, or speculate on the outcome. Since there was no clear evidence of blood poisoning, however, and the rest of the Chinaman's arm and body in general seemed in good health, the signs appeared favorable.

As for Waite: he was preoccupied with his toothache, kept rubbing at his jaw and trying to hold back the soft sighs of a man in considerable pain. He too was trying to sleep, and Miranda must be similarly exhausted, mentally if not physically.

It seemed to Gill the ideal opportunity to hold a think-tank session with the rest of the group, in which he included Fred Stannersly. If they were ever to get out of this mess and back to the lighthouse in any sort of shape, the pilot was the only one who would be able to transport any relevant information to the authorities on the mainland. Which meant that from that point of view he was the most important member of Gill's party and should be privy to everything that went down.

"Jack, Angela, Fred." Gill stood up. "Let's have a scout around outside, make sure we're safe here." And to Waite, who stirred himself and seemed half-tempted to join them: "George, you and Miranda take it easy. Keep Sung company. If he were to wake up and find us all missing, he'd think we'd deserted him. We won't be going very far. Give a yell if you need us . . ."

The four moved out, found a place maybe fifty yards away where they could talk. It was a teepee of collapsed scaffolding, not quite on the edge of the gorge but furnishing excellent views through an arc of a hundred and eighty degrees.

"Just like old times," the big minder grunted. "A think tank, eh? Concentrate the power of the mind, right? *Huh!* Well at least there are three of you!"

"In this situation," Gill told him, "your ideas are just as valid as anyone else's." Which wasn't exactly a pat on the back—or the brain—but Turnbull knew what he meant. "And anyway," Gill went on, "it was you who first voiced your concern over Ki-no Sung, and about . . . well, something else. And so far I believe you've been right both times. Or if not *both* times, at least one tends to prove the other."

"Eh?" Turnbull straightened up from where he'd been leaning against a stanchion. "Did you say I was right? And the one proves the other? What does that mean? What's on your mind?"

"Yes, what?" Angela wanted to know, looking utterly mystified.

"Now hold on." Gill held up his hands calmingly. "I could still be wrong. This is all guesswork. But Ki-no Sung—oh, I don't know—I can't seem to fit him in. When he's more surely on his feet again I'll have to have a little talk with him. So far . . . there hasn't been time for much of anything, let alone questioning someone who isn't too well versed in English."

"But what's bothering you about him?" Stannersly pressed. And Turnbull at once stepped in to explain the outsider theory that he and Gill had put together.

"So you see," the minder finished, "it was the same last time. Except Jon Bannerman was a big bastard and this bloke is just a little fellow."

"You're saying there may be an alien inside him?" Stannersly looked doubtful. "Well if so he's a damn good actor!"

"Oh, he is," Gill answered. "A *bloody* good actor! And inside a man-like environment suit—a synthesized construct—he also has the strength of three men, so size doesn't count." He glanced at Turnbull. "And that arm of his . . . doesn't hurt?"

"That can be tested," the minder grunted. "That stump may be healing, or it may be in the process of—what, resynthesis?—but if one of us was to stumble and accidentally gave it a sharp knock . . ."

"Jack, don't!" Angela pulled a face.

And Turnbull sighed, "Drastic, I know. But isn't it a matter of life or death?"

"It could be eventually," said Gill grimly. "But actually I'm torn two ways. I mean, there's something else that's bothering me. If that really was Sith up on that screen, how could he be inside a Ki-no Sung construct at the same time?"

"Couldn't." Stannersly shook his head. "I was with Sung at the time; frankly, he was intent on staying alive, keeping well away from the edge of the machine gorge. Take it from me, there isn't any way he could have been connected with what was happening on that screen. Oh, he was keeping an eye on what was going on, all right, but he was looking out for himself, too."

"So then," said Angela, "if there is something fishy about Sung, what is it? Could he be a construct, a spy synthesized by Sith to, well, 'keep an eye' on us?"

"A spy?" Gill looked at Turnbull.

"Why not?" the minder answered. "And his being Chinese is his cover.

We can't question him too closely because as you say he doesn't understand English too good. His injuries could be a part of his disguise, too. It's a hard man who'll take against a cripple."

Gill looked about ready to agree, then bit his lip, shook his head. "No," he said. "It doesn't work."

"What doesn't?" Angela asked him.

"Trying to pin anything on Ki-no Sung doesn't. When I cut Jon Bannerman, he didn't bleed. Or he did, but only on the outside." They remembered, and Turnbull said:

"That's right! His fingers were fingers right enough. But when you used that weapon of his to slice through a major part of his body, namely his legs, in order to immobilize him—"

"There was no bone in there," Gill cut him off. "Just a flexible metal tube where the bone should be. Oh, and a cupful of alien juices inside the tube. But Sung has lost a hand, and we all saw the stump. His wrist was flesh, blood, and bone all the way through."

"Spencer, *don't!*" Angela turned her face away.

"So, he's a man," said Stannersly.

"A man with a scar on his neck," Turnbull growled.

Gill shrugged, said, "Yes, we have to consider that, too. But I have scars. And so do you and most other people."

"Let's take a vote on it," said Angela, practical as ever. "I vote we take care of him—but that we also watch him like a cat with a mouse. The first time we notice anything odd, that's when we look at him more closely. But . . . there is something."

"Oh?" said Gill.

She nodded. "He *has* been acting strangely. I mean, I don't claim to understand Chinese psychology, but Ki-no Sung has been performing as if in a dream, as if nothing around him is, well, real. Oh, I know there could be a simple explanation—like, is *any* damn thing real in this place? *We* accept it because we know what it is, but how do we explain it to him? Also, it's highly likely he's still in shock; I'm pretty sure I would be."

"If you were entirely human," said Gill. "But on the other hand, is he *enough* in shock?"

"I vote yes to Angela's proposal," Stannersly said.

"Me, too," said Turnbull.

And Gill agreed, "Okay." But as they all relaxed a little: "And then there's George Waite," he said . . .

"George and his toothache." Jack Turnbull had been waiting for it.

"His toothache?" Angela frowned—then clapped a hand to her mouth. And after a moment: "The one . . . *the one proves the other!* Now I see what you were getting at. If one man's flayed face can heal itself in just a couple of hours—"

And Fred Stannersly finished it for her: "What the hell is George Waite doing with a mere toothache?"

"I've been thinking about it," said Gill. "There isn't any reasonable explanation for what he's going through. Well, there is one: that Miranda was right and it's his tumor. Which is to say, he only *thinks*—or maybe hopes?—it's a toothache. But this is the Castle, a synthesizer, a House of Doors, and Houses of Doors are benign, sympathetic; they're supposed to automatically cure illnesses. So, maybe with something as serious as a tumor it takes longer. I don't know . . ." He shook his head.

"But we do know that he was taken by that Ggyddn mansion," the big minder reminded them. "Okay, they didn't keep him long, but long enough that when they tossed him out again he was in a bad way. And anyway, why the hell did they give him back? Since they seem intent on killing us all off, why not get rid of poor old George right there and then?"

"All of that." Gill nodded. "I've been going over exactly the same things."

"So, let's find out the truth," said Turnbull. "We take a look at his tooth. If it's not that, then it's his tumor. And whichever, if it doesn't start to ease up pretty quick then it . . . has to be something else?" He scratched his head, frowned, said: "Does that make sense?"

And Gill found himself obliged to grin. "Stop kidding us, Jack," he said. "We know you're a hell of a lot shrewder than you'd ever be willing to admit."

"We've been out here some time," said Angela. "Maybe we'd better get back now."

"In a moment," Gill told her. "But there are other things you should know."

"Good or bad things?" Stannersly looked anxious.

"Depends how they work out," Gill answered. "But some of them could work in our favor. Shall I go on?"

"Quick as you like," said Turnbull.

"First, while Sith Bannerman was actually looking at us through that screen, he couldn't see things *off*screen. So it appears he is limited in what he knows about our locations at any given time. If we were to split up— and no, I'm not advocating that—it would definitely be harder for him to pin us down. Next, when you were offscreen, Fred, along with Miranda, George, and Sung, Sith talked about our 'three' traveling companions. But only three? There were four of you. I think that was a slip of the tongue, a mistake. And an easy one to make, because—"

"Because the fourth man, or woman, wasn't *our* friend." Stannersly nodded.

"Strike woman," said Angela. "Miranda might seem bitchy, but take it from me she's a hundred percent human."

"And all woman," Turnbull said. "Well, if you'd give her a chance." He coughed, went a little red when he noticed they were all looking at him. "Anyway, she doesn't fit our picture of an outsider at all."

"Agreed," Gill said with a nod. "Also, I think we're all satisfied that neither is Fred here an outsider. So yet again we're left with Ki-no Sung and George Waite. One or the other."

"A spy?" It was Angela's turn to ask the same question.

"Possibly," said Gill. "Unless Sith wasn't aware that Ki-no Sung had also been taken. If he wasn't, that would make his 'three' traveling companions statement a truth. From his viewpoint, anyway."

"All very confusing," said Stannersly.

"But all to be checked out." The minder narrowed his eyes. "My job, I think."

"When I give you the word," Gill told him. "But let's not jump the gun; let's not 'alienate' anyone just yet."

"So, is that it?" Angela was getting nervous. And Gill had long since learned to trust her woman's intuition.

"What is it, sweetheart?" he said. "What's bothering you?"

She looked all around, frowned, and answered, "Probably all this talk about spies and what have you—but did you ever get that feeling someone was watching you? Like eyes burning a hole in your back?"

"Okay," said Gill, contracting her nervousness, "let's get on back to the others."

But a few minutes later, as they maneuvered a buckled catwalk back to their mighty digger sanctuary, he caught a glimpse of Ki-no Sung apparently standing guard outside the bucket. And whether or not the yellow man had seen them, he chose that very moment to duck back out of sight through the gap between two of the scoop's massive steel teeth . . .

Miranda and George Waite came starting awake at the clatter of boots on steel. But Sung made no pretense of waking up; he was on his feet, slowly and carefully peeling the bandages off his face. "Is itch," he said, when Gill went to him. "Face is itch. Arm, too. But face feel . . . good?" The *expression* on his face was one of genuine astonishment.

"Let me," said Gill, and removed the last strip of bandage and the pad beneath it. Then, stepping back, lost for words, he silently shook his head. And Turnbull said:

"Plastic surgery's got nothing on this! Smooth as a baby's bum! Not even a dent or a pimple."

"Turn around," Gill instructed, guiding Ki-no Sung by pulling his shoulder. And without protest the other turned a slow, full circle. The minder took the opportunity to brush aside the black hairs high on the back of Sung's neck, then said to Gill, "He's almost completely healed." Gill knew what Turnbull meant: not that Sung's face had healed but that the tiny scar had very nearly disappeared now.

But Sung was looking at his arm, the bandaged stump where a hand used to be. "Arm itch," he said, and looked at Gill.

Gill nodded. "Okay, we'll see about that next."

And Sung at once held out his arm, allowing Gill to unwrap the bandages, soak the stump's padding with a little water, and remove it, and gently examine the plastic seal. The plastic was peeling back, taking the old dead skin with it. As for the skin underneath, on what should be the "raw" rim of the stump . . . it was as clean and fresh as if an old scab had recently dislodged itself and fallen away.

"Wrap it again," said Angela. "Let's keep it covered overnight to be on the safe side. A simple bandage this time." Her voice was little more than a sigh. Even knowing what they knew, still they found the curative powers of the House of Doors astonishing, awesome.

Turnbull said: "I know a couple of gents in Harley Street who would pay a fortune for a lease on this place!" But under his breath he whispered to Gill, "So, are we still undecided?"

And again Gill knew what he meant. If Ki-no Sung was safe—*if* he was safe—then what about Waite?

Waite didn't seem too interested in anything. Holding his jaw, he was rocking to and fro against one of the bucket's curved teeth. But Angela noticed the way Gill and the minder were looking at him and guessed what was coming. "George," she said, preempting them. "Would you mind us taking a look at that tooth of yours?"

At which he slowly stopped rocking, tentatively worked his jaw this way and that, frowned, and finally offered Angela a puzzled look. And sighing his relief, his disbelief, he said: "But isn't it always the same? The moment someone threatens you with the dentist—"

"The pain disappears," said Gill. But he wasn't smiling. And: "I think we should look at it anyway," he added.

Maybe it was the way Turnbull was moving closer that activated Waite; maybe the look in Gill's and Angela's eyes, or all of these things. But the way he suddenly started to his feet . . . the minder wasn't about to start taking chances. There followed the solid smack of a rock-hard fist on

Waite's jaw, and he flew backward, tripped, and went sprawling. Out cold, he lay where he fell.

Breathing easily but pulling a wry face, Turnbull rubbed at his knuckles and said, "Ouch! Sorry about that, but if he's been got at we don't know how much he's been got at. Whichever, now maybe we can look at that tooth—if he's still got it."

He did have. Gill found it with the help of a tiny pocket torch from Angela's pack, and at once knew what he was looking at. But to be doubly sure—concentrating his machine empathy—he used the tip of the torch to prod the leaden metal cap on Waite's tooth . . . which at once gave to his touch and indented like a blob of mercury, then sprang back to its former shape.

And straightening up, grim-faced, Gill said, "Thone metal, or Ggyddn. But whichever, a bug for sure!"

And Angela gasped: "Jack was right. The Mansion . . . !"

"What? What on *earth*—?" Miranda couldn't keep up. To her mind they'd all gone mad—and a moment later madder yet.

"Out of here, now!" Gill snapped.

"What?" Miranda cried again. *"What?"*

"We're sitting ducks in here," Angela told her. "That bastard Sith knows where we are."

And Stannersly said, "What about him?" He indicated Waite.

"He's coming, too," Turnbull grunted. "But not his tooth." And to Gill: "You go on. I'll be right behind you."

"Will you know where we're going?"

"It's my guess we're going down," the minder answered as he searched through a pile of junk in one corner—looking for a piece of "dental" equipment, Gill rightly supposed. And Turnbull glanced at him and lifted an eyebrow. "Down to the tracks in the bed of the gorge. Am I right?"

Gill nodded. "We still need a way out of this place. Since it appears to be a precise replica of my original machine world, and if it works the same way—"

"And if that sound is what I think it is," said Angela.

They held still, listened. Faintly, coming up in a series of dull, distant vibrations through the floor, now they could all hear it:

Gong-*bang!*—Gong-*bang!*—Gong-*bang!*

"The train now arriving on platform two . . ." said Turnbull nasally. And: "If you want to catch it, you'd better be on your way!" Nodding grimly, and glancing at the unconscious Waite, he cleaned the dirt and rust off something that looked like a tiny tire lever, held it up to the light speculatively.

"Right," said Gill. "Let's go."

And Stannersly said: "You go on with Sung and the ladies. I'll stay and give a hand with George. Jack would need to be a bloody fireman to carry him down there on his own!"

The gong-banging was a little louder now and Gill daren't wait any longer. Until Miranda realized she no longer had executive status she was going to need a lot of help. As for Sung: he looked agile enough and would probably be able to take care of himself. But still Gill's party could use a head start.

"Don't hang about any longer than you have to, you two," he said needlessly. "I mean, make it seconds rather than minutes, okay?" And then he led the others out of the bucket . . .

CHAPTER
19

A BUG?" MIRANDA STILL wasn't getting it.
"When George was taken by the Mansion, yes," Angela told her as Gill scouted out the way. "Sith or whoever was in control planted a bug on him, or in him—in his tooth. So while we've been sitting back there thinking we were safe—"

"He could have sent another one of those awful scorpion things after us?"

"Now you're getting it, yes."

"And this train we're catching?"

"It was in our reports," Angela said.

"My God!" Miranda gasped. *"That* train?"

"Yes. A big lunatic thing with all kinds of arms and periscopes and what have you. A huge box on wheels, that runs—or clatters and bangs—on those tracks down there."

"And . . . and goes out into the rust desert," said Miranda, quietly now. "To the rust-worm mounds. I remember."

"Right," said Angela, also quietly. "The one door we know of for sure is in the base of one of those mounds or hives."

"Oh, my God!" Miranda said again, in such a way that Angela knew quite definitely that she had read their reports. Yet a moment later:

"But surely *that* train, engine, box-thing, was destroyed?" Miranda was starting to live it for real now, beginning to see what they had gone through.

"Yes," Angela answered, "but this is a freshly synthesized version of the same world. It's like . . . like replaying a videotape. The same setting every time. Except that's a bad analogy, for in this world there *can* be changes, depending on our behavior; that is, the changes are brought about by us, by our actions. But should we ever come back here—"

"If we ever get *out* of here!" Miranda interrupted.

"It will start off in more or less same way. Like a reprise that always goes back to square one."

Miranda nodded. "The train hasn't been wrecked yet."

"Correct . . . I think."

And Gill said, "And we haven't caught it yet, either. And we won't, if we don't get a move on."

"I'm not sure I want to," said Miranda.

"Well *get* sure," Angela told her. And: "Look, we know this is nightmarish, but we've been here before and survived it. Now save your breath for climbing . . ."

They were halfway down to the bed of the gorge when Turnbull's shout echoed down to them. Looking back and up at the high horizon of mechanical debris, Gill shaded his eyes and waved at the three figures outlined there. The big minder was carrying Waite over one shoulder in a fireman's hoist position, but even for a man like Turnbull it wasn't going to be an easy climb. Standing beside him, Fred Stannersly waved the minder's machine pistol.

Looking at them, suddenly Gill gave a start. And frowning, casting all about, he muttered, "Oh, *hell!*"

"What now?" Angela's voice wasn't nearly as steady as she would like. So far she had managed to keep a measure of control over her outer facade—and thus over Miranda—but inside she was nervous as a cat.

"It's Barney!" Gill answered. "Damn! I thought he was with Jack and Fred."

"The dog?" Miranda said. "Why not call him?"

"When we're closer to those tracks down there," Gill told her, "then maybe I will. But not from here. In fact, I wish Jack hadn't yelled like that."

"Someone might hear him?"

Gill shrugged. "I just think we should keep a low profile. Angela feels eyes on us. Myself, I . . . I'm not sure what I feel. Like this place doesn't like us, maybe? Like it knows we're not supposed to be here." He shrugged again, disgustedly. "Hell, of course we're not! And as for Barney, I can't see how he'd make it down here on his own anyway. So no use calling him."

Greasing their hands in a metal barrel of what looked and smelled like rancid axle grease, they slid precariously down vertical sections of scaffolding pipe at the corner of a never-to-be-completed engine block the size of a two-story building, made their way cautiously down the sagging concertina of a spiraling metal stairwell that swayed and threatened to come loose from its moorings at every step, and so continued the hazardous descent. And both Gill and Angela were surprised and not a little relieved to note that Miranda Marsh was looking after herself without further complaint, and that even Sung—now that he was used to the idea that he was minus a left hand—wasn't finding the going too hard. The real battle was going on overhead, where Turnbull and Stannersly shared the extra burden of George Waite. They managed somehow, however, and even appeared to be catching up.

But as Gill and his three paused to get their second wind where a section of catwalk had half collapsed, forming a chute of steel latticework something like a giant cheese grater down to the next level, so Miranda said, "That awful racket seems a lot louder now."

Gill nodded, and said, "Yes, but believe me it's going to get much worse."

"And soon," said Angela, pointing along the slick-shining ribbons of the great tracks back into the heart of the machine city. "Here she comes!"

Miranda looked where Angela directed, gaped, finally husked, "A train? That? But it's . . . well, it's like you said: an enormous spiky box on wheels. Like something a mad child would build from all the world's Meccano sets!"

"Exactly," said Gill. "But don't knock it. It's more than likely that I'm the mad child! Anyway, that's our one means of conveyance out of here. So come on, for we're not there yet."

He had found a good length of rusty but serviceable chain, attached one end to a stanchion, and now tossed the rest of it down the throat of the cheese-grater chute. But: "Don't slip," he warned as Angela went first. "That metal latticework would cut you to bits." There was no time for niceties, just truths.

With his heart in his mouth Gill watched the women lowering themselves backward down the chute, hand over hand along the chain. They managed it without trouble, however, and Gill went next in order to take Ki-no Sung's weight in the event he should slip. But again all went well and in a few minutes they were all four down onto the last but one level. Then:

"Do you recognize this place?" Gill wiped sweat and rust from Angela's forehead.

"Unfortunately, yes." She nodded, pointing along the catwalk. "That

tangle of scaffolding over there. We climb down it to that sheet-iron platform. And that's it—that's where the beast refuels."

"What?" said Miranda, very nervously now. "The beast?"

"The train, engine, whatever," said Gill. "It stops under that platform."

"We're going to have to jump for it?" Under the rust, her face was pale.

"No," said Gill. "This is one part of the report you must have missed.
Once we get onto that platform, the rest is automatic, out of our control."

"Please," she said, "explain, will you? I mean, I'm sorry now that I
wasn't more attentive to your bloody reports, but I really do hate mysteries."

Gill nodded. He was pretty sure she was going to hate the facts even
more. But before he could begin:

"Spencer!" Turnbull's bull roar came echoing down to them. And it
was full of urgency, an as yet unspoken warning.

Gill looked up. The minder and his companions were at the top of the
mighty engine block where it was sheathed in scaffolding, but they hadn't
started down yet. And George Waite was on his feet now, apparently only
a little the worse for wear.

"What is it?" Gill cupped his hands to his mouth, shouted back.

"Look . . . *Look* . . . *Look!*" The answer echoed back, and the figure
standing at the rim of the scaffolding canyon pointed an arm and hand.
Gill and the others looked—

All with the exception of Ki-no Sung, who seemed intent on checking
out their current location. They looked—and Angela saw it first: one of the
giant screens on the other side of the tracks, but on the same level over the
bed of the gorge as they themselves. It was coruscating, throwing out arcs
of electrical energy, giving off flashes of intense white light—and in the
process leaving no one in any doubt as to what was coming next.

"*Shit!*" said Miranda softly, and no one gave it a second thought.

"Spencer! . . . *encer!* . . . *cer!*" The big minder again. "Get the hell . . .
the hell . . . *hell,* back up here! . . . *up here!* . . . *here!*"

The crab-scorpion came trundling through the screen, scanned the
gorge and looked across it directly at Gill and Co., and began clambering
down the wall of compressed machine parts like a tick negotiating the wool
on a sheep's flank.

Gill licked desiccated, rust-dry lips, looked all about, this way and that,
and tried to think. Like himself, his half team was close to exhaustion; it
was a temporary condition, he knew, but still the energy they would have
to find in order to climb back up to the minder and the others before the
scorpion intercepted them . . . it seemed hopeless, impossible.

Necessity was ever the mother of invention, however, and out of Gill's desperation, suddenly an idea struck home. Then, putting aside everything else from his mind, as he watched the hunter-killer descending to the bed of the gorge and the crazy gong-banging train approaching along the giant track, he began calculating the odds. And:

"Go!" he told the others, urgently. "Go now. Go back . . ."

"What?" Angela grabbed him as he started along the catwalk toward the festoons of dangling scaffolding. "Go where? Without you?" Fearful now, but angry, too, she stuck out her jaw in that certain way she had. "No way, Spencer Gill!"

"Trust me," he said, turning to her and taking her shoulders. "Trust me—but do it quick. The train's almost here, and that bloody scorpion is very nearly down onto the tracks."

"But, Spencer, what are you doing?" She saw plainly enough the desperation—and the determination—on Gill's face. And she knew that whatever was on his mind, her safety would be top of the list. Yes, even at the expense of his own.

"If things work exactly the same as the last time, we have a chance," he said. "A very slim one. But remember, sweetheart, this isn't for us. There's a lot more than just the seven of us swinging on this one. There's five and a half billion."

"Spencer," she said again, uselessly, as he kissed her and turned her about-face.

"Try to get back up to Jack and the others. I have to give this a shot. At the very least I might be able to slow the bastard down." And then he was gone . . .

Along the catwalk to the scaffolding where it hung like a tangle of roots from the side of a bank; without pause scrambling into the maze of it, and climbing down to a position only a few feet above the loading platform. And from there he looked back up, thinking:

If this doesn't work, that damn thing will pick me out of this metallic fuzz like a monkey grooming its mate for fleas—except I'm not a flea. And I'm definitely not its mate!

With that he let himself down as gently as possible onto the flat sheet-iron surface of the fueling platform, which was vibrating like a tuning fork to the monotonous hammering of the gigantic mechanism on the tracks.

Gong-*bang!* Gong-*baang!* Gong-*baaang!* The thing was slowing down, ready to load up on fuel. And this lunatic device, engine—train, for God's sake!—seemed to be the only thing in this entire world that made any kind of mechanical sense. Which formed in essence the basis of Gill's idea or hunch: that in fact the train *was* his escape route from nightmare.

He knew that everyone has his bolt-hole from a bad dream, that usually when a nightmare becomes too fearful to bear, its author will find himself shocked awake. But this was a synthesized dream, a dream made solid, and since Gill couldn't wake up from it—because he wasn't in fact asleep— maybe this was his let-out clause. It had worked before when the train had carried him and his original crew out into the rust desert, so maybe it would work again, albeit a little differently this time.

The scorpion was coming across the tracks, scuttling like a hugely magnified version of its tiny namesake, its mandibles raised in a threatening attack mode and its stinger arched. But as it approached the nearside tracks under the refueling platform, so the pointless but no longer useless engine groaned to a halt directly in its path and blew a piercing, almost derisive whistle.

And now Gill knew that he did in fact have a chance. Just the one slim chance.

There was a handful of nuts and bolts, scraps of the usual junk metal that can be found by the side of every ordinary railway track, scattered over the surface of the platform. He took up a handful of these metallic odds and ends, stood at the edge of the platform in plain view, began to rain them one at a time down over the train onto the armored carapace of the momentarily stalled scorpion.

The thing looked up, scanned Gill coldly with its stalked eyes, and stood up on its rear legs as if to judge the distance and height. And a moment later it began to climb up the side of the train. This was neither an "instinctive" nor a blind mechanical response; Gill's intention hadn't been to "anger" or irritate the hunter-killer, but simply to apprise it of his location; he'd wanted to be sure it knew where he was, and at exactly the right time. The platform was forty feet high; held aloft by a single stanchion buttressed to one corner, it made Gill impervious to attack from the ground. Therefore the scorpion's easiest route to its target was straight up the "spiky" side of the train, and so onto the platform.

Timing was everything, and by God it seemed to be working for Gill! Knowing what he would see—or at least *praying* that he knew—he looked off to one side. And there it was, a giant crane on a gantry: another device that actually worked in this mechanical madhouse. And as if simply looking at it had called it to life (though that wasn't the case) the crane jerked into spasmodic action. Clanking, it trundled forward along its own tracks, and with a rattle of chains began to lower an enormous steel-jawed bucket toward the refueling platform.

This was exactly what had happened the last time Gill was here. Then, he hadn't been expecting it. This time he was, and instead of throwing himself flat he clambered back up into the scaffolding. Not a moment too soon; he was still climbing when the scorpion reappeared from behind the massive, boxlike bulk of the train and hauled itself up onto the rim of the loading platform, its mandibles scrabbling on the flat steel surface.

But on the very rim it paused, tested the platform with a heavy claw while balancing itself there at one corner, astride two of the platform's rigid sides. Damn the thing; it saw that the platform was hinged, spring-loaded! Gill's weight—indeed the weight of half a dozen people—wouldn't suffice to spring that trapdoor and send them down on top of the train. But the scorpion must be the weight of an armored personnel carrier, and it seemed well aware of its own limitations.

For a moment more it poised there, and Gill thought: *Now! For Christ's sake, let it be now!*

And it was.

Intent on Gill, the construct hadn't noticed the refueling crane and its huge steel-jawed bucket. Now that it did, it was far too late.

Reaching the end of its tracks, the crane jerked to a halt and swung its bucket at the loading platform. It smacked headlong into the scorpion, loosening its grip and tilting it over onto the trapdoor . . . which at once cracked open, dropping the hunter-killer onto a second spring-loaded hopper on top of the train. And again the construct's weight quite literally let it down, as it fell in a frantic threshing of limbs into the vast belly of the greater, far less terrifying beast on the tracks. And the trapdoors sprang shut above it.

"Got you!" Gill yelled, clinging to the rusty tubing with his legs and shaking a fist so hard that he set the whole mass of scaffolding trembling and swaying all around him. "Got you! I damn well, bloody well, *fucking* . . . well . . . got—?!"

—Or maybe not.

The train whistled again, but a shrill, tortured sort of sound this time, which almost precisely matched the rending of metal from below the trapdoors. Then, out from the gap between the top of the train and the loading platform, a huge, hinged, torn, and battered sheet of metal screeched where it ground its way into view, finally coming loose and clanging down onto the tracks forty feet below. And from its hinges Gill knew what it was: one of the trapdoor flaps from the train's hopper!

He was galvanized into activity, climbed higher still, and hauled himself up onto the catwalk. And below him the fueling platform's doors clanged, again and again, and actually showed dents where they were being pounded on the underside. And with every clang they jumped on their hinges and sent scabs of rust flying, until one flap tore loose and twirled like a leaf down onto the tracks, while the other was grabbed by a chitin-plated pincer and twisted to one side.

And as Gill clung to the rail of the catwalk as if frozen there, which indeed he was, the head and mandibles of the scorpion rose up into view, and its eyes stared up at him—

For a moment.

Until the jaws of the crane's great bucket opened, letting loose its load of "fuel": maybe fifteen tons of scrap iron! And down went the hunter-killer as if poleaxed under all that metallic debris. At which the train whistled a third time, a strangled, muted whistle of mechanical desperation, and began to pull erratically out from under the now skeletal platform. Then:

Gong-*bang!*—Gong-*clank!*—Gong-*clatter!* The train shuddered its way along the track, wobbling and throbbing, and Gill wondered what engineering miracles or idiocies were going on in the thing's highly unlikely engine to convert scrap iron—and now Ggyddn metal?—into fuel. And, indeed, he also found himself wondering if it was even possible for the train to convert something as huge, grotesque, and alien as the scorpion.

The answer came when the train was maybe sixty yards away. And the answer was no.

With a deafening blast the thing blew! Its seams ruptured, its roof came off, and its wheels went bounding in all directions under the pressure of an explosion that turned it into so much more junk in this junkyard city. And as Gill felt the hot air wash over him, gripped the catwalk's rail even tighter, and ducked down, so he began to hear the clang and spatter of nuts, bolts, and lesser debris raining from the sky, and the occasional secondary explosion as the train made its final complaints.

After a count of three, when he dared to look up—

He saw a great blackened patch in the bed of the gorge, and smoke rising from train remnants scattered in a radius of a hundred or so feet around the involuntary suicide's last observed location. Of the scorpion:

A scored, blackened mandible twirled lazily in the smoky air, and finally smacked down onto a pile of rubble on the far side of the gorge. But apart from that, and the tinkle of lesser litter still falling from on high, nothing stirred and there was a quite wonderful silence . . .

Jack Turnbull came down to meet them, joined up with Gill and his party halfway through the weary climb back up the wall of the scrap-metal canyon, and helped them through the rest of it. Along the way, while the women and Ki-no Sung paused to rest, Gill and the minder moved a little apart to have a chat in private.

"So that's that." Turnbull shrugged, after Gill explained the wreck of the train. "It looks like we won't be hitching a ride out into the rust desert—not unless there's more than one train?"

"Not even then," Gill told him. "When the train blew, it took a section of the tracks with it. They were buckled out of shape. And anyway"—he managed a grin—"I never worked out the timetable." Then he let the grin slip and said, "There's something else that bothers me."

"Really?" Turnbull said. "Just one thing? Well do tell."

"Did you get Waite's tooth?"

"Yes, and just as well, because it was loose and starting to flap. I jammed it into a chunk of scrap, threw it as far as I could manage into the gorge. Right now poor old George is up there holding his jaw. But so what? This place won't leave him in pain for too long."

"You threw it into the gorge? *Hmmm!*" said Gill.

"Oh?"

"Well, that could explain why Sith sent the second scorpion out through a screen at the bottom of the gorge. Since the bug was down there, he thought that was our location, too. The bastard was lucky; it *was* in fact my location, if not everyone else's."

The minder shook his head. "Doesn't work," he said. "See, I didn't think to get rid of the tooth until *after* I heard the train blow. By then, we'd almost made it back to our original entry point, the junkyard cave."

"So how did Sith know where we were?" Gill scratched his chin and thought about the presence—the eyes—that Angela had been sensing. "But anyway, and since he did know . . . maybe he knows where we are right now, too! But how?"

Again the minder's shrug. And wearily he said, "One down and one to go, maybe?" He glanced casually in the direction of the women and the Chinaman, let his eyes linger a moment on Ki-no Sung. "But anyway, it's like you said before: all guesswork until we have proof. Meanwhile, Spencer my boy, this is Sith's game. It's his fucking game, and while Sith's the gamesmaster you can bet your life the snakes will come a damn sight faster than the ladders."

"Bet my life?" Gill answered. "I thought we already had?"

"Bad choice of words," said Turnbull.

"Oh!" Gill suddenly remembered the dog. "Have you by any chance seen Barney?"

"Last time I saw him was when we were near the cave."

"Near the cave?" Gill repeated. "Where we first came through?"

"That's the one." Turnbull nodded.

Gill's frown lifted, and likewise a little of his gloom. "Let's get going," he said, and the minder sensed something in his voice. Could it be hope?

"Did I say something, tell you something?"

"You might have, Jack," Gill answered. "Indeed, you just might have. And that old dog, he could be trying to tell us a whole lot more. I think it's time we started listening to him. Perhaps more carefully from now on . . ."

CHAPTER
20

"S OME OF THE screens are doors," Gill summed the situation up as best he could. "It could be that they're all doors, but we daren't try them. If we go near them Sith is likely to see us, and by now he's got to be just a bit pissed at us. So we don't want to go running about in the open giving him too many chances to even the score. Our second-best bet was a door that we know exists in the rust desert in a rust-worm mound. The only way to get to that—and by no means a safe way—was aboard that rattletrap of a train. But the train has blown itself to hell, the track's knackered, and that route is definitely out. So, here we are right back where we started in this mechanical mausoleum, our so-called 'cave.' It's now late afternoon, and we have food and water for maybe three or four days at most." He looked from face to face. "Any ideas?"

They had each eaten a bite or two of food, taken a sip of water. But in trying to conserve what little remained, they'd left themselves unsatisfied, still hungry or thirsty or both; and all of them ached from their heads to their toes. In fact that last wasn't so bad. Though aches and pains weren't injuries or "illnesses" as such, still they knew that the House of Doors would restore their strength far more quickly than they could ever hope for in the "real" or unsynthesized world. But with regard to food . . . quite simply, there was no compensating. When the food ran out, then they must weaken.

"Ideas?" Miranda eventually, tiredly answered Gill. "How to get out of here, do you mean? That's your department, Spencer. On food: I could eat a horse! As for drink: a gin and it will do just fine, thank you. Oh, yes, and I know that should I ever sleep again I'll dream of bathing. Sorry, but those are the only 'ideas' I'm able to come up with right now. Well, no, there is one other. Not even an idea, really, but more a self-appraisal: that I must be a complete *idiot* to be wearing what I'm wearing in a godless, god-awful, goddam place like this!" And they all knew that for once Miranda wasn't complaining—just stating a fact.

She was still dressed in her trouser suit, which was rust red now, especially around the seat and knees. As for her white blouse: its frills were crumpled, greasy, and flecked with rust. Worst of all, the heels of her fashionable shoes had long since broken off and been discarded, leaving her feet housed in shallow, scratched, battered relics of shoes that wouldn't see her through another morning. And there she sat, rocking herself in the hollow curve of what looked like a tractor's mudguard, and tenderly massaging her feet.

The rest of them, apart from Ki-no Sung, had come fairly well prepared, at least where clothing was concerned. And even Sung was wearing one of Turnbull's hand-me-downs, an old ex-army pullover. Stannersly had the protection of his flying suit and boots, and when Turnbull had equipped himself in Newport, he'd also picked up gear for George Waite. So in that respect, they weren't badly off . . . except for Miranda. Tall, slim, and leggy—and very lovely, and no less dirty—she looked like . . .

"Like a fireplace elf!" said the minder, grinning.

Miranda looked up, seemed surprised at first, then angry to discover that his comment was directed at her. Finally she scowled at him, and snapped, "A what?"

"An elf who lives in the fireplace," he said, straightening from where he kept watch at the exit hole. "Dirty and cute, and—"

"Cute?" Miranda had never been called cute before, never in her life; which was because boys and later men had usually been frightened or in awe of her. But there wasn't a lot that frightened a man like Jack Turnbull. "A cute, dirty elf?" She clenched her fists . . . then relaxed them and, despite herself, grinned with him. "So what does that make you, Mr. Turnbull? A caveman, or perhaps a troll?"

"Just Jack, to my friends," he said. And then, shrugging unselfconsciously: "And a troll, yes, if you fancy—*especially* if that's what you fancy!—but a damn good-looking one, you have to admit. So let's settle for troll-*like*, okay?"

"Too true." George Waite rubbed his jaw ruefully. "I can certainly vouch for the fact that you *hit* like one!"

"Sorry about that," said Turnbull, and he meant it.

Meanwhile Angela had noticed the state of Miranda's shoes. And feeling guilty (though in fact she knew she shouldn't, because it was proving hard enough simply to look after herself) she dug into her miraculous sausage bag and brought out a pair of rugged walking shoes. "My boots will do just fine for me," she told Miranda. "But you might like to try these on."

Miranda tried them, said, "They're maybe just a fraction too small. But you know what? I don't give a damn! Thanks Angela. I won't lace them up too tight, that's all."

And Gill said, "Is that it? No more ideas?"

"Well I know you have one," Turnbull told him.

"Oh?"

"You've been perky for a couple of hours now," the minder said, "ever since we met up on the canyon wall. Tired but optimistic. So why don't you let us all in on it?"

"Because that's all it is, an idea," Gill answered. "I'll keep it to myself for now, till after we've rested up. Then, if it doesn't come to anything, at least we'll be refreshed. And I personally won't feel like such a failure."

"You're not a failure!" Angela started to protest. "No one could possibly have foreseen—"

"Idea," said Ki-no Sung abruptly, stopping Angela dead in her tracks and startling them all. Seated upon a massive anvil, he thumbed his chest and said again, "Me, idea. No, *two* idea! I got."

They looked at him, waited.

"One: is dream," he said, opening his arms to indicate the others, the cave, everything. "Is *all* bad dream! This." He held up his stump, completely healed now. "Bad dream. This place not real, bad dream. I come and go, slip in and out. I here—I not here. I remember . . . things. Not remember things. Is bad dream, ev'thing."

"Well, he's right there," said Gill, when it appeared that Sung was done. "It's at least built from a dream, and a bad one at that: my worst nightmare. But what in hell is all this other stuff about? He says he's slipping in and out? And there's something wrong with his memory?"

"Two," said Ki-no Sung, holding up two fingers. "If no bad dream, if real . . . we got food!" He pointed at Barney sleeping in a corner, where he had been since they got back to the cave. "We eat dog!"

"*Christ!*" Turnbull exploded. But Gill held up a hand, and said:

"Calm down. Sung's an oriental after all, and they do eat dogs. At least I think they do. And he doesn't understand that Barney is . . . important to us."

"Or maybe he does," said Angela, suspicious of the Chinaman as never before, and furious to boot.

But Gill quickly glanced at her—at Turnbull and Stannersly, too—and his single meaningful glance contained a warning. If Sith were listening, a verbal attack on Ki-no Sung now would let the alien know that *both* of his spies, or his spying devices, had been discovered. That was, of course, if Sung was in fact Sith's dupe. But now that he'd advocated eating Barney, it could be seen how he might be just such a dupe. It was obvious that Angela thought so, anyway.

In any case the three got Gill's message and at once settled down, leaving Waite and Miranda to wonder what it was all about.

And Sung looked at them, one after the other, shrugged, and said, "Me idea no good? No matter. Wake up soon . . . maybe." But he couldn't stop his eyes from swiveling toward Barney.

Before the others could start up again, Gill said, "Ki-no Sung, it's your watch I think." Indicating the cave's exit, he touched a finger to his cheek just under his eye. And as Turnbull searched for a place to make comfortable, Sung uncomplainingly replaced him at the exit.

But it was as if Barney was aware that he'd been under discussion; perhaps he had been about to wake up when he heard his name spoken. Now, looking exhausted, he came out of his corner, shook himself into a cloud of red rust motes, limped across to Gill.

"It's okay, old son," Gill told him. "You're not about to be eaten. In fact, it's the other way about." The dog's nose was dry, his paws rough; indeed, when he pawed Gill they left blood on his combat jacket. Also, the red streaks of rust on Barney's coat seemed stuck there as if by sweat that had since dried. So what kind of exertions had the dog been getting up to?

Gill opened a can of corned beef, sliced it up, and fed it to Barney piece by piece; no one said a word. He took his water bottle, poured a little into his palm, and let the dog lap, then moistened a handkerchief, dampened Barney's nose, and wiped rust from the corners of his brown eyes. Barney blinked, looked up, and up, and . . .

Gill followed his gaze. To the compacted metal ceiling of the cave nine feet overhead.

Rust drifted like dust from on high, getting into everything—getting into your eyes, too, if you were looking up at the ceiling. But what was Barney looking at? Or . . . what was he looking for? And what had he been doing, to cut up his paws like this?

And Gill thought: *Maybe I should tell them what my idea is right now. But if I do and if I'm right, what if it's a case of out of the frying pan into the fire? But on the other hand, how could anything be worse than this?* The trouble was, of course, that he knew it could.

The dog was still looking at the ceiling and beginning to whine, and

Fred Stannersly had noticed. "Is he losing it?" The pilot came over to where Gill sat with Barney. "Is he cracking up?"

Gill shook his head. "I don't think so. I think that while we've been climbing up and down—or down and up—that bloody canyon, Barney has been busy as hell. But the task he'd set himself was just too much for him." And now Gill, too, was looking at the ceiling.

Stannersly frowned, said, "Something up there? Junk metal is all I see. About a million tons of it. And I don't much like it. No, I'm not claustrophobic, or not much, but it's the open skies for me every time. And when I think about what's pressing down on us . . ."

"Try not to," Gill advised.

Jack Turnbull had joined them. Elbowing Gill gently in the ribs, he whispered, "Look!"

The light coming into the cave was very dim now. Outside, glimpsed through the roughly oval entrance, the atomic sun was setting way out over the rust desert. And sitting in that entrance, Ki-no Sung seemed strangely hypnotized. He sat still as could be, with only his eyes moving, shining in the gloom. And they moved first this way—and after a few seconds that way—and so back to square one, where the sequence started again.

Stannersly whispered, "Is it this place, or what? I mean, are we all slowly going mad?"

George Waite and the two women were getting to their feet. They were aware that something was going on, but what? Gill motioned them to silence, crept up behind Ki-no Sung, looked where he was looking.

Across the gorge, something glittered in the last rays of the sun. Sung was looking at it. And as he turned his head, so Gill followed his line of sight. The second thing the Chinaman looked at was similar to the first: a point of silver-gleaming light maybe a quarter mile away, along the wall of the canyon. Then, after a moment, back to the first point of light, and so on.

Gill moved to one side a little, stumbled on machine junk, put a hand on Sung's shoulder to steady himself. And the little man took no notice whatsoever, just kept looking at the distant glimmers, their reflections mirrored in his own dark eyes.

Morse code? No, not that. There was no message here; only Sung's gaze was repetitious. Radio beacons? Uh-uh. Or could it be the sun reflecting off giant screens? Whichever, Sung definitely formed part of a triangle here.

Triangulation!

And even as Gill started in sudden realization—in the knowledge of what was going on here, if not how—he saw something more than just a glimmer. On this side of the canyon, the second "reflection" was no longer reflecting . . . it was putting out zigzagging arcs of electrical fire and brilliant bursts of incendiary fireworks. A screen, yes, which was now a door!

"You lousy spying bastard!" Gill cried, grabbing Sung by the front of his pullover and shaking him. But the expression on the Chinaman's face didn't change; he just wasn't there. He *really* wasn't there; he'd "slipped out" again. So what use for Gill to take his spite out on him? It wasn't him—it was the person or thing on the other side of Sung's eyes that Gill was mad at.

And turning to the minder, he said, "He doesn't know. He's just like George, bugged and he doesn't know it. But it's different with Ki-no Sung, it goes deeper. Literally deeper. You're right, Jack—it has to be an implant."

"I'll implant the little—" Turnbull advanced.

"Hold it," said Gill, alarmed. "Can't you see it's not his fault? He's been got at."

But Sung had slipped in again. Since he'd served his purpose this time around, Sith was no longer controlling him. And, "Look!" Sung cried, slumping as Gill released him. "You *look!*"

Gill stuck his head out of the exit—and at once shrank back inside. "A scorpion," he said. "The last rays of the sun, glancing off its armor. It's maybe four hundred yards away and coming straight for us. But this canyon wall isn't the easiest of terrains. Getting here will take time."

"Another scorpion?" Miranda gasped, hopping from one foot to the other. "How many of those things are there?"

"As many as Sith needs," Angela told her breathlessly. "He makes them, synthesizes them."

"Time for us to move out!" Turnbull slung his machine gun over his shoulder. But Gill shook his head.

"Maybe, maybe not," he said. "Jack, give me a hand."

"Eh?"

"There's a section of ladder outside. It's a mess of rust, but usable I think."

"To do what?"

"To get me up there, or to get Barney up there." He looked at the ceiling.

And Fred Stannersly got it. "We dropped out of there," he said. "Like from the sky. So obviously we fell from somewhere."

"From that swamp in the Castle," Gill said with a nod.

"We're going back *there?*" Miranda shrilled.

"Not necessarily," Gill said, leaving the cave with Turnbull close behind.

"Not necessarily?" the minder repeated him, but under his breath. "Or is it that you're just being hopeful, cheerful, for their sakes? For mine, maybe?"

"Hopeful, cheerful?" Gill answered. "Jesus, Jack—I don't even know what I'm doing! *I* don't, but Barney does—I hope. He didn't get cut up trying to climb that wall of junk in the cave for the fun of it. Didn't work himself into a sweat, half blind himself, fall asleep from sheer exhaustion for nothing."

"No, he did it to go back to that swamp!"

"Wrong. It's all in the nose, Jack. And when he's hungry, that Barney has one hell of a nose. It's my bet he smells something good. And as for myself, I can't remember one good thing about that swamp. Ergo: Barney was trying for somewhere else."

"You're sure?"

"No, I'm not sure. How can I be sure? But didn't Sith say he'd reprogrammed the synthesizer to play a game of Snakes and Ladders? What kind of a game would it be if every fucking move landed us on a snake? So like I said, maybe Barney was trying for somewhere else."

"Okay," the big minder said. "You've convinced me. I want to try for somewhere else, too. Let's do it. *Huh!*—and with a real ladder, too!"

Fred Stannersly had joined them along with Ki-no Sung; between them they wrested a length of rusty ladder from the junk jumble that made up the mountain of mechanical scrap. But even as they passed it through the cave's door there came a screech of rending metal from somewhere not too far removed, and a moment later the thunder of dislodged debris cartwheeling into the canyon.

The sun was almost down now, leaving a dusty (no, a *rusty*) haze, a great many angular shadows, and a momentary silence. So that the minder paused to sniff the air, and said: "What do you reckon, Spencer? Did our ugly pal lose his balance back there—I hope?"

"No way." Gill shook his head. "Don't you remember? One of those things climbed down a sheer cliff with me clinging to its back! No, that was just him clearing the way ahead—on his way to us."

Inside, they wedged the ladder in the middle of the floor, held it steady while Gill took Barney under one arm and climbed to the top. Then, wrapping a leg around one of the uprights, he took the dog in both hands and held him up to the tangled metal ceiling. Or tried to. But Barney only let Gill lift him so far, until his back paws found purchase on Gill's shoulders. Then he kicked—kicked upward! And with a yelp (a glad one, from the sound of it) he left Gill's arms . . .

And disappeared!

"*Shit!*" Turnbull gaped, his jaw falling open. But a moment later he was hoisting Angela onto the ladder.

"Come on, let's go!" said Gill, moving onto the other side of the ladder to balance the rickety thing and let Angela pass.

Passing him, she kissed him between rungs, said, "Don't be last. I couldn't take the suspense."

His hand under her backside, pushing her through into the next world, was Gill's only answer.

Miranda came next, and Gill could hear her breathing, "Oh, damn! Oh, hell! Oh, shit!" as she climbed. And from outside as she vanished, the shriek of tortured metal and clatter of collapsing scaffolding.

"The bastard's coming!" Turnbull yelled.

"Fred next," Gill shouted. And as the pilot climbed past him, so a deceptively soft, feathery feeler began to probe the cave's entrance—only to be withdrawn a moment later, making way for a pair of great claws that begin ripping at the hole's sides, enlarging it.

"Now you, George," Gill yelled. "For Christ's sake, move it!" And George moved it. Then it was Turnbull's turn, but as he and Gill came face-to-face, Gill hoarsely whispered: "Sung will be next. As he emerges—well, wherever—take no chances but put him on ice."

"My plan exactly," the minder muttered. And followed it up with: "I didn't know you were in the circus?" Then he was gone, and Gill suddenly knew what he meant.

But despite having only one hand, the Chinaman might well have been in a circus! He came swarming up the ladder, balancing the thing as he came. By which time everything was shaking, even the cave itself, as the scorpion tore at the entrance and thrust its head and mandibles inside.

Sung climbed past Gill, reached up . . .

And the scorpion crashed into the cave, its mandibles scything at the foot of the ladder, slicing right through its rotten frame and rusty rungs.

At the last possible moment Gill let go his hold on the ladder, stretched his arms upward, tried to leap for the ceiling. Instead of propelling him up, his kick pushed the crumpling, swaying ladder down. And all around the cave was collapsing, its walls caving in on the invading monster.

And:

Oh, hell! Gill thought—then went blank as he felt his right hand gripped and his body drawn upward.

For a moment that he'd thought must be his last, Gill had closed his eyes; now, opening them a crack, he saw Ki-no Sung's grin framed in a full moon, and alien stars wheeling in a night sky. Then, opening them farther, he saw the others all gathered around, felt solid ground beneath his back, and an unbelievably sweet breeze blowing through the rustling leaves of what could only be a forest.

And finally Gill saw who it was who was still gripping his hand, the lithe yellow arm that had drawn him up out of hell.

"Ki-no Sung!" he said, stupidly, as the little man's grip slackened, and his grin, too, when the big minder hit him . . .

CHAPTER
21

"OUCH!" SAID GILL, wincing. "I felt that one myself."

"Yes, but don't go thinking I enjoyed it," Turnbull growled, looking at his handiwork where Ki-no Sung's sprawled body made a dark shadow on the ground. "I didn't, but I didn't see any alternative. And I was only following your instructions."

George Waite got the idea, said, "Like the three wise monkeys in one, eh? See no evil, hear no evil—speak no evil."

But Miranda had taken the minder's arm and was glaring at him face-to-face, hers pale in milky moonlight. "Jack Turnbull, what on *earth* are you doing?" she demanded. "I mean, didn't I just a moment ago see that poor little man save Spencer's life by dragging him out of . . . out of *there*, into . . . into *here*?"

"Miranda," Angela intervened, sighing. "Can I ask you: do you by any chance know where 'here' is?"

"No, of course not! Back home, I hope. It certainly feels like it."

"But it isn't," said Angela. "Not unless we suddenly have a second moon!" And there it was, floating over the horizon. A shining disk half as big again as the first one.

Miranda looked, saw, deflated a little. After a moment she said, "So what's your point? I mean, what's that got to do with Jack hitting people?"

"But isn't it obvious?" Angela said. "Since this isn't our world, it's one of Sith's. Sith has been using Sung as his eyes and ears. Sung has some kind of implant. Through him Sith knows where we are—even if we don't. But if Sung can't see or hear, then Sith's blind, too—we hope."

Miranda let it sink in, and said, "But in George's case it was a simple bug."

And as Gill shakily stood up and brushed himself down, he explained: "That's true, but we actually *saw* Ki-no Sung in action, acting on Sith's behalf, or at least obeying his commands. So you see Angela's right. Whether it's involuntary or not, Ki-no Sung isn't going to be spying or following anyone's instructions while he's out cold."

"And you'll . . . well, keep him that way? But how?" Miranda had a point.

And Turnbull said, "There is a way to keep him that way—and permanently. But I don't think I'm up to that just yet. And God knows I hope I never am. But if it comes to it . . . it seems to me the vote's six to one. Our lives against his."

"No," said Gill, looking around in the twilight; but a predawn or an evening twilight, it was hard to say. "It won't come to that, not ever. We'd simply ditch him first."

"Ditch him?" From Fred Stannersly.

"We would go our way, and he would go his," Gill answered grimly. "After that, the next move would be up to Sith."

"But . . . that poor man *helped* you!" Miranda knew that Gill was right; her protest sprang from the sheer frustration of the situation.

"It's like Sung himself said," Gill replied. "He 'slips in and out.' When he's in, he's with us, but when he's out . . . then he's with Sith."

"And for now?" George Waite was down on one knee, checking on Sung's condition.

"Oh, he's *out* all right," said Turnbull, "but right now he isn't *with* anyone."

"Tie his hands," Angela said—then shuddered and corrected herself, "I mean his feet. Blindfold him, too. That way, if he doesn't know where he is Sith won't either."

"Good!" said Stannersly. "That makes sense. But while he's unconscious, shouldn't we first get away from here? Won't Sith have these crossover points between worlds mapped out? How long before he starts looking for us again? Sooner or later, surely he's bound to look right here—wherever here is."

"And for that matter," said Miranda, who was really thinking now, "why hasn't that bloody dreadful thing, that scorpion, followed us through?"

"My turn to do the carrying," Gill said, hoisting Sung across his shoulder in a fireman's lift. "We move, but with caution." Then, to Miranda: "As for the scorpion: the last time I—*uh!*—saw him, he was having a bad day. I think he pulled the whole cave down on himself, for which we can all thank our lucky stars. But you never know with those damn things, so we'd better get a move on."

And they did . . .

Dawn!" Fred Stannersly said some thirty minutes later. "Dawn, and coming up a lot faster than on Earth. The only time I ever saw the sun rise as quickly was when I was flying east."

By then they had made their way out of what seemed to be a walled, circular, overgrown garden (the place where they'd materialized), fought through a strip of densely grown rain-forest type vegetation, then climbed the huge stone steps of an amphitheaterlike structure. That last had been something of a climb—maybe four hundred feet vertical—and now exhausted they sat on the topmost steps, rested bone-weary bodies, stared out over a warm, tropical jungle world, and watched the sun come up.

"Any ideas?" Turnbull said, where he tore an arm from Ki-no Sung's pullover, cut a hole in it for the mouth, and pulled it down over the Chinaman's head. The minder had already fastened Sung's good right arm and hand to his side, immobilizing them, and the little man's ears were stuffed with wadding. If he couldn't hear or see what was going on, then neither could Sith. That was the theory, anyway, but for the moment it was academic; Sung was still out like a light.

"Ideas?" said Gill. "Do you mean like where we are? Well somewhere we've never been before, that seems certain. These ruins look real enough to me. In a way they're familiar, like old Aztec stuff, maybe? But the stars are all wrong, and the vegetation in that jungle was really different, sort of prehistoric? Hazarding a guess, I'd say this was a world the Thone looked over one time but didn't settle. Or maybe they did and then moved on. Anyway, it's obviously a part of their synthesized 'library,' shelved from previous visits."

"Thone?" said Miranda. "I thought we were up against the Ggyddn now?"

"But the Castle is a Thone synthesizer," Angela reminded her. "Sith may be Ggyddn now, but he's still using the previous owner's technology." And:

"How about that?" said Turnbull. "This Thone-Ggyddn thing? I mean, how come Sith now claims to be Ggyddn."

Gill could only shrug. "Beats me," he said. "But right now anything would beat me. *I* am beat! Dead beat. And I'm hungry. I suggest we eat, wait for the sun to come up more fully and get some idea of our surroundings, and then sleep. We'll also need to keep a watch, if only for Sung's sake; make sure he doesn't 'slip out' again and try to get up to something sneaky. And"—he looked all around, sighed deeply, and offered a second weary shrug—"and wait for Barney to catch up with us."

"Damn!" said George Waite. "Why must that dog keep doing this to us?" For quite some time and with the single exception of Sung, Waite had been the quietest of them all. But now he seemed to be leaving his general air of gloom behind. His tooth was no longer problematic; even the gap it had left at the back of his jaw had long since healed. But best of all, he no longer suffered from the constant, nagging headaches that had plagued him for months.

That last had been on his mind, though, for which reason, out of the blue, he now said: "It's a hell of a thing, but you know, just when I get the feeling that this is working—that being here in the House of Doors is actually killing this lump in my head—I'm beginning to doubt if I'll ever get back home to enjoy the feeling!"

Gill almost commented, *Or how long you'll have* left *to enjoy it if we do get back!*—but he somehow managed not to.

And meanwhile the sun had come up—except there were two of them! Two moons, and now two suns to match.

And Turnbull told Stannersly, "I'd be willing to bet that you never saw anything like *that* when you were flying east!"

The larger of the suns was Sol size; golden, it could be Earth's sun. The other was small, hot, and white. And it constantly gave off plasma streamers that warped and twined about each other, and were almost as long as the parent body's diameter.

"A fiery little bloke," Fred Stannersly commented thoughtfully, and added: "Would you just look at this place? It might easily be the Amazon . . ."

Miranda nodded and said, "A South American jungle, you're right. Or maybe Mexico, with all these amphitheaters, temples, altars, and such. But inhabited? Surely it must be."

And all of them scanned far and away across the canopy of a forest that reached to the horizon and was only broken where enormous circular structures reared, or partly collapsed ruins in the tiered shape of olde-world beehives like vast, circular step-pyramids. But the hives of what gigantic bees? And glyph-carved monoliths spied through the treetops, and lesser ruins in the green-tangled deeps.

"Personally," Angela said, but very quietly, "I hope that it isn't inhabited. Yes, I very much hope that it isn't . . ."

They all looked where she was looking. Behind them on the rim of the great amphitheater, standing stones had been carved with other than glyphs. And the pictures that came to light as the shadows fell back and the twin suns rose higher yet told a story all their own. A tale not only of alien intelligence but also of war, or slaughter, primitive worship, and bloody sacrifice.

Gill got up, went to the nearest stele or menhir, and followed the weathered carvings with his fingers. He sensed ages of time sped by, antiquity oozing from the pitted stone, the desolation of the eons. Yet paradoxically the stone was empty to his sixth sense, the creature who had carved it had known little or nothing of science, machinery, or tools as man knows them. These marks, pictorials, patterns, stories, were all—

"Hand-carved," said the minder quietly from behind him. "Or claw-carved, certainly. On their 'hands' or forelegs there, those jointed, prehensile index claws. Really great for cutting grooves in stone. Or for cutting anything for that matter. Razor sharp, I'd guess . . ."

The rest of the party had spread out; they were examining other standing stones, following their story. And the artists of the race who had written it had left little to the imagination.

However primitive, the pictures were detailed, stylized in their presentation of the planet's principal life-forms, namely the ones who had carved or "clawed" them. They were—or *had been,* as Angela and now the rest of Gill's party desired it—insects or insectlike, but large: man-sized and then some, and warriors! Like weird hybrid mutations, perhaps a cross between giant stag beetles and the Minotaur of Earthly legend, the creatures had gone on four rear legs, holding up the smaller forelegs before them to bear arms.

Barbed spears seemed to have been their principal weapons, with shields of chitin or giant fish scales. But since many of the scenes showed warriors with broken "stag" horns, obviously their grotesque head adornments, too, had been terrible weapons of war. They had also worn armor to protect their joints, and carried banners with staghorn insignia.

"They took prisoners," said Turnbull. "For sacrifice . . ."

"Lesser creatures," said Miranda, "more primitive yet, yet more like us, too. Animals at least, as opposed to insects. But six-legged animals?"

"Six-legged cave-or forest-dwellers," Gill murmured quietly. "See, they wore loincloths, covered their parts . . ." Then, as Turnbull touched his shoulder, he gave a start and withdrew from his musing reverie.

"Are you sure we weren't here before?" the minder said.

Gill knew what he meant. "What, the forest world?" he answered. "The world of the Mansion and those poor, wild fawnlike creatures that Haggie wanted to eat?"

"It was Earth-like," Turnbull insisted. "And while we didn't see all of it, still it had its share of six-legged stuff, too."

"All nature has its share of those," Gill said, shrugging. "Which includes our own world. But no, I don't think so. You're forgetting the two moons, and the twin suns. The world of the Mansion had only one of each."

"Yet I know what Jack means," said Angela, frowning. "This place . . . it *feels* much the same, you know?"

"They used to cut out their hearts," said Miranda faintly, still morbidly fascinated by scenes of sacrifice. "They daubed their horns with their blood, and laid their eggs in the bodies of their victims." Shuddering violently, she said, "God, I hate this place!"

"We all do," Waite told her. "But isn't that the problem? How to get out of here?"

"Somewhere, there has to be a door," Gill said, trying to shake off his weariness both mental and physical, and failing.

"Like the last time?" Miranda sounded hopeful. "Where we came in, maybe?"

Gill shook his head. "Too accessible. And I need time to think. And to be truthful, I'm knackered. All of us are, must be. It's only adrenaline—terror—that's kept us going this long. But I find that I can't think straight. So I say again: let's eat, sleep, wait till the suns are more fully up."

"*Huh!*" said the minder, opening his pack to break out rations and pass them around, though no one seemed eager to accept them. "Sure, we could all use some sleep. The problem is, will we be able to? Sleep, I mean."

"Give it a try anyway," Gill advised.

"No," Turnbull answered, seating himself with his back to a standing stone. "I don't reckon I will. Instead, I think I'll take first watch. That's if no one minds."

"And I'll stay awake with you," Miranda shivered, sat down beside him in the shade of the stele.

"Are you cold?" he said. "You'll warm up when the suns are up. And listen, the forest is coming awake!" There were hooting noises, bird sounds, gentle rustlings from the jungle.

She snuggled closer to him, and closer yet as she felt the warmth from the minder's body. And as exhaustion conquered fear, the others began to make themselves as comfortable as possible. In a little while they would all be fast asleep.

And they were, while Turnbull and Miranda huddled together to greet the sun . . .

*   *   *

But as the temperature rose, and drew up a mist to wreathe the treetops—like a lake of milk that gradually covered the canopy of the sprawling woods—Miranda said, "You know something, Jack Turnbull, you're full of surprises."

"Really?"

"Oh, yes. I overheard something you said to Spencer, about the creatures who carved these stones: their 'jointed, prehensile index claws.' "

"So?"

"Well, it was hardly the kind of statement or sort of observation a person might expect from someone like you. I mean, it was out of character, somehow."

He nodded. "Meaning I look much too dumb—too brutish?—to be talking that kind of stuff, right?" He turned toward her and grinned with strong, even teeth. And before she could answer: "Miranda, my letting you hear me speak like that was a mistake," he said. "The sort of thing that can blow a man's cover, ruin his image. Me and my big mouth! But now that you ask:

"See, all my life I've made the wrong choices. When I was a kid, I was into marine biology, archaeology, paleontology, all the ologies you can mention. But I couldn't settle on a single one of them and so lost them all—lost my chances, if you see what I mean. And anyway, there were girls out there, and adventures to be had, exotic places to be seen. My body wasn't built for sitting behind a desk, or in a museum, and my hands weren't made for scraping dust off old bones. I had a lot of energy and nothing much to do with it. By the time I hit eighteen the army seemed a good idea; and it was, in that it led to other things. Military Intelligence, gunrunner, mercenary . . . hey, you name it. I tried them all, finally settled for minder: close protection. But stupid? Me? Ask Gill and he'll tell you otherwise."

"I didn't mean—" she began to say, but he cut her short with:

"*Shhh!* The others will wake up, hear what you're trying to say. Then my image will really be shot! Anyway, you're one to talk. You're not quite who you seem to be either."

"Oh?"

"Naaaah!" he growled, still grinning. "What, you? The big iceberg? Hard-hearted Hannah? The iron maiden? When I was obliged to deal with George, you were mad at me. When I smacked Ki-no Sung, you were really upset! And the pictures on these obelisks, menhirs, or whatever: these were *alien* things, and by the age of the stones, the looks of the creatures on them, they're long gone from this or any other world. But you . . . you really *felt* for the little guys, like they were your personal friends and it had all happened yesterday. So there you go—I've got your number. You have a soft center, Big Boss Lady."

She looked about to argue, then changed her mind, snuggled closer still, and said nothing.

"Still cold?" he said.

"Uh-huh. Tired."

"So go to sleep. It's okay. I'm the solitary type."

But as Miranda Marsh began to breathe more deeply into his collar, and finally, softly to snore, the minder told himself:

Or at least I used to be the solitary type.

So maybe this time he'd make the right choice for once. And anyway, weren't opposites supposed to attract? It certainly worked from Turnbull's point of view. Now all he had to do was convince her . . .

Barney woke them up; all of them except Angela, who was keeping watch. And Barney had brought them breakfast. He woke them with his whipping stump of a tail, his mincing about and wet ministrations, his barked greetings.

Gill examined Barney's catch, got a fire going. "Six-legged rabbits!" he said. "No wonder the old dog's fond of this place. He's been here before. And since he doesn't seem much afraid of our surroundings, maybe we shouldn't be either."

As he gutted and cooked the rabbits—for that's what they were, more or less, or two legs more—Angela said, "Aren't you worried they could be poisonous?"

"See that dog?" Gill said. "He was scrawny the last time we saw him, downright miserable-looking. But right now he's as fat as butter. What do you reckon he's been eating?"

"Rabbit," she said, nodding. And: "You're probably right. He was a gamekeeper's dog after all. He should know what's good and what isn't."

"Just smelling that roasting meat"—Waite grinned—"I can tell you what's good! The way my stomach is rumbling, I'd probably risk it anyway. And come to think of it, what have we got to lose?"

And so they ate; Ki-no Sung, too, through the hole in his sleeve mask. But the little Chinaman wasn't himself; or rather, he was different again—though in what way it would have been hard to say, for they didn't know him well enough. But while he made no real effort to break free of his restrictions, still he kept stretching his neck, as if something was bothering him. He sighed and groaned a lot, too, and barely touched his food.

"I didn't hit him that hard." Turnbull shook his head. "I didn't think so, anyway. Maybe he's just depleted. Which isn't surprising. Things are starting to catch up with me, too."

They ate in silence, wolfing the good meat. Between them Barney's rabbits didn't go too far, but at least they filled a gap. And as they finished up, Gill said, "I needed that sleep. For me, sleep has always been the clearing house of the waking world. I leave all the crap behind in dreams and come out with only the good stuff. Anyway, good or bad, I've been thinking."

"We're all ears," said Turnbull.

"Do you remember the last time?" Gill said. "Okay, I know you do. But I'm talking specifics now: namely, how we got saddled with Sith's nightmare scenario."

"You mean where the worlds we entered were all *our* worlds, created from our worst dreams come true?" This from Angela.

"Exactly," said Gill. "Or not exactly. But anyway, do you remember how it worked?"

"Sure," said the minder. "The first one through the door, whichever door it happened to be, set the scene. For me it was a bad time I had in Afghanistan. For Angela it was—"

"It was a paradise," she cut him off. "Until Sith filled it with replicas of my husband! And for you, Spencer—"

"It was the mad machine world," Gill took it up again. "That's right. So what I've been wondering is, is it the same this time? Is that how it works? Snakes and Ladders, Sith said. But he didn't say who was to roll the dice."

"You mean, *we* might be rolling them?" From Stannersly.

"Well sure we are," said Turnbull. "We're the players!"

"Who was first through that door in the swamp?" Gill was excited now. "I was. And where did we end up? The mad machine world. Because it had been on my mind from the moment I realized that things weren't right. Okay, let's work on that. Who was first through the invisible door in the roof of the cave?"

"I was," said Angela, looking mystified. "But what do I have in common with this place?"

"Nothing." Gill shook his head. "You see, that's just it. You *weren't* the first through. Barney was . . ."

"But Barney's a dog!" George Waite protested.

"And single-minded," said Gill. "*And* a player. Like it or not, Barney is part of the game. Personally, I like it. He's a dog, sure. So what? He's a very sane, very smart dog. And he's on our side."

"You were thinking of your machine world," Turnbull mused. "And you knocked on the door. Barney was thinking of six-legged rabbits, presumably. He came through first, and we all ended up here. Okay, that works for me. So . . . who's next for the dice?"

But Gill only nodded and said, "Let's work on that when we find the door."

CHAPTER
22

DOORS!" SAID GILL. "Or rather *the* door. There's got to be one or else there's no game. The problem is finding it, and as yet we don't have a clue. Well, personally it's not the first time I haven't had a clue. In the past I've usually stumbled across them as I've gone along—clues, I mean. And doors, too, come to think of it."

"But as we go along where?" George Waite looked out over a green expanse that reached to the horizon in all directions. "I mean, it strikes me that if we set out to go anywhere, we're as likely to be heading away from this magical door as toward it."

"Right," said Gill. "And that's precisely why we won't be going anywhere too far. See, when I said 'as we go,' I meant as we get on with the business of surviving. Look down there." He pointed down tiers of crumbling, creeper-grown steps on the outside of the amphitheater, through the forest canopy to a sparkling ribbon glimpsed through the leafy cover. "Water. A stream. God only knows when or even if we'll get another chance to top up. What I'm saying is, when we do find our door it might well be a case of out of the frying pan into the fire, you know? It could be that we're currently on a ladder, and our next throw will send us sliding down a snake. Well okay, but I would like to be prepared. We're very low now on our original food supply, and here we are surrounded by forest, game, fruits—who knows what other good things to eat—*if* they're good things to eat? So since for the moment we aren't going anywhere . . ."

Turnbull got it, said: "We should put the time to good use and do some harvesting? *Wow!* Here's me a hunter-gatherer, just like the little six-limbed types on these standing stones." And then, more seriously, "Teams?"

"Absolutely," said Gill. "No one is to go off on his or her own, and we all stay within hailing distance. Now that the morning chorus has quietened down a little, that last shouldn't be too difficult." Putting his hands to his mouth, he gave a loud halloo, which came echoing back again and again.

"Okay, teams," said the minder. "Me and Miranda. Er, someone should look after the weaker, fairer sex, right?"

"Right," said Gill, smiling despite their predicament. "And I'm sure she'll take good care of you! I'll be with Angela."

Stannersly looked at Waite, said, "So who's doing what? And for how long?"

"You and George, collect water," Gill said. "Take our empty bottles and top them up. *But* . . . I'd suggest you test the water first."

"How?" From Waite.

Gill thought about it, said, "Take the dog with you. If he won't drink, then we're probably out of luck."

"Those rabbit-things must drink," Miranda said.

"Right, but we don't know what from," Gill told her. "They could get their fluid nourishment from roots or leaves for all we know. What I'm saying is, play it by ear—but carefully."

"Okay," said Stannersly, "Barney accompanies me and George. And in the event he snaps up a couple of rabbits along the way, well so much the better."

And Turnbull said, "Myself, I think I'll try out the fruit. There were gourds in that overgrown patch in the middle of the garden last night. Also some weird-looking fruits in the trees. Why, this could be a regular Garden of Eden." He gave Miranda a sideways look that she avoided, but Gill was surprised to see a sudden flush on her unmade-up cheeks.

"Myself," said Gill, "Angela and I . . . we'll be looking for the door."

"With no clues?" Turnbull reminded him.

"No clues"—Gill shook his head—"but maybe a sixth sense." He tapped his nose. "These doors are gateways from the synthesizer into—I don't know—parallel worlds? Into spaces between the spaces we know, anyway. They're machine-made or conjured by a machine, like a file on a computer disk. And as you all know, I have a 'thing' for machines. So while you're off hunter-gathering or provisioning, I'll be trying to track down the door."

"Won't Barney know where it is?" said Waite. "If he's been here before, I mean?"

"He probably does," said Gill. "But have you tried seeing this from his point of view? Barney has companionship. And down there in the forest there's food aplenty. And he *knows* he doesn't like the other places he's visited. So . . . what would you do?"

"Nothing," said Waite, glancing enviously at Barney where he had curled himself up at the foot of a squat standing stone, half in, half out of the twin sunlight, and lay there blinking at his humans with one ear cocked.

"Damned right," said Gill. "But on the other hand we can't afford to lose him. So put him on a leash."

"I have some strong twine in my bag," said Angela. And as she went to get it, Gill continued:

"Timing. We daren't get split up, or stay too long apart. So let's all be back here in one hour. As for Ki-no Sung . . ."

"Leave him to me—" said the big minder.

Miranda gave a start, and at once said, "Jack!"

"And I'll bind him to that stone with a creeper," Turnbull continued. "We'll leave food and water close by, and I'll free his right hand and arm up to the elbow." Then, turning to Miranda innocently: "Er, was there something?"

A few minutes later when they were ready to set out, Gill said, "Okay, let's be back by midday. That is, when the major sun is about as high as it can get—maybe a little more than an hour, okay?"

They all agreed and set off in various directions down the outer steps . . .

And an hour later were back, as agreed. Turnbull and Miranda took just a few minutes longer than the rest, and looked just a little paler when they finally struggled up the broad outer circle of weathered steps.

"Problems?" Gill took Miranda's hand, drew her up onto the level.

"Some." She nodded weakly. "The fruits are out. And I mean definitely."

"Most of them," Turnbull added wrily. "The gourds are okay though; they're full of sweet water and helped to flush our systems. And believe me we needed to! You know what got us? Just a taste—I mean like the tips of our tongues—to a thing that was indistinguishable from a pear."

"And delicious," said Miranda. "But as Jack says we didn't eat, just tasted, then laid them aside to see what would happen. What happened was minced rabbit and corned beef. So, my stomach is back to square one—empty!"

"I, er—" Turnbull looked sheepish. "I tasted several different types of fruit. Just a taste, I promise. But the rest of them were just as vile, bitter, and volcanically, er, laxative? So it's like Miranda said: strike fruit."

And Fred Stannersly said, "But the nuts are great!" And in fact both he and Waite looked in fine fettle, buoyant and exuberant. They had brought back great clusters of nuts in the general shape of pineapples, that fell apart very easily into individual thumb-sized, soft-skinned kernels. And Stannersly went on: "These are what the rabbits eat. When these things fall out of the bushes, those little six-legged fellers are on 'em in a flash. And they get so pissy-eyed drunk that they're dead easy prey. Good old Barney here caught a couple more of 'em, as you see." He held up a brace of the creatures in question.

"How many nuts have you eaten?" Gill was concerned.

"Jus' a couple each," Waite affirmed. "They're damn good, Shpencer." And to Turnbull: "Hey, Jack! You could ferment some heavy-duty shtuff with these things!"

"Don't you just hate them?" Turnbull murmured to no one in particular. "It's like arriving late at a party to find everyone's stoned but you."

"How about the water?" said Gill.

"Watersh fine," Waite slurred it out. "Barney drinked—dranked—drunk—Jesus, am I!—drunk it, so we drunked it, too. 'S fine. Bottles all full." He sat down with a thump.

"Very well," said Gill, though he wasn't at all sure that it was. "We'll divide the nuts into our packs, and likewise the water and these small gourds. Later, we'll cook the rabbits for immediate consumption. But I would warn you off eating any more nuts for now. Let's see if there are any aftereffects—other than the obvious ones, that is."

"I could try . . . maybe one, do you think?" Turnbull licked his lips.

But Gill said, "I don't think *you* should try any!"

Meanwhile Miranda talked to Angela. "Obviously, you didn't find the door," she said.

Angela shook her head. "We went down outside the amphitheater, started to circumnavigate. But if this place is some two hundred and fifty yards across, that makes it about eight hundred yards around. Almost half a mile, and most of it dense jungle. Gill thought we might find a door down there. But no such luck. We got more than a third of the way, but knew that if we carried on we'd miss the first deadline. So we turned back."

As she finished speaking—coming out of the blue, startling them all—Ki-no Sung said, "Gill . . . Spencer Gill. It's time we talked, you and I."

The little Chinaman had loosened his bindings sufficiently that he'd been able to bend his body, reach up, and pull off his headgear. But that wasn't what stopped the others dead in their tracks. *That* was his voice— his dull, booming, ominous voice—which scarcely sounded like Sung's at all.

It came and went, fluctuating like a bad radio signal. And it was a voice that Gill knew and dreaded.

"Sith!" He sprang to Sung's side, tried to look him in the eyes. But Sung was turning his head, looking around in his own right, until finally he paused to gaze full upon Gill. Then:

"And so I am right. You returned to this place." At which Gill knew that it was Sith.

"Just a lucky throw," Gill answered—taken by surprise, not knowing what else to say—as he stared into Sung's black, unyielding, and now penetrating eyes. But:

"No," said Sith/Sung. "An *un*lucky throw!" And the eyes in Sung's face left Gill and turned upward to the twin suns, for just the merest moment, before returning to Gill. "Do you know where you are?"

"Do you?" Gill was recovering, felt strengthened when the others gathered around him.

"No word games, Gill," said Sith. "You have just ten minutes to live. Will you waste them being clever?"

Jack Turnbull was looking where Sith/Sung had looked. The suns? Was there something wrong with the small one? "That small sun is acting strange," the big minder said. "It's throwing out streamers like crazy, bulging or blistering at the equator. And it seems to be drawing closer to its big brother."

"That is not its brother, Mr. Turnbull," said Sith. "That is the reason the Thone didn't claim this world—or why they did, only to desert it three thousand years ago. It's also the reason why the Ggyddn didn't want it. For this was foreseen: the advent of an invader into this system, and a collision, resulting in the destruction of both suns *and* this world in a mighty nova!"

"Christ!" said Waite, desperately trying to sober up. "Did he say ten minutes?"

"But how can you know that?" Gill cried. "How can you know when?"

"I know *exactly* when," Sith told him through the medium of Ki-no Sung. "I know *precisely* when. What? But do you think this is happening now, Mr. Gill? Ah, no—it happened three thousand years ago! And the last time you were here—did you think what happened was happening then, at that very time? *Hah!* The simple minds of primitives. We *recorded* it, Mr. Gill! And these are the replays. But where you are concerned, why, it *is* happening now! The only difference being—"

"That we're in it!" Gill gasped. "But . . . you said that we had *returned* to this place. And you've talked about the *last* time we were here."

"Ah!" said Sith. "The twin suns fooled you. And the moons, which arrived in a great orbit around the small white star and finally fell under the influence of this planet."

And Angela gasped, "So this *is* the world of the Mansion—but at the end of the recording, a lot later than our visit!"

"It's the other side of that world," said Sith. "Which is doubtless the third reason you failed to recognize it."

And Turnbull groaned, "The fourth being the poisoned fruit . . . *Jesus!*"

"None of which is important," said Sith, "for your presence here won't make the slightest difference . . . and there are only eight minutes left." His voice came and went, waxing and waning but growing fainter all the time. "Alas, it seems I'm about to lose my eyes, ears, and voice," he said, sounding so disgruntled that Gill could even picture the scowl on Sith/Bannerman's face.

"A defect in your implant?" Gill said, beginning to sweat. "Your technology isn't as perfect as you'd like us to think, is it?"

"But way beyond yours, Mr. Gill. Seven and a half minutes."

"And so the game ends and we fry," Gill snapped. "Well at least we'll be rid of you!" It was a ploy; he was begging Sith to let it end here, and not throw them in the briar patch.

"Rid of me?" said Sith, his voice falling to a new low, a whisper of stuttering static. "The other way around, I think! Except . . . I'm not yet ready. For you deserve a lot more pain, and I'm enjoying it oh so very much, and it looks like I'm not going to be able to see . . . see it through to the end. Which I so dearly *want* to do. So think, Mr. Gill, think . . . for the dog knows the way!"

Barney? Gill looked around, couldn't see him.

Turnbull had loosened Sung's bonds. Now he hauled the little man to his feet. But Sung was cramped and cried out against it. And the pain in his eyes told them that he was his own man again. The implant had failed and Sith was locked out.

"Where's Barney?" Gill yelled.

"There!" Miranda pointed.

They all looked: one-third of the way around the curve of the high perimeter of standing stones, to where Barney was even now cocking his leg against a huge squat menhir. He made water, presumably, in the split second before lightning from the stone stiffened his hair and knocked him sideways off his three feet, sending him sprawling down the first four inner steps!

For a moment Gill was stunned, but then he yelled, "That's it—that *must* be it! Barney pissed on the door and earthed the thing. He's only a dog after all, doesn't know that you mustn't piss into the wind—or onto electrical appliances!"

Turnbull snatched up Ki-no Sung, hoisted the cramped Chinaman to his shoulder, said, "We'll have to run for it. What is it, three hundred yards? And we have maybe five minutes left?"

They ran . . . at least *four* of them ran, and Waite and Stannersly stumbled. But even the powerful Turnbull was suffering; not only from the additional weight he was carrying, but mainly as a result of tasting the poisoned fruit. He and Miranda Marsh had both been seriously depleted.

Three hundred yards in five minutes; in normal circumstances they would make it in less than two, but these weren't normal circumstances.

Two-thirds of the way to their objective, the amphitheater's standing stones and the surface of its uppermost tier had long since crumbled away, leaving stony debris inside and outside the huge structure. They had to climb down quite some way, then over the rubble and back up onto the level, before finishing their run. By which time they were just about all in.

By then, too, all eyes were on the twin suns, glancing at their brilliance at every opportunity, fearful yet unable to ignore the inevitable, final battle of these cosmic combatants. Pseudopods of plasma were sweeping like great tentacular arms from the natural mother of the system to the invader, and the lesser star's shape was elongating as its own plasma extensions were swept away and the gravity of the greater sun began to pull it apart. It couldn't go on much longer.

But at least Sung was on his own feet now, and sheer terror had brought sobriety to Waite and Stannersly, so that they no longer stumbled. As for Barney: alive but dazed, lying where the shock had thrown him, he was lifting his head and whining, struggling to get back on his feet.

Gill, marginally ahead of the runners and almost dragging Angela along behind him, made it to the enigmatic menhir first and went down the steps to the dog's aid.

"The door," Gill shouted, over a sudden rumble of thunder and flash of lightning, as great dark clouds rolled up out of nowhere. "Angela, get ready to use the door!"

Gasping, fighting for air, she looked at the great squat stone and wondered how they'd failed to notice it before; distance, she supposed. But where the rest of the encircling megaliths were all evenly spaced, this one was at odds and didn't belong. Moreover it had a single iron ring or manacle—or in fact a knocker?—swinging from a pivot some three and a half feet above its base. But iron, or indeed any metal, as a relic of a society with no tools as such, in a place built entirely out of stone such as this? And so Angela knew that this was in fact the door.

Then Gill's instructions finally got through to her, that she should get ready to use the door. But:

"Not without you, Spencer Gill," she shouted down to him as he took up Barney into his arms.

By then the rest of the team had arrived—and then, too, the rain. But rain such as they had never seen before. Torrential, tropical, terrible, it fell in sheets, its droplets as big as their thumbs! And it fell with force, drenching them in seconds, battering them, and sending them staggering.

And there was Gill crawling up the shuddering steps with the dog under one arm, and Jack Turnbull reaching down to haul him the rest of the way. Which was when the last scene in the life of a world, indeed of a star system, was enacted.

They all saw it—in the sky, through a moment's break in the roiling clouds—the collision, the nova!

The two suns merged, wobbling like jelly, burning bright, and brighter yet, as the sky turned a blinding white! And the light came right through the clouds themselves. And a terrible heat came with it.

But in the moment before this happened, vast seismic convulsions had seized the planet; its orbit was changing even as the suns changed and merged, and storms were brewing that would never have time to unleash their fury. The earth was shaking in the grip of the ultimate quake, the amphitheater steps crumbling beneath the feet of the small party of humans.

No less than the others, the little Chinaman stumbled and staggered. But falling to his knees, Ki-no Sung sought support. He saw the ring in the standing stone, reached out, and managed to grasp it—but only for a moment, before the tremors shook him loose.

And in that same moment, however unintentionally . . .

Ki-no Sung knocked!

CHAPTER
23

I T WAS STILL raining like mad, despite that the world—or the planet—
seemed to have somersaulted. Gill had seen it happen: the megalith with
the iron ring, indeed that entire area of the amphitheater's sweeping perimeter, rising up in an almost liquid wave, and turning itself upside down on
the heads of him and his team; followed in short order by a dizziness and
a darkness that might easily be death.

And yet he wasn't dead, and it was still dark despite that common sense
told him the nova couldn't have switched itself off, and commoner senses
that told him he was wet as hell from a deluge that had somehow avoided
turning to superheated steam along with an entire world.

So what had happened here? The answer was obvious. To Jack Turnbull, anyway.

"Who knocked?" The big minder groaned or grunted, sitting up amid
a tangle of jungle tree roots and large-leaved shrubbery in the mud and the
slop of a subtropical rain forest.

But then—as Ki-no Sung stopped gasping and wallowing in a pud-
dle of his own, looked all around in the hissing, streaming gloom, then
grasped and examined a handful of leaves from a shrub that was gradually being flattened by the sheer weight of water, and cried: "We home!
We come *my* home! We come China!"—then they knew who had
knocked.

"China?" Miranda Marsh gasped, staggering to and fro until Turnbull
reached up, caught her, and drew her to a standstill.

And: "China?" From George Waite, thoroughly tangled in the branches of a shrub where he'd materialized. And stupidly: "But . . . China on Earth? Asiatic China? China as in the Orient?"

Or perhaps not so stupidly . . .

Barney whimpered in Gill's arms, licked his face, kicked to be let down. Then Angela came stumbling out of the drenched darkness, anxiously calling ahead as she searched for a special someone. Finding him, she sobbed her thanks and collapsed with a splash beside him.

"China," said Gill, holding tight to Angela, with the dog between them. But a moment later, as his mind stopped spinning and he accepted the weirdness of it: "Where's Fred?"

"Here," the pilot choked and sputtered, a mud-thing levering itself up from between a pair of rotting tree stumps. "I'm here. But . . . did I hear someone say we're in China?"

"When, or if, the sky clears," Gill answered, "then we'll know for sure. But Ki-no Sung seems to think—"

"Not think, Spencer Gill, *know!*" said Sung, holding up his arm and one good hand in the downpour and pointing the way through the rain-sodden trees. He tried to stand up. "That way is . . . is Yellow Sea. My . . . my house." But he couldn't struggle to his feet. And sighing, he let his arm drop to his side, his chin to his chest, then toppled over and fell facedown in the slop.

Turnbull reached down, grabbed the Chinaman, drew him out of the mud. "Got him," he said. "The poor bastard's all in."

"Come on," said Gill, climbing unsteadily to his feet and helping Angela to hers. "Sung pointed this way, said something about his house? If he actually recognizes this place—I mean if he's right and not simply delirious—well anything has to be better than this."

They fought through bamboo, soaking shrubbery and entangling vines, finally stumbled across a trail through the jungle that led them to a rise overlooking a shoreline. And the night sea was indeed yellow. And there at the edge of the forest—

A house, of sorts. And, as Gill had pointed out, it had to be better than the night and the rain, most definitely.

The house had no lights; deserted, its door flapped a little in the dying wind off the sea. But it had oil in lamps, and water in jugs, a place to cook and a place to eat. And it had a good roof on which the rain fell with a constant, lulling susurration as the storm began to abate.

Behind dividing bamboo walls, they found low wooden beds, rush mats, and even a pair of huge easy chairs woven of raffia.

Ki-no Sung's house? Well, perhaps—but hadn't he made his home on a ship? They would doubtless find out all about it when he woke up. Until then, this place would do very nicely.

Gill's party had just enough strength to clean up a little—a very little—before sheer exhaustion set in, and then they slept wherever they found suitable places . . .

Gill woke up with a start to a distant clap of thunder. Angela was curled in one of the great chairs and he was parked on the floor beside her. Shivering, he got up and went to a window—to a window space in the woven bamboo wall, anyway—and looked out and up at the night sky. It was clearing, and the constellations were those of Earth.

Thank God! he thought, and at once rephrased it: *Well, for now, at least.* Then he quietly returned to Angela and went back to sleep—

Only to start awake again after what might have been minutes or then again hours, when a large hand touched his shoulder.

"*Shh!*" Turnbull cautioned. "Don't wake them all up. I just thought I'd tell you: the little guy's in some kind of pain."

"Pain?" Gill came more fully awake. "Little guy?"

"Ki-no Sung. He was moaning in his sleep. Nightmaring maybe? Well, I could understand that. But he's mobile and seems to be very uncomfortable."

"Mobile?"

"Moving about, restless, hurting."

Gill went with him to a small room where they had lain Ki-no Sung on a pallet and thrown a blanket over him. And there he lay, muttering in his sleep and stretching his neck, pain etched deep in his face.

"He was doing that in the last place, too," Gill said. "We thought it might be simple exhaustion, remember? But look, he's trying to claw the back of his neck."

"That scar," said Turnbull. "Now what the hell . . . ?"

They turned the Chinaman onto his stomach and examined the back of his neck. There was some fresh blood in the scar, where a sliver of something dully metallic poked out from inside.

"Sith's implant!" Gill said.

"Eh?"

"You know how a spelk will sometimes work its way to the surface, as if the body were rejecting it? Well I reckon that's what's happening here. Do you remember how Waite's bugged tooth bothered him?" Gill grasped the projecting tip of the thing between thumb and forefinger, slowly drew it out. "Sith's implant is a foreign—indeed an alien—body, and Ki-no Sung has finally rejected it. Which might explain why, just before the twin suns went nova, Sith had trouble communicating through him. It appears that Thone or Ggyddn metal and human flesh don't mix."

And as Sung gave a low, almost grateful moan and relaxed again, they examined what Gill had taken from his neck. It was no thicker than a match stalk and only half the length. But at one end, the last to come out of his flesh, it had tiny trembling filaments as fine as those in a lightbulb or maybe finer. Bloody as it was, Gill had to wash the thing before they could see these tiny wires. But finally there it was in Gill's palm: five-eighths of an inch long, a tenth of an inch thick, and of the same dull metal used to cap George Waite's tooth.

"And that—a thing as small as that—gave that bastard jellyfish complete control over him?" The minder shook his head in amazement.

"Not complete control," said Gill. "But near enough as to make no difference. What annoys me is that I didn't detect the thing, for after all it is a machine. But so very small! And of course in my machine world my talent was drowned out, or fenced in, by all of that useless, pointless junk all around us."

"But not on the lighthouse rock," said the other. "And not in those ruins on the world of the big roaches."

"No," Gill said, "but Sith was sparing in his use of Sung. He didn't use him in my machine world except maybe the once, to discover our whereabouts. Likewise in the forest world: he didn't use Sung until the little fellow had uncovered his eyes and Sith was able to see where we were."

"So no way they were in cahoots?"

Gill shook his head. "I shouldn't think so. But Sith obviously had time to work on Sung, which he didn't have in George Waite's case. Hence the difference in the design and quality of these bugs. This one was a classic. But as I said, human flesh doesn't make a good home for this 'intelligent' metal. Or maybe in this case it's simply the House of Doors doing its own automatic thing, 'curing' the illnesses of the people or creatures under test. I mean, surely if a body is housing something injurious, that would be akin to being diseased? Especially if that thing could *cause* a disease? I remember you saying that Waite's tooth was so loose that it was—how did you put it?—'flapping in the wind'? Well maybe it had been loosened by the House of Doors as the first step to getting rid of it. And that would account for all the pain it was putting poor old George through. Anyway, I'm feeling just a bit guilty about Sung. No offense to you, Jack, but it strikes me that maybe we didn't take the best possible care of this poor little bloke."

Turnbull disagreed. "Ki-no Sung was seen to be Sith's instrument," he said. "It was six lives to one. We would have been justified to simply ditch him, even to kill him. But we didn't, and I'm very glad for that. Especially if this is China—*our* China, I mean . . ." And he looked at Gill in that certain way of his.

"I know well enough what you mean," Gill answered. "That's why you couldn't sleep, right?" He knew the other very well indeed.

"And why you're as jumpy as a cat with a flea in his ear." For Turnbull had developed a similar rapport with Gill. "Spencer, old son, you started awake almost before I'd laid a finger on you. So just between the two of us, what do you reckon?"

Weary, Gill sat down with the minder on the edge of Sung's pallet. "I reckon we'll have to wait until morning," he finally answered. "At least till Sung comes out of it and tells us yes, this is home. But to be truthful, if it *is* home I can't see *how* it is. The constellations are Earth's stars, true, and it would seem that we're in China, yes. Also, it appears proven that the one who knocks is the one who throws the dice, fine. Yet when I knocked we ended up in my machine world. And old Barney's throw couldn't have been that much better, or we wouldn't have materialized in a world with only a couple of hours left to exist! So if all of these synthetic worlds are worst-case scenarios created from our nightmares, how can Sung's throw have brought him home? Or is he just lucky?"

"Or is his nightmare still waiting to happen?" the minder quietly inquired. "And not only to him but to us, too."

"A game of Snakes and Ladders," Gill mused, scratching his chin stubble. "The aim of the game being to get home safely."

"In an ordinary game, yes," Turnbull answered. "But didn't Sith say something about making up the rules as he went along?"

"In that last place we were on a snake," Gill continued to talk to himself. "*Huh!* Were we ever on a snake! So even if this place isn't all it seems—even if it isn't China—maybe now we're on a ladder at least."

"But that still means that the game's not over yet," Turnbull sighed. "I hate to sound gloomy, but that's how I see it. And hell, I'm beginning to wonder if this damned game ever *had* any fucking ladders in the first place, or if someone left them out of the box!"

"Maybe he did, maybe he didn't," said Gill. "But one thing is certain, we won't know until we know."

"And meanwhile, what do we tell the others?"

"Nothing," Gill answered. "Let them stay happy awhile, if only to pick up the bits and pieces of their shattered nerves."

"Is that fair on them?"

"I don't know." Gill shook his head. "But it's fair on me. At least it will stop them asking me what comes next, when they must know by now that I don't have any bloody answers!"

"Don't get riled up, Spencer," said the minder. "Keep your cool. But I know what you mean, and if it comes to that I suppose that I'm just as bad as the rest. But hey, I mean it when I say you're a pillar of strength. Maybe not my kind of strength, no, but *real* strength. That's why we all lean on you so much."

Gill looked at the Thone metal implant in his hand. "Meanwhile I have this to work with," he said. "Unlike George's bug, which was quite simply a bug, this is a tiny machine. And me, I used to have a thing for Thone machines."

"I'll leave you to it, then," the other answered. "And now that we've resolved one or two things, or haven't, perhaps I'll be able to get some sleep."

"Oh, good," said Gill, wryly. "Thanks a lot . . ."

Long after the minder had left, Gill was still there, much too tired to move, the tiny implant feeling cool and strange in his hand, and his weary eyes on Ki-no Sung, whose breathing was much easier now. And while Gill sat nodding there, the Chinaman slept his healing sleep and dreamed his unguessable dreams—

In what little time was left before they would turn to nightmares . . .

Gill's dreams were the clearinghouse for all the debris of his waking mind. He had frequently made that point, as had many others before him. And indeed it worked for him. So that when Angela gave him a shake and said, "Spencer, it's morning," he came awake immediately, his mind refreshed and already in gear.

Jack Turnbull was in with Ki-no Sung, who was beginning to stir. "I'm letting him lie," Turnbull said, when Gill inquired as to Sung's well-being. "I've just been watching him, letting him sleep on, wondering where he keeps his razor. Lord, I could use a shave!"

"I've an idea," Gill said. "Something I woke up with. Help me with this, will you?"

Sung was on his back again; as he began mumbling protests, they turned him gently onto his side so that Gill could inspect the back of his neck. Guessing what was on Gill's mind, the big minder grunted his approval, and together they looked at Sung's wound . . . or rather, at the narrow white strip of perfect scar tissue where it had been.

"Healed," Turnbull said.

"Completely," said Gill. "Damn it to hell! And last night, there we were, arguing all the pros and cons. And all the time the true answer was right there in front of us."

"Eh?" said Turnbull.

"The Yellow Sea," said Gill. "Which by now, in our world, must be green!"

"*Shit!*" said the minder under his breath.

Miranda stuck her head around the bamboo screen that served as a wall. "Good morning." She had washed, looked good, or at least a deal better than last night, said, "I was thinking: it would be a good idea if we made a decent breakfast. If I am going to have to deal with Red Chinese officialdom—which it appears I am—then well fed and mentally alert is the way to go." Apparently she was the old Miranda Marsh again. But then, suddenly aware of the looks passing between Gill and Turnbull, her smile turned to a worried frown. "Is there something . . . ?"

Fred Stannersly came on the scene, his face full of foam. "I was up early," he said. "The stars were out, and they were our stars. That doesn't solve the big problem, I know, but at least we're home. And it seems Sung is one Chinaman who actually shaves!" He beamed, then frowned. "Or is it the Japanese I'm thinking of? Anyway, I've scavenged up a blunt razor and a bar of decent soap. So who wants to go . . . next?" For by then he, too, had noticed the air of gloom around Gill and Turnbull.

Then Angela, who had been looking around the place, called out shakily from the other room, "Spencer, it . . . it's the sea. I think we should talk about . . . about the sea." She had been out on the shack's rickety verandah, and she had noticed—or remembered, or realized—the selfsame truth: that the Yellow Sea should be green.

As the rest of the team except Ki-no Sung himself joined Angela in the main room, George Waite sat up on his pallet in one corner, yawned, and said, "What's that about the sea?"

Since they were all together now, and both Turnbull and Angela knew the truth, Gill saw no further advantage in keeping it from the rest. "The Yellow Sea is, well, it's yellow," he said. "We should have noticed it last night, but obviously we weren't up to scratch. It's yellow, and it should be green. Why? Because this is where the Ggyddn Pagoda materialized . . ."

For long moments there was silence—until Miranda Marsh caught on and exploded, "But that's ridiculous! Are you trying to say that this isn't our world? We're in *China*, Spencer! Naturally it doesn't look like England, but that doesn't mean it's alien. Fred says the stars are right, and Ki-no Sung said this was home. Well, it certainly *looks* like his home to me!"

"But the sea isn't green," Gill insisted. "And Sung's neck wound is all healed up. It healed overnight . . ."

Again there was silence, until:

"Okay, right, we get the idea!" said George Waite, furious without knowing what at. "So the scene isn't right and there's no weed. But . . . couldn't this mean that our boys have somehow beaten the invasion off, that these alien jellyfish have left, gone back where they came from, and that their filthy weed has died? I mean, isn't that as good a reason as any why Sith would dump us here, set us free?"

"No, it isn't," said Gill and Turnbull, almost as one. And Gill went on, "In fact he'd kill us first—just like that, out of hand. But no, we're alive and the game goes on."

"Jack"—Miranda turned to the big minder—"don't you hear what Spencer's saying? I mean, don't you have a point of view, too? Don't you wish that—"

"Wish?" Turnbull cut in. "Don't I wish? Sure I do. But in that one word you've said it all. That's what you're doing: wishing or hoping—and don't stop, because where there's hope there's life. But right now reality looms large, however unreal that reality may seem. So until you prove Gill wrong, I have to tell you he's probably right."

Miranda burst into tears, and Angela almost joined her.

And Stannersly said, "You know, if only I had a chopper I could prove it one way or the other."

"And if we had bacon we could have bacon and eggs," George Waite told him, "if we had eggs."

"No, seriously," Fred said. "If this Pagoda node is as big as it's made out, it wouldn't be hard to find from the air."

"Pagoda?" said Ki-no Sung, standing ragged as a scarecrow in what passed for a doorway to his screened-off room. "Did you say Pagoda?" And while his English had a pleasant oriental accent, still it was perfect English!

"Ki-no Sung." It appeared that Miranda hadn't noticed the discrepancy or was too worked up to let it concern her. "Can't you tell Gill how wrong he is? That this really is your home?"

"I . . . remember," Sung said, twitching spasmodically and touching his brow dazedly. "I remember . . . something. About a Pagoda? About . . . *the* Pagoda!" Then his jaw fell open, and his eyes stopped blinking. "Pagoda! Out there." He pointed at the door to the verandah. "Out there in the Yellow Sea!"

They had all heard it: the fact that he *was* speaking Chinese, but that it only manifested itself as a muted background wash or echo, submerged beneath the English. So who was doing the translating?

"What the hell . . . ?" said Waite, gaping.

"And now maybe you'll all listen," said Gill, his brain working over-time. "This is Ki-no Sung's world, yes, but it's a synthesized world, the world of Sung's worst nightmares. Okay, they haven't happened yet—but it's a safe bet they're going to. And not only to him."

"What?" said Angela, feeling faint and clutching his arm.

"We're all in this game together," Gill tried to explain. "And we're meant to be terrified, as we've been in all of these places so far. But there'd be no terror in it if we didn't know what was going on. So it's been fixed that we do know. The synthesizer is doing the translating to make *sure* we know!"

"The Pagoda!" Sung said again, making for the verandah.

They followed him out, saw him put his good hand to his forehead as a shield against the dazzle of the rising sun. For a moment he stood stock-still, apparently scanning the horizon, then staggered and almost fell, and clung to Gill in a mixture of shock and disbelief. Shaking like a leaf he said, "There's no Pagoda, so maybe it was a dream after all. Tell me it was a bad dream, Spencer, and that I didn't get taken by the Pagoda? But if that's true, then what are you people doing here? I remember most of . . . most of *that* clearly. Or . . . am I a madman?"

Gill shook his head. "You're not mad, Ki-no Sung. The Pagoda was real—and it must have taken you, yes—but this isn't your world."

"Not my world?" Sweat stood out on Sung's brow. His black eyes were wide, pleading.

"No," Gill told him. "It's like those other places you've seen, foreign, alien. Yet in a way—in a crazy sort of way—it *is* your world. I mean, just like the mad machine world was made from my nightmares, so this place is made from yours."

Sung looked deep into Gill's eyes, knew he told the truth. "I'm living—*we* are living—in my nightmares?"

"For the moment, yes we are." Gill nodded. "Whatever your worst dreams are, they're going to happen to all of us."

It was like an invocation, and Sung's slanted eyes opened wider yet. "Lotus!" he gasped. "My wife, Lotus!" And as he flew in search of her, back inside the house, Gill had no choice but suppose that the first of Sung's nightmares was fast developing. For as yet he hadn't seen any sign of anyone called Lotus . . .

CHAPTER
24

LOTUS! MY LOTUS!" Sung ran wailing through the house with his arms held high, shaking them in a typically oriental gesture of despair.

Gill ran after him, caught him, said, "She isn't here, Ki-no Sung. Last night, when we came in to shelter from the storm, no one was here. The house was deserted."

"No Pagoda, no Lotus, no left hand, no sense to . . . to *any* of this!" The little man trembled in all his limbs, and grabbed hold of Gill again, as much for support as anything else. "Gill, Spencer Gill," he cried. "Will you please, *please* explain these things to me?" But before Gill could even begin to answer: "No, there's no time. I have to go to the village. My Lotus is pregnant and has returned to her people to have the child. She must think I'm dead. I *have* to go to the village!"

"Wait!" Gill blocked his way, held him tight. "Your nightmares are waiting for you, Ki-no Sung. Better if you first try to understand what's happening here."

Angela took Sung's elbow, guided him into one of the easy chairs. "Listen to Spencer," she said gently. "He can make it easier for you to understand."

"A tall order," Gill sighed, but tried anyway.

It took maybe an hour. And while Gill talked, checking now and then to ensure that he was understood, Sung gratefully took sustenance—the first real food he'd had in some time—from Miranda Marsh. And:

"So," Sung finally said. "You believe that none of this is real. Or it is, but that this isn't our world."

"That's right," said Gill. "It only looks like our world. But it's a place where all the things that frighten you can and probably will happen, and they can hurt you. Like in the swamp; we could have died, *really* died, in that swamp. Or in the machine world, or in the world of the twin suns. The thing is, you mustn't believe the things that happen. Or believe them if you will, insofar as they can affect you, but at the same time try to remember that they're not happening in the real world."

"And you hope to get back there? You hope to find another door and get back . . . home?" The little Chinaman slowly shook his head; it was all so hard to take in.

"Ki-no Sung," said Gill. "Can you speak English?"

"A few words," said the other. "Very little."

"Do you understand English, then?"

Sung shrugged. "Again, a few key words," he said. And Gill waited—

Until Sung caught on and his jaw fell open. Then:

"Exactly," said Gill, nodding. "You *are* speaking it. We *do* understand you, and you us. Now tell me: how can that be, Ki-no Sung? And so I ask you again: is this the real world?"

"I . . . I hear myself speaking in Chinese," Sung said.

"We hear it, too," Angela confirmed. "Beneath the English, or parallel with it, we hear your natural language. But what do *you* hear when we speak?"

"Since we got . . . here, I hear Chinese!" said Sung. And he nodded. "Very well, I believe what you have told me. I have to, for I saw the first of these invaders land here! But still this looks like my home, and still I have to seek out my Lotus."

"If you find her, it won't be Lotus." Gill shook his head. "Lotus is on our own world."

"But I must at least *look* for her, in case . . . in case . . ."

"Sure you have to look for her," Turnbull told him, in his very softest voice. The minder glanced at Gill, and Gill understood what he was saying: that since this was Sung's nightmare, it might make good sense to follow his lead. For he was the one most qualified to discover the way out, to escape from himself, to find the door.

"Let's finish up here," Gill said. "Finish washing, have a shave, make ourselves as presentable as possible. Miranda, depending on the scenario, you may still have some diplomatic work to do; we won't know until we go into the village. But at least we'll have Ki-no Sung on our side. So let's pack up and—how do they say it, break camp?—and be on our way."

And as patiently as possible, Ki-no Sung waited for them to make ready . . .

The village stood in a large clearing overlooked by a terraced knoll rising to the rear. A dozen large, quality wooden houses climbed the steep sides of the knoll, and paths threaded their way through the gaps between the gardens. From the foot of the knoll, many lesser homes sprawled toward the jungle, principally along a half-metaled track that wound off into the trees. Seaward stood the lowliest of the dwellings, places much on a par with Sung's house. Beyond these, the lashed-together plank catwalks of fragile-seeming jetties stuck out like spokes from the pincer arms of a harbor formed of boulders welded in position by seaweed and years of oceanic concretions.

"Mainly, a fishing village," Ki-no Sung told his guests, leading them along the main street toward the knoll. Several female inhabitants came out of their houses to stare, and Sung explained: "The women are fishermen's wives, and strangers are a rarity. Also, you must excuse them; they are mainly of peasant stock. Lotus, however, is not. Her parents are wealthy and most honorable; her brothers own half of the fleet of vessels and many houses; her uncle fixes engines, and he also runs the general store. Alas, they do not care for me. For I own my own house, my own small boat, and do my own repairs—*Ah!*" For suddenly he'd remembered; all of that had been in the real world, and he didn't know how things stood in this one.

But he was about to find out.

The women had started to babble, and while they spoke in Chinese, it was only there as background static. Rising above it, Gill and the others heard English:

"Huh! Ki-no Sung! He dares to return! Can you believe it? He steals away poor Lotus from her loving parents, forces himself upon her and gets her with child, finally deserts her and runs off into the jungle." This from a scrawny harridan, shaking her fist at Sung.

And another called out: "Oh, and is it Ki-no Sung the rapist? Did someone tell you that poor besotted girl was pregnant, then, and you're back to stake a 'legitimate' claim on her family fortune? *Hah!* Little do you know, Ki-no Sung. Her brothers will kill you and use you for fish bait! Aye, and these damned foreigners with you!"

Sung went white and began to shake, then came to a sudden halt as two well-dressed young men burst out from the garden of one of the quality houses at the foot of the knoll. One of them was big, the other small and thin as a reed. "You!" the big one called out, hurrying toward Sung. "Rat turd! Stinking son of a scum-sucking, fish-peddling Korean! What? You dare to come back here? I'll cut out your rotten heart!" He pulled a long-bladed knife from his belt.

"Her brothers!" Sung husked.

"Oh-oh!" said Turnbull as Gill heard the minder's weapon make its typical ch-*ching* sound. But:

"For God's sake hold it, Jack!" Gill said in a rush. "The gun has to be a means of last resort." And to Ki-no Sung: "Are there any weapons in the village?"

"Knives," the other gasped. "Maybe some shotguns, air guns, small arms for hunting. But modern weapons, no. Not that I know of." He turned to the minder. "But in any case, you can't possibly use that! What, would you make me a murderer, too, on top of all these lies of which I'm accused?"

"This isn't your world, Ki-no Sung," Turnbull told him, at the same time reminding Gill of what was going down here. "If I have to use it I will, anything to keep you safe." He took up a position at the head of the group, braced himself, and aimed the machine pistol ahead and at the ground. And: "You two men," he called out. "Stop right there!"

"Foreign dog!" the one in the lead shouted and waved his knife, just a moment before the minder split a cobblestone directly between his feet—which stopped him in his tracks. And as the sharp, resounding *crack!* of the shot died away:

"The next one is going into that great empty space behind your eyes," Turnbull growled, marching right up to Lotus's brothers. Following with the rest of the group, Ki-no Sung stepped forward to intervene, but Gill took his arm. "Jack's right," he said. "If anything happens to you we may not get out of here. I mean, *none* of us will get back. And that includes you."

"You're right," Sung gasped. "This isn't my world. It simply can't be. Lotus's brothers don't like me, but they wouldn't kill me! And everything you heard about me is a lie."

"Low-born dog!" The real troublemaker of the pair crossed his arms on his chest and scowled at Ki-no Sung. "Scummy Korean *bastard!*" He was overweight; so that despite seeming tall for a man of his race, he looked squat. He had a thin mustache, piggy eyes, and black pigtails shiny with grease.

"Honorable brother-in-law." Sung bowed from the waist. "I only want—"

"Want?" the other broke in. "You *want* something? You *dare* address me as your brother, you filthy dog turd! And . . ."

But the "and" signaled the end of it, for that was when Turnbull slammed the folded-down butt of his gun into the man's gut, and whipped it up under his flabby chin, stretching him on his back. One minute the bully was on his feet, the next supine, his knife clattering on the cobbles.

The younger, scrawny brother gawked and took a pace to the rear, but Turnbull was on him at once, prodding his belly with the muzzle of his gun. "You," the minder growled. "Do you want to insult us, too?"

"I . . . I . . . no, not at all." The other was almost fainting. And Ki-no Sung's courage was bolstered.

"If I no longer have any face," he said, "then what I say or do in this village no longer matters. Now you, *listen!*" And he grabbed the scrawny brother by the throat with his one good hand, but a hand with the terrible strength of fury in it now. "Everything those . . . those *crones* said about me is a complete lie," he said. "As for what my so-called 'honorable' brother-in-law said . . . that was also a lie. Now, I want to see Lotus. Is my wife well? She had better be. Where is she?"

The scrawny one scowled—until Ki-no Sung shook him like a terrier shakes a rat. Then:

"In my uncle's house, there," and he pointed. "Lotus will give birth soon, perhaps even now."

"I know your uncle's house, idiot!" Sung thrust him away, so that he stumbled and went to his knees on the cobbles. Then, stooping to pick up the fat one's knife, Sung got in step with Turnbull and headed for the house in question. "My Lotus." His voice trembled, belying his bravado. "She is having my baby!"

That was when the stones began to fall. The village women were throwing them, shouting in unison, "You have no face, Ki-no Sung. You're a faceless Korean dog!" And then for the first time Angela produced Turnbull's 9mm Browning, and put a shot not too high over their heads. As by magic, the street cleared at once and stood empty. And Gill's party proceeded to Lotus's uncle's house where it stood at the foot of the knoll . . .

Without pause Ki-no Sung rapped on a wooden panel in the rather flimsy door. A face appeared briefly in a bead-curtained window but apart from some furtive movement within that was all. Turnbull wasn't about to be hindered, and he certainly wasn't going to be ignored. Putting a massive shoulder to the door, he shattered it inward, almost tore it from its hinges. First inside, Ki-no Sung very nearly came in collision with a fat woman carrying a bowl of steaming water, and clean towels draped over her arm. That told the whole story.

"Where is Lotus, honorable aunt?" Sung growled, and for once was given no argument. Perhaps the midwife had noticed his injury, his missing hand; or it might have been his disheveled appearance, the wild look in his eyes, or the way he said "honorable." Whichever, the midwife saw that he was in no mood to brook any kind of argument.

"There!" she shrilled. "The poor child, poor sweet Lotus, is in there— *beast!*" She pointed to a door with swaying bead curtains. At which a girl's voice called from within:

"Ki-no Sung?"

It was sweet, that voice, yes, but . . . trembling fearfully? Well naturally Lotus would be afraid. She was just a young girl, about to give birth. (At least, Gill hoped that was what it was.) But since Ki-no Sung had lost so much face, who could say how much more was still to be lost?

"Lotus!" Sung cried, starting forward—and the bead curtains parted, revealing a squat man with a gleaming scalpel in his upraised hand. He saw Sung and swept the razor-sharp blade at his face.

But his wrist met the barrel of Turnbull's machine pistol, so that he dropped the scalpel and yelped his pain. The minder reversed his weapon to club him, and Sung cried, "Jack, no! My uncle . . . is also the village doctor!"

Turnbull stopped his lunge barely in time, and Gill propelled "the doctor" back into the room.

And there lay Lotus, her belly grotesquely distended, legs spread wide and bent at the knees like the nether limbs of some monstrous white spider. Sweat rivered her face, her flesh quivering as if under the lash. But seeing Ki-no Sung . . . there was no joy in those staring eyes—neither joy nor loathing at the appearance of the man who had put her to such pain—but there was fear! And Ki-no Sung saw it.

"Lotus! The way you look at me, no!" He sobbed and fell on his knees by the delivery table. "They have lied to you. Everyone has lied. Whatever they say about me, it's not true! Surely you know that?" He reached out and tried to take her hand where it gripped the table's rubber handles.

She jerked away from him, cried out in sudden pain, closed her eyes, and lay there panting, hissing.

"Heartless dog!" said her uncle, pushing Ki-no Sung aside. "What, and do you think we don't know how it was? Do you think she was too afraid to tell us? Well she did tell us, and we do know. When she refused your advances, you stole her away, took her by force, and left her for dead. Oh, you faceless one!"

Lotus cried out, shrill, gasping, and terrified. Her eyes were bulging black orbs in her white skull face. And her uncle turned again to the table.

"This baby," he mumbled, almost to himself, in something akin to desperation. "He is too big, and Lotus cannot push him out. I'll have to cut."

But in fact he wouldn't have to . . .

"That poor girl's belly," Miranda Marsh cried out. "She's huge, enormous!"

And Angela said, "You men, other than Ki-no Sung: out of here. Go and guard the house."

Gill agreed with her. Bundling the men back out through the curtained door, he said: "Position yourselves as best you can. Albeit this is an alternate, synthesized China, it looks pretty authentic to me. Which means it's probably a Red China, too. If so, there's bound to be a Communist watchdog or dogs somewhere. Choose a window and keep your eyes open for what's going on outside."

They did, and sure enough a party of men was coming from the heart of the village and heading for the house at the foot of the knoll. Three of them wore olive-drab uniforms with flat gray caps and red-star insignia, and they carried shotguns.

"The law," said Turnbull grimly. "Military law at that. I think we're about to become fugitives!" Smashing out the panes of his window with the butt of his weapon, he went on: "On the other hand, if this is all they have going for them, we should be all right."

But Lotus's sudden shriek from the delivery room, her cry that went on and on, and climbed higher and higher—and Ki-no Sung's exclamation of uttermost horror—told them differently, that it wouldn't be all right after all. Not from Sung's point of view, anyway.

Gill met Angela and Miranda as they came back out through the bead-curtained doorway. He saw the looks on their faces and the way they staggered; the way Miranda held a hand to her gasping, choking mouth. And yanking aside the beads, he looked in on the scene in the delivery room . . .

Or tried to. But the doctor, Lotus's uncle, came flying headfirst, spraying red as he came. Except the term "headfirst" wouldn't fit, because he had no head! His corpse hurtled out into the corridor, crashed to the floor, and lay there twitching.

At first Gill thought this must be Ki-no Sung's doing, but then he stepped through the curtains . . . and just couldn't take in what he was seeing. Lotus was giving birth, yes, but she was doing it from *every* orifice, and doing it all at once!

Or rather *it* was doing it to Lotus.

A bloodied chitin pincer with gleaming, scallopsorlike cutting jaws—gleaming, at least, where the chitin showed through the gore—was protruding from her lower body, sticking up through a gash that reached from Lotus's pubic region to the base of her rib cage, and which had obviously been snipped from within.

Despite that her body was jerking, inwardly mobile on the table, Gill knew that Lotus herself was quite dead. The pain of this emergence alone would have killed her, without the actual damage to her tissues. Her lower body was literally in two halves, no longer joined above the thighs but lying in two joints like a part-butchered carcass. And there was semisentient, or semi*mechanical* movement at least, within that raw red cave of guts that, even as Gill stood watching in his horrified paralysis, extruded an unfolding nest of feathery feelers.

Even the girl's neck, head, and face were not excluded from the monstrous internal, now external, violation. Her neck grew as fat as Gill's thigh, until the skin began to split and roll back on itself like red paper; her dead eyes bulged hideously, were dislodged as her entire face began to open. Her upper lip split, likewise the teeth and jaw beneath it; and as her mouth became a ghastly gaping hole, so her bottom jaw was dislodged and hung loose.

Then, with an eruption of blood and brains, Lotus's entire head split open, blossoming upward and outward as if on hinges and revealing . . . a curved scorpion stinger, rising up and up, finally bursting the column of her neck in a scarlet welter of chords and pipes!

Gill stepped back—*fell* back, on rubber legs—as Lotus's chest peaked in the middle, her sternum squealing, then audibly *cracking!* open, allowing a second razor-edged clawlike appendage to thrust its way into view.

Vacantly aware of—remembering—the doctor's fate, Gill drew back yet more as the thing snapped at the empty air, once, twice, a third time, with lightning-fast changes of direction, all around the area of the bed.

The girl's body was now completely gutted . . . no other way to describe it. And gazing blankly at Gill from that mutilated shell, from between her flopping puppet legs, he saw a pair of those emotionless, faceted scorpion eyes that he knew so well. The awful thing was growing bigger, expanding even as he watched, like an insect under a magnifying glass as the lens draws it into clearer definition—*that* quickly.

Impossible, of course, because no newborn creature could ever grow that fast. But Gill already knew what he'd witnessed here: not a birth as such, but an arrival certainly. Lotus had been a door; not the way out, no, but a way *in* from the synthesizer to this terrible world of Ki-no Sung's worst nightmares. And the grotesque mess on the table had been the very worst of them: that something should go wrong with his wife's pregnancy.

Stuttering gunshots sounded, yanking Gill out of his morbid hypnosis. For the first time he saw Ki-no Sung where he had flattened himself to a wall, with the fingers of his good hand stuffed deep in his mouth. It would do little good telling him to move, Gill knew, and so manhandled him out through the bead curtains.

Seen from the corridor through the minder's shattered window, three Communist soldiers lay dead outside the house, their olive-drab uniforms spattered red. But the crowd they'd brought with them was rapidly dispersing. Gill took one look, and said, "Let's go." At least he did his best to speak, but only managed to croak the words out on his second attempt.

"Go where?" Turnbull rasped, turning to him.

Gill grabbed the lapels of the minder's jacket, bared his teeth, and snarled at him. "Where?" And then in full voice—as a great plated claw ripped away the curtains from the delivery-room door, and the walls bulged, and the floor shook—he yelled, "Anywhere, Jack! *Any* fucking where!"

No one needed any further urging.

In moments all seven of them had exited from the main door of the house, and jostling Sung into motion they headed for the cover of the jungle. From behind, cries of outrage, of pursuit, sounded. And the phrase, "Come back, you faceless Korean bastard," was only one of many that followed their tracks under the canopy of the trees.

But not a single member of Gill's ragged group was in the least concerned about *human* pursuit. No, not in the least . . .

CHAPTER
25

THE "JUNGLE" WASN'T as bad as Gill and the others had thought. Despite many subtropical species of birds, animals, and plants, it was more broadleaf forest than true jungle; so that in fact it felt like walking through some vast, uncut wooded region in England rather than China. But in last night's rain and storm-tossed darkness, it had certainly seemed like jungle. Even now there were areas that were completely choked with tough creepers, which must be circumnavigated, and places where the trees appeared to have collapsed en masse under the weight of vines, crushing the underbrush and making the terrain extremely hard going.

After about an hour, when their pace had slowed literally to a crawl and the last of the catcalls and furious threats had long since been left far behind, the minder said, "That's about three miles, by my reckoning. Poor going, but it seems that the village people found it just as hard. Either that, or they didn't want to risk their necks against our superior firepower. Or . . ." But he let it go at that, offering a shrug instead.

Gill knew what Turnbull's "or" meant: the scorpion. The minder had thought better of putting a name to his fear, that was all; he hadn't wanted to mention it out loud, and neither did Gill . . .

He and Angela were helping Ki-no Sung keep pace, assisting him where the going was rough, simply *being* with the poor, dazed, zombielike creature and offering him companionship.

But as the group halted to take a breather, and Turnbull and Miranda sat down on a fallen tree trunk, Gill joined them, leaving Ki-no Sung with Angela.

"Sung says there aren't many roads in this area," he reported. "That's when he was still talking, but for the last mile or so he hasn't said much of anything. He did tell me, however, that even the smallest village has its Red Army Observer Corps, paramilitaries on the lookout for incursions from Korea across Hwang Hai, the Yellow Sea. And we could have been seen as just such a force: spies for South Korea. Which means the word will have gone out by telephone to whoever's in command of the nearest military base. So, if I were you I wouldn't worry too much about the villagers, but we'd all be well advised to watch the sky. For Sung also said that reconnaissance aircraft, choppers mainly, are a regular feature over this forest."

The big minder nodded, but it was plain his thoughts were elsewhere. And knowing they would have to talk about it sooner or later, and deciding it might as well be sooner, he said: "I know that no one wants to go into this just yet, but you know, villagers and paramilitaries and helicopters, they aren't our only problems. I mean—hell, you *know* what I mean!—there's Sith's god-awful bloodhound, our ugly chum from the synthesizer to think about, too. I find myself listening for him, glancing back the way we've come, and wondering what's keeping him."

"The forest," Gill answered. "It has to be. We've seen one of these fellows get bogged down once before, remember? In that dried-out river-bed in the forest world? I mean, this foliage is pretty densely grown, and some of the vine patches are close to impenetrable. Maybe the scorpion is cutting his way through, in which case we could well have lost him. Still I wouldn't bet on it. Those things are tenacious. They don't just quit."

"Oh, my *God!*" Miranda shuddered. "Jack, Spencer—must we talk about that terrible thing? I shall never, *ever* forget what I saw in that room in that house if I live to be—"

"Hush!" Turnbull said softly, and thought: *She seems to be forgetting that she may* not *live to be.* But out loud he only said, "Of course you won't. No one could. But by God I feel for that poor bastard." He looked across to where Angela sat beside the little Chinaman—Korean as it now appeared—at the mossy bole of a tree. And to Gill: "Was it really that bad, Spencer?"

"It was"—Gill shook his head; he didn't have words for it, still didn't want to dwell on it—"one of the most terrible things I ever saw. If I didn't know, if I wasn't absolutely sure, that this was a synthesized world . . . well, I think it might easily have driven me mad. And as for Ki-no Sung . . ."

"*No!*" Angela's sharp cry of denial brought them all bolt upright. Fred

Stannersly and George Waite, who were closest to Angela and Sung, saw what was happening and leaped to her assistance.

For at first sight it appeared she was fighting with Sung; but in fact the little man wasn't trying to hurt Angela—only himself. He had the knife that he'd taken from his fat brother-in-law, and seemed intent on drawing it across his own throat!

Angela had managed to grab his arm, and because Sung had only the one hand he wasn't able to fend her off. Nevertheless, and with the strength of a madman however depleted, he was winning the struggle. So that by the time Fred Stannersly reached them, Angela had almost given in and Sung's blade was actually touching his neck, quivering as he strove to slice through his throat just above the Adam's apple.

The pilot's additional strength saved the day—in fact saved Sung's life—as George Waite forced the knife from the little man's clenched fingers and tossed it away. Ugly though the knife was, it was a weapon; Jack Turnbull picked it up and secured it through a loop in his webbing belt.

Gill had gone to Sung, knelt beside him. "Ki-no Sung—what in the name of . . . ?" But in fact he knew what in the name of. Ki-no Sung was on the verge of madness. Up until their arrival here, he had understood little or nothing of what was happening; indeed, and despite all Gill's explaining, he'd thought it was a bad dream. Then, upon reaching what he had believed to be his own or his adopted country, the *real* nightmare had commenced.

Betrayed by his people, denied by his wife, exposed to uttermost horror in the shape of Lotus's death as she gave life to an alien monster—allegedly the product of his raping her—little wonder he'd slipped over the edge.

Now Sung stopped fighting the people who were holding him down, looked at Gill through eyes as black and empty as space, and said, "I have no people, no wife, no face. I am as good as dead, wherefore I may as well be dead. I *should* be dead!"

Gill shook his head, licked his lips. "Lotus is only dead in this place. The horror you saw in the village only happened in *this* place. And as for your loss of face . . ."

But here he paused, stared harder into Ki-no Sung's eyes, and drew back a little. Now what the hell . . . ?

Maybe it was only the way Sung was holding his face, the strain he was under, but his yellow skin was suddenly tight as a drum across his cheeks. His nose, scarcely prominent in the first place, had likewise seemed to flatten a little, no doubt as a result of the tightening of his skin. But his mouth—

Was little more than a gash, *and getting smaller!*

From behind Gill's shoulder, Jack Turnbull hissed, "Jesus, Spencer! What's happening here?"

In an equally reduced voice, unable to take his disbelieving eyes from Sung's metamorphosis even for a moment, Gill replied, "Jack, let's face it, *anything* can happen here. This is a world of the imagination, of Sung's imagination. It's his nightmare world, a synthesized world, and in nightmares reality gets warped all to hell. Have you forgotten Clayborne's world?"

"Clayborne believed in the supernatural," the minder answered. "His world was bound to be full of demons."

"Ki-no Sung's demons are in his breeding," Gill said. "And in his situation, the fact that he's been made to feel that—"

"He has no face!" Miranda Marsh cried.

Or almost none.

Ki-no Sung's face had flattened out—literally. From his forehead to his chin: a flat, almost blank expanse of stretched skin, with tiny teardrop-shaped pinpricks for nostrils, slanted slits for eyes, no lips or mouth at all, and ears that were welded over into blunt, blank triangular outlines on the column of his upper neck. His mop of black hair looked like an untidy wig or something you might stick on top of a scarecrow.

His good hand went up to touch what had become of his face—or to discover that he didn't have one, or that the one that he had was blank—and his head arched up and back in a scream, which was the very worst thing of all. For of course his scream was silent.

The *whup-whup-whup* of helicopter vanes and a sudden wind from overhead was all the warning they had.

"Shit and damnation!" Turnbull yelled through a flurry of flying leaves. And: "Run, get out of sight. The cavalry's arrived, but they're not on our side!"

Released as the rest of the team was galvanized into panicked activity, Ki-no Sung sprang to his feet, went rushing off into the forest with his arms held high over his head, shaking them in a display of oriental terror and desperation. Gill and Angela took off after him, likewise Waite and Stannersly.

They ran for maybe a quarter mile, always within sight of Sung but never quite able to catch him. Until finally exhausted he stumbled into a clearing, tripped, and went flying face—or no-face—down. And Gill and the others were on him at once. But as they pinned him down, looked at each other, then looked around . . .

There were two helicopters at rest in the clearing, and a ring of startled Red Chinese soldiers were quickly recovering their wits and beginning to close in on them. Angela got to her feet, brought her pistol out of a pocket, had it slapped out of her hand as a soldier stepped in close.

Then he grabbed her by the throat, and Gill kicked him in the groin—

And in the next moment it felt like this entire synthesized world had fallen on him . . .

Gill dreamed of the dog, Barney, in a dream where he kept calling to him and getting no answer. So that when he woke up, forgetting for a moment all that had gone before, he cleared his throat and casually asked Angela, "Where the hell has that dog gone to now?" Or he tried to, but his mouth was full of dirt.

"Eh, dog?" said a harshly authoritative voice that wasn't anyone's Gill knew, a moment before he felt someone's boot probing under his ribs to turn him over onto his back. "What? Are you calling me a dog?" The voice was double-tracked; underneath it spoke Chinese, but it reached Gill as English. *Then* he remembered what had gone before, and with a start jerked into a seated position on a cold earthen floor.

There were three of them, soldiers, Chinese, all scowling and seeming very threatening. And Gill was in a "cell," or at least a room of sorts, with bamboo walls and ceiling, no windows, and only a little light that struggled its way in through tiny chinks in the thick bamboo. The soldier directly in front of him—the one who had spoken, he assumed—was holding the butt of a rifle toward him, where the merest flick of a wrist would doubtless cause Gill considerable pain.

"Dog? You?" Gill mumbled. "No, I was only dreaming. We've lost our dog again, that's all." He was still groggy, had difficulty balancing himself and staying upright. The fact that his hands were tied behind his back didn't help much either.

"And so you're the leader, eh?" said this same soldier.

"Leader?" Gill tried to look blank, which wasn't too hard right now. "But I have nothing to lead. I don't even know what we're doing here, or why we're being treated like this."

The soldier laughed harshly, looked like he might use the butt of his weapon on Gill, thought better of it, and said, "You are foreigners, traveling with a murdering Korean traitor, and you don't know why we're treating you like this? Well, believe me, so far you've been treated very kindly. But not necessarily so when the colonel gets here from Yancheng!" He stepped back a pace, spat at Gill and missed (for which Gill was glad), ordered his men out of the cell and went with them. For a brief moment the open door let in daylight before all was dark and musty again.

But in that brief shaft of light Gill had seen figures sitting against the

walls, and now he called out, "Angela? Are you there? Miranda? Jack?
Fred . . . ?"

"We're missing two members," said George Waite's voice out of the
gloom. "Miranda and Jack . . . aren't here. Maybe they got away, or it could
be they put up too good a fight."

Gill took that in, said, "Angela?"

"She's beside me, over here," said Fred Stannersly. "They knocked her
on the head. After they'd belted you she really got mad at them! That's
some little woman, Spencer."

Gill tried to get up, discovered that his feet were bound, too, fell over
on his side, and wriggled in the direction of the voice. "But is she . . .
okay?"

"Snoring quite peacefully," the pilot answered. "The rest of us are
okay, too. Just a bit shaken up. But Ki-no Sung . . . well, he's not much
interested in anything. Can't say I blame him, really."

Gill was there; he knew Angela's smell—her sweet scent, which all
the dirt in the world couldn't obscure or hide from his nose—and
pushed himself up alongside her, between Stannersly and her sleeping or
unconscious form. And to the pilot: "Does anyone have free hands or
feet in this place?"

"I don't think Sung was tied up," the pilot answered. "He was so obviously out of it, in a world of his own, they didn't much bother with him."

"Too true," Gill grunted. "You've got it dead right. This is just exactly
that: a world of his own. His own nightmares."

Angela stopped breathing for a second, then gave a start, and her arms
went around Gill's neck. "Spencer?" She hugged him, wouldn't let go.

"You'll choke me," he said, and she finally relaxed. And:

"Oh, my head! Someone must have clubbed me," she groaned.

"They did," he told her. "But you're okay?"

"I think so, yes."

"And you're not tied?"

"Maybe they thought I'd be out for a while. Or that being a woman
they didn't have to worry about me." Wrong, for already her hands were
looking for his knots.

And now Gill's thoughts could return to Turnbull and Miranda. "The
minder didn't make it, eh?" To Stannersly. "Likewise Miranda? Well,
don't write them off. That bloke's been in worse places, I can tell you. He
thrives on this kind of stuff. And he's taken to looking after Miranda. As
for Sung . . ."

"It's all right," that one cut in from the gloom in a far corner, his voice
a whisper, a whistle, thin as a rustle of leaves. "It's coming back. My san-

ity—my face, too—they're coming back." Something struggled to its feet, wove totteringly forward into a thin shaft of light from the ceiling.

"Ki-no Sung?" Gill felt the last of the knots loosen; when his hands jerked apart he was scarcely able to keep from crying out loud as his blood began circulating more freely. Yet a moment later he was rubbing vigorously at his wrists to accelerate the process. And again he said: "Ki-no Sung? You're . . . you're speaking?" (A stupid thing to say, for of course the little man had been speaking.) "And your face . . . ?"

"My face is returning. My thoughts are clear. Do you know what sustained me, Spencer Gill? Your faith. All of you. Yours, Angela's, everyone's. And your message."

"Our message?"

"That this world isn't real. Of course it isn't. My Lotus loves me. That was *not* my Lotus! And that *Thing* she gave birth to: like the creature in your machine world. Therefore this is *not* my true world. I knew it wasn't—saw many differences—but in dreams we accept even the strangest things. So then, if my thoughts, my darkest nightmares, created this world . . . maybe they can help destroy it, too."

Sighing his relief, and working at the thin rope tying his feet, Gill thought: *If only Clayborne could have had that kind of strength.* Now that his eyes were a little more accustomed to the gloom, he could make out the others more clearly.

"George?" he called out softly across Angela. "You okay?"

"I'll be a lot better when Angela gets these ropes off my hands," the other answered. "But yes, I'm okay."

And now that Gill's feet were free, he turned to Stannersly and went to work on him. As for Ki-no Sung: he got down by the pilot's feet, did what he could with his one good hand.

And Gill asked him, "What did our guards think of . . . of your face?"

"They didn't see it," Ki-no Sung answered. "And that too told me that this was a false place, not real; that these horrors were only meant for me—and for you people."

"You're sure you're okay now?"

"No, I'm not okay," the little man answered, very softly. "I'm angry. I want revenge. Against this world, and the one who made it happen—Sith? If I can't go back to my world, then at least I want to do some damage to this one—as it has damaged me."

"And have you given any thought as to how you'll achieve that?" Gill asked him. "I mean, we aren't in the best possible situation here." Stannersly's hands came free; Gill set about massaging the pilot's cramped wrists and fingers while waiting for Ki-no Sung's answer. And finally:

"My father was in the war," Sung said. "He saw the results of that war and was made afraid by them. That's why we moved to the forest and the sea, to fish for a living. But his fear transferred to me. In my real world, there are places like this one—even in the forest, yes—where men prepare for war. There are silos like this one, where rockets sit waiting for the commands that will speed them across the Yellow Sea to Korea. And others in Korea, that face in this direction. In my nightmares I've seen them coming, seen them land . . . the devastation. And when I was awake I was always waiting for it to happen. It was a waking nightmare as well as a dreaming one. And they are the worst sort . . ." Sung paused, and Gill waited. Everyone was free now, easing their cramped limbs.

Eventually Ki-no Sung went on. "Please understand—I did not fear so much for myself as for my wife and unborn child. I feared for the innocents. But in this world it strikes me there are few of those. It is an evil world, sprung from evil dreams. And if a dream is a subconscious thought . . . what power may lie in a conscious one?" He fell silent.

A dangerous line of reasoning. But in any case Gill didn't answer; there were other things to worry about. "I don't think we'll be left alone much longer," he said to everyone. "And personally, I can't say I like the sound of this colonel from Yancheng. He sounds like an expert in interrogation to me. Sung is absolutely right: this is an evil place, and it's all set up to take its spite out on us. So I say we move first. But before we try to do anything, I would like to know how we arrived at this camp. Can someone help out? How did we get here?"

And George Waite told him. "After that small ruckus in the forest clearing, the soldiers herded us—carried you and Angela—aboard those two helicopters. They flew us here. Not far, maybe a mile or two. I got a good look at the place as we came in. From what I saw, it's like Sung said: a military defensive position in the woods. Lots of camouflage netting, a couple of dirt tracks leading in and out, some accommodation well hidden in the trees, and a concrete bunker near the central area like at the hub of a wheel. A missile silo? Yes, I suppose it could be, though the staff don't appear too thick on the ground. But then again, why would they want to be? This is mainland China, after all, and the alleged enemy is a long way off."

"Very well," said Gill. "It sounds a bit dodgy to me, but I did like the bit about these people being thin on the ground. And us being civilian types, and a female included, they probably won't be too worried about us trying to get away." He gave a shrug. "I mean, where would we escape to? So apart from that, what else do we have going for us?"

"The element of surprise, maybe?" Waite was up on his feet now, prowling to and fro in the restricted space. "The next guy that comes through that door—wham!" He positioned himself to one side of the door.

And Gill thought—*George, I'm beginning to see your other side. And I like it a lot.* While out loud he said, "What else?"

"I'm a chopper pilot," Fred Stannersly spoke up. "Yes, *you* know that, but these Red soldiers don't. If we could get to one of those machines . . . it may be a squeeze, but I think it would take us all."

"Good," said Gill. "In fact, great!"

Ki-no Sung moved toward the door. For a moment he turned and looked at Gill, said, "You people are brave. Beside you, I feel like a coward."

"You're no coward," said Gill and Waite together. And Gill went on: "Where plenty of others would have broken down permanently, you're still in one piece and looking good." And in fact Sung was. His face was almost back to normal—it was in place—and his mouth more a real mouth than a whistling slit. Even as Gill stared, the little man's face was improving, reshaping itself.

"I may have to stay here, in my nightmare," Sung answered, "but you people deserve to get away."

Gill was suddenly alarmed. It was as if he could hear Sung thinking, and he didn't like what he heard. But the little man had already turned away, gone to stand on the other side of the doorway, faded back into the shadow of the wall opposite Waite.

While from some way off, but rapidly growing louder, there came the sound of a helicopter's *whup-whup-whupping* fan, making Gill wonder if this was it.

Angela was obviously wondering the same thing, when out of the gloom her hushed voice said, "Oh, my *God!*" And: "Spencer—what odds that's the inquisition?"

It was a joke they had between them, something from Monty Python. So that Gill heard himself almost automatically answering, "Don't mention the inquisition."

And in fact he wished she hadn't . . .

CHAPTER
26

THE CHOPPER SOUNDS got louder, died down, finally cut out and left a pregnant silence in their wake. There were muted voices from beyond the bamboo walls, but nothing loud or clear enough to be intelligible.

There came a sharp *crack!* (and everyone jumped) as Ki-no Sung forced his good hand into a gap in the tightly woven wall to break off a long knuckle of bamboo that tapered to a needle-sharp point: a vicious knife of sorts. George Waite would have followed suit, but there was no time.

Heavy, stamping footsteps sounded, and Waite and Sung lay back against the wall in their respective positions. Gill, Angela, and Stannersly got down on the floor in the darker corners—the ones farthest from the door—and tried to make themselves or their outlines look as bulky as possible. The footsteps halted outside the door, and harsh orders were given; the door opened inward and three Chinese soldiers entered. One of them strode forward and the others fanned out to flank him.

Without pause Waite and Sung struck.

George Waite didn't need a knife after all; his binding cord was still fastened to one wrist; it made a splendid garrote. And Ki-no Sung's man went down with scarcely a gurgle as the vengeful fisherman used his "blade" to deadly effect.

The senior man was unarmed. He was in the middle of the cell before he knew what was happening, by which time it was too late. Gill and Stannersly came up off the floor together, their resounding blows driving him to the ground. He was out, but that didn't satisfy Sung. With a strangled little cry of personal pain, or perhaps relief, he leaped forward and drove his bloodied knife through the officer's throat to put an end to things.

A startled query sounded from outside, and a moment later an unsuspected guard cast his shadow in through the open door. He took a pace inside, stood there with rifle and bayonet extended.

Waite hit him from the side, the rest of them were on him in a flash, and yet again Sung was beyond restraint as he worked out some of his fury and hatred on his synthesized enemies. But not before the guard had screamed a curse and high-pitched warning . . . at which Gill and the others knew they'd been here long enough.

Ki-no Sung was satisfied with his knife; the other three men snatched up the fallen weapons of the dead Chinese guards; they all ran for it, out of the open door and across the clearing.

"The choppers!" Stannersly called out. "Head for the nearest chopper!" But their flight had been seen.

There were cries of alert and outrage from behind, coming from the entrance to the bunker and a group of camouflaged huts around it. Shots began to whistle overhead. And cannons mounted in the nose of one of the helicopters swung in their direction.

"Christ!" cried George Waite, going to one knee and aiming at the gunship, while Gill and Stannersly turned and looked for targets behind them. Waite got off a couple of shots, probably useless from an unfamiliar weapon—

Or there again not.

There came a prolonged stuttering of fire, and just as the chopper's cannons opened up and sent the dirt spouting at their feet, so the plane itself exploded, blowing itself to bits in a ball of white heat, followed by billowing black smoke rings and a long tongue of red-and-yellow flame that licked for the sky.

"You got the fuel tank!" Stannersly cried. "Hell! Anywhere but the tanks! Don't aim for the fucking tanks!"

"But I . . . I don't think I hit anything," Waite protested.

And in fact he hadn't. For as seven or eight Chinese soldiers came running from the bunker, firing as they came, so that somehow familiar stutter sounded again—from the trees at the edge of the clearing. And as a handful of the pursuing soldiers were hit and crumpled to the dirt and the remainder took cover, so Gill knew where he'd heard that deadly sound before.

"Turnbull!" he yelled as the big minder stepped out from under the trees, hosing fire, only pausing to point at the next helicopter in line and wave his intentions. Then he was making a weaving run for it, and Miranda Marsh right there alongside him. Yes, and Barney the dog, too.

"It might just take us all," Stannersly gasped in the sudden lull. "It's quite a big machine; a five-star chopper, probably used by the big brass. An unusual design, from what I can see of it. But if it can fly, I can fly it."

Sirens went off, starting low but quickly winding up to a banshee's wail that rang out over the forest. "Just a bit late for that," Angela said, feet flying as Gill almost dragged her along. "These people, *uh*, aren't too quick off the mark."

But it was a little after noon, the military had probably eaten very recently, and this must be, after all, a totally unique experience for them—the element of surprise, yes. Gill thought these things and others but didn't bother to give them voice. Instead he saved his breath, and his group closed in on the command chopper.

Then a loud-hailer system replaced the siren with a tinny Chinese voice overlaid with English, that kept hysterically repeating: "Incoming! Incoming! Incoming!"

There was a high-pitched whistle, and some few miles away a white streak in the sky with a tail of smoke and fire. It was like a shooting star at noon, plunging down out of sight beyond the horizon of the forest. Then, seconds later the near-distant explosion, and a concussion that trembled up through the ground into their feet. Into Gill's brain, too, as Ki-no Sung snarled:

"Got you running now, you honorable bastards! Ah, but the next one will be right on target!"

And now Gill knew what he'd found so ominous in the little man's question: *If a dream is a subconscious thought, what power may lie in a conscious one?*

It was his world, after all, the world of his worst nightmares. So why not dream a really good one? Or for that matter a really nasty one? And:

"Ki-no Sung," Gill gasped, "I know what you're doing. This is your war you just started, right? But we're right in the war zone. In fact, we were almost ground zero . . . !"

Far away across the treetops, a mushroom cloud was rising on a tall, thin stem. But surely, if this place housed a missile silo, it must have been designed to hit back?

"It will keep until you're in the clear," Sung said with a grim smile. "But you had better be on your way. Their instruments will have told them where the next one is targeted." And he pointed back toward the camouflaged complex.

White-smocked technicians were fleeing the bunker now, and the Tannoy or whatever was back on, screaming: "Incoming! Incoming! Incoming!" And no one, but no one, seemed any longer interested in Gill and his group.

Or perhaps someone was.

"The return of the return of the magnificent seven," Turnbull growled as the group converged at the command helicopter. "Nice to see you all in one piece, not pieces."

But Ki-no Sung was anxious now. He hopped from one foot to the other, saying, "I can't stop this thing. It's going to happen. Fred, can you fly this machine? If so, then go. All of you—go now!"

"His nightmare's out of control," said Gill. "It's time we got aboard this . . ." But there he paused abruptly, and his mouth fell open as he looked up at the cockpit. A figure had appeared and was staring down at the group through the curved window.

It was a Chinese officer, a colonel, in uniform . . . but at the same time it wasn't. The figure was too big, too powerfully built, too white.

"My God!" Angela hissed. For despite the theatrically slanted eyes, the Fu Manchu mustache, and the regalia and insignia of a senior Red Chinese officer, the man in the cockpit was unmistakably—

"Jon Bannerman," Turnbull snarled. "Also known as Sith!"

"And the chopper . . . isn't," Stannersly groaned. "It looks like one at first glance, but it's an imitation. Like something off a cheap movie set. It would never get off the ground."

An imitation, yes, Gill thought. *Something knocked together in a hurry by the synthesizer. Oh, it's a transport, all right, but not for use in this world. Only into and out of it. Just a part of the game.*

"Sith?" Ki-no Sung's voice had hardened now. "The one who caused all of this? Then if it's over, let it be over for him, too. Let it be over now!"

"Incoming! Incoming! Incom . . ." And then a continuous buzz from the speakers as the last of the technicians fled the bunker and control center.

Sith/Bannerman in his Chinese guise was grinning down on them, a sardonic grin that would indeed have suited Sax Rohmer's fiendish creation, Fu Manchu. But when the figure in the mock-up helicopter actually burst into laughter, then Gill and the minder were prodded into the same wild action—or perhaps not so wild, for they had both arrived at the same conclusion.

They swung their weapons up, aimed them directly at Sith's face and form through the plastic window of his "machine." And his slanted eyes widened in shock as he fell back and tried to squeeze himself down out of sight.

"Oh, God!" said Miranda Marsh, but so faintly they barely heard her. "Someone pressed the button. But he's too late."

Her companions looked where she was looking: toward the center of the camp. The low whine of underground machinery and a grinding of gears told their own story, as an area of camouflage netting near the bunker quickly folded back on itself and the nose of a missile elevated into view. But Miranda was right and it was too late. For high in the sky, a silver dart with a white tail was already arcing down to its target.

The one will set off the other, thought Gill. *Two tactical nuclear explosions for the price of one. We're goners!*

There was an electrical hum and crackle. Sith's "helicopter" shimmered, faded, and was gone . . . but the crackle and the shimmer remained. Just exactly what Gill and Turnbull had been hoping and indeed praying for. A door: a means of transporting not only *into* but *out of* this synthesized world.

Gill grabbed up Barney, yelled, "Now, *quick!*" and thrust Angela ahead of him into the space where the fake or disguised machine had stood. They all crushed forward into that intimidating space, that doorway—all of them except the big minder, who paused to sweep up Ki-no Sung like a sack of rice.

In fact, as Turnbull hurled himself and the little yellow man into the trailing end of Sith's nexus, he feared that he'd left it just a second too late. But no, for while the intense white light that suddenly surrounded him was blinding, it was also cold and seemed to last for only a moment. Then . . .

The Castle!" Gill croaked, trying to stand up and not making it at first, then finally staggering to his feet and reaching for Angela. "The control center."

"And undamaged," Turnbull groaned from where he sprawled in an untidy tangle with Ki-no Sung. "Still in one piece—or several colors—despite that I might easily have shot it to bits when I wrecked that screen on your machine world."

"Thone machinery," said Gill. "Self-repairing." And:

"*Sith!*" cried Ki-no Sung, pointing as he got to his feet.

It was Bannerman, no longer in his Chinese guise but *the* Jon Bannerman as Gill, Angela, and the minder had first known him, and known him only too well, during their previous journey through this incredible maze of worlds:

Tall, firm-limbed, and well muscled, with a blocky figure, a broad chest, and a short thick neck bearing a modestly handsome head of gray-streaked, crew-cut hair; and with a straight nose and narrow cynical mouth—"foreign" features in general, especially his dark eyes, defying speculation upon his nationality—Bannerman wouldn't go entirely unnoticed in a crowd. But neither would he attract too much attention.

Not at first sight, anyway.

But look closer . . . and his unusual eyes never seemed the same color, while his powerfully built body appeared just *too* . . . too what? Too well put together? Constructed?

Foreign, built, constructed: fashioned. That was it. All taken together, the impression he left was just exactly that: of someone who had been fashioned. And despite that his exterior was modeled on a real man, in *sum total* Bannerman seemed other than human.

But only seemed? No, of course not; for Gill and the others knew the facts of it. And: *Too damn true!* Gill thought. *We know you, Jon Bannerman. You weren't born. You were made, synthesized, copied. But God alone knows about the genesis of the fucking thing inside you!*

The construct had appeared from behind a bank of controls unlike anything Gill could ever have imagined. But being Gill, no sooner had he seen it than he *did* understand: that this was indeed the node's control center. It was the heart of the Castle, the synthesizer itself. And Sith/Bannerman was in a hurry.

His blunt hands fluttered, almost blurred, over an array of glowing areas that changed color even as he instructed the vastly complex computer. Gill was aware that many of the great machine's more basic functions could be brought into play telepathically, similiar to voice activation in Earth-type instruments; *knew* that this was so because he'd actually interfaced with this very computer. But that was when he'd had a key, and when he'd had time to "study" the thing; since when a new program or "disk" had been inserted, and entry restricted.

But while he wasn't as yet able to get into the new system, that didn't mean he couldn't try to stop someone else from using it.

Gill looked for his gun, grabbed it up. Useless—he was either out of ammo or didn't know how to prepare the unfamiliar weapon for firing. The few shots that he had managed to get off in "China" had been made ready by the previous user. And George Waite and Fred Stannersly had the same problem. But Jack Turnbull was something or someone else. And he still had his original machine pistol.

The minder was on his feet, lumbering across the weirdly resistant floor in the direction of Sith/Bannerman and bringing his weapon to bear as he went. Sith saw him coming and his activity at the controls became a frenzy of motion. Then, following a final, frantic pass with his hands over the light array, he backed off from Turnbull and bared his teeth in a snarl—a savage glare of hatred from a supposedly "higher" intelligence!

But in the next moment—as the entire "console" began to glow with a pulsating reddish light—Sith's snarl turned to a grin, then a baying laugh of triumph.

And Gill thought: *Jack, if you're going to shoot the bastard, for Christ's sake do it now!*

No such luck.

The "room" elongated, became a tunnel with flowing, multicolored walls, with Sith and the console of lights at one end and Gill's party at the other. And the tunnel stretched itself like an infinitely long rubber tube, carrying Sith at accelerating jet-plane speed away into the distance! So that even if the minder had fired, still his bullets wouldn't have had the velocity to catch up with the departing Sith, not unless they, too, had been possessed of the same acceleration; in which case they might just have caught him. But Turnbull didn't fire.

And in fact, having moved several paces away from Gill and the others, the "stretch" had carried the minder almost a hundred yards away before he'd cut short his pursuit. And Sith continuing to zoom off like a message down a wire, becoming a dot, and then a speck, and finally vanishing in haze and distance . . .

A moment more and the incredible tunnel contracted again, bringing Turnbull back to the group and returning the "room" to its origins, except now there was no console and no Sith, only the sick-making, soundlessly flowing walls.

"Why didn't you shoot him?" Gill was furious.

But the minder only said, "Spencer, will you calm down? I wasn't trying to shoot him. I *couldn't* shoot him. For the same reason I didn't shoot him in that fake chopper of his. I don't have any ammo. I used the last of it on those Red soldiers. So I thought my best bet would be to try to frighten him, put him off whatever he was doing at those controls. And it looks like my little ploy worked well enough. But on the same subject—why the hell didn't *you* shoot him? Any of you?"

Gill looked sheepish, likewise Waite and Stannersly. And throwing down his weapon in disgust, Gill said, "Because I don't know how to cock the bloody thing!"

"Same story here," said Waite. And Stannersly, looking miserable, offered a wry shrug.

"Fred and George I understand," Turnbull said, glancing at Waite and the pilot. "But you? You with your machine thing?"

"I was baffled, too," said Gill. "But see, these only *look* like Chinese guns. They were synthesized, along with everything else in that world, from what the Castle knows of China."

"No," said Ki-no Sung, "from me. My head. My bad dreams. I know—I *not* know—guns. Not know 'bout guns.'"

"His English is back to square one," said Miranda.

Gill nodded. "The game has moved on. We're down that snake and it's time to roll the dice again."

"But who rolled them last time?" Angela still didn't know how they had got here.

"Sith," Gill explained. "When he took flight from 'China,' we hitched a ride on the tailgate of his truck. I suppose you could say we cheated."

"So these guns are useless to us." Stannersly tossed his weapon aside. "Shit!"

But the minder said, "Hold on a bit. If the synthesizer manufactured those rifles from the little bit that Sung knows about guns, how come they weren't mock-ups like Sith's helicopter? I mean, those Chinks from the bunker were firing away like crazy!" He picked up Stannersly's weapon.

"What's your point?" said Gill.

And Turnbull grinned at him. "You're not working at maximum revs, are you, my friend? Where else would the synthesizer have obtained knowledge of a gun's working, do you suppose, if not from Sung's mind?"

"From yours." Gill shrugged. "Or from mine? No, more probably from yours."

The minder half shook his head, said, "Well, maybe—but more likely from the bullets I sent through that screen on your machine world!"

Gill gaped as Turnbull checked the alien gun, said, "Jammed," then yanked the magazine off and examined the ammunition. And as a broad grin spread across his face, Gill knew what the other was doing.

"It copied your bullets!" he said.

"Right," said Turnbull. "So let me have those magazines, boys, and at least one of our guns will be back in action."

"Spencer," said Angela, who was looking anxious again. "I don't know or care whether Sith moved away from us or moved us away from him. But I do care that he knows where we are. Can't we move on now . . . well, wherever?"

"She's right," said Gill. "If there's anything else that needs working out we can do it later. But right now I think we should be getting away from here."

And Ki-no Sung said, "Go Barney?"

Barney!

Gill looked around, gave a nervous laugh when he saw that for once Barney hadn't deserted them. And as soon as he called to the dog, Barney came to him and whined, and licked his hand. "Not a bad idea," Gill said then. "We go Barney. Except—how do I tell him where we want to go?"

"Tell him to seek," said Turnbull. "And when he goes seek, we follow him."

"You're on," said Gill. And to the others: "We may be taking a chance, but . . . are you ready?" Everyone could see there was no time to waste, and so Gill crouched and patted the dog's head, and said, "Seek, Barney, seek!"

And the old fellow cocked his head on one side, went running to one of the walls with his stumpy tail wagging, sniffed around for a moment, then gave a single bark and stepped stiff-legged, straight into the swirl of sickening colors . . .

CHAPTER
27

NOTHING WAS SOLID in the house of doors. Even the "solid" walls only seemed that way in that they refused penetration; not like a man-built wall that hurts if you fail to acknowledge it, but an initially gentle resistance that only grows harder in answer to your insistence, like opposing magnetic forces.

But the wall Barney had chosen wasn't in the least solid. It allowed access, and you could walk right through it and out the other side. For of course the dog had the advantage—or perhaps not—of having spent time here; not alone in the synthesized worlds, but right here in the guts of the synthesizer itself; time that he had probably used on the run from Sith or one of his constructs. And out of necessity he'd worked it out for himself which walls were and which weren't.

But here in the House of Doors there was nothing good for a dog to eat, and that had been Barney's other incentive. Just how he had first discovered his way into the synthesized worlds of Gill's, Angela's, Turnbull's first ordeal still wasn't understood; but since then the program had been changed, making even more speculative the assumption that he could still do it. Not that the seven had any huge desire to explore alien worlds, but they would certainly like to get back to their own.

That last was true for the majority of them, at least, but Gill and the minder weren't so sure. Yes, they would like Angela and Miranda out of it—and maybe Sung, Waite, and Stannersly, too—but their own choice (if they were to have one) wouldn't be so easy. For they knew that getting back to Earth, or rather back to the world they knew, wouldn't solve a thing. The alien nodes would still be there; the Ggyddn weed would be everywhere; the countdown had already started. And whether the Ggyddn destroyed Mankind or Mankind destroyed itself trying to destroy the Ggyddn, the end result would be the same. In short, the place to stop this invasion was right here, in the synthesizer or in one of its many projections.

In any case, it was unlikely that Barney could find his way back to his own world; he hadn't done so the first time around, so why expect it of him now? No, the best (or worst) they could hope was that he would show them the way into a more acceptable world, and then that Gill would have the time or opportunity to attempt an interface with Sith's new program.

Meanwhile:

"Will he know where we are, d'you think, even if we're mobile in this bloody place?" George Waite asked of no one in particular. For like everyone else, Waite had sensed Gill's growing frustration when people aimed their questions directly at him, as if he were omniscient.

Yet still Gill chose to answer him. "While we're here in the House of Doors," he said, "it's entirely possible that Sith knows where we are at all times. There's no way we can know for sure. But if we're always in motion and he's kept busy tracking us, maybe it will slow him down in the preparation of whatever little surprise he's cooking up next. Better still, we won't be sitting ducks if he sends another scorpion after us."

"Meanwhile, we just keep following Barney," Turnbull added, making it sound like a statement and not a question as such.

"The good thing about that," said Gill, "is that the dog seems to be moving at random, simply following his nose. If we don't know where Barney's heading, then Sith can't guess where we're heading either."

"So in fact we could go nowhere forever or until we starve to death," said Miranda, unemotionally but wearily. "And we've not even nearly been going forever, and here I am already worn out!"

"But not as tired as you'd be if all this had happened in our own world," Angela told her. "For the fact is the House of Doors *is* good for you . . . when it's not being bad for you."

Waite gave an odd little laugh and said: "I'm pretty sure I've got this lump—this bloody tumor—beaten. So to that extent, Angela, you're dead right: in the event it doesn't kill me, the House of Doors will have been good for me!"

"At least you have hope now," said Stannersly.

Waite gave an emphatic nod. "Damn right! So whatever else comes of all this, I'm better off."

"For now," said Gill—and again silently cursed his own lack of diplomacy.

"What's that?" Waite put on speed, came up level with Gill where he followed close behind Barney. The rest of them were in line, with Turnbull at the rear watching their backs.

Gill knew that it was too late to back away from the conversation he had started, and so said: "We all have bad dreams, George. You've seen something of my nightmare world, also Ki-no Sung's. But that's just the two of us; others of us have still to visit the worlds that only their dreams can conjure. Come to think of it, maybe it's a good idea to air our fears right here and now. That way we might find out what we'll be up against at the next throw of the dice . . . that is, depending on who throws them."

"Or who knocks on the next door?" said Miranda.

"Same thing." Gill nodded, glancing back at her where she plodded ahead of Turnbull. "So why don't you start us off, Miranda? What does it for you? What's your worst nightmare?"

And as the walls of swirling color flowed past, and the group kept moving through the House of Doors' mainly conjectural "spaces," along its mazy corridors and through its dizzying yet claustrophobic rooms, she thought about it and eventually answered:

"It was a long time ago, really. And actually, I've never been much of a one for nightmares. Maybe I'm too down to earth or something."

"Tell us anyway," the big minder prompted her in his softest tone. "That is, if it's not too painful or private."

"No, nothing like that," she said, uncertainly. "But I was just a girl at the time. I mean, it hasn't bothered me for many a year now."

"But it did at the time?" said Gill. "What, was it recurrent?"

"Nightly!" She gave a small shiver. "Oh, very well, if you really think it might help to know:

"I was a bit of a tomboy . . ." And, mainly to Angela: "Well, maybe I don't much look like one now—or perhaps I do, in the mess we're all in—but I was. And I had fallen out of a tree, breaking my right arm and dislocating my shoulder. At the hospital, they got my records mixed up, gave me a shot that didn't agree with me and left me only half-sedated. In fact I was delirious when they fixed my arm, and the shot hadn't worked so I wasn't exactly out. I *felt* most of what they did to me, and it was bloody awful!

"So that afterward, well, that was it: a recurrent nightmare. About this group of terrible, silent, white-coated giants standing all around me, looking down on me, swimming in and out of focus and breaking my limbs one at a time, then fixing them, and then starting all over again. I used to wake up screaming, sure that all of my bones were jelly!" She paused and shivered again, then said, "That's it. Nothing more to tell . . ."

"*Phew!*" The minder whistled. "Well, I think we can all do without that. What, a world of concentration camp doctors carrying out experimental operations without anesthetic? Miranda, you won't be knocking on any doors while I'm around!"

"And what about you, you great thug?" She fell back beside him. "Or do you only *give* nightmares?"

"I have my fair share," he said. "A couple of bad times in Afghanistan. Another about a colleague of mine who got crushed by a truck."

"Crushed by a truck?" Her hand flew to her mouth. "Jack—what a terrible accident!"

"No." Turnbull shook his head, looked her straight in the eye. "It wasn't an accident," he said gruffly. "That's why I have nightmares about it."

And Miranda's eyes widened as at last she began to understand something of the man behind the wisecracks, also to recognize some of the cracks behind this occasionally not so wise man. The big minder wasn't about to reveal any more weaknesses, however, and so passed the buck to Stannersly. "What about you, Fred?"

"Mine's a spatial thing," the pilot answered, stepping out apace with Ki-no Sung, but keeping his eyes glued to the floor or straight ahead but in any case averted from the walls. "You saw an example of it when we first arrived in here, inside the House of Doors, I mean. I wasn't going to get up off the floor, tried to dig my fingers in, couldn't open my eyes. Like I told you then, I think it's a result of my being a flyer. It's like all my senses are tuned to it: tuned to three dimensions, that is. I have to be—what, free as a bird?—free as the sky? It isn't claustrophobia but it could be related. So personally, I don't think you need worry about me knocking on any doors. *This* place is my worst nightmare! I don't think it can get any worse than this, and I mean right now! I feel so sick, disoriented, I could just throw up. I would, if there was anything in my stomach."

Gill was interested. "You mean you think that if you were to roll the dice, knock on a door, we'd end up back here? Well that's an interesting idea in itself, and one that's worth remembering."

But while listening to Stannersly, Gill had also been rethinking this thing. Maybe it wasn't such a bright idea to get all of these phobias out in the open after all. Surely it would only serve to bring them all back into focus, make them all the more vivid, easier to remember. And easier to conjure?

And besides, he certainly didn't want Angela talking about her thing:

the constant terror she had lived in, of her brutal, rabid, rapacious ex-husband, Rod Denholm. He was dead now, yes, but his memory was a nightmare in itself. So maybe it was time to change the subject. And so:

"Other things," Gill said abruptly, in an attempt to arrest their minds, turn them aside from such morbid subjects. "We got split up back there in Ki-no Sung's China. Maybe now is a good time to fill in some gaps. I remember waking up in that bamboo hut yapping about Barney. That was because I'd been dreaming he was lost again. Yet he turned up with Jack and Miranda. Do you know what happened there, you two?"

"Happens I do," Turnbull answered. "Or I might. Barney was with us in the rain before we found Sung's place; likewise the next morning when we went into the fishing village. After that . . . the last time I saw him he was sniffing around a couple of the village dogs. I reckon he was doing his own thing a while there, and when he was through he picked up our trail again."

And Miranda said, "When we all ran into the forest, Jack and I got separated from the rest of you. I was lucky, I suppose. Being with Jack, I was that much safer. He's good at that sort of thing—escape and evasion and such. We saw you taken, and also the direction those helicopters took. So, we doubled back to where we'd been surprised, picked up what we could of the stuff you'd dumped, and we were just starting out again—heading for that army base, the silo—when Barney found us."

Turnbull took it up. "We only salvaged one sausage bag," he said ruefully. "Going on all the odds and ends it contained, it had to be Angela's. We pocketed the best of the stuff, left the rest. Hey, we had to make speed and couldn't lumber ourselves. But there was also one dead rabbit in there. Maybe it was a bit suspect, I don't know, but Barney didn't think so. So we let him get on with it and he caught us up later as we arrived at the Red base. Other than that, there were a few high-octane nuts and a couple of bars of chocolate, and that's it. So much for rations." He dug in his pockets, handed out chocolate.

And again Miranda: "When I saw that place, those soldiers—the camouflage netting, the whole termite's nest—my every instinct said flight. But Jack's said fight. And the rest you know."

Waite said, "I thought it was all over, and then you two stepped out of the trees. You know, that was the closest I've ever been to a combat zone? Up until then I only made contingency plans for soldiers—I never tried my hand at being one. Not a real one, and not for very long, anyway."

"And not just a soldier," the minder reminded him. "A spy, a guerrilla—a cancer in the enemy's guts—working behind his front lines. That's why I became a minder. Close protection is dangerous enough, but hell . . . I was getting *too* damned old for that really tough stuff! Ten years ago I was too old for that. Face it, twenty-five is too old! And the fact is, I quite like the idea of getting old. *Now* I do, anyway." And pacing forward, he put a supportive arm around Miranda, said, "You okay?"

"I'll live . . . well, for the time being," she said.

"This maze of worlds is working against us," said Angela thoughtfully, "and it's working for us." She had been thinking things out, puzzling over the apparent paradoxes here. "Ki-no Sung worked it out, came at the problem from a fresh angle. If it was his nightmare, why not make it work for him? Something seems to be keeping—I don't know—a crazy sort of balance here? For sure enough he did make it work for him."

"Yes, and nearly got us killed in the bargain," said Stannersly.

"Not you," Sung said, from where he trotted in the middle of the pack. "I not want you get hurt. My bad dream—*I* hurt, not you."

"Yeah, but that's not how it works," Turnbull said. "What kills you is likely to kill us, too. So no more heroics, Ki-no Sung."

"Stupid!" The little man shook his head.

"Me or you?" said the minder.

"I stupid," Sung answered. "Think it finished. So make *all* finished. Stupid."

"Ki-no Sung," said Gill, "some of us have done this before—and we won, got back to our own world. Keep telling yourself that. You *can* go back to your own world, and to Lotus. The real Lotus, I mean."

And the little man nodded, munched chocolate, kept going.

"Well, we have no more packs to carry," Waite sighed. "No more food, either. Hell, we deserve a ladder. I've had it with all these snakes."

And Gill said: "Angela, sweetheart, what you were saying about the synthesizer maintaining a crazy kind of balance has got me thinking—and crazy is the right word for it. So if I stray from what little we know, somebody put me right. Anyway, this is how I see it:

"Whatever else is out of whack, cockeyed, in our continuing existence, *we* at least are the real thing. I mean, we're in our real bodies, no matter which world we find ourselves in. That much is clear from the fact that we've retained our usual bodily functions, which weren't much apparent the last time we were trapped in a House of Doors; and additionally we get hungry, weak, bearded, et cetera. So this *is* us . . . lousy English: *we, are us!* We aren't the synthesized dummies that we were the first time around. That time, only Rod Denholm and Alec Haggie were the real thing. One of them, Haggie, got into the game by accident, and Rod Denholm was an additional little menace that Sith dreamed up. For some reason he used the real Rod; probably for his personal titillation."

Gill paused, frowned, said, "It's easy to lose track. So many combinations of ideas or guesses that can be right or not so right or totally wrong. Anyway, I'll try to go on. Now Sith said that this time around poisons can kill us, alien atmospheres can kill us, and just about anything can kill us, because we *are* real. Being real, our energies get depleted and we can be worn down body and mind and soul. Depleted and destroyed.

"Well, that's what *he* says . . . but what about the synthesizer? The way I see it, it must have basic rules for testing the specimens under examination. I mean, this is a Thone machine, and at floor level the Thone weren't bad people. You can reason with them. I talked to the Grand Thone; he didn't come over as some kind of monster; Sith was the odd man—or thing—out. So if certain rules are basic to the synthesizer, maybe Sith was putting on the frighteners about poisons and inhospitable atmospheres and such. In which case, maybe the synthesizer's computer *does* keep some kind of crazy balance."

"Basic rules?" Turnbull sounded skeptical. "But didn't he say this was his game now? Didn't he tell us he'd reprogrammed the thing and could make up the rules as he went along?"

"Yes, he said so," Gill answered. "But can he? What if the thing has fail-safes, built-in principles that just can't be bypassed—not by Sith or anyone else. After all, we know that it has one such. I got knocked on the head when those Red soldiers grabbed us in that clearing. So did Angela. Okay, so I've got a bump and she has a bruise, but they're healing fast. And apart from that we're fine . . . we were put right. And George has been fixed up, too. And Ki-no Sung, to the best of the synthesizer's ability, anyway. So obviously that part of it still works. See what I'm getting at? What good is a test where all the control specimens must eventually die?"

"Let me get this right," said Turnbull. "What you're saying is . . . that first time, up in Scotland, we couldn't die or come to harm, not physical harm, anyway, because it wasn't us. But we could be harmed mentally, driven mad with fear, because we *thought* that we were us. We didn't know we were synthesized because if we had known it would have defeated the purpose of the test, which was . . . which was—"

"To drive us to the end of our tether," Gill cut in on him, nodding. "And then to see if we fell off the edge. And as it happened some of us did: Clayborne and Anderson. But as for the bulk of the test group, we survived both mentally and physically, even to the extent of beating Sith at his own cheating game. So obviously we were worthy. That's why the Thone backed off and let us be."

"Okay," said the minder. "So this time Sith would *like* to have changed the rules—and he would like for us to *think* he has—but in fact the program is fixed, immutable. Is that what you're saying?"

"Right," said Gill. "Something like that. Maybe. But just think: wouldn't it make sense in worlds that couldn't hurt the test specimens physically—in worlds that were suited to them—to test the actual specimens and not just their replicas?"

This time it was Angela querying, "Couldn't hurt them physically?"

Gill shrugged. "Well, barring accidents, of course. I suppose what I'm talking about is worlds with compatible atmospheres and gravities—in our case Earth-type worlds—where the specimens might actually survive."

"But if that were the case," Turnbull again, "then why didn't Sith put the real us through it the first time around?"

Gill frowned again, and said, "You know, Jack, sometimes you're too damn logical by far?" But then he snapped his fingers. "But you also supply your own answers."

"Eh?"

Gill nodded eagerly. "Do you remember when that poisonous insect-thing clamped itself on your hand? If that had been the real you, you would have been a dead man there and then. But you survived and went from strength to strength."

"So," said Waite, "there's some kind of justice, a system of checks and balances. For every snake a ladder, and vice versa."

"Possibly," said Gill. "Which means that Sith isn't as all-powerful as he would like to make out. And, Jack, think of this. If our synthesized bodies were the only reason we lived through that first ordeal, what about Haggie and Denholm—and Barney? They lived through it, too, most of it. Mostly on alien worlds. I mean, we know Sith's a cheat, so why not a liar, too?"

"So what it all boils down to," Turnbull said, "what you're actually saying, is that we have more of a chance than he's led us to believe. And that the only difference between this visit and our last visit is that this time it's really us."

Gill nodded. "And one other thing," he said. "This time *we know the score!* This time, if we get scared, terrified by something monstrous, we know that that's what it's all about. Okay, so let's be scared by all means— but let's *not* be driven over the edge. Sith's counting on us going a little bit nuts or maybe entirely insane while he stands off and laughs at us; counting on us being scared witless, when, at the last minute, he'll step in for the coup de grâce. In fact he's already tried that once, in 'China.' This is his idea of the big payback. So what we have to do is hang in there. And meanwhile, what *I* have to do is get back in touch with the bloody machine, or the purely mental part of its brain."

"And you're the only one who can do it," said Angela.

"And," Gill tried not to snap, "this is the ideal *place* to do it. But it takes concentration and I could use an edge, and at the moment I don't have either one."

Nor was he likely to have them just yet, for that was when Barney's hackles went up as he fetched an abrupt halt, growled low in his throat and went all stiff-legged, and began backing up so fast that Gill almost fell over him . . .

CHAPTER
28

FOR QUITE SOME time now there had been no "rooms" as such, and Gill and his party had been walking along a narrow winding corridor between parallel banks of the sickening color swirl that served as walls. Since doors into other sections of the synthesizer were invisible, they couldn't see the one that Barney had shied from. His instinctive reaction, however, had told them it was there, and what was now coming through it confirmed it.

"Here we go again!" Jack Turnbull grated, as feathery feelers like the plankton-seeking legs of some grotesque, gigantic barnacle came snaking out of the swirl only a few inches ahead of a blue-gray chitin-plated pincer and a set of baleful, swiveling crystal eyes.

"Arachnid rex!" George Waite gulped, backing off. But Gill grabbed him and dragged him past the emerging bulk of the scorpion construct.

"We know what's back that way," Gill shouted. "Nothing. So we have to go this way—forward!"

They all followed suit, hurling themselves past the swaying feelers, the threatening pincer, and the glinting faceted eyes; and those emotionless eyes followed them every inch of the way. But as Miranda squeezed by along the wall opposite, so the groping feelers drifted toward her. They may or may not have been a threat in their own right; it could be that they were purely sensory equipment additional to the eyes, giving the construct or its pincers something to lock on to in places where the eyes couldn't go. Whichever, it appeared to the minder that Miranda was threatened.

Bringing up the rear, he ducked under the feelers (which at once curled back on themselves, as if they sensed the draft he'd created), actually grabbed hold of an eye stalk, and tried to hack it loose with the knife he'd taken from Ki-no Sung. He was immediately batted aside by the great claw, fortunately in the right direction, and sent sprawling. But his reflexes were lightning fast; quick as a flash he turned on his back, scrambling out of reach as the scorpion came in a sideways scuttle through the invisible door, its stinger swinging out from the sickening colors to hover over the spot where he'd fallen.

Turnbull dug his heels in then, propelling himself backward, partway out of reach, and Gill and Stannersly were on hand to drag him the rest of the way.

Following which . . . they were all seven running, and Barney in the lead making eight, and making very good time as he fled down the corridor with his stumpy tail between his legs. Except the corridor was now more a tube, a funnel of swirling colors that curved overhead and underfoot, as if the party of humans raced for their lives along the eye of a horizontal tornado blowing from the mind of some crazed surrealist painter.

And like a tornado, the thing curved and twisted ahead of them; while behind the scorpion came scuttling, seeming better equipped to negotiate the sluggish floor and gradually gaining on them. Then, as they followed Barney around a sharp bend—

"A door!" George Waite shouted, from where he now led the group. And as the rest of them came around the bend—there it was, a circular plug of dull gray metal, by its looks as dense and impenetrable as the door on a bank vault. Indeed, and except for one major difference, it might be just such a door. It had a knocker: a heavy ring on a swivel, set central in a surface of studs, bolt heads, and overlapping plates of welded fish-scale styled armor. Waite reached for the knocker, and . . .

"No!" Gill yelled. "We didn't get to *your* nightmares yet!"

And as Waite hesitated, so Angela stepped forward. "But I know all about mine," she said, "and he's dead and gone." Cold and untypical of her as it sounded, still it was the truth and she didn't have time for niceties. None of them did.

She grabbed the knocker, lifted it, and even if Gill would have stopped her he couldn't. The scorpion was coming around the conduit's bend; it was almost upon them; if it got much closer it would be coming right through the door with them.

Turnbull went to one knee, snapped off three rapid shots on single-fire, and heard them spang uselessly off the construct's alien armor as the thing lunged closer still.

Then, several things in rapid succession:

Barney gave a howl—someone whispered, *"Jesus!"*—Angela saw the agony of indecision on Gill's face, then his sharp nod—and because there was no time left and nothing else for it, she knocked . . .

They were falling. Those of them with open eyes saw a rotating wheel of colors, but at least the colors were acceptable:

Blinding golden sun . . . blue sky . . . white sand . . . green trees (palms?) . . . blue sea . . . and back to blue sky. And so on until the sea was everything. Then deep, deep *into* the sea. And down they went, the big (and heavy) minder even touching bottom maybe three meters down, which at least gave some indication of how far they had fallen. And all of them took in water, because their mouths were open, or they didn't have enough air in their lungs and tried to breathe at the wrong time, or from the sheer shock of splashing down.

But then they were on the calm surface, gasping, spluttering, coughing, and swimming or floundering for the beach—most of them. But Miranda cried out; she couldn't swim; she flailed her arms like a mad thing and slid back under. Turnbull grabbed her hair, drew her to the surface, coolly and calmly struck her hard under the jaw. It was fifty yards to the beach and he knew that he—and she—wouldn't make it if she fought him. There simply wasn't enough of anything left in him. Or in any of the others, for that matter . . .

Parrot," Gill mumbled, spitting out sand some hours later.

Turnbull was already awake. Naked to the waist, sitting on the beach, he kept the glare off Miranda Marsh. And in so doing he was obviously enjoying the sunlight. The rest of them—with the exception of Barney—were still asleep and recovering from their exhaustion. They lay wherever they had crawled and crumpled, on the soft white sand of the beach.

"No," said the minder when Gill spoke. "It looks like one, I agree, but there are subtle differences. Webbed feet, mainly, and the fact that it's flightless. It was probably the big beak that fooled you, that and the brilliant colors. But the beak's for cracking open bivalves which they fish out of the shallows. I've been watching them do it."

Gill sat up. "Barney, too, apparently," he said. The mongrel dog was some five or six paces away, guarding the dead body of his latest catch, the bird in question. "But he hasn't eaten it yet."

"I don't think that's to question its edibility," Turnbull said. "Simply means he hasn't got rid of the rabbit yet. I suspect the bird's for later."

Gill looked around, felt something of urgency return, and said, "Where the hell are we?"

"Well it certainly isn't hell," the minder answered. "More like paradise if you ask me."

And then Gill recognized the place. A world of oceans and beaches, blues skies and seas, grassy plains and flowering forests. An Earth-type world of warm-blooded creatures that variously walked, flew, or swam and were in the main small, pretty, and fairly unintelligent—in the main, yes. Yet paradoxically, this had been the world of Angela's nightmares. Except, and as she had pointed out, *he* was dead now . . .

The word "dead," just thinking about it, added fuel to the fire of Gill's urgency. "The rest of them," he said, getting to his feet and finding his legs weak as jelly. "Are they okay? How long have we been out? What's been happening?"

"Whoa!" said Turnbull. "Ease off, or you'll wake them up and scare them all to death! We're okay . . . I think. I've been awake maybe an hour. If that sun's like our sun, I calculate I was down maybe two or three hours. Which means you've each had about four hours' sleep. I would think that's right. Certainly I feel refreshed. Here, have a drink." He passed Gill a co-conut, or something almost exactly like a coconut, with the eyes punched out at the blunt end, and added, "Go ahead. I mean, if it's poison, then it's the best I ever tasted. Well apart from Schultheiss anyway."

"Schultheiss?" Gill drank, and the milk of the nut was as cool and sweet as wine to his parched lips and throat.

"German beer, from Berlin," Turnbull told him. "God, when Waite's people found me in that bar, I should have kicked hell out of them and run for it!"

"Angela!" Gill gasped, and made staggeringly for her small sprawled figure.

Ki-no Sung groaned and propped himself up, and Gill handed him the coconut as he passed. A moment later he was down on his knees cradling Angela in his arms, and just as quickly she woke up.

"Uh?" she said, for a moment fighting him. But then she saw who it was and her arms at once tightened around him. "Spencer! What happened—?" She looked around, saw the beach and the sea, and remembered. And: "*That* place." She grimaced, and wiped sand from the corner of her mouth.

"But not quite the same," he told her with a smile. "You're not alone this time, and there's nothing to fear from . . . well, from him."

Turnbull was waking the others. He'd poked the eyes out of more nuts, and soon all of the group's members were sitting or kneeling, slaking their thirst and beginning to ask questions. Gill rightly supposed that he was the only one who'd be able to answer them (Angela wasn't quite herself yet), and being fully awake and safe for now, for once he felt capable of doing so.

"Let's get some shade," he said, "and then we'll talk. But I can tell you now, this isn't a new place to me and Angela. We were here before. The story isn't very pretty, but this time at least it should be different. For while this is definitely the place of Angela's own personal nightmare, the bad dream itself has long since gone away." (Gill hoped so at least, but in the back of his head something had already commenced niggling away at him.)

Behind the beach, the forest fringe started where the sand turned to loose soil. And as the party moved into the shade, so the undergrowth came alive with furtive rustlings.

"No shortage of food here," Fred Stannersly commented. "A little pig-creature just went rushing off through those bushes there. And the fruit on these trees . . . okay, okay, I know!" He held up his hands placatingly. "We can't be sure. But they certainly *look* edible."

"And those big palm nuts are excellent," George Waite gave his opinion. "If their flesh is as good as their milk—"

"It is," the minder assured him. And Waite went on:

"Then we aren't going to starve. And don't tell me that an ocean as beautiful as that doesn't have any fish."

"It has shellfish, certainly," said Turnbull.

"Fish!" said Ki-no Sung excitedly. "Me fisherman. Show you how catch fish!"

"Yep," said Turnbull, "and the fowl seem decent, too—at least Barney thinks so. So there you go: fish and fowl and food afoot in the forest green. Some kind of paradise, yes."

"But it wasn't always," Angela shuddered . . .

They were a ragged bunch, their clothing soiled, ripped, or in tatters; their bodies bruised, scratched, cut, and in the Korean's case mutilated; their faces showing bruises and hollowed eyes, and the worry lines of constant stress. Miranda's smart modern clothes had long since given up the ghost. Now she made do with whatever was half or even in small part decent. Panty hose were no more; they now formed an elastic belt to hold up a pair of the minder's baggy winter long johns. He had explained to her that this wasn't normal wear, but in the House of Doors one never knew what to expect. Her midriff was bare, where she tried to hide her belly button under a knot formed of the tattered, dangling lower ends of what was once a blouse. The upper part was little more than a rag that scarcely hid her bra. But then, Miranda's joining the party had been a last-minute decision.

Ki-no Sung was the most ragged of all. He had looked like a scarecrow from day one; but thin as a rake, and with his mop of black hair forming a fringe all the way around his head, and the ugly stump of his left hand plainly visible because he had nothing to cover it . . . he seemed a hopeless case. But if hardiness is a virtue, then Sung was most virtuous of all . . .

They made themselves comfortable in a small clearing under a tree much like an oak, and Gill started to tell the story:

"When we got separated during our first—well, call it an adventure, if you like—Angela ended up here. Then as now, we were experiencing our own worst nightmares. At that time Rod Denholm, Angela's husband, was alive and unwell. Rod was a pretty sick man: sick in his mind, that is. He was an insanely jealous alcoholic—jealous with no cause, I might add—and just as hard on his friends as he was on the booze. As is usual, his nastiness went hand in hand with his drinking. But worst of all from my point of view, he was hardest on Angela, saw her as the reason for all his many problems . . ." Gill paused. He was uneasy with doing this, as his hesitancy indicated. So Angela took up the story:

"Rod didn't make love," she said bitterly. "He raped. You think a man can't rape his wife? Well you don't—didn't—know Rod. When things went wrong he drank; when they went very wrong he soaked in it. I didn't see this side of him until after we'd married, when it was too late. But you can only take so much of jealous accusations, and fights and bruises and . . . and . . . and the things he did. So I ran off.

"I didn't know Spencer—I'd only just met him—when the House of Doors, or the Castle, took him. But because I was with him, it took me, too. Likewise Jack and one or two others. Sith knew about Rod . . . don't ask me how. It probably came about because Rod was following me, threatening me.

"So Rod ended up here. The real Rod, captured by Sith and . . . and *injected* into this world to foul it up. And to foul me. But he couldn't do it without booze, so Sith saw to that, too. And as if that weren't enough, Sith duplicated—constructed—a whole gang of Rods who pursued me like . . . like . . ." She shook her pretty head, looked away. And Gill said:

"Paradise? Not under those circumstances. More like some kind of hell. But Angela came out of it unscathed when Rod—the real one—fell into a giant clam and . . ."

"A clam?" Miranda Marsh spoke up, frowning. She had been rubbing the spot under her chin where the minder had hit her, and looking at him curiously. But glancing at Angela: "Do you mean like an oyster, a sea-shell?"

"A bivalve, yes." Angela nodded. "But a big one. There's a stretch of beach not too far away where the surface is more mud than sand. At night, these large crabs come out of the sea into the forest to eat green stuff. They're pretty timid things. When they get panicked they flock down the beach, and the clams are waiting. Only touch one of their siphons—they sense food and open up to feed. Some of the shells I saw were maybe, oh, as much as seven feet across."

"*Ugh!*" Miranda shuddered.

But Turnbull said, "Clam chowder! *Wow!*"

"I like!" said Ki-no Sung.

And for a moment the conversation faltered, changed direction, actually lightened up a little.

Gill and Angela were sitting close together, Gill with his arm around her protectively; and now Miranda slid closer to the big minder. "You really hit me," she said, looking at him with that same curious expression. "I remember tasting salt water as I went down, and being dragged up by the hair. And then—"

"I hit you, yes," he said. "Or you would have drowned, maybe. And it's possible I would have drowned trying to save you. And I don't think I'd have given a damn if I did."

She took that in, said, "You saved my life."

For a moment Turnbull looked back at her, his expression as serious as any she'd ever seen . . . until he grinned, which ruined the whole effect. "Of course I had an ulterior motive."

And Miranda blinked, shook her head as if to clear it, and said: "I owe you one, Jack Turnbull."

"Anytime," he said, smiling at her warmly and genuinely.

The rest of them exchanged speculative glances, and George Waite coughed and turned to Angela, saying, "Okay, so this Rod fellow, your husband, slipped and fell into a giant clam. And?"

Angela gave a little shrug, pulled her shoulders together, and in a small voice said, "It was the end of him. The siphons whipped back inside and the lid—the upper half of the shell—ground shut. He was gone."

Gill took it up. "Tridacnae on Earth are cockles by comparison. And they can weigh hundreds of pounds. But wait; there's something else about these clams." The change in his voice got their immediate attention. "Angela made her escape through one of them."

"She what?" From Fred Stannersly.

"The other Rods, those damned constructs, were still after her," Gill explained. "Angela knew what they'd do, knew exactly how it was meant to end, because that was her nightmare . . . and Sith's twisted little joke."

Angela took over again, continuing in a very small voice. "On that same beach, as those terrible, lusting bastard things were closing in on me, I tripped another of these giant clams, tridacnae or whatever. But inside . . . there was only the yawning blackness of a great pit. It was the color of space—it *looked* like space, out beyond the stars. One look in there and I knew exactly what it was. It was a door, a tunnel to another world. And before the Rods could get to me, I jumped in."

"A door!" George Waite was on his feet. "Where, along the beach?"

"Hold it!" said Gill. "Things change, are rearranged, by the House of Doors. By the computer, the synthesizer. We don't know if it will be the same this time. Also, these crabs only come out at night, which triggers the clams. What would you do, dig for six-or seven-foot clams? Well I don't know if you ever tried digging up a razor shell back in our world, but believe me it's no easy thing. And they're only six inches long!"

Waite slowly sat down again.

"Also," Gill continued, "I needn't remind you that we're hardly at our best. We're hungry for decent food, tattered and dirty, quickly running out of steam."

And Turnbull said, "He's right. This is our chance for a little R and R before old *Sarcoptes scabiei*—or is it Arachnid rex?—comes back on the scene. Because I don't know if you've noticed, but if we sit around in any one place for too long, that bloke with lots of legs and a big stinger shows up like some kind of copper on the beat saying, 'Now move along there, you people, move along!' "

"Food," said Gill. "We get it however we can and eat our fill. And we wash these stinking clothes before they run the hell away. And we bathe in that gorgeous ocean."

"We can do better than that," said Angela. "I know where there's a river of sweet water less than a mile from here and toward the beach with the clams."

"And then we sleep," Gill went on, "and get as much as we can. Passing out on the beach there has only made me long for more of the same. But in a safe place and one that we can protect."

"Er, which might be difficult," said the minder.

They all looked at him. "The good swimmers among you," he said, "had better come with me. Or maybe we eat first and then you come with me. My gun's gone, and I want it back."

"Gone?" said Fred Stannersly.

"In the sea," Turnbull told him. "I was knackered, floating Miranda, needed at least one hand. I know the gun isn't too big, but still it felt like an anchor. I let it go in some ten feet of water. If we can recover it without too much delay, it will be okay. It was well oiled, and the magazine greasy. Then, if there's no damage to the ammo . . ."

"A few ifs," said Waite.

"But it's an iffy old world," the minder said with a shrug.

And Gill said, "In fact it's several of them, in fact a veritable maze of worlds . . ."

CHAPTER
29

THERE WAS NO question as to what they would do first. Sleeping on the beach had refreshed them; the milk and flesh of the coconuts had given them back a little of their strength; now they could use more of the same, and also attend to matters of personal hygiene.

The small forest pig-things were impossible to catch; get a hold of one, he would instantly exude grease and slip out of your hands. Fish were something else. Ki-no Sung quickly discovered how to wade out slowly and quietly into the shallows, cover the local guitar-shaped flatfish with his shadow, which seemed to immobilize them, then pluck them out of the water and toss them onto the beach. And for meatier meat: Fred Stannersly used the minder's knife to kill and skin four fat, slow snakes, which went onto a spit over a fire built by Miranda. Barney still hadn't eaten his catch, however, and so the "parrots" were safe for the moment from the group's attention.

Meanwhile, Turnbull and Gill had swum out from the beach and found the gun on a sandy, shell-strewn bottom. This hadn't been an easy thing to do. The weapon had half-buried itself in the soft sand; several large, weed-bearing conches had decided to take up home on it or in its vicinity; the gun had been hard to spot. Now the minder stripped and cleaned it while everyone ate, and Gill sat thinking about their next move.

Their *very* next move was obvious . . . they followed Angela to the river and swam or simply laved, easing all their aching parts and joints in the cool water, and hammering the dirt out of their clothing. And this was also

the ideal opportunity to spend a little time in private with Nature, something the lack of which had been getting to all of them.

By which time it was middle to late afternoon, the light came slanting
through the trees, and the forest was slowly quietening down . . .

Gill had picked up some half shells on the beach; their rims were razor
sharp and could take your finger end off. They were pretty good on bristles,
too. While the men shaved, Angela and Miranda sat on flat rocks at the
water's edge and talked.

Occasionally Miranda's eyes would stray to the big minder; his phy-
sique was imposing, yes, but there was a great deal more than that to him.
Angela saw the other's glances and asked her, "So, what do you think of
Jack?"

Miranda shook her head. "I don't exactly know what it is," she finally
answered. "Maybe it's just what we've been through that's getting to me
and not him at all. But *that* is a man! I thought I knew them all well enough,
but not that one."

"I feel the same about Spencer," Angela said. "The only difference is,
he knows it." It was a trap—and Miranda fell right into it.

"Of course, it's totally impossible, unthinkable," Miranda said, more
to herself than to Angela, before she even realized she was saying it. But a
moment later she did, and said, "I mean—"

"I know what you mean," Angela said, chuckling. "But let me tell you
it isn't impossible. If we get through this with all of our bits intact, you can
make up your mind then. Meanwhile he's looking after you like a baby—
and our bits *are* intact. So far at least."

"That's maybe a bit personal," Miranda said. But then she smiled. "I
don't know what you think, but I'm . . . well I'm not exactly a virgin, you
know."

Angela grinned, tossed her hair. "Well you can certainly bet that Jack
isn't! Anyway, it's none of my business. But if ever anyone needed a setting
for it, this place would have to be it."

And she was right. All that was missing was the music and the cham-
pagne.

"What are you two talking about?" Gill had a rag around his waist,
was pulling on his none-too-dry combat trousers.

"I was just saying that there's a great waterfall maybe a quarter mile
upriver, around that bend," Angela lied. "And if there are caves behind it,
that could be our refuge—our fortified position—for the night. Naturally
fortified, that is."

"Good!" Gill answered. "But the night's a while away yet. We'll check
out your cave theory first, but then we'll have to get back to the beach and

see if we can find those mighty mollusks. We can collect food along the way; Ki-no Sung can do a little more fishing before the sunlight goes entirely; and we can gather some more big nuts to fill our two remaining packs. But if there's a waterfall back there, then there will have to be cliffs, too. Cliffs means caves, so one way or the other we should find a refuge, yes. Everyone ready?"

And everyone was. They were all weary to their bones, but they knew what they had to do and wanted to get it done . . .

The caves were there, as Angela had expected, but to the sides of the waterfall rather than behind. It was ideal. An incursion from the white water wasn't likely; there were rugged cliffs to the rear; the caves were somewhat elevated from the forest, making for good observation across the ninety-degree arc of vegetation that would form the only likely route of any hostile invasion.

Without pause the group returned to the beach, and they were now brave enough to try some Earth-type fruit—or fruits that at least looked like those of Earth—along the way. They were delicious, however exotic, and no one fell ill. The route to the river, the waterfall, and caves was now reasonably well known to them; it wasn't likely that they would get lost when darkness fell.

Ki-no Sung caught more fish while there was still sufficient light; the rest of the group collected up his catch. Then, with the fall of twilight, it was time for Angela to lead them a third of a mile along the beach to the mud flats.

By then the sky was dotted with a handful of small, varicolored moons; they gave adequate light as the sand firmed up and became mud. "It isn't quicksand," Angela quietly informed her companions. "Your feet shouldn't sink in more than an inch or so. But we should start moving away from the sea and toward the forest now. That way we'll scare up the crabs that I told you about, and you'll see what you'll see."

The moons brightened up as the last rays of the sun made a fan over low, distantly silhouetted mountains, and the coconut palms at the rim of the forest cast shadows in which the group quietly moved forward.

But not quietly enough.

Suddenly there was a rustling of leaves and undergrowth, a commotion in the forest fringe! Then, in a madly tumbling rush, the first of the land-going crabs emerged. They were timid creatures, as much as a foot across but lacking pincers, and they shied, reared up, and sidled past Gill's startled party before continuing their frantic sidelong scuttle for the sea.

"Now!" Angela cried as the rush became an avalanche. "Down onto the beach and you'll see what happens. Trip the siphons if you want to look inside the clams—but for Christ's sake don't trip yourselves and fall in!"

Leading the way as hordes of crabs went sidling or tumbling past them to the sea, Angela cautiously pointed ahead. By the strangely weaving moonlight, the group could make out what looked like lengths of slimy rope lying like ridges on the mud surface. But as the crabs scrambled over them—

They writhed, slithered, carried the message back to their owners that it was feeding time. The ropes were siphons, snorkels sent up through the quivering sand to lie in wait for the prey; when the crush of crabs hit them, they triggered the great clams. The flat, upper shells of the bivalves were opening all along the beach. Lying just beneath the surface, they slopped mud aside as their scalloped rims rose like trapdoors, which was exactly what they were. Crabs in their dozens—literally scores, hundreds of crabs—went tumbling into the deep cups of the lower shells whose mobile, living innards slopped over them. And when those great, gorging mollusks were filled to capacity, then the upper shells ground shut again.

But Angela had been in a hurry, panicked in that previous time, and understandably so; she had underestimated the size of these monsters. Some of the great horny shells were easily ten and maybe more feet across!

"God!" said Miranda. "And to think that when I was a kid I used to collect seashells."

"You'd need an articulated truck and a crane to collect one of these babies," the minder told her. "Yes, and I think we can forget the clam chowder!"

The party separated, cautiously spreading out across the mud flats and carefully triggering those clams that hadn't as yet been activated. But they discovered no "great black hole the color of space," no secret door to another world, in any of them.

"Apparently," said Gill, calling off the search, "doors come and go. Maybe Angela's test run had come to an end. When the synthesizer calculated she wasn't going to break no matter what the pressure, it offered her a way out and so maintained the status quo—well, so to speak. The door was created especially for her, and after she'd used it it was withdrawn."

Back at the edge of the forest, Turnbull said, "But hasn't it been doing that all along? I mean, could it be that we don't really have anything to fear, that the synthesizer will call it quits even on the very rim, when it can drive us no farther? In your machine world we found the door in the ceiling of the cave right at the last minute. And likewise in the six-legged rabbit world, just before the suns went nova."

"I don't think so." Gill shook his head. "This time Sith's taken the gloves off."

"What makes you so sure?" The minder wasn't convinced.

"You keep forgetting," said Gill. "That first time around 'we' couldn't be killed, because it wasn't us. But this time it is. If we hadn't got out of my machine world we would have been pulped when the cave collapsed, and in the other place the nova would have fried us along with the entire planet."

"But we *did* survive that first time around," Angela said. "We were synthetics—yes, even though we didn't know it—but we did survive."

"That's right," said Gill. "Do you know what I put it down to? Partly to the fact that we're pretty clever, us humans, but mainly to the fact that we were bloody lucky . . ."

For a long while as they walked back the way they'd come, Turnbull let that sink in and made no reply. But eventually he said, "You're not always right, but I guess this time you probably are. In which case we have to hope that we can *stay* bloody lucky."

"Check," said Gill with a nod . . .

The caves were small—even the roomiest wasn't big enough to take the whole group. But leftovers from a time when the river had run this way, they were plentiful and literally honeycombed the cliffs. Gill's party of seven chose a close-packed nest of them, lighting fires in front of them on naked earth. And they broke up dry, fallen branches, piling them within easy reach to keep the fires going through the night. Also, they stripped the living branches from soft-leaved bushes for beds, and drew lots for watch duty (two people on watch at all times, for additional safety), before settling down to sleep. By which time they were more than ready for it.

Gill and Waite had drawn the first watch, and Turnbull sat up with them awhile. Angela and Miranda had drawn second watch, and Ki-no Sung and the minder the third; then Waite would be on duty again with Stannersly. And so the pilot was the lucky one: he at least would benefit from a mainly unbroken night's sleep. As for Barney: the mongrel dog was already snoring in front of a fire.

"Why don't you get some sleep?" Gill asked Turnbull.

"Things on my mind," said the other. "I wanted to ask you how you were getting on? If you'd progressed any toward getting back in touch with the synthesizer? That kind of thing."

"Because time in the real world is narrowing down?"

"I reckon."

Gill shook his head. "The more it narrows down, the more pressure I feel. The more pressure I feel, the less capable I appear to be. And as for the synthesizer: I haven't a clue as to how to get back in sync with it, no."

And Waite said, "So how did you do it the first time?"

Gill shrugged tiredly. "We were lucky—again, yes. Sith came after us on Earth, in Scotland, with a Thone weapon; more properly a tool. Jack shot it out of his hand, took a couple of fingers with it. I learned how to use the weapon. It was a machine, after all, and that's what I do. But the thing was damaged and leaking power. Then we came across a scorpion that was also damaged, and we were there when it did some long-distance refueling like that crippled tick-thing on the Isle of Wight. So I gassed up the weapon, too, and learned yet more about how it worked."

As he paused, the big minder took it up. "Then, on a desert world, the world of Clayborne's worst nightmares where the supernatural was real, we came across a door like a giant crystal. And finally, using his machine empathy, Spencer was able to put two and two together. He crashed into the synthesizer's mechanical mind, 'talked' to the thing, gave himself an edge."

And Gill finished it. "Sith made a couple of bad mistakes. We took advantage of them and won. Not only did we win, we took him out, chased him right back across the universe to God only knows where. And because he'd been cheating—because he'd wanted the Earth for his own reasons—the Thone punished him."

Turnbull again: "Now, apparently, he's been recruited by the Ggyddn. And this time he's out for revenge. The worst of it is that while he's giving us hell in here, wherever here is, we know that the real world is going to hell out there!"

Waite was thoughtful. "So, it all started to come together when you got hold of that weapon. But where is it now?"

"When I deactivated the House of Doors, the Castle on the slopes of Ben Lawers—*this* Castle we're inside now, yes—I left the weapon inside," Gill answered. "It wasn't the sort of thing, the kind of technology, that should fall into the wrong hands. Or any hands . . ."

And Turnbull said, "What about that probe or bug or transmitter that we took out of Ki-no Sung's neck?"

Gill shook his head. "It was broken, probably by you when you rabbit-punched him. And it's lost. I put it inside the cap on a ballpoint pen . . . lost the pen. Anyway, I would have to have something a sight bigger than that if I . . . if I . . ." He paused. For suddenly he'd seen what Turnbull was getting at.

The minder nodded. "Let me think about it," he said. "But it seems to me we may have been running away from Arachnid rex for too damned long. Maybe it's time we got you something bigger to work with, know what I mean?" He got up and headed for his cavelet.

"Sleep well," said Gill, watching him go.

"Damn right!" said the minder . . .

Gill's intention had been to mull things over before he went to sleep, to let loose his feelings, his machine empathy, into the atmosphere of this synthesized world and perhaps to the synthesizer itself. No such luck; from the moment he laid his head on his folded jacket he was asleep. As deep and dreamless a condition as any he'd ever known—

Until Ki-no Sung shook him awake.

"Eh?" Gill sat up. "Eh? What . . . ?"

"Jack asleep!" Sung said, dancing with agitation in Gill's and Waite's scoop of a cave. "Him no wake up. And ladies gone!"

That did it. Gill was up onto his feet so quickly he almost brained himself on the low ceiling. "What!? The ladies—"

"Gone," said Sung again. "Not here."

"Shit!" Gill pulled his jacket on, gave George Waite a nudge with his toe. "Ki-no Sung, go wake the others. Go, for Christ's sake, *go!*"

Outside, the fires were burning low. Loping next door to the cave shared by Angela and Miranda, Gill tossed dry tinder onto the glowing embers, sent sparks flying. Sung was right: the girls weren't there, weren't anywhere that Gill could see. And with a hammering heart he entered the next cave: Jack Turnbull's. The minder was on his back, snoring. Beside him, a bowl of something that smelled mildly—what, alcoholic? His breath, too.

Gill took up the small bowl, saw that it wasn't a bowl at all but one half of a big coconut. Now what the hell . . . ? Fermented milk? Gill took it outside and looked at it by the light of a fire. Turnbull had drained the milk, but stuck to the inner wall of the coconut, its flesh, were five or six masses of well-chewed pulp that the minder had obviously spat out. There was also one other item that hadn't as yet been chewed: a nut, from the world of the twin, doomed suns. An *alcoholic* nut!

"You bastard!" Gill ducked back into the cave, kicked the minder awake. "You big, dumb, drunken bastard!"

"Eh? Eh?" The other grunted, sat up groggily.

"The girls," Gill yelled. "Gone! *Fuck* you, Jack Turnbull! You and your bloody addiction!"

Gill stormed from the cave, bumped into Waite and Stannersly. "The girls are gone," he said. "Don't ask me where or why. Ki-no Sung woke me when he couldn't wake Jack."

"Yeah," a voice growled from the shadowy cave mouth. "Well I'm awake now. Jesus, my head!"

Gill rounded on him. "The girls are gone, you . . . you . . ."

"Me . . . me what?" Turnbull snapped. "They were supposed to wake me. Well, no one woke me. So why blame me?"

"You've been chewing those bloody alcoholic nuts," Gill accused. "And washing them down with fermented coconut milk. You were *drinking*, Jack. Bloody drinking!"

And finally it got through to the big minder that in fact he'd slipped up. "God, I remember," he groaned. "I couldn't get to sleep. My mind was full of Miranda and all kinds of shit. I thought the nuts might help a little, didn't realize they were pure rocket fuel! But, Spencer, I'd have been asleep anyway."

"But you might have heard something." Gill was calmer now. "I mean, didn't anyone hear or see anything?"

"We were out like lights, all of us," Stannersly said.

"I hear, I wake up," Ki-no Sung said. "A thing—things—move. Make noise in night, soft. Hear lady choke. Then quiet a little time. Then Barney, he make noise, but quiet. I get up."

"Barney?" said Gill. Then his eyes went wide, and, *"Barney!"* he hallooed, cupping his hands to his mouth and directing his cry out across the forest. And from along the line of shadows formed by the base of the cliffs in a direction away from the waterfall, the dog's faint bark came echoing back.

Gill set off at once, in near-frantic haste, but the minder was on him, catching his arm. "Spencer, we've no idea what we're up against."

"I don't give a shit what we're up against!" Gill snarled.

"One of the scorpions?" George Waite's face was pale in the light of a white moonlet.

"No," Gill answered. "Or we'd have heard it coming through the woods or clattering down the cliff. And what would it want with the women? Or *only* the women?"

"What, then?" said Stannersly.

"Something quiet, furtive." Gill broke free of Turnbull's grip. "Something . . . like us? Oh, God!" There was no restraining him then. But in fact no one wanted to restrain him.

Turnbull caught up with him as he plunged recklessly into the shadows. The minder had taken a brand from the fire. "Spencer," he panted, "you can take it out on me later, but for now start using a little common sense, okay?"

"Or what? Or you'll slug me?" Gill said. "And is that all you're good for, Jack—a slug of this, a slug of that? Angela and Miranda are in trouble. They've been taken."

"I've never seen you like this," Turnbull grunted, lighting the way ahead. "If you know what's got them, why don't you say so?"

"Because it scares me to fucking death!" Gill answered, and stopped dead—so suddenly that the minder ran into the back of him. And the rest of the group right there behind them.

"Look!" Gill pointed. Turnbull swept the ground ahead with his torch. There were footprints, paw prints, too, in the sand at the foot of the cliffs; but Gill saw only the human prints. The small prints would be those of the women, while all of the others . . .

Were man-size. Naked, male, human feet had made those prints, and there were plenty of them.

Then the smell hit all five of the trackers at once—a fish stink that seemed to waft up to them from the impressions in the sand. And the prints were wet with some kind of slime.

"That shit's like the slop in those giant clams." Stannersly grimaced and turned his face away.

"Natives?" Waite gasped.

Gill gave his head a wild shake. "I don't think this world has any natives," he choked the words out. "Did you see any evidence of natives?"

"Then what?" Turnbull rasped from a dry throat.

But Gill only looked at him wild-eyed, and hurried on into the night . . .

CHAPTER
30

"G OD, WE MIGHT have known it!" Gill husked, forging along the sandy, boulder-strewn fringe at the foot of the cliffs.

"What?" said Turnbull, keeping pace with him. "What might we have known?"

"We were left alone too long on our own," Gill answered. "What, a whole day of good food, cleanliness, a little relaxation? It was a ladder we were on, one of Sith's damn ladders. Ask yourself this: why didn't that scorpion follow us through the door in the tunnel? It was hot on our heels, after all."

"The sea?" said the minder. "It can't swim, maybe?"

Gill shook his head. "No," he said. "Those things would have to be amphibian, like the Ggyddn crab or scabies constructs back on Earth." He snarled his frustration. "Christ, I wish I could stop thinking like that! We *are* on Earth, in the Castle, on a barren jut of rock, somewhere off the southwest coast of England. And yet we're here, too."

Waite was directly behind the two leaders. He, too, had grabbed a torch from the fire. As the trail under the cliffs broadened out, he came up to flank Gill on his left. "So why would those things have to be amphibian?" he panted.

"Because there are bound to be lots of watery worlds in storage just like this one," Gill answered. "Or like our own Earth. See, it isn't the construct's normal function to be a hunter-killer. They're normally used as—I don't know—vacuum cleaners? For the removal of extraneous refuse from, and the general tidying up of, stored worlds *after* contamination by any particular group of beings under test."

"You know that for sure?" Waite pressed.

"I knew a whole lot once upon a time." Gill's voice was hoarse now, with fear. Fear for Angela and Miranda. But talking was keeping him from cursing, howling his agony of frustration, losing it completely. "It's how the synthesizer's memory is kept clean and uncluttered by events taken place since the original recording and storage," he continued. "The scorpions are like eraser cursors that move across or within the synthesizer's three-dimensional 'screen' sweeping up all the debris."

"Okay," said Turnbull. "So now I'm asking myself why the scorpion didn't follow us? But I'm not getting any answers."

"Try this one," Gill spat the words out. "It didn't follow us because Sith had us where he wanted us, on a world that could terrorize the girls, and through them the both of us."

"The girls?" the minder repeated him. "A world that terrifies the . . ." And then he gasped out loud. "That Rod character? Is that what you mean? Angela's bastard of a husband? But he's dead!"

"I don't think so," said Gill. "I think he's in the computer, in limbo, just waiting to be synthesized—or he was!"

"But in any case he's just one man," George Waite put in.

"Right," said Turnbull. "And if he's responsible for this, then when we get him I'll personally wring his neck. Construct or not, the bastard's going down for good!"

"Aren't you forgetting something?" said Gill as the big minder spat his disgust, hurled his burned-out faggot far into the forest, and they went on in the faltering light of Waite's flickering torch. "You can put him down as often as you like, and just as surely Sith can bring him back again. Rod Denholm, *if* this is his work, is just a copy. And Sith has the copier. God, we don't know how many of him there may be!"

Turnbull unslung his gun from his shoulder. "I don't know, and right now I don't especially care. Bannerman couldn't take a bullet, and neither will this bloke. Okay, he's a copy. But a copy of a man. And even if we can't kill 'em, we can certainly knock 'em down."

And Gill knew that Turnbull was stone-cold sober now. The grit was back in his voice.

At which moment Waite's torch flickered and went out in a small shower of sparks. And Ki-no Sung said: "See!"

Now that the shadows fell in earnest, a glow was apparent in the forest not too far away. "Quiet now!" Gill cautioned in a harsh rasp. And:

"Single file," whispered the minder. "That way only one of us bumps into something."

"Who?" said Gill, acknowledging Turnbull's superior authority in this kind of situation.

"Me." Turnbull stepped out away from the cliffs and under the trees—and almost immediately bumped into something.

"Barney—*Jesus!*" he rasped.

And Gill sighed his relief, reached down to pat the head of the wildly wriggling dog. Then . . . an idea. "Poachers, Barney!" said Gill under his breath but urgently. "Poachers, old lad. Find 'em, Barney—*find 'em!*"

But Barney didn't have to find 'em; he already knew where they were.

Gill's group followed the dog through the forest, and the glow in the trees grew brighter. Also, a pair of saffron moons swung up from the black, false horizon of the cliffs to dapple their path to the fires in the woods. And the closer they got, the quieter they went.

This was old hat to Barney; he had known poachers before. Apart from an occasional snuffle, a rumbling growl low in his throat, he was as quiet as the group of five vengeful men that he led unerringly to their quarry. But even if he'd barked, or if one of the men had stepped on a dry branch, it was doubtful that the sound would be heard over the *other* sounds now coming from that patch of flickering light, that red and yellow firelight that grew steadily brighter.

They were almost a chant, those sounds, like an unearthly chorus, and this despite that the voices making it—their guttural, throaty timbre—sounded hideously wrong. But certainly there were names in it, repeated over and over: Angela and Miranda.

And now, ahead, a clearing.

The . . . *men* in the clearing were vague figures at first, shadows that glowed and flickered in the flickering firelight, merging into silhouette as they blotted this or the other fire with their oddly jerky movements about the clearing, then coming into sharper focus as they passed between the fires.

But men they most certainly were. And, Gill noted with a thrill of horror, they were costumed.

His rescue party had come to a halt on the dark side of dense bushes; they could see over the tops of the foliage, but keeping low were well hidden. And as the chanting—that guttural, hoarse, whistled and hissed litany—went on, the minder whispered, "What the hell? Ku Klux Klan?"

"No." Gill's voice was more hoarse yet. "No pointy headdresses here, just face masks. But gauze face masks? Sith has changed the rules again.

And those aren't sheets that they're wearing. They're white surgical gowns!"

"What?"

"Notice how each of these figures is precisely the same? Duplicates, Jack. Well, that smacks of Rod Denholm to me. But dressed as doctors?"

"Miranda's nightmare!" Turnbull hissed.

"Or maybe two nightmares in one," Gill answered, feeling the minder tighten up beside him, and hearing the for once muffled ch-*ching!* as he drew back the bolt on the cocking mechanism of his weapon. But:

"Wait!" Gill warned. "Do nothing until we know what's happened to the girls."

They didn't have to wait too long.

There were four white-gowned figures in the clearing. They were busy around a flat-topped boulder, roughly oblong in shape, over which they threw a sheet to transform it into a table; but a table that sloped a little, like a broad, out-of-skew coffin shape sunk deep in the earth at the narrow end. And Gill's unidentified feeling of dread had gone up by several notches when, just before the sheet was deployed, he'd seen a number of iron rings hanging from staples around the uneven sides of this . . . this what?—this altar stone?—and a row of five rings top to bottom of its upper surface, dividing it into two sloping beds or, indeed, tables. But *operating* tables? That was the overall impression as his eyes received it.

And Gill wasn't the only one with eyes to see. Beside him, Jack Turnbull was straining like a bulldog on the leash. A very short leash.

There was a disturbance in the bushes on the other side of the clearing. The four robed figures about the small fires went stiffly to the aid of four more as they appeared from the shadows. But Gill and the minder were much more interested in what or who the newcomers brought with them than any sudden increase in the enemy's numbers.

It was the women, Angela and Miranda—naked, gagged, with their hands tied behind their backs—manhandled into sight by these four slow-moving, white-gowned, face-masked, and identical figures. And as they were prodded like cattle, but still kicking, into the clearing, so the chant was taken up again. And at last Gill, Turnbull, and every member of the rescue party could hear the actual words. Maybe Ki-no Sung didn't understand them, but to the rest of the party they were perfectly clear:

"Here's to Rod! *Fuck! Fuck! Fuck!* Here's to the all-powerful rods of Rod! Of the many Rods! *Fuck! Fuck! Fuck!* Here's to the hungry rods that will rip these cows and soak them in their seed! *Fuck! Fuck! Fuck!*" This from four of these now nightmarish figures, their heads thrown back to allow the words to come gurgling out of their throats. And from the other four, a sort of answering cry, but done in giggly-girly yet at the same time sickly voices:

"We are ready for you, Rod! *Fuck! Fuck! Fuck!* Ready for all the rods of you Rods! *Fuck! Fuck! Fuck!* And I, Angela, as I have been in life, so shall I be in death! *Fuck! Fuck! Fuck!* It's what I did best, and what I shall continue to do, even until I join you in your lowly, rotten estate! *Fuck! Fuck! Fuck!* I left you to die, Rod, when all you wanted was to *fuck! Fuck! Fuck!* Now we shall fuck until I die! Thus I, Angela, repent my sins. *Fuck! Fuck! Fuck!*" And, in a different, slightly deeper, gurgly-girlish voice:

"I, Miranda, have no sins to confess, not against Rod of the rods. But I, too, would know the utter joy of being *fuck, fuck, fucked* to death, to be one with all of you in your lowly estates! But I have dreamed a dream, and it is this: my agony shall be your pleasure, and all my joints broken so that I may scream out the louder as you *fuck, fuck, fuck* me!"

Through all of this, a fetor had been spreading outward from the clearing. It was, beyond any doubt, the stench of the open tomb. But it was more and worse than that; there was, too, the fishy, cesspool foulness of the giant clams about it. Jack Turnbull's head, still aching from fermented coconut milk and "high-octane" nut pulp, reeled from the stomach-wrenching nausea of it—and still more so from the passion he felt boiling within.

"Spencer . . ." the minder growled. "*Spencer . . . !*"

"Wait," Gill ground the word out. "You can't fire while the girls are in the way." But already they could see that the girls wouldn't be in the way. The eight "doctor" figures were tying them to the rings in the altar stone—tying them naked, on their backs, side by side and with their legs spread wide, at exactly the right height for—

"*Fuck! Fuck! Fuck!*" the eight gurgled, spat out the words into the night air. Then one of them snatched the gags from the mouths of the girls, while the rest took up huge rounded stones from the ground and moved in a body toward Miranda. And:

"Fuck, fuck, fuck you, too!" roared the minder.

Gill, Ki-no Sung, and Barney burst from the bushes on one side, Turnbull, Waite, and Stannersly on the other. The obscene chattering of the minder's weapon froze the tableau like a photograph, until its message flew home. Six of the robed figures crumpled, letting their stones fall. The other two ran straight into Gill's party. Barney fastened his teeth in the gown of one of them, tearing it from him, while Gill tripped the other and Ki-no Sung leaped astride him and twisted his head on his neck. A good move—and yet a bad one, too.

The head came free, rolled from Sung's hands, and lost its mask. And underneath it was a second mask: the mask of death!

It was little more than a skull. A skull that slopped the digestive juices of mollusks, and maggots, and rotting fluids. A skull with a matted crown of hair, grinning teeth in blackened gums, and eyes that burned sulphur yellow!

Sung cried out loud—a strangled shriek of terror—and leaped erect as if jerked upright by some master puppeteer. He took a pace to the rear, tripped, and sat down. Meanwhile, Barney had backed stiff-legged away from his quarry, letting fall the thing's smock . . . or its shroud, as might well be the case. But in the next moment a single, well-aimed shot from Turnbull shattered the corpse's spine and it, too, crumpled—and *crumbled*—to the earth.

It wasn't over yet. Waite and Stannersly were freeing the girls, helping them find their clothes behind the bushes. Turnbull was using the rounded stones to pulverize the wormy skulls of the corpse constructs. Everyone kept his eyes open for more dead Rods; everyone except Sung who was gagging in the shadows. And Gill stood trembling, his fear and fury in front of the maggoty head—

Which suddenly spoke to him!

"Spencer Gill," it said in a hollow scratchy whisper, like an old-time record player with the volume turned low. "Gill, my old friend," as the yellow eyes seemed to focus upon him. "Well and you're certainly meeting my expectations. Up a ladder, down a snake. And the game goes on, eh?"

"Sith!" Gill croaked, bent down, and reached for a stone.

But before he could use it the voice gave a final chuckle and died away, and the lights behind the eyes went out . . .

There were undoubtedly Thone or Ggyddn mechanisms here for Gill to study. But cloaked as they were in rotting flesh he couldn't even consider it, didn't think of it until much later. And then it would be far too late. His party had taken stones and broken up the bodies, piling their skeletal remains on the fires. And wherever a bone or skull was broken to let out the alien liquid within, so the fire burned brighter.

It was the work of madness, carried out in a lunatic silence, under small alien moons that looked down dispassionately on scenes never before witnessed in this or any other world. A nightmare scene, yes, but one that would never threaten Angela or Miranda again *except* in their dreams.

As for Gill and Turnbull and all the others who walked in horror from the clearing that night—well, they would have a new nightmare to dream. Probably forever and forever.

Later—much later, and in private—the minder would ask Gill, "Spencer, those things were dead. Okay, they were synthesized dead things, but close enough as to make no difference. Now tell me, how could dead things hope to—?"

"Stop!" Gill would cut him off. "Jack, there are things I won't question, questions I won't answer, stuff I really don't want to know. And that's one of them . . ."

Back at the caves, Gill said, "From now on, three to a watch. No matter where we end up, there will always be three of us on watch during the night. That's one extra to watch the watchers. And it was really stupid of us, or of me, to let the two girls do a shift together."

Despite that it had taken Angela and Miranda some time to let go, they were now asleep, and they were probably in shock. But sleep being the best healer—and especially since in this place there was nothing else for it—Gill and the minder were glad that they were getting their rest, however troubled. Angela was the tough one: Gill had sat beside her awhile, and in her sleep she'd growled, lashed out. Miranda on the other hand whimpered. Well, and if ever there was a place to grow up fast and find yourself, it would have to be the House of Doors. No matter that Miranda had been powerful in the world they'd left behind, here she was just another victim.

Gill and Turnbull were on their own. Ki-no Sung had said he wouldn't sleep; he sat on a ledge higher up the cliff face, scanning the night forest through anxious eyes. Still not completely in the picture, the little man's terror was that much larger. Compounded by night fears, and by the unknown and its apparent unpredictability, to Sung this was a *total* nightmare.

In a way, his sleeplessness was a good thing: he made up Gill's three; he was the third watcher. But in fact Gill suspected that Waite and Stannersly wouldn't be getting much sleep either. All of them had experienced a horror that wasn't going to go away for a long, long time.

Turnbull handed Gill his gun. "There's maybe ten rounds left," he said. "One up the spout. Go ahead and shoot me."

"Don't be fucking silly," Gill told him. "Without you we don't have a chance and wouldn't have got this far. Time over you've pulled us out of trouble. And we all know you're by no means the dumb ox you sometimes pretend to be. So tonight you were dumb, so what? It was going to happen anyway, one way or the other. Sith would have seen to that."

"I fucked up as a minder," the other growled. "What good is a minder who doesn't mind? Anyway, if it eases *your* mind, take note of this." He dug in his combat-jacket pocket, came out with a handful of nuts, tossed them onto the fire. "It's done with. If I can't control it, damned if I'll let it control me!"

"You've said that before," said Gill.

"I've said it for the last time," Turnbull growled. "If anything had happened to those girls . . . you wouldn't have to shoot me, Spencer. I'd do it myself."

Gill looked at him. "Miranda?"

"Too true." The other nodded. "She's better than booze, that one. Or she would be. Miranda's something for a lifetime, and mine's not getting any longer. It's not so much the years, it's the mileage. Time I quit this shit."

They both started as a voice from the shadows of the cave behind them said, "Jack?" It was Miranda, a little tremulous, hugging herself for warmth, coming closer to the fire.

"You okay?" The minder got up from the rock where he was sitting, took off his jacket, and draped it over her shoulders.

"I . . . couldn't help overhearing what you said," she answered. And Gill said:

"Er, could you use a little privacy here?" He made to move apart.

Turnbull started to say, "No, that's not nec—" But Miranda cut him short.

"That's very thoughtful of you, Spencer." And when she was alone with the minder: "I said I heard what you said."

"I talk too much," he answered.

"And I don't listen enough," she said. "I think . . . well, I don't know what I think. Maybe I'm just scared of this place, the House of Doors. Or maybe it's something else. And maybe if I don't find out now, I never will find out. But what you were saying . . . did you mean it?"

"Hell, no." He grinned, then stopped grinning. "I've been drooling over you since the first time I saw you."

"And is that all it is, drool?"

"It's whatever you want it to be," he said in all seriousness now. "Maybe it's what keeps me going when everything else looks like going to pieces."

She nodded, and shivered again. "We mightn't have too much time, you know?"

"I know."

"The fire in front of your little cave needs building up."

"I know that, too." They moved toward the fire, found a broken branch each, and positioned them on the embers. And suddenly, in a rush of words, she said:

"Is there room for two, I mean, in this little cave of—"

But then she was in his arms, and the big minder was lifting her, crushing her to him, and it felt *that* good. To both of them . . .

Watching from the shadows, Gill thought, *Damn! There goes my third watcher again.*

But it was okay. There was a blush on the horizon; an hour or two more, it would be a new day. So let them have their hour or two. All of them. It could be that their time was very precious now.

And overhead on his ledge, Ki-no Sung kept silent watch on the forest . . .

CHAPTER
31

I T WAS STILL early morning. Gill had caught himself nodding off on two or three occasions, but however brief his naps or lapses they seemed to have done the job; he felt reenergized. And anyway, Gill excused himself, Ki-no Sung was still at his post on the cliff face, Angela and George Waite were up and about, and Barney had been on the prowl for hours. Also, and perhaps surprisingly, so had Jack Turnbull.

The minder had gone on up the cliff with Sung, who had discovered an easy route to the top. Angela had freshened herself up at the river, and finding herself for the moment alone with Gill, she told him: "Spencer, about last night . . ."

"Are you sure you want to talk about it?" Gill was at once concerned.

But she nodded. "I'm over it now, yes. Being able to understand it makes it easier. I mean knowing *it*—or *they*—weren't the real Rod or Rods . . . well, at least *I* understood it. But as for poor Miranda . . ."

Gill told her about Miranda's and Turnbull's get-together at the crack of dawn, and she said, "Thank goodness for that!"

"Oh?"

"It gives them both something to go on for. Something extra to work toward. Where there's a future, there's hope for that future—right?"

"Whatever you say," said Gill. "But Jack and Miranda? One thing for sure, it will be interesting." And then back to the previous subject: "Okay, what about last night?"

"It was the smell that made it easier to bear."

"The smell?" Gill was taken aback. "Of rotting flesh?"

"The other smell," she told him. "The soupy fish stink of the giant clams. When we were snatched, I knew from square one what was happening. It was Rod, or the Rods, resurrected from his, er—his clammy death? No pun intended, believe me—and duplicated by Sith. The fact is that once I knew what we were dealing with, then it wasn't so bad. The worst thing about it was that all I wanted was for him to be dead again. But . . ."

"Yes?"

"There's something I don't understand. Those things being constructs, why didn't Sith make them stronger? Jack cut them down like so much straw, like the moldy dead things they were made out to be. They . . . they came to pieces too easily. If we had known—if we hadn't been so overwhelmed—Miranda and I might well have fought off the four who snatched us. Well, perhaps not. I suspect we were both half-asleep, didn't know what had hit us."

"Same goes for all of us," Gill answered. "This place had kind of lulled us into a false sense of security. We should all have known better: that in the House of Doors there is no security. Only the strength of the individual, from which the group as a unit draws its strength. But the more I see and know of us—all of us, I mean—the better equipped we seem. Okay, we're a new team this time. But we're a good one. And I think that at last Jack's learned his lesson. Anyway, from now on there'll be no opportunity for him to indulge himself." He paused a moment, then returned to her question:

"As for the corpse constructs—the dead Rods, their apparent weakness—but haven't we already worked that one out?"

"Did I miss something?" She looked at him questioningly.

He nodded. "I would say it's the synthesizer's basic program coming into play again, the equalizer, the one that Sith can't seem to override. If you introduce a new terror into the game, it can't be any worse than if it were the real thing. And since dead creatures really *would* come apart that easy . . ."

She thought about it, said, "You think that the synthesizer is maintaining the balance?"

"The way I see it, yes," he answered. "Remember the first time we were taken? You, me, Jack, and the others, we were also constructs, but we were only as strong as our real selves. So, maybe that's the answer. But who can be sure about anything in the House of Doors? One thing I do know, though: you must have had some really hellish nightmares since that first time!"

She shivered a little and said, "You know I did. But that was in the past, almost forgotten, until this awful place woke it all up again."

Gill put an arm around her, kissed her, and was disturbed by a clatter of pebbles as the minder and Ki-no Sung came down from on high. "Up there, yes," Turnbull said, angling his head and narrowing his eyes, peering at the high rim of the cliffs. He had a very satisfied look on his face. "It's ideal."

"What is?" Gill wanted to know.

"The cliff, for what I have in mind. Ideal."

Miranda came on the scene and as she passed on her way to the river said under her breath, "And what do you have in mind now?"

Turnbull grinned, let her get out of earshot, then stopped grinning and said, "She's had enough of shocks for now." And before Gill could make any comment, if he would: "You *know* what I mean! No sooner are we out of one nasty situation than I'm making plans for the next."

"Of course we know what you mean," said Angela diplomatically.

And the minder looked at her suspiciously, too. Until Gill said, "You were saying? About what you had in mind?"

Turnbull nodded. "Okay. What do you reckon would happen if a scorpion fell off the edge of that?" He indicated the heights again.

And Gill said, "He'd probably break something."

"Damn right! So that's my plan."

"Explain."

And the big minder explained. "Sooner or later," he said, "probably sooner, Sith's going to send one of his chitin-plated pals to prod us into activity. Especially if we just sit around here not doing anything much. So that's exactly what we'll do—nothing much. Well, except we'll rig a booby trap up there. The cliff at the top is made for it."

"But what good will it do us?" Angela was puzzled. "Wrecking one of those things isn't going to get us anywhere, is it?"

And Gill told her, "It's Jack's notion to get me something to work with. A piece of Thone or Ggyddn machinery I can tinker with, which might help to get me back in sync with this thing."

"Do you think that would help?" Angela looked worried now. "And anyway, who'll bait the trap? I mean, who'll be the scapegoat, bell the cat?"

"We split into two teams," Turnbull said. He had obviously been giving it some thought. "One team at the top of the cliffs, the other down here. And we keep a twenty-four-hour watch until it happens."

"Go on," said Gill. "Until it happens?"

"Until old king crab comes on the scene," Turnbull continued. "If he appears from up there, the party on top lures him into the trap on their way down. If he comes out of the forest down here, the other party nips up the cliff and we nail him from the top."

Gill began to feel excited. "How will the trap work?"

"I'll show you," Turnbull said. "And anyway, it will take all of us together to rig it up. And it won't be easy work."

Returning from calls of nature in the forest, Stannersly and Waite had heard some of this. Approaching, they asked what was required of them. The minder waited until Miranda was finished at the river, then showed them all the easy route up the cliff. Using wide, zigzagging ledges and easy climbs, it was no great problem.

"But it might prove a little more difficult for a scorpion," George Waite panted as they reached the top.

"No," Gill told him, shaking his head. "I've been carried down a steeper cliff on the *back* of one of those things! He'll make it, all right, but probably not as quickly as us. Despite that scorpions are tenacious, they don't ever seem in too much of a hurry. They need time to work out how to negotiate stuff. Anyway, let's listen to what Jack's got to say."

And then Turnbull explained further . . .

Right, look down there," the minder said. "See that boulder, about a third of the way down? It's loose and right on the rim. That's why I shepherded you all carefully past that point. When that rock goes it will probably take a whole lot of rubble with it. Okay, now look at the way we came up through this gap here, which must have been caused by a recent rockfall. There's maybe three feet of topsoil on both sides of the gap, which from now on I'll call a defile, and it's only held together by roots and moisture and its own rough texture. It's overhanging pretty dangerously. If something heavy steps on that overhang, it's going to give and launch the heavy something into space. Sith's scorpion bloodhounds aren't stupid, more's the shame, but they are heavy and easy to figure. Where we go, they follow.

"So, if the high ground party is approached from the woods back there"—Turnbull thumbed the air to the rear—"they scramble for the defile and make their escape down the cliff. Except they don't go all the way to the bottom. I'll explain. Note how the route zigzags; if you look straight down, it zigs thataway, zags thisaway. So when you're making your escape, you wait at that end of the zig, *away* from the big loose boulder!

"But two of the men stay back; they stay right there *with* the boulder. And they have a couple of good strong levers stuck deep into the loose soil at its base. That rock's actually teetering and shouldn't take much to shift.

"Meanwhile, Arachnid rex has tested the rim, doesn't much like it, and he's coming through the defile. This guy has lots of legs; he's bound to put one of them in a noose while negotiating the defile. When that happens, the blokes with the levers topple the boulder. Of course, the other end of the noose is fastened to the boulder. And off balance, our chitin-plated pal does the big nosedive. Crunch!" The minder nodded, grinned, and said, "I like that."

"Noose," said Gill. "I know you've thought about it. What do we use for a rope?"

Turnbull pointed out some nearby tree whose boles were fat as old oaks. "See those parasitic vines growing up those trees? They're thin as rope, tough as power lines. I tried one and did a damn good Tarzan! They're anchored to the trees by thin rootlets that Ki-no Sung's knife goes through like butter. Okay, so I said 'noose.' Make that nooses, the more the better. You have enough rope there to fully rig a couple of old schooners!"

"Good," said Waite. "Sung and I can get on with that. But before we do, what's the plan if the scorpion attacks from down under?"

Turnbull looked at Waite and grinned. "There's always got to be a troublemaker," he said. And: "No, I'm kidding. It's a good question. If the scorpion attacks from below, well that's the easy bit. The downstairs party scrambles up the cliff, and they *all* wait for the scorpion at the big boulder. See how the route up the cliff passes right underneath it? When the construct gets under the boulder, then they topple it onto him. The thing must weigh nine or ten tons or more. Enough to knock the big fellow right off the cliff and carry the ledge away, too." He turned to Gill.

"After that, a few well-aimed shots at a mainly crippled monster—to take out his eyes and wreck his feathery bits—and you'll have five or six tons of junk to mess with. What do you think?"

"I think you're a genius," said Gill.

Turnbull shook his head. "Just a minder," he said. And: "Okay, let's get to it. Vines to collect, nooses to make and bury under a scattering of soil, some good strong branches to break off and sharpen for levers. And I do mean branches, because even though that big rock is loose, you're not going to shift it with twigs!"

And Gill said, "Miranda, Angela: let us handle this heavier stuff. But look, there's a lot of food left from yesterday. We don't know when we'll see its like again. Why don't you get a fire going, cook us all up some fish or snake or whatever?"

Fred Stannersly chuckled, and Gill thought, *Someone actually laughing? Maybe things are looking up!* Out loud he asked, "Fred, what's tickling you?"

"Oh, I was just thinking," the pilot answered, still grinning. "A silly old joke from way back. It's a pity there are no pigmies in the forest."

"Really?"

"Yes," said the other. "Then we could have snake and pigmy pie!"

No one laughed and Stannersly looked embarrassed, explaining, "Er, you know? Steak and kidney . . . snake and pigmy?"

"Jesus!" said Turnbull in disgust . . .

Later:

It was early afternoon, the work was done, and they were still at the top of the cliffs where they had all recently finished eating. And now, too, a thought they'd all been thinking was voiced by Angela. "What if he doesn't come?"

"Then it will be time to start looking for the next door," Gill answered. "Fact is, we can't sit around forever, and Sith knows it."

"Something else has been bothering me," Angela said.

"Oh?"

"How does Sith know where we are? I mean, how does he know where to send his damned scorpions?"

"Nice one," said Turnbull. "It's something that's bothered me on occasion, too."

And Gill answered, "In the Castle, I mean in the House of Doors, that wouldn't be too much of a problem for him. We'd be like some kind of virus in the computer or an anomaly on those wall screens of his. Maybe for him it would be as easy as hearing a floorboard creak when he knows that no one's supposed to be home. See, it's Sith's environment . . . he would simply *know* if something was out of kilter, if there were uninvited guests.

"But once we're assimilated into a test situation—once we're shanghaied, inserted into a synthesized world, or on this occasion into Sith's bloody game—things aren't quite so easy for him. I mean, on both occasions we've been in the Castle, he knew exactly where we were. The first time he sank us up to our knees in a swamp, and the second time he turned a corridor into a tunnel and put a door in it; a door that brought us here, to a place where he could work his nasty stuff on us. But no, he doesn't automatically know where we are. He'll know what world we are in simply by checking with the synthesizer, seeing what program it's running. But I shouldn't think he'll know where we are within that world.

"Why do I say that? Well, if he knew where we were at all times, he wouldn't have needed to fix Ki-no Sung up with a seeing-eye bug, or George with a locator for that matter. So while it's more than likely Sith can always find us, still I think he needs a little time to do it.

"And maybe we have the proof of that right here. The game, or program, has been rigged to reproduce our worst nightmares in whichever worlds we find ourselves. And while we are playing those nightmares out, Sith uses the time to figure out where we are, and maybe insert a little more unpleasantness in the program. In my mad machine world, which was quite literally synthesized, unreal, actually manufactured from my nightmares, the problem didn't exist. Since the computer had created the place, albeit from images hidden in my mind, still it *was* computer-generated; we could be found just like any other 'file,' and Sith had instant access. He was able to get to us through those big screens, the synthesizer's windows on our progress or lack of it. And the scorpions were literally his cursors—with which he tried to erase us. Well, perhaps not—but he certainly used them to move us on!

"But in a 'real' world—like the doomed planet of those extinct six-legged species—Sith had to rely entirely on Ki-no Sung to follow our movements . . . which he couldn't because Sung was blindfolded. Not knowing exactly where we were, Sith wasn't able to create a door and send in a scorpion to speed things up a bit or guide us in the right direction. So in fact he had to rely on Barney's memory or our intelligence or sheer good luck, that we'd find the door out of that place. And if we hadn't . . . then we'd have died, fried. But even so Sith had fixed it to be there, watching it happen through Ki-no Sung's eyes.

"Okay, this is all guesswork—but you must have noticed that there was no scorpion in that doomed world? Maybe if he'd had a little more time after he found us, Sith might have sent one. But then again, knowing that bastard Sith, maybe not . . ." Gill paused, giving Angela a chance to ask:

"And is that why he hasn't yet sent one to this place? Because he can't be sure just exactly where we are?"

"Maybe." Gill shrugged.

"But those Rods knew where we were."

"Because they were your nightmare, programmed right out of your own head, your own thoughts," Gill answered. "Just Like Ki-no Sung's alternate 'China' was programmed from his."

"That doesn't work." Turnbull shook his head. "After the fight in the clearing, Sith spoke to you from that 'dead' head, remember? He knew where we were."

Gill chewed his lip. "Guesswork, like I said. Maybe when the synthesizer creates its constructs, Sith can use them like bugs."

"There's a whole lot of maybes here." Stannersly shook his head.

And Gill agreed. "Always has been," he said. "But you know, we've talked our way through them before, and talking seemed to work well enough then."

"So how about Sung's alternate 'China'?" Turnbull queried. "There was both a scorpion *and* Sith himself in that place!"

Gill nodded, thought about it. "Yet again, we'd been there for some time," he said. "We stayed the night at Sung's place. Maybe Sith got tired of us sitting around, and brought himself into play to speed things up."

And Ki-no Sung said, "Scorpion was my bad dream. That thing part of *my* nightmares!"

Gill snapped his fingers. "Of *course* it was! Hell, it emerged from a woman, from a synthetic Lotus! We saw it grow out of her. It wasn't one of Sith's constructs but something Sung himself dreamed up!"

And Sung nodded eagerly. "My bad dream. I *scared* that scorpion thing!"

"You, me, and all of us," said Miranda. "In fact, I'm scared of everything."

The minder was still puzzled. "Okay, but how did Sith actually find us in that weird China?"

"He put himself into the game," said Gill. "Taking the role of a Red Chinese officer, he sent out his goons to look for us. After they picked us up in the forest, they called Sith and he showed up in his fake chopper. But then, *everything* was a fake, created from what little Ki-no Sung knows of how things work."

For a while there was silence as they all thought it over, until Waite said, "You know, this whole fucking thing is dizzy-making? Sorry, ladies. A slip of the tongue. But if ever a situation was designed to make a man curse . . ."

Angela agreed. "And not only men," she said.

"Anyway," Gill took it up again, "you can't take anything I've said as rock-solid fact. But until I know better, it's all I have to go on." He stood up, went to the rim of the cliff, and looked down. "Maybe it's time we split up, took up our positions. Things have been too quiet for too long."

"Me, Miranda, and Fred," said Turnbull. "If it's okay with you, that's my team and we'll stay up here. Oh, and we'll keep Barney with us, too. You have the 'luxury' of the caves, and we get Barney's early-warning system."

"Huh!" Gill scowled, but good-naturedly. "Well, you're welcome to him. He wasn't much good at his job last night, that's for sure. Anyway, he makes up your four, and I've got my four. So unless there are any objections, I vote we move out now."

There were none, and they did . . .

*   *   *

Half an hour later Turnbull stood at the top of the defile and watched for Gill's wave from the foot of the cliffs. He and his group were safely down. The minder waved back, returned to Miranda and Fred where they were taking it easy in the shade of a tree. Barney was off hunting in the forest. Every now and then Turnbull would hear him barking.

Miranda wasn't yet completely over last night. She looked half-asleep, maybe fully asleep; her chin bounced and her eyes started open as the big minder sat down beside her. And seeing him, she grabbed hold and hugged herself to him. "Jack! Jack!"

"Hey, it's okay," he said, stroking her hair.

"Oh, my God!" she said. "My God!" And slowly the tension went out of her. "I . . . I was just beginning to dream."

"In a place like this, that's to be avoided," he said.

"I was back on that slab, in that clearing." Miranda shuddered. "And I could feel . . . I could feel . . ." Suddenly her eyes opened very wide and her jaw fell open.

"What is it?" Turnbull was instantly concerned for her.

"When I was lying on that slab," she said, her hand flying to her mouth. "There was a metal ring right in the middle. When they threw me onto the slab, I felt it in my back—a big ring under that white sheet. Then I bounced off it, but it was pressing against my hip through the sheet."

The minder frowned. "There were rings all over that slab," he said, "like staples hammered into the stone. They used them to tie you down."

"But this one was a *big* ring." Miranda stared at him. "It wasn't a staple. And it was loose. When I moved, it moved—on a pivot!"

"A pivot?"

Wide-eyed, she nodded. "Like a knocker!" she gasped.

Turnbull said, *"Christ!"* and jumped to his feet.

And as he ran toward the defile, he heard Gill's frantic shout of warning echoing up to him from below . . .

CHAPTER
32

THE SCORPION HAD come out of the woods. Ki-no Sung, the moment he'd got himself comfortable at his usual vantage point a little way up the cliff, had promptly fallen asleep. Last night's vigil, and all the climbing and work he'd done since then, had finally taken its toll of him. And because it was still broad daylight, Gill, Angela, and George hadn't been as observant as they might normally be. In short, the tranquility of the place had lulled them yet again.

Also, since the forest was close to Earth type—almost a summery English or North American in fact—the trees were set well apart. This had allowed the scorpion to approach without making too much commotion, though whether this had been a deliberate ploy or simply expedient was another matter. But in the end it had been a series of unnaturally loud cracklings in the undergrowth, culminating in the shattering of a large, dry, fallen branch, that had alerted Gill's party to their danger.

After that and on sighting the grotesque thing as it came lumbering through lesser underbrush, there had been only sufficient time for Gill to yell his lungs out in a warning to Turnbull and his team up above, before he and his group had set out in full if not panicked flight back up the face of the cliff along the proven and approved route of ledges and easy climbs.

The scorpion, of course, would follow them along that same route. That was how they'd reasoned it out, anyway.

But that wasn't how it worked.

Looking down from the first "zigzag," where the ledge went slantingly on but the group must now essay a short climb to the next higher ledge, Gill saw what he should have foreseen, especially since he had once ridden upon just such a construct: that sheer cliff faces were in no way an obstruction to such as this mechanical beast. The thing gripped with its many pincer appendages, scrambled with its legs, clung like a limpet to the sheer face. And in the many places where the face was less than sheer its progress was frighteningly rapid. Indeed the one good thing about it was that the scorpion appeared to be following a ruler-straight line up the cliff that would take it to a point directly beneath the teetering boulder. So that now the only problem would seem to be how to get to the boulder before the construct got to the ledge beneath it.

But after completing two more zigzags, Gill and the others could see that they simply weren't going to make it. For then, briefly, when the scorpion hauled itself up onto the very ledge that they were occupying but at the other end, they saw that in fact its elevation was a little higher than theirs. And when it came trundling down the sloping ledge toward them in its weird half-sideways fashion, only the fact that they were so positioned as to be able to scramble up to the next ledge saved them. That stopped the thing, and after a moment's hesitation it went back to its original direct assault upon the face.

So it went—with the construct constantly, effortlessly closing the gap, while the group's fear and exhaustion grew in direct proportion to the thing's proximity—until finally they arrived on the ledge beneath the great, teetering boulder, only to find that the scorpion was there before them. And this time there was no easy climb overhead but an impossible overhang!

The construct had climbed onto the ledge at its zag end, and there paused directly under the boulder to scan Gill's party where they stood panting, clinging to each other at the zig. Beyond the scorpion's prey the ledge petered out; above them an overhang bulged outward; beneath them a descent they no longer had strength or time enough to negotiate in reverse.

In short, they were trapped.

The scorpion's many legs clattered as it adopted its diagonal, side-on charging stance. Its stinger vibrated, curving up and forward. And finally the thing scuttled to the attack.

Or it would have, if Turnbull and Stannersly hadn't chosen that precise moment to apply pressure to the previously located levers. Then, as the first pebbles bounced off its upper carapace, the thing's swivel eyes looked up . . . in time to recognize the danger as the boulder peeled away from the rim immediately overhead, turned lazily, once, amid a cloud of dust and stony debris, and came crashing down.

The scorpion had half reared up, extending its forward pincer claws . . . but that was a mistake, for there was no deflecting the mass of the great boulder. The egg-shaped rock hit with its sharp end at the rim of the construct's carapace, cracking it and driving the thing's rear legs over the rim of the ledge. For a moment its rearward pincers gripped, but as chunks of the ledge broke free the pincers lost their purchase.

In any case, the weight of both the scorpion and the boulder was too much. The ledge collapsed, and the construct, boulder and all, went sliding and bouncing down the cliff face, were chuted out over a slight overhang, spun free, and seconds later landed jarringly in a dust storm of rubble and an avalanche of pebbles at the foot of the cliff. And behind the initial bomb burst of rock and rubble, the whipping, trailing "ropes" of the booby trap brought a secondary avalanche of lesser debris, like a dusty waterfall plummeting into the depths.

Gill gave a hoarse, throaty cheer—was surprised to discover that the others were cheering, too—hugged Angela close, and stared in morbid fascination as the dust cloud below slowly settled. But for the moment at least there was no movement down there.

Then Barney came scampering, and the minder and the others of the high cliff party not far behind. And Gill couldn't help it—didn't want to help it—but hugged Turnbull, too, before finally gasping, "What kept you?"

"I ran along the rim up there until I could see what was happening below," the minder answered as Fred Stannersly came on the scene with Miranda in tow. "When I saw that the scorpion was going to beat you to it, it dawned on me that we were closer to the boulder than you were, and also that it would be much easier for us to climb down to it than for you to climb up. So that's what we did. Even so, we only just made it in time."

"I was never so glad to see anyone in my life," Gill told him, a sentiment that was heartily, noisily endorsed by George and Angela.

"Save it," the other told them. "Jack Turnbull's the name, minding's the game." Then he sobered and said, "Get your breath back while we go on down and see what we can salvage. But don't hang about, for there's something else you should know . . ."

Gill and his team didn't hang about. And shortly, as Gill gave Angela a hand down from the lowest ledge to the sandy floor at the foot of the cliffs, they heard the sharp *crack! crack!* as the minder loosed two close-range shots. When sounds of shattering crystal followed, they knew what he'd been firing at.

"The damned thing's eyes," Turnbull confirmed it as they came upon him and his team at the scorpion's crash-landing site. "Would you believe that little tumble it took didn't 'kill' it? Hell, no! It was still casting about with its eye stalks, and you can see for yourself that its stinger is mobile even now. From the looks of it, I would guess it landed feetfirst, and then the boulder smacked down on top. Cracked it wide open."

Piled up at the base of the cliffs, and still cascading from on high, a mound of dirt dotted with rocks and stony debris quivered and quaked. The great boulder, still intact, lay some way off in the forest where the boles of two close-grown trees had brought it to a halt, but barely. Their great roots were half torn from the earth, and they leaned backward away from the boulder's bruising tonnage.

But the quivering of the avalanched matter continued, and Gill could see why. It was just as the minder had said: a pair of shuddering eye stalks projected from the rubble, while above them the construct's stinger swayed jerkily to and fro, squirting spasmodic jets of pale yellow fluid blindly from its needle tip. At the top center of the mound, the scorpion's chitin carapace showed through; indeed it was cracked, and its overlapping plates were deeply indented. Hurled outward from the pile, several insectile legs or pieces of claw lay inert among the outer scattering of rubble.

"So, what bits would you like?" Turnbull inquired. "And if they can be cut or broken off, you've got 'em."

"An eye," Gill answered at once. "The complete assembly at the end of one of those eye stalks."

"Well, not quite complete." The minder rubbed his chin. "I took out the outer lenses, just in case someone was watching."

"Wish you hadn't," Gill answered. "You might have damaged the inner workings, too. And as for 'someone' watching, I just couldn't care less. He already knows where we are—has known it since last night at least. But I understand why you did it: you just didn't like—"

"The idea of having that bastard watching us!" the minder finished it for him. And: "Okay, let's get you an eye."

"But watch out for that stinger!" Gill warned as Turnbull went to climb the quivering mound. Then he saw that he needn't concern himself; the stinger was stationary now, barely trembling, pointing up and out like an antenna across the forest. And at last it had stopped dribbling its poisons.

And as suddenly as that, Gill knew what he was looking at. It was his talent (which he had started to believe had deserted him) *telling* him what he was looking at. The word "antenna"—in fact a thought rather than a spoken word—had triggered the thing in his mutant mind, and his machine empathy had done the rest.

The stinger *was* an antenna! And why not, since it formed the highest part of the construct's body? Quite definitely, it would be the most logical place to house a communications link with the central computer, the synthesizer. But more than this, the constructs were self-sufficient, even self-repairing. When it was required, they were capable of requesting and receiving Thone energy broadcasts direct from the synthesizer. And while this specific scorpion was perhaps beyond repair, that wouldn't stop it from trying. Certainly it would be programmed to report its location and situation in the event of an accident or breakdown. And that's probably what it was doing right now.

Gill stood there among the stony rubble, fascinated by the idea, rapt in thought—until Angela saw the expression on his face and said, "Spencer, what is it?"

He glanced at her, then called out to Turnbull, "And, Jack, see if you can get me that stinger, too—especially that bulge in the casing just behind the actual sting." He stooped to pick up a shattered section of curved, chitin-plated claw maybe fifteen inches long. It was surprisingly light but had a keen cutting edge. "See if this is any good."

The minder was sawing at the junction of one of the eyes and its stalk with Ki-no Sung's knife and getting nowhere fast. He stuck the knife in his belt, accepted the scallop-edged claw from Gill, and used it like an ax—then swore vividly when the eye stalk parted as cleanly as a piece of dry old kindling. And Gill was right there to catch the bulbous eye as it fell. "Now the stinger," he said.

Again a single blow sufficed, and Turnbull said, "What do you know? A case of fighting fire with fire, right?" He slid on his backside down from the heap of dirt and rubble. And handing Ki-no Sung his knife, he tucked the claw section in his belt in its place.

By now the buried construct was vibrating and clattering within its cairn of earth and rock shards, making a sound much like a mechanical death rattle. And in fact that was precisely what it was. For as Gill and the others turned away, the thing suddenly fell quiet and the swaying stinger arm collapsed atop the pile.

Meanwhile, Gill had picked up the bulbous stinger mechanism with its now retracted needle. George Waite had the sausage bag; Gill gave him the eye and stinger for safekeeping, turned to the minder.

"So what else is it you wanted to tell me?"

"Miranda tells it better than me," said Turnbull, leading the way into the woods in the selfsame direction that the scorpion's stinger had been pointing. "But while she's telling it, we'd better be moving on. The way I see it, that scorpion back there is just so much junk now, and sooner or later some other construct will be along to clean up the mess. That is what you said, isn't it? I mean, that's how it works?"

"Right," said Gill. "I think so, anyway."

Then Miranda told them about the so-called altar stone in the woods; about the large ring at the center of the slab, and how she'd finally remembered it in a dream. "I'm sure the ring was a knocker," she finished.

"It makes sense," Gill told her. "Well, if anything makes sense in the House of Doors. But that's where the Rods were, so that's probably where they came through. Likewise the scorpion: it came from roughly the same direction in the forest. And its stinger—which I think is an antenna—was pointing back that way, too."

Fred Stannersly was looking puzzled. "But doesn't that mean that if we use that door we'll be reentering the synthesizer?"

"Not necessarily," said Gill. "What we know—or what we're going to find out—is that it's *probably* a door. But where it leads to will be up to Sith's program. So far he's been shuttling us about between worlds created from or adapted to simulate our worst nightmares. But we haven't all been there yet. We still have George's, Jack's, and your own nightmares to explore. So it looks like it will have to be one of you three."

"My nightmares . . . you don't want to know about," Turnbull said at once, pausing to look back from the lead position where he hacked a way through low underbrush with his new pincer weapon. "How do you reckon you'd make out in a war in Afghanistan, or an IRA bomb scare in Belfast?"

"As for yours truly," said Stannersly, "I'm not even sure I have nightmares!"

"And I'm sure I don't," said Waite. "Believe me I'd like to help out, but I can hardly remember dreaming a single dream."

"So maybe you're our best bet," Gill told him.

And Miranda said, "If it was up to me—and if my life was the only one at stake—I'd say let's stay right here. I'd say let's make Sith come to us. Meanwhile we could enjoy this place. But I know that while we were enjoying it people would be dying. And I suppose we would, too, in the end."

"I know how you feel," said Angela, "and I can sympathize. I'd gladly spend what little time I *might* have left with Spencer in this place. But I know Sith wouldn't leave us alone for a minute, you can bet on that. And meanwhile the real world is still out there."

"Still out there," Gill repeated, "still going to hell, and still capable of surviving. But only if we keep going. Give in now . . . that's the end. Of everything."

"But of course we can't, and won't," Jack Turnbull growled. Then, changing the subject: "Look here: tracks from last night. Our tracks. Another hundred yards or so, we'll find the clearing and the stone. So on you go, Barney—sniff it out, boy!"

Barney took the lead, went bounding off through the trees, led them straight to their destination.

Then it was decision time . . .

They sat around the clearing not saying a lot; mainly psyching themselves up, Gill suspected. And he sat alone (though not too far from Angela, who knew enough to leave him alone for the moment) with the artificial eye and the stinger device-cum-antenna, if that's what it was. These items were machines, yes, or parts of machines, and Gill had a way with mechanical things, a weird rapport. But right now these were "dead" machines, and his empathy was at a low ebb.

Within the severed eye a concave, dishlike surface (a lens of sorts, Gill supposed) reflected an inverted image of his own face, his frowning gaze. It told him nothing, merely confirmed that this had been an eye. As yet he hadn't had time to find a way to disassemble the eye and study its inner workings, but it was important that he do so eventually. For it was only by understanding such "lesser" intricacies that he might eventually get in sync with that greater mystery known as the synthesizer.

As for the bulbous part of the cylindrical stinger appendage immediately behind the telescopic syringe itself: Gill believed it to house not only an antenna but a direction finder, and possibly a "conduit" for beamed Thone energy. But this was "intelligent," flexible metal; indeed, it might even be caused to flow like water, and uphill at that, if only he was able to focus his talent upon it—give it his total concentration—in the almost forgotten luxury of peace, quiet, and privacy.

An antenna or receiver, yes, for power beamed direct from the synthesizer. An antenna . . . *which even now was working!*

Gill almost dropped the thing, very nearly started to his feet. But no, it wasn't actually working, merely . . . what, resonating? Reacting, maybe, to some unseen presence? It was like a fine wineglass humming to the note of a tuning fork. And yet only a moment ago it had been stone dead in his hands—would still be dead, to anyone except Spencer Gill. And from moment to moment, the vibrations were growing in intensity.

Sheer instinct brought him lurching to his feet then, but with such jerky, puppetlike movements that Angela and the rest of the team were startled into following suit. And:

"Get away from that slab." Gill's throat was dry as dust. "Get away from that damned door, and as quickly and quietly as you can! Follow me into the woods." The woods on that side of the clearing farthest from their previous camp in the caves at the foot of the cliffs, of course.

They followed him without question, until they were well into the undergrowth, where Gill got down on the far side of a huge, fallen tree trunk. And while he tried his best to concentrate on the detached antenna, tried to will the device to "silence," his baffled colleagues joined him behind the great mossy bole where it had welded itself to the earth. Then, very gradually Gill succeeded, or the antenna gave up the ghost, until at last it lay quiescent in his hands. But only just in time.

"What's going on?" Turnbull wanted to know.

Gill held a finger to his lips, signaling, *Be very quiet! Something is happening.*

There came a rumble from the clearing and the earth shook under their knees. They ducked down more yet, squinted over the rough curve of their bark-clad barrier, saw a whirlwind or dust devil careering around the perimeter of the now mainly obscured clearing. Then, abruptly, the wind ceased . . . the massive slab was no longer visible; it seemed simply to have disappeared.

"Wait!" Gill hissed. And even as he spoke the rumble came again, and again the earth shook, this time accompanied by geysers of dirt, leaves, and twigs that jetted high into the air. And when the dust settled the huge slab was back—and so were *two* blue-gray, chitin-plated scorpion constructs!

Gill didn't have to issue any further warnings, wasn't required to say or do anything more. As a single unit, the seven held their breath; even Barney quit wriggling where Ki-no Sung held him fast.

The scorpions scanned the immediate vicinity of the clearing, both of them scuttling in tight circles, with their stingers extending up and forward. There was a moment's hesitation . . . until without further pause they set off through the forest toward the cliffs along an arrow-straight route that Gill guessed would take them directly to their wrecked colleague.

And when the sounds from the underbrush were sufficiently diminished, the seven came out from behind their log and returned to the clearing. And now there could be no putting it off.

"Your dice, George," Gill said. "It won't be long before those constructs are back. If they're only here to clear up the mess, they may not be interested in us—not yet. But once the job is done—then they'll *definitely* be interested."

Waite looked at him, looked at the great ring that was set slightly off center in the slab. Maybe he was trying to stall; in any case he licked his lips, said, "I'm damned if I can remember seeing that ring when we were here last night."

"It was under the sheet," Miranda reminded him.

"And where the hell is that sheet now?" Waite was nervous. "And where are the remains of those . . . those damned *things* we burned?"

"Cleaned up," Gill told him. "Last night's rubbish, removed back to the synthesizer."

And Jack Turnbull asked, "Why are you stalling, George? The sooner we're out of here the sooner we can get on with . . . with whatever we've got to get on with."

Waite nodded, bit his lip. "See," he said, "I've only ever had one real nightmare—and I've beaten that now. I just don't like the idea that this fucking House of Doors could give it back to me again."

"Your tumor?" Gill said, and Waite nodded.

Gill shook his head. "I can't see how a tumor can threaten all of us. And anyway as far as I understand it it's one of the synthesizer's functions to cure things, not to infect people."

But before Waite could answer, if he would, Gill felt something. No, he *sensed* something. A force that radiated outward from the sausage bag over his shoulder. It lasted only for the merest moment—a buzzing, a vibration, the last spastic throb of a dying bumblebee's wings. But in the woods, the diminishing sounds of construct activity ceased on that selfsame moment . . . and in the next started up again, *moving back this way!* And:

"George, this is it," said Gill as the seven clustered to the great stone slab. "Blow on those dice and let them roll."

"Oh, shit!" said Waite, white-faced. But there was no avoiding it. And quickly he leaned forward over the slab, lifted up the iron ring, and let it fall . . .

CHAPTER
33

THE TREES AND shrubs around the clearing leaned inward, were *sucked* inward, shedding a multitude of leaves and twigs as a second whirlwind sprang up out of nowhere to blast counterclockwise around the perimeter. Choking dust and dead forest debris whirled in that mad circle; the seven felt their breath sucked out of them; they leaned forward across the great slab, clasping each other's wrists. Barney was actually snatched up into the air, had barely enough time to yelp before Turnbull threw up a hand, grabbed him, and hauled him down again.

Then the ground trembled underfoot, and the slab sank down into the earth. Indeed a huge circular plug of earth—with the slab at its center— sank down into the earth. It was as if the great stone stood upon a mighty elevator cage, which was now on its way down. A circular wall of raw earth rose up all around, and the weight of the seven fell away almost to nothing as they plummeted. Overhead the sky dwindled to a circular patch of dim light that quickly turned gray and blinked out altogether.

Swiftly then the descent came to a halt and their weight increased, and more yet as the great hydraulic ram lifted them up again. The sky came back into focus; the wall of earth hurtled downward; they were actually lifted some inches off their feet as motion ceased with a geysering of dirt and dust . . .

And a dim gray world sprawled all about them. Letting go of each other, the seven sprawled, too, stumbling and falling from the shock of sudden stillness.

Stumbled and fell—but were unhurt! Neither a jolt nor a bump—neither the rustle of leaves nor the melody of birdsong. Neither strong, clean sunlight nor the starlit skies of night, but a dirty gray twilight on a landscape that reeked and fumed and felt rotten underfoot. And no slab or altar to be seen but the same monotonous sub-monochrome desolation all around.

"Where in the name of all that's bloody hideous . . . ?" Jack Turnbull began to wonder, letting it trail off as the echoes of his words came shuddering back from near-distant walls of mist. Then (but in a whisper this time) he tried again. "I mean, are there really worlds like this? If so, thank God for Earth!" It scarcely sounded like the minder speaking at all, such was the awed yet despondent texture of his voice.

They got to their feet, sinking ankle deep into gray . . . flock? That was what it—the "ground" underfoot, the desolate landscape, or flockscape—seemed composed of: tufts and rags of lifeless gray wool, or flaky desiccated vegetable fiber. It was as if a million sofas or fifty million padded postal packages had been ripped open and their stuffing scattered over the entire surface. Oddly shaped flaps of the scabrous *slough* fluttered in feeble irregular updrafts, as if something down below were breathing.

And the stuff was obviously rotting down. In places there were sinkholes where the matter slumped toward smoking, blackened centers that gave of vile-smelling fumes. Almost as far as the eye could see the entire region was pockmarked in this way; the rolling mists were in fact banks of stench, rising from the blackened, diseased areas. And the fumes were acrid, poisonous; they stung the linings of the seven's nostrils, snatched at the backs of their throats.

"Christ!" Fred Stannersly gasped. "We could die slowly in this place."

"Or rather more quickly than that," Miranda choked, clinging to the minder's arm.

"Spencer, what now?" Angela's eyes were watering, stinging from contact with the acidic, drifting mist.

And Ki-no Sung wondered out loud: "Who bad dream this?"

Taking the stinger out of the sausage bag, Gill glanced at George Waite. But Waite seemed to be in some kind of shock. Turning in a slow circle, he gaped at the rot and reek all around, and his bottom jaw was hanging slack. Gill thought he knew why: that this was indeed the world of Waite's nightmare given form, though perhaps not the form he had expected. Neither Waite nor Spencer Gill for that matter.

"God knows we can't stay here," Turnbull choked, finding a handkerchief to cover his nose and mouth.

Gill silently agreed, but didn't waste time or air on an answer. Instead he held up the stinger, concentrating on it as best he could, and himself began turning in a slow circle.

"Water divining?" Stannersly inquired. It was an innocent enough question, humorous in its way despite the circumstances, but by no means sarcastic. Gill knew what Fred meant, ignored him anyway. And Turnbull said:

"Life divining, more like. But for now keep quiet and let him get on with it. And meanwhile, find something to cover your mouths and noses. It's a fair bet that breathing this stuff is about as healthy as sucking on an exhaust pipe!"

Gill sensed something: a pull in his mind, a tugging, the same indefinable *buzz* of weird attraction that he'd felt back in the clearing. And holding the stinger—the antenna—as gently as possible, he swung it through a gradual arc until he reached a point where the attraction was strongest. Then:

"The synthesizer," he choked the words out, "or at least something like or *of* the synthesizer—something anomalous to this place, anyway . . . perhaps a door?—lies in that direction. So let's go."

He helped Angela along, and Turnbull and Miranda followed immediately in their plodding tracks. All of the team were very badly affected by the fumes—except perhaps for Barney. Keeping his nose low to the ground, he raced ahead. His human companions, feeling as ill and helpless as they did, could scarcely avoid noticing this; Gill especially was struck by an idea.

"Crouch down," he told the rest. "Keep as low as possible to the ground. It seems the higher this stuff rises the denser it gets. But closer to the ground the air's much cleaner. Barney seems to think so, anyway."

He wasn't entirely right, but for the moment his advice sufficed. Then, up ahead, a veritable cloud bank of the stuff rolled up out of nowhere. "On your hands and knees," the minder choked the words out. "Crawl, if that's what it takes. But whatever you do don't stop!"

The ground was rising, and the flock was much looser now where it flapped around their knees. Waite, trailing the group with Ki-no Sung, made continuous hacking, choking sounds. Stannersly fell back a half-dozen paces to help Sung drag Waite onward and upward. Looking back, Gill saw that they were losing the battle and didn't understand why.

Then, as suddenly as it had come, the "fog" thinned out; a bare hill of what looked like furrowed soil rose ahead; behind Gill, Turnbull, and the two women, a slowly tumbling sea of the stuff rolled in every direction as far as the hideous horizons.

"That vapor, or whatever it is, is layered." Gill pointed a trembling finger at the fog billows. "But up here it seems to have thinned out. We can actually breathe."

"That's true enough." The big minder nodded. "But, Spencer, your door had better be up here, too, because we can't risk going down into that stuff again."

As if to deny him, there came a cry from behind them. Down in the wreathing fog, dim figures seemed to be fighting with something. Gill groaned and said, "Can't risk going back down? Well it seems we may have to."

Miranda and Angela, collapsing onto the rubbery, strangely ridged "soil," were left coughing and retching, comforting each other as Gill and Turnbull descended once more into the reeking vapors. And there they found Sung and Stannersly battling with the slough . . . that appeared to be attacking George Waite!

Long, frondlike flaps of the stuff were sprouting at his feet, bloating like weird fungi, wrapping around his legs, his thighs, his waist. Fluttering leprous tendrils seemed alive . . . they *were* alive, where they groped at his face, nostrils, ears, and mouth. And George was sinking down into it; a fuming sinkhole was forming directly beneath him; it was sucking him into its squelching center and bubbling acid wetness.

"What the hell—?" The big minder couldn't take it in, but Gill believed he knew well enough what the hell.

"This is Waite's nightmare," he said, coughing in the sick stench of the place. "Don't you know what this filthy stuff is? What this place really is?"

But Turnbull was already fighting alongside Sung and Stannersly, which was as well. For if Gill had explained his theory to him . . . even the minder might have quit and gone back up the hill into the cleaner upper atmosphere.

That was what Gill felt like doing—what most men would have done—but he was stronger than that, and knew that this was the House of Doors and that he, they, his whole party, were being tested; and poor Waite was being tested to the limit in this, his personal nightmare.

"Leave me!" Waite was shrieking. "Get away! Go, before it gets you, too! Can't you see it's alive? It was alive in me . . . and now it's alive *outside* of me. But still it wants me . . . God . . . oh, God . . . *it still wants me!*"

The sinkhole opened more yet, and Waite cried out again as he slipped farther in. Stannersly and Ki-no Sung had one of his arms, Gill and Turnbull held fast to the other. But the suction was incredibly strong, and the pulp beneath their feet was shuddering, turning black and sick yellow as the sinkhole's circumference widened, threatening to suck them down, too.

And sentient, purposeful now, the groping tendrils forced their way into George's mouth, nose, and ears . . . and his face turned red with blood that spouted from their entry points!

Made powerless by horror, the four men jerked back away from that unbearable sight, felt George's arms, hands, and fingers slip through theirs, and heard the slurping, *gloop, gloop* sounds of the vile earth as it literally ate him! And all that was left of George was the sausage bag, floating on the mobile surface . . . Following which it was as much as they could do to hold to each other and struggle their way back up the hill . . .

Spencer." Angela looked up at him as he staggered closer. She held up a hand and he drew her to her feet. Then she looked at the men with him: Sung, Stannersly, and the big minder. But . . . where was George Waite? Her eyes opened wider as she saw their expressions; those haggard looks and hollow eyes, and not only as a result of the fumes. "George . . . ?"

Gill shook his head, said, "George . . . he went down in the rot, into a sinkhole. That filthy slough is alive. Some kind of life, anyway. It . . . it ate him."

"In fact, it *was* him." Turnbull helped Miranda to her feet, looked to Gill for corroboration. And Gill knew that he needn't have worried about him, that the minder had already guessed the truth.

"Something like that, yes," Gill answered. "This is Waite's nightmare world, and that stuff *is* his personal nightmare. Some kind of cancerous growth infecting the whole—what, world?"

Even as he spoke, the ground trembled under their feet. It trembled again, shaking them, throbbing with some inner activity. "Volcanic," said Stannersly. "It can only be. Those gases are the result of volcanic activity. And this isn't soil but a kind of pumice, lava. It's soft, warm, and gives underfoot. The furrows or convolutions are caused by slow ripples as the stuff flows to the surface. And that dull red glow underneath is maybe the actual lava flow, bubbling up from below."

Miranda shivered uncontrollably in Turnbull's arms, clung to him, looked down at the ridgy surface. "It's like some kind of ugly brain coral," she said. And Gill knew he would have to tell them the worst of it.

"Soft, warm, convoluted, and ugly," he said. "Yes, all of those things. But it isn't volcanic and it isn't lava or coral. The reason it looks like a brain is because—"

"Because . . . it's a brain!" Angela tried to lift her feet from the surface, almost pulled Gill down with her.

"God Almighty!" Jack Turnbull cried, his face ashen gray, even as gray as the loathsome landscape. "Waite's nightmare: a cancerous brain! Down there, down the hill, that's the diseased area. The sinkholes are the cancer's spread, and those foul emissions are the stench of its rottenness!"

As he spoke, all six of them began to step lightly, glancing at the trembling surface underfoot, noticing as if for the first time the pulsing veins of dull color that swept like an undercurrent through its mass.

"A . . . a living brain." Miranda staggered and almost fell. "Poor George's brain, in a way, in the last stages of a terminal disease!" She was about to faint; only Turnbull's arm around her waist held her up.

"Jesus, Spencer!" the minder cried. "Where's that fucking door?"

Following the hopeless fight to save Waite, Gill had snatched up the sausage bag and placed the stinger inside for safekeeping. Now he ripped the bag open, took out the antenna, and pointed it up the hill in roughly the same direction as before. Maybe it was the urgency of the situation, or perhaps his talent was coming back into its own; whichever, the mental tingle was still there.

"Up there!" he gasped. "It has to be up there."

"There's nothing up there." Angela licked her lips, shook her head. "Just the dome of the . . . the hill." But in fact she meant the dome of the vast brain.

"No." Gill gritted his teeth. "I tell you I can sense it. Something *has* to be up there."

They struggled to the top, treading as lightly as possible on the pulsating—*matter*—under their feet. But at the crest of the dome there was nothing to be seen. Only an ocean of filthy gray fog swirling all around.

Yet as they had neared the top so Gill's arm had gradually swung down from the horizontal until it now pointed at the ridged contours of the brain itself . . . pointed vertically down at the "ground" underfoot. And shaking his head he said, "I . . . I don't understand."

"Then we're all in the same bloody boat," Stannersly said, "for I know that I don't understand a damn thing!" And he felt uncontrollable laughter suddenly bubbling up in the back of his throat. But he knew that he had to control it, that everyone's terror was at least as great as his own. "I . . . I'm sorry," he said then. "But, God—this is really getting to me!"

"That's what it's supposed to do." Turnbull grabbed him by the shoulders. "And what you've got to do is not let it!"

But as if that were some sort of invocation, now Miranda began dancing from one foot to the other, skipping on her toes to avoid something she'd seen, crying: "Oh, my God! Oh, my good God! Look! *Look!*"

They looked, shrank back, stared at one another in absolute dread. Gray sinkholes were forming in what they had believed to be firm brain matter. And out from the sinkholes spewed a flood of rotten gray loath-someness, bloating as if in an updraft! Cancer, alive and apparently sen-tient, and living in Waite's nightmaring brain! Ragged tendrils and palps followed the cancerous slough, unfurling into the air, groping in the direc-tion of the six. Barney yelped, skittered as a tendril lashed out, wrapped about him. But Turnbull hacked through it with his claw weapon and it fell writhing onto the ridgy brain—and there burrowed its way in!

"It's spreading!" Angela gave in momentarily to her terror—and just as quickly pulled herself together. And: "Spencer," she said. "Spencer Gill. Just you get us the hell *out* of here!"

Even as the sinkholes, the cancerous cells, came floating to the surface and commenced rotting the hitherto healthy matter all around, so Gill stood there pointing the alien antenna at the "ground." And his voice was shaky as he answered, "It's here. It's really here, deep inside . . . this. And its attraction is getting stronger all the time. Jack, Angela, all of you, hang on. Don't let go now, for God's sake. Something . . . something is coming."

The great brain was throbbing now, pulsating, and a dozen sinkholes had surrounded the six and were sending up their tendrils, their drifting flaps of cancerous slough and gut-wrenching fumes. Worse still, the tendrils seemed to know where Gill and the others were; their palps came curving inward, closing all the time.

"Jesus!" Turnbull croaked. "We're breathing this filth. I mean, it's *touching* us!" It was even getting to him now, mainly because there ap-peared to be no possible way out. All the strength and determination in the world weren't going to get the minder, or Miranda, or any of them out of this one. And it seemed so unfair because poor George had already paid the price.

But Gill was still gasping, "It's coming. It's coming!"

And in the next moment *it* came. The ridged contours of the great brain underfoot suddenly bulged, split open like a bursting boil as thick flaps of gray meat folded back on themselves. And up from the throbbing pulp underneath came a pair of shuddering feet, ankles, legs . . . the entire lower trunk of a human being. And from its clothing they knew that it was George Waite. He had gone down feetfirst, and he was coming up the same way. His legs kicked spastically as they flopped over the rim of the eruption, and the rest of his body kept right on coming. It was as if the great brain were giving birth.

He slid out of the mush on his back; his heaving chest and wildly threshing arms appeared from the slop, then his neck, and finally his head. George's terrible head.

His eyes were open, bulging. His jaw, too, hanging slack, and his mouth making sounds that no human voice should ever be capable of making. But his head seemed held back, and his chin pointed sharply upward as if something were trying to pull him down again by the hair. Then, behind him, the gray, corrugated surface bulged more yet and began to split like a huge overripe melon. And finally . . . finally the six saw what was holding him down.

It was simply the weight of his own head—or of what his head had become.

For as the split widened and frothed yellow, gray, and red gore that ran through the brain's coral convolutions like paint flooding the channels of a maze . . . so the *rest* of Waite's head came to the surface. And this was the actual cancer, a hideous mutation of a growth that outstripped its host body twice over.

Behind George where he lay twitching and mewling like an idiot, the rupture in the great brain's convoluted surface—in the surface of the domed hill—was maybe three feet long, but the *thing* that was bulging upward, forcing its way to the surface, widening and extending that monstrous gash or split, was all of that and two to three feet wide. It was a monstrous tumor, growing out of the top center of George's skull where the skin and bone was yellow, soft with rottenness and fretted and discolored like an apple hollowed by wasps. And this terrible sack of cancerous juices, all veined and tufted with hair, lay throbbing with a ghastly life all its own, its roots buried in Waite's head and the rotten pulp that had been his real brain!

And yet perhaps something of that brain remained even now, for suddenly his mouthings made sense.

"Kill me!" he begged, his mouth drooling slop and his claw hands scrabbling like white spiders to and fro across the pulsating surface of the ruptured dome. "Kill me now!" Then George's bulging eyes focused and looked straight up at the big minder. And: "Jack," he drooled. "For the love of God, end it . . ."

The tendrils closed in, palps swaying, groping, searching. But the minder's only thought was for Waite: to do as he begged be done and put an end to his misery. Turnbull uttered a weird, half-strangled cry, then went to his knees and lifted his claw weapon—

And Gill yelled, "No!" and flung himself at the minder, turning his downward-sweeping blow aside. And instead of coming down on George's extended throat, the scalloped claw struck the junction of his riven skull with the cancerous bladder, slicing it free. Moreover, the weapon drove deep into the diseased mush of the giant brain on which they were all standing.

And the brain caved in!

It fell away under their feet, pitching all seven of them, and Barney, too, into what should have been a loathsome death.

But wasn't . . .

CHAPTER
34

WHEN THE GREAT brain opened up, Jack Turnbull was on his knees. He fell in that position, fell for a split second that might as easily have been an hour, for a moment that went on and on, yet wasn't long enough for him to straighten his legs and fall feetfirst. Thus he came down in the same position, knees first, and so off balance that he very nearly keeled over and had to lower a hand to the rain-slick pavement to avoid falling on his side. Actually (by virtue of the fact that there was no shock or pain to his legs), it was entirely conjectural whether he had fallen or simply moved. Or not so simply moved.

But "moved" he certainly had.

To a wet pavement and cold rain slanting down, and passersby, most of them with umbrellas, looking at him curiously, and . . . Berlin?

He knew it at once, knew exactly where—for it was one of his favorite places—and for several seconds thought he knew when, too: now, of course. But it wasn't. Or rather, now wasn't when he thought it was. Which was just as dizzying as the fall.

God, when had he last seen Berlin looking like this? Had he *ever* seen it looking like this? Yes he had, as a young soldier not yet nineteen years old. But that had been way back in 1970! More recently, well, the city had changed, perhaps indefinably, infinitesimally in this special place, but definitely. The minder knew that because he had been here only—what, a week ago?—less than a week? Well, since Waite's people had picked him up, whenever that was. So what was going on here? A dream? A nightmare? The whole thing? Could this be what happened to you when you died: you simply went back in time?

Or was this *his* nightmare? His nightmare world!

He had done it, yes! He had "knocked" on the door that was George Waite's rotten tumor! And:

I'm gibbering! he thought. *To myself, but gibbering nonetheless.*

Directly ahead of him, on the pavement within arm's reach, stood one of those tall, circular advertising pillars peculiar to German cities. At the bottom, near the curb, the column was dented where multiple layers of posters an inch thick had been ripped away from one corner, probably as the result of a vehicle bouncing the curb. The poster that showed—the one at the bottom, the oldest of them—was still firmly glued to the pillar. And a date was visible. 1967.

Turnbull, still on his knees, inched forward, grabbed the soggy, torn section, and stripped away a great swath of papier-mâché. And the poster said:

April 1967

—SPORTPALAST—
Norman Granz Produktion

RAY CHARLES!
Das Ray Charles Orchester!
Die Raelettes!

April 1967

Turnbull stared, and stared. That poster must be at least three years deep. That would make it, what, 1970? 1970 *now*? In Berlin? But wasn't that just exactly what he'd thought when he first arrived . . . here?

Damn, he'd *been* to that show! He even remembered the numbers: "Chitlins with Candied Yams," "Busted," "Unchain My Heart," "I Don't Need No Doctor," "Georgia"—all of those great songs. And, of course, "What'd I Say" to close the show.

Okay, okay, steady now, he told himself. *But . . . I'm still on my knees.* And people were beginning to notice him now. Someone's hand fell on his shoulder, slid under his armpit, hauled him to his feet. It took a big man to do that. And it *was* a big man! A black man, immaculate in his USMP uniform, with the armband over the cape near his right shoulder and a burnished two-stripe brass chevron pinned to the armband.

And here was Jack Turnbull, in disreputable ex-army combat dress,

with darker patches still showing at the shoulders where insignia or badges
of rank had been removed. Jack Turnbull, minder . . . wearing day-and-a-
half-old stubble, a folded-down machine pistol over his shoulder, a chitin-
clad claw-thing clutched in his hand, and a bleary yet wild-eyed look
twisting his gauntly disbelieving face.

"You okay, buddy?" the corporal grunted.

"No," said Turnbull at once. And, "Yes," in the very next breath.
"I . . . am fine. Slipped, that's all. The wet pavement." He offered a shrug,
a grin, tried to bring his whirling senses back under a semblance of control.

The other nodded, narrowed his eyes. "Gets like that when it's rainin',"
he said. "So what's happenin' here?" And looking at the weapon on
Turnbull's shoulder he frowned more yet. "You *is* military, right? Frog,
maybe?"

It was Turnbull's out. "Brit," he said at once. And, wondering what the
penalty would be for impersonating an officer in a divided city that was
still officially occupied: "I'm Colonel Jack Turnbull, Intelligence Corps."
For of course he wasn't and never had been.

The corporal straightened up a little, released the minder's arm. "Yassir!" he said, and looked at Turnbull again. "Er, is this suthin' to do with
that war game they's playin' at the stadium?" He meant the 1936 Olympic
Stadium, HQ of the British Sector, Berlin. Another out.

"You're well informed, Corporal," the minder said. "I had no idea you
Americans knew about that. But yes, I'm the leader of an escape and evasion team." Which in its way might be true enough.

The corporal shook his head. "Well, ah has heard you Brits play rough,
but . . ." He shook his head again, looked Turnbull up and down. "Any-
thin' ah can do, sir? Can ah help in any way?"

"No." Turnbull shook his head, and again changed his mind. "Well,
there is one small thing."

"Yassir?"

"You've got your police notebook with you?"

"Yassir," and he produced it.

"I need proof that I was here," Turnbull told him. "A sort of schedule
of progress, a checkpoint, you know?"

"Sure. So what do ah do?"

"Write down, 'Saw Colonel Jack Turnbull outside the Bahnhoff, Charlottenburg, Berlin,' " said the minder. "And the date and time, then sign
it." And when the corporal was done: "Now tear out the page and give it
to me."

"Eh?" The big MP frowned. "But, Colonel, sir, that be mutilation of
an official document."

Turnbull nodded. "It's okay—I'll sign the next page as your get out. How many colonel's signatures do you have anyway, Corporal?"

"Nary a one!" The other grinned. "Till now."

Turnbull took the small tear sheet, looked at the time and date. 1800 hours, April 24, 1970. And that settled that. But now he reeled as all the implications of the situation finally came down on him. And the huge corporal said, "Is you sure you is okay, Colonel sir?"

Hell, no, Turnbull wanted to say, but instead said, "Yes, I'm fine. Just tired and hungry." He patted his pockets. "They, er, don't give you any money, you know?"

The corporal brushed aside his cape, took out a wad, said, "Would this be considered cheatin'?"

"Not at all," Turnbull said. "It's called initiative. And that's something I have plenty of." *Damn right!*

"Will twenty do it?"

Twenty deutsche marks? In Berlin, 1970? A few beers, a damn good meal, a flophouse, and breakfast tomorrow morning—well, if there was going to be a tomorrow morning. But: "No, I can't do that," Turnbull said, and asked himself: *What? Why the hell not? He's not real? He's how I remember things, that's all.*

"Sure you can, Colonel sir. Ah means, it's mah privilege. You has mah name on that there notebook page. When your game's all over, you can send me mah twenty."

"You're a damn fine man, Corporal." The minder shook his hand.

"And maybe ah could drop you somewheres?" The big man inclined his head toward the road, at the USMP "vee-hicle" that was standing there. And Turnbull at once knew where he wanted to go—where he more than anything in the world wanted to go, and right now. Oh, he would really like to go wherever Miranda was. But since he couldn't and didn't even know where that was, this other place would have to do. A beer, a meal, a flop, and breakfast all in one. If it lasted that long. If nothing happened to stop it lasting that long.

"Er, the Alt Deutscheshaus?" He looked at the other inquiringly.

And again the corporal frowned. "That place? It be out of bounds, Colonel sir."

"Right," said Turnbull. "Exactly why they won't expect to find me there. And it's my next checkpoint. It's just along the road here, you know? But see, I can't afford to be seen walking it. Hey, look at me! It's obvious I'm an escapee!"

The corporal helped him into his vehicle, a kind of small, black Maria, and got into the driver's seat. Behind them in the cage that was the body of the van, two badly beaten black soldiers in uniform, Americans, gazed back at Turnbull through the small, steel-barred window. "Shit," said one under his breath. "We gets picked up out of bounds—he gets delivered there!"

"Privilege of rank, soldier," Turnbull told him, and slid the door of the window shut in his face. And then, to the corporal: "Is that why you're here, in the British Sector? Picking up those two? Where were they?"

"Where they should'na aughta bin," said the other, grinnning hugely. "They was in the Alt Deutscheshaus, Colonel sir!"

Turnbull nodded, said, "And you did that to them?"

The corporal shrugged. "Minimum amount of force, sir. They is AWOL, full o' beer, and they resisted arrest."

"Good work." Turnbull nodded again, and felt very glad his combat suit was British. "But tell me something: why didn't you check my ID? For all you know you could be helping a criminal."

"Uh-*uh*." The other shook his huge head. "When you said you was Intelligence I knowed it was so. That gun there? Brit? See, ah knows suthin' 'bout guns—Have Guns, Will Travel, you dig?—but ah never seed that one 'afore. Special arms for a e-lite corps, right? And anyways, if you was a criminal, how the hell long you think you'd stay on the loose in Berlin, eh? And how'd you be gettin' *out* o' here? Ain't no way, Colonel sir. Berlin, it be the biggest damn jail in the world!"

"You're a credit to the MPs, Corporal," Turnbull told him. "And anyway I don't have any ID. The enemy picks up an escapee, finds his ID, he's a goner. Especially a colonel in the Intelligence Corps."

And the corporal nodded his understanding. "Ah can surely see how that would be, sir. Yassir!"

And a few minutes later he dropped Turnbull off at the Alt Deutscheshaus . . .

The Alt Deutscheshaus was one of *those* places. It had fascinated Turnbull as a young man. Talk about "kultur"? In the world he'd temporarily (he hoped) left behind, if the Hard Rock Cafe had been called the Hard Cock Cafe, and been decorated to suit, then there'd be an Alt Deutscheshaus in every major or capital city in the Western world. And Turnbull knew that in fact there had been several such dives here in Berlin, and in Soho, and on Straight Street or "The Gut" in Malta, and in Hamburg, and Paris, etc., etc. He knew because he'd frequented most of them. Er, on duty, of course.

Of course these days—the days of *Last Tango, Deep Throat*, home skin flicks, and magazines where the *in*sides of female bodies were shown as frequently as the out—it would be old hat.

Huh! These days! But it was 1970, and this was Berlin. Or a damn good look-alike anyway. Damn right it was a good look-alike, for it had been fashioned right out of his mind. Unless he *was* right out of his mind! Occupied, divided, goldfish-bowl Berlin, where so-called "Kultur" and Decadence went hand in hand. Or in places like the Alt Deutscheshaus, dick in hand.

Turnbull's looks were disreputable. The Alt Deutscheshaus "clientele" wouldn't much care. But his pistol's skeletal frame was folded down; it didn't much bulge out the loose material of his combat jacket. And so what if it did? Since Turnbull looked like a bum it was probably a bottle. And it was balanced on the other side by the scorpion's claw, which he had likewise tucked into one of his huge inside pockets. Anyway, there was no doorkeeper on the Alt Deutscheshaus.

Inside was just as he remembered it (naturally), but still Turnbull paused for a moment—more a moment of ageless, ever-fresh astonishment than true nostalgia—to gaze at the walls. For above waist-high wooden paneling, those walls were cinema screens; or they served as such. Painted off-white, they flickered with jerky life, displaying pornographic movies projected from the opposite sides of the room. But the *whirr* of the projectors was lost in the babble of patrons, and their beams cut through wreathing cigarette smoke. Occasionally someone would get in the way, teeter uncertainly across the floor, and nipples or other parts would float across his unsuspecting back or face, or both if he stood where the beams crossed.

Turnbull ducked under the beams, went to the bar, ordered a Schultheis from a sweaty woman who might easily be an ex-tank commander in drag . . . or maybe his tank.

"Und ein Zimmer?" he inquired as she delivered the frothing half-liter glass. "You know, a room? *Was kostet?"*

She cocked her head, grinned, said, *"Mit oder ohne?"*

With or without. And she didn't mean a bathroom. The minder shrugged, looked at his beer. *"Nach fünf oder sechs,"* he said, *"es macht nicht."* After five or six beers, it wouldn't matter a damn.

"Den trinken sie nur drei!" she said, laughing.

And Turnbull laughed, too. Then he should only drink three, she had told him. Oh, really? But looking at the beer, his mouth was already watering. Draft Schultheis—ye gods!

He offered her money but she said no, the first was free. And because he seemed such a nice fellow, she'd even bring him a second drink to his table. Free if he was staying and buying. Er, he was staying, wasn't he? And he would be buying?

Turnbull began to nod an affirmative, then paused. Alarm bells rang in his mind . . . or was it only guilt? He thought of Miranda, Angela, Gill, and the rest of the team—then nodded anyway. Yes, he'd be staying. Not only that, but he was beginning to understand why he'd come here in the first place: instinct. And all he needed was a little time to think things over, work things out in detail.

"In die ecke," he said, indicating a small corner table in the niche of a partition wall; a bead-curtained alcove, where a couple might find a little privacy. But in a place like this, a couple of what?

His table was up two uncarpeted steps and stood behind a pair of large, bedraggled-looking potted plants in precariously balanced terra-cotta tubs; from this slightly elevated vantage point, he had a decent view of almost everything on his side of the arching partition. Taking his seat with his back to the exterior wall, he looked around the room. Not that there was much to see. There had always been a kind of perpetual gloom in the Alt Deutscheshaus, even in broad daylight.

The place wasn't packed yet, wouldn't be until maybe ten, ten-thirty. Then they'd flock here, mainly the losers. As for the gays: they'd be heading for the Twilight Drei und Dreizig close to the Bahnhof, the Charlottenburg railway station where he had just come from. And the "purists," those who were only here for the beer, they would be linking arms and swaying left and right to the tunes of a lederhosen-clad, knee-slapping umpah-umpah band in the Hofbrauhause in Kurfürstendamm.

God, he had loved this city as a young soldier! And now he would love to be out of here. And meanwhile every root of every hair on Jack Turnbull's head was tingling every time he looked at the whitecap of foam on his beer. As he picked up the glass, the minder's hand shook. And as he touched it to his lips, his whole body trembled. Free beer, here in Berlin. And Schultheis at that! And no Spencer Gill to say him nay, no Angela Denholm to get mad at him, and no . . . no Miranda.

Jack Turnbull's personal hell? Okay, so what did that make him? A fallen angel? In that case—and apart from the absence of Miranda—it could only be that he'd fallen in reverse, from hell into heaven!

And again he asked himself: *Oh, really?* But that wasn't how these synthetic nightmares were supposed to work, was it . . . ?

Again he looked at and listened to the room. Low, murmuring voices; the chink of glasses, bottles; the sound of a jukebox, probably from upstairs. Shadowy figures seen through the drifting cigarette smoke; the glow of cigarette ends; faces in profile, flickering to the whirr of the projectors. And the monochrome, moving pictures on the walls, distorted bodies, grotesque acts. And the smell of beer and schnapps.

Turnbull lifted his glass again. To be or not to be? Hell, or heaven, or a mixture of both . . . ?

A few minutes later the *kellnerin*—the panzerlike barmaid—came to him with a second beer. She'd noticed that his glass was empty. And:

"Essen," he said. *"Haben sie etwas?"* He slapped his twenty note down on the table, leaned forward, and squeezed her thigh.

"Bockwurst?" She slapped his hand playfully. *"Oder schinken-brötchen?"*

"A ham sandwich? Yeah!" said the minder. "And a bockwurst? A hot dog? That'll do it. With potato salad—I mean, er, *kartoffel salat?*"

She nodded and asked, *"Und senf?"*

"German mustard," Turnbull sighed. And: "Damned right!" He smacked his lips. Then, as she turned from his table, he picked up his second glass . . .

Sith of the Ggyddn was delighted. From his previous time here, as a Thone invigilator, Sith understood something of humanity's addictions. And something of its lusts, too. On the Royal Mile in Edinburgh that time, that New Year's Eve, he'd seen alcohol imbibed at a frantic pace; seen what it did to men, too. And he had witnessed at first hand the sluts it could make of certain women.

Of course, all such were "alien" concepts to him, but the Thone (and now the Ggyddn) were experts in the ways of aliens. When your business is colonization, you have to be. And as for the great computer, the synthesizer, the House of Doors: without that it could get into and decipher the thoughts, feelings, emotions of alien minds, none of this was possible at all. But it could, it did, and what with the synthesizer and Sith's previous knowledge, he fully understood Jack Turnbull's predicament. Sith's delight sprang from the fact that Turnbull had succumbed to that predicament, that addiction, and moreover, that soon he would be called upon to pay the price for it.

A protector—a "minder"—Jack Turnbull? *Hah!* Only take away his formidable strength, his resolve, then taunt him with his own weakness and the corruption of everything most dear to him . . . it would destroy him utterly!

Watching him this past hour, Sith had observed Turnbull's gradual descent into an alcoholic stupor. Well, not quite that, not yet . . . but be sure it was coming. The big minder's hell on Earth? Oh, yes: it was quickly catching up with him, right here in this variant Berlin. Sith had confirmed and agreed to the synthesizer's original projection, its plan of attack, but he'd also exercised what he could of a veto on the cutoff point. For of course he wanted to enjoy the minder's torment right to the bitter end. However, and because the computer was a Thone machine, it had built-in fail-safes. Even now Sith could not say for sure just how far the synthesizer would allow things to go. He supposed it would depend largely on the degree of Turnbull's mental degeneration toward the end. But so far the computer seemed to have accepted Sith's additional directives.

Accepted them, yes, and yet . . . it was disconcerting; for at the same time it had shut him out. He could watch the ordeal building, watch its effect upon the subject, Jack Turnbull, but he couldn't "tune in" and experience it from the minder's point of view. Presumably the synthesizer considered that to lie outside its moral guidelines; it was one of its fail-safes, that an invigilator should not be allowed to enjoy the torments of his victims . . . (or rather the trials of the test specimens).

But in any case Sith was enjoying just watching. Watching the beers being delivered, seeing the minder sinking them, and watching this . . . this *Neanderthal* sink with them. A pity that the light wasn't better in the Alt Deutscheshaus. But the way Turnbull slumped there against the wall, his legs outstretched under the table; the way he rocked first this way and then that as the alcohol soaked into his system; and his droopy eyes on the wall opposite—looking directly *at* Sith, in fact, but without seeing him, of course—oh, it was obvious that fatigue, both mental and physical, had taken its toll of him. He'd eaten a meal, true, but that had only served to relax him. It had done nothing to alleviate the stupefying effect of the beer.

The minder's personal hell? This drunkenness, the achievement of which gave him so much pleasure? Well, not *yet* his hell—not just yet—but it was very close now. In fact the timing was entirely at Sith's discretion, for he had arranged to initiate the thing personally.

He himself would set it in motion . . . and watch Turnbull's world and mind disintegrate into a chaos that could only result in complete and irreversible madness.

And that last was such an inspiring thought, which came at such an opportune moment (for the minder's elbow had slipped on the wet table, sending his glass crashing to the floor, and his head had jerked free of his cupped hand and lolled uncontrollably on its drunkard's neck) that Sith decided to wait no longer but do it now . . .

CHAPTER
35

WITH ANGELA'S CRY of horror ringing in his ears, Spencer Gill fell, or seemed to fall, for a long time. And: *If that brain was an actual brain,* he thought, *and if we're falling right through some gigantic person from head to toe, then we'll all be dead before we hit. Or immediately after.*

A crazy thought, yes . . . but then, wasn't that the idea? That the synthesizer take them to the very limits of madness? No, that wasn't the idea. That *had been* the idea, before Sith changed the rules. But now there were no limits. Unless they had been imposed by the synthesizer itself.

And Angela would be falling, too—*was* falling, because he could still hear her echoing cry—and Miranda, Fred, Jack, Ki-no Sung, Barney, and (amazingly) even poor George Waite. Or maybe not so poor if they survived it and if George's mind was still in one piece. These were some of Gill's thoughts in the seconds, minutes, or however long they fell.

Then:

Crump! And a thin crust of sand gave under his feet, spilling him down the steep slope of a dune. Gill didn't see all of this; he felt rather than saw it because his eyes had been half-shut. Expecting pain or even death, he hadn't wanted to see the Old Boy arrive. It was the same principle he'd used as a kid in Cyprus, when he would face down a breaker in the warm Mediterranean Sea: hold his nose and close his eyes as the breaker hit. Or in this case as he hit. So that where he'd landed only felt like sand, and because it was heaped he'd automatically taken it for a dune.

Well, and what's a dune if it isn't a heap? But it wasn't a heap of sand.

Gill knew that as soon as he'd spun head over heels and come down on one shoulder and his face in the stuff.

He had known immediately where he was, too.

Not sand but rust, and not a dune but an embankment. God, a railway embankment, but for the strangest kind of train anyone could ever imagine!

And then Angela came tobogganing into his back, knocking what was left of the wind out of him. "Spence*eeeer!*" she shrilled, and grabbed him fiercely as she opened her eyes wider and stared wildly all about. And then, but in a gasping, disbelieving whisper now: "Spencer, do you know . . . know where . . . where we are?"

He nodded, began to answer, or would have if Barney hadn't arrived with a yelp and a cloud of rust. Then, spitting out red flakes of the stuff, "Oh, yes, I know where we are," Gill finally said. "And it's still nothing like Kansas!"

Ki-no Sung was sitting to the left; with shaking hands, he brushed rust out of his mop of hair. Beyond Sung, George Waite lay prone, head down the slope, half-buried in red grit. Groaning, he just lay there motionless. Miranda Marsh and Fred Stannersly had come to rest to the right of Gill and Angela; apparently unharmed but shocked to their roots, they simply huddled there.

Then Miranda gave a start, shook herself, looked all about. And she noticed at the same time as all the rest . . . that Jack Turnbull wasn't with them.

"Jack!" She stumbled to her feet, turned this way and that. "*Jack!*"

"Miranda," Gill went to her. "Miranda, take it easy. He has to be here somewhere."

She fought him off. "Jack! Where are you? Oh, you big fool! Where the hell *are* you?"

Angela had already got a grip of herself. Standing up, she told the others, "Look for the minder." It was the first time Gill had ever heard her use that term . . .

But it was no use. The rest of them were here, even Barney. So Turnbull should be here, too. And wasn't.

"Jack!" Miranda was wailing now, stumbling and going to all fours where she started to climb the embankment.

Ki-no Sung was on one knee looking at George Waite. Angela went to him, said, "Is he okay?"

And George spoke for himself. "I can't, daren't move," he said in a whisper. "My . . . my *head!*" His head was turned on one side; his breath blew small plumes of rust away from the corner of his mouth; the rest of him remained motionless.

"Does it hurt?" Carefully, Angela brushed rust from Waite's hair. Then, a little less carefully, she searched his scalp minutely at the top and back of his head. Not a mark—not a sign, no evidence at all—that he'd ever been anything but perfectly normal! Every trace of the thing that had grown out of his head had completely disappeared.

"Is it . . . ? I mean, am I . . . ?" George twitched, tightened his muscles as if testing them, and knotted his fists at the ends of his spread-eagled arms.

"You're okay!" Angela sighed. And exerting all her strength she turned him onto his back. George slid a little way downhill, rolled to one side, braked with his hands, and sat up. "You beat it," Angela told him. "Just like we all have, you beat your own personal nightmare."

His face was half red with rust, made darker yet by all the blood that had rushed to his head. But the twitching grin that curved his lips was less than normal, and the light in his eyes was just a little too bright.

Angela moved closer, held out her arms to him. "You're okay, George!" she said. But:

"Uh-uh." He shook his head. "Not quite." Then, suddenly he reached out, grasped her shoulders, began shaking her. "No, I don't think I am okay, Angela!" And now his grin was a kind of crazy grimace.

Gill caught hold of George's grimy collar, dragged him to his feet, hit him a backhander that caught him off balance and sent him flying down the slope. Gill followed him, stood over him, snarled at him in a way that was almost as mad—but mad with passion, not madness. And:

"Listen," Gill growled. "We've lost Jack Turnbull. We don't know how, but we have. That's driven Miranda half-crazy. So the last thing we need is for you to take it all the way. Angela is right: you've beaten your own personal nightmare. So congratulations, George, but don't go giving *us* nightmares! Me, I *really* don't need any more than I've got right now."

And slowly the too-bright light went out of George's eyes, and finally he blinked and shook his head. "A . . . a nightmare?" he said then. "But God, Spencer, you should have been in there with me! You should have *felt* it!" His voice was one long shudder . . .

"Spencer!" Miranda's quavery, frightened cry sounded from on high. "From up here I can see the sun. But it's *your* sun. I mean, this is *your* world. Your mad machine world."

"Keep your voice down," Gill called back, but softly. "Get down and stay low. Yes, this is my machine world, and we're out in the rust desert. But there are some machines you don't know about yet." And to George: "Are you going to be okay now?"

"Probably not ever," said the other. "But I won't give you any trouble, no."

Fred Stannersly still hadn't moved. Gill went to him, said, "Fred, what's up?"

The other looked at him. "It's my spatial thing," he whispered. "I'm just trying to get it nailed down, that's all. That fall of ours. It was weird."

"You mean you couldn't figure the time? Me neither. It went on forever, but it didn't."

Fred nodded, gulped, said, "Something like that. I felt we were falling through some weird places, Spencer. Or rather, no place at all! This thing of mine: it isn't claustrophobia, agoraphobia, or any phobia you can stick a name on. I suppose I'm just very much aware of our three mundane dimensions. And what we've just been through wasn't any of them."

Miranda came sliding down the side of the rust bank. "Spencer, Jack cut that thing loose from George's head. He—"

"He knocked on the door, yes," said Gill. "That giant brain was a door."

She clutched his arm. "So why are we here, and Jack's not?"

Gill shook his head, looked away.

"He's in his own personal hell?" Miranda's hand flew to her mouth. "Without us? But how can that be?"

Angela had come to them. She said, "The first time we were taken by the House of Doors, the same thing happened. Only then it was worse. On one occasion, we *all* went our separate ways."

"But we all got back together again," Gill quickly put in. "And it could happen that way again. So it isn't over just yet. Miranda, just remember this: wherever Jack is, he'll be trying to get back to you. And we'll be trying to get to him."

Miranda looked at him, and set her jaw in a way he recognized. The iron lady he'd known back in the beginning. "Right," she said. And: "Come on, all of you." Amazingly, she started up the embankment again.

"What?" said Gill.

She turned and looked down at him. "Where do those trains go?"

"Trains?" he repeated, frowning. "You mean like the one that blew up when we were in the dying machine city?"

She nodded. "Where do they go?"

"Both ways," Gill answered with a shrug. "Some of them go out into the rust desert; others go back into the city."

"Well, there's one coming," she told him, "and I think we should catch it. We have to catch it, because Jack's not here, and we have to go where he is."

For the first time Gill heard it, very faint but utterly unmistakable, the alien clatter of a crazy Heath Robinson device: Gong-*bang!* . . . Gong-*bang!* . . . Gong-*bang!* Anywhere else he would have known it, felt it, sensed its presence at once, but in this place his machine talent was right out of kilter. Surrounded by weirdness, in a weird machine universe, the static was like the hum of a giant dynamo in his head. He had to concentrate *not* to hear it.

But Miranda was right. If it was coming this way—from whichever direction—they should try to thumb a lift. Indeed they should, for while the train was harmless there *were* other machines that Miranda, Fred, and Ki-no Sung hadn't seen as yet, and they "lived" out in this red rust wilderness.

Angela clutched Gill's arm. "What if it's heading out into the desert? I mean, farther out?"

"There's a lot more than just a couple of rust-worm hives out there," Gill answered. "There's a House of Doors—and we know exactly where it is."

"But if the program has been changed?"

"We must hope that this part hasn't."

"And if the train's on its way back into the city—?"

"We know where there are doors." Gill nodded. "Also, we know which ones to avoid. Come on, let's go."

Ki-no Sung and Fred helped George, who seemed fragile as a paper doll. Miranda didn't need any help; she had someone else to worry about now; she went back up the embankment as if she'd been born here. And Barney of course beat them all to the top.

Up there: "That way's the city," said Gill, pointing. "And the other way's the rust-worm hives—and the House of Doors."

"Rust-worms?" said Fred and George together, a little anxiously. The latter had probably read about them in Gill's report, but he was still dazed, in no fit state to try remembering much of anything right now.

"Just pray we don't bump into any," Gill answered.

Angela pointed along the silver ribbons of the tracks at a near-distant lumbering object that got bigger every moment, and said, "That train is coming *from* the city. Which means we'll be heading for the hives."

"Right," Gill said, nodding. "Same train, same hives, same bloody story. Which means we'll probably see rust-worms, too, yes."

"Same train?" said Miranda, puzzled.

"The one that blew up," Gill answered. "If I'm right, then things should work out more or less similar all around."

"Same old same old," said Fred, displaying a little of his accustomed sense of humor, however shaky.

But while George was much steadier on his feet now, still he looked confused. "The one that blew up?" He frowned.

"Everything is as it was," Gill tried to explain. "Except we've entered the program at a different time, different location. This time around we weren't in the city, so there was no scorpion to get jammed in the train's guts, so the train didn't blow itself up."

"So," Angela continued, "from here on in it has to happen pretty much like last time. But . . . how do we get on board?"

"Look for some good-sized bits of rubble, junk, anything," said Gill. "We'll pile it on the tracks. This fellow clears the tracks, does running repairs, as he goes. When he stops to work on our obstruction, that's when we board. Okay?"

And they all got to work. Even George . . .

In the Alt Deutscheshaus, in a 1970 Berlin that never existed except in Jack Turnbull's mind and memory, something was finally happening. It started with the pornographic films flickering in lewd procession over the screens. Or more properly, over the very *special* screen above the bar, the one that faced Turnbull directly where he sprawled in his corner niche.

The unaccustomed color was the first thing to catch his attention and draw his droopy gaze, the fact that the film was no longer monochrome. Both that and its sudden high quality—meaning the quality of the film itself as opposed to its dubious subject—caused the minder to focus his concentration so much more intently upon it. Indeed he jerked in his seat, very nearly starting bolt upright, as this new piece of larger than life pornography began to unfold in glorious Technicolor right there before his eyes.

The color, vivid detail, seeming proximity of the actors where they filled center screen—and finally the actors themselves—drew the minder's eyes like iron filings to a magnet. There were just two of them; only two actors, or more properly players, in a well-lit room with cameo drapes and neutral carpets where everything was perfectly coordinated to draw the eye of the viewer to the central, black-sheeted, circular bed. And to the players, of course.

The players:

One of them was Sith/Bannerman, standing naked, arms akimbo to one side of the bed, and facing the audience; facing Jack Turnbull, in fact. There could be no mistaking Sith's handsome, human/inhuman face—or rather the face of the Bannerman construct that hid his true, alien form—

but Turnbull might oh-so-easily have mistaken his body. For despite that it was the same body, there was one huge difference.

The original construct—the Sith/Bannerman whose weapon hand the minder had blasted into so many crimson sausages that night in Killin, in Scotland; the Sith/Bannerman who had attempted to trample him like a great crazed bull before making his escape into the night—had been just that, an alien construct. And a construct, alien or otherwise, (unless it's that type of "doll" favored by persons who have difficulties with entirely human relationships, or perhaps a clever model for students of anatomy) does not need the "gear" with which this one was equipped. In fact, the original Sith/Bannerman had been quite sexless. Oh, it had looked like a man, but what use has a deep-sea diving suit—or a spacesuit for that matter—for a penis and testicles?

But where "a great crazed bull" had been Turnbull's description of Sith/Bannerman in his original construct form, "hung like a bull" was the only way he would describe this new creation. Nor would that be an exaggeration.

A gasp of astonishment had gone up from the rest of the Alt Deutscheshaus's clientele. This was a new one on them, too. Of course it was, for it was the synthesizer's progression of the minder's nightmare. Or rather, it was Sith's sadistic addition to the program.

As for the other actor—or actress—she was on the bed which was now seen to be rotating, but oh-so-slowly. She was on her knees, legs apart, her arms spread wide and shoulders down. And she had her back to the audience. Everything was displayed, in black, pink, and deeper pink, against the cameo of the room's drapes and the silken black of the bedsheets, as the bed's rotation gradually brought her into profile, but facing away from Sith/Bannerman.

That was what was happening on the screen; it was the prelude to a scene of explicit and even awesome sexuality. And off the screen: the Alt Deutscheshaus's audience had fallen into a completely uncharacteristic silence. They were accustomed, even inured, to cheap, trashy, warts-and-all skin flicks . . . but this was something else. And in Jack Turnbull's mind a dull, distant roar was sounding, growing louder second by second, and drowning all else out, as the black bed continued to rotate and the erotically posed female figure upon it gradually turned toward the audience.

But her face was angled away from the camera, looking back the way she had come, and her hair cascaded over cheek and chin so that as yet the minder couldn't see her face . . . couldn't be certain of what he more than half suspected. Sith/Bannerman, on the other hand, was very sure. Even cocksure. Plying his monstrous, rearing member with two hands, he waited until the woman was in precisely the right position, then climbed onto the bed behind her.

And God, she was ready for him! She pushed herself backward onto him! And her face hung off the far side of the bed, and her breasts bounced beneath her as he rammed himself home, again, and again, and again.

And the bed continued to turn . . .

Sith of the Ggyddn looked out through that same screen, looked at Turnbull where he sat in his corner, his square jaw hanging slack, blue eyes no longer glazed under droopy eyelids but popping from his head, his body stiffly but (Sith supposed) impotently erect. And Sith knew precisely what Turnbull was seeing, for the same scene was being enacted on one of the computer's screens right there in the control room.

Indeed Sith was hard put to decide which subject he might best concentrate upon: the real man, or the entirely fictional, computerized event that was part of the man's nightmare—yet only *half* of its real substance. For the other half was surely Turnbull's own impotence, brought about by his addiction!

And there he sat, frozen in his seat—with all the blood draining from his face, and spittle, foam, or the froth of his last beer still clinging to his unshaven chin—and now a tic jerking the flesh at the corner of his mouth. The Neanderthal, the minder, Jack Turnbull, impotent of restraint in respect of his drinking, and now made more impotent yet by virtue of such excesses. And the black bed still rotating, but already turned to a degree where finally Turnbull was allowed to see the face of the woman. The face of Miranda Marsh!

But *such* a face. A face full of indescribable lust as her breasts pounded and her hand went back and up between her legs to grasp and tug on the madly lunging Bannerman's balls. A salivating, gasping mouth, twisting in a grimace of pain, passion, and unbearable pleasure. Nostrils gaping, drawing madly on air to fuel her exertions as she drove backward almost as hard as the *thing* drove forward!

And then her eyes meeting those of her audience—specifically those of Jack Turnbull—and her slavering, oh-so-knowing smile! And Sith/Bannerman's silent but uproarious laughter as he pushed her buttocks together on his great pole of a penis and continued to drive it home, while gazing directly into the minder's eyes!

Sith's attention was now riveted on the sex act. The synthesizer had outdone itself. The only thing he couldn't fathom was why he had been allowed to watch for so long. For this must be the cruelest of all torments, the point where Turnbull must surely descend into animal madness. But no, no—that would be the *next* act, when the big minder was dragged away, tossed into a cell, and left to rot; and his *mind* rotting, too, in the awful knowledge of what he had just witnessed.

And here it came: the big black provost corporal and two lance corporals, from behind the arching partition wall, starting up the steps and reaching for the sodden, sobbing Turnbull. And all three of them angry as hell where they confronted him.

"Motherfucker!" the corporal yelled. "Ah done checked with the 'lympic stadium guardroom, and they checked with Int Corps, and they *'aint* no Colonel Jack Turnbull! And you owes me twenty deutsche marks and a whole mess o' hurtin'. Hold 'im, boys."

After that, all was chaos . . .

CHAPTER
36

SPENCER GILL SAT in four of five inches of vile, fish-smelling oil, in the narrow moatlike trough that formed the rim of the train's loading platform. He appeared to be bathing in the filthy stuff! Angela Denholm, too, letting the oil trickle through her fingers down the neck of her torn, rust-stained jacket, and rubbing it into her lower thighs and legs where her once-trousers had been shredded down to little more than shorts.

Watching them, Fred Stannersly shook his head, said, "What the hell . . . ?"

Gill grinned at him humorlessly, told him, "You'd be well advised to do the same. The rust-worms are metal-eaters."

"We are not metal," said Miranda Marsh, distantly. She was interested in only one thing: to get out of this place and find Jack Turnbull.

"No," Angela told her, "but the rust-worms don't know that. When Spencer said metal, he really meant machines. They cripple machines, make dead metal of them, and then eat them. Machines move, you see. So since you also move, you're liable to be mistaken for a machine."

"And the oil?" said Fred.

"It's like shark repellent," Gill came back in. "But don't ask me why." He shrugged. "Maybe the worms see it as indicative of a well-oiled, 'living' machine—something that's not to be eaten, not quite ripe for rustville—I can't say for sure. But David Anderson, who was Miranda's and George's predecessor, was here with us the first time we were taken. He was grabbed up by a rust-worm. It got him in its mouth, spat him out again. And I reckon it was because he stank of this oil."

Fred came on hands and knees to the rim of the moat, sniffed at the oil, stripped off his jacket, and gave it a thorough soaking. "I'm convinced," he said.

Miranda did the same as Angela: dribbled oil down what was left of her blouse, and rubbed it into her arms and legs. Ki-no Sung actually grinned while following suit. "Is like the fish!" he commented. While no one shared his enthusiasm, they couldn't other than agree. As for Barney: he'd been "assisted" aboard by Gill and Stannersly, and during the scramble he'd fallen in the moat. Now he sat alone looking morose. George Waite looked much the same; he said nothing, did nothing, until Gill told him:

"George, you've got this far in one piece. We *are* going to come out of this, you have my promise." He was bragging, but if he was wrong he knew he wouldn't have to apologize. He probably wouldn't get the opportunity.

And George sighed, moved to the moat, dipped his hands, and daubed along with the rest of them. "When we started out, I had something growing in my brain," he said. "Now there's something else in there—in my mind, anyway. And I don't think I'll ever get rid of it."

"It'll fade," said Gill. "You can fight it."

"Like Anderson?" George looked at him.

"You're younger, stronger," said Gill.

"Maybe," George answered uncertainly. "Anyway, what I went through had to be the very worst of it. And that's over now."

Gill said nothing more, but wondered: *Oh, really? The very worst of it? Over? Well, I hope so.*

Miranda put her hands on the outer rim of the moat, looked over the edge. The train was like a spiky, not-quite-oblong box on wheels; six pairs of them in fact, massive steel wheels running on tracks all of a foot wide with a gauge of at least forty feet. The box was maybe thirty-five feet high, some fifty long, and was skewed or imperfectly angled in just about every direction. Its so-called "spikes" were a multitude of grasping, cutting, or hammering appendages decorating its four sides like the tools on some maniacal, gigantic Swiss Army knife. When she had first seen the thing close-up, Miranda had doubted that she and the others could ever get aboard it. But . . .

After the train had put up a swiveling multijointed periscope and subsequently gong-*banged* to a clanging halt, the appendages at the front had quickly cranked into weird mechanical life. Concertinaing or otherwise extending themselves, they had removed the scrap that Gill and his colleagues had piled on the tracks. During that operation, the six human beings and one dog had climbed the projecting flanges of the immobile tools to the rear.

Then, with a snort and a jerk, the train had set off again. And now they were here, wherever here was, going somewhere else but not necessarily anywhere they really wanted to go. Yet Miranda was satisfied that at least she was mobile. And if she was headed in Jack Turnbull's direction in time and space, that was good enough for her.

And meanwhile the scenery was startling, dramatic . . . and terribly samey; so that in less than half an hour it had become utterly boring. Nevertheless, and with nothing else to do, Miranda observed the red, barren "landscape" all around. Spencer's machine world. But apart from their weird piggyback ride there wasn't too much evidence of machinery out this way. Well, there was, but only in the endless iron-oxide dunes, the dust and debris and ultimate death of machinery. As for the machine city:

Quite obviously they were heading away from it. When first they had scrambled aboard the train, the junk-and rust-riddled city had been visible only as an irregular, slumping, skeletally spired red hump on the rearward horizon; but at least it had been a distraction, something you could focus your eyes on. Now it was lost in distance and ahead there were only the dunes . . .

Or perhaps not.

There was also, for instance, the "sun." Spencer Gill's sun. Two or three times as large as Sol, it hung there in the sky defying acceptance. A giant, silver ball-bearing peppered with blowholes that blasted out spokes of fire and light and radiation in a never-ending chain reaction of nuclear energy; a *machine* sun set centrally in a machine system of worlds. At first, it had hurt one's eyes to look at it for too long, but not quite so much now. Because soon it would be setting, and the machine planet's atmosphere had robbed its slanting rays of much of their ferocity. It was more than three-quarters of the way down the sky, and the dune-cast shadows were steadily lengthening.

But the sun wasn't everything, and Miranda blinked, frowned, and looked again. She'd seen something else just then . . . hadn't she? If so, then like the blink of her eye it was there and gone, so that she couldn't be sure even now. But still she kept looking . . .

Gill and Angela were out of the moat now. Oily, disheveled, exhausted, they sprawled in each other's arms on the riveted-iron loading platform. Barney, his tongue lolling, whined and grumbled at Gill's feet. Fred, George, and Ki-no Sung sat with their backs against the moat, nodding and falling asleep where sleep was almost humanly impossible. And the train gong-*banged* monotonously, deafeningly on.

But Miranda stayed wide awake worrying about the big minder, Jack Turnbull, who for a certainty had "minded" her. He'd looked after her for all he was worth. And damn it to hell, he was *worth* a lot! Everything that Miranda was capable of giving, anyway . . .

She scanned the forward horizon—*and there it was again!* Now what the . . . ? For a while now Miranda had seen nothing worth noting; well nothing definite, anyway. No crumbling girders, no burnt-out boilers oxidizing their way to a rusty red heaven, no metal parts at all save the bright steel ribbons of the tracks reaching out interminably fore and aft. And on both sides wave upon wave of rust sifted as fine as sand.

But now, above the false horizon of a dune up ahead, three dark knolls or roughly cone-shaped structures had become visible as a direct result of the declining sun silhouetting their fretted outlines in sporadic rays of silvery-red fire. And as the suddenly laboring train dropped a gear to attack a rising gradient, so the structures appeared to rear up into view that much more rapidly.

And yet Miranda looked at them without really seeing them, for she was searching for something else. It wasn't the knolls that had attracted her attention but some transient thing that came and went almost as fast as her aching eyes could register its presence. And what do you know, even as the thought occurred . . . there it was yet again!

A spray of rust, a spouting geyser against the red-litten horizon, maybe half a mile away between the crest of the great dune and the train. And another, and another . . .

And: "Spencer?" Miranda queried, much too quietly. Gill's chin was on his chest and he merely twitched a little; the sudden increase in the engine's din as it climbed the gradient was drowning Miranda's voice out. She crawled across the shuddering roof, grabbed one of his scuffed and battered boots, and yanked on it. "Spencer, wake up. I think something's happening."

"Eh?" He started awake. "What? Huh?"

"Look." Miranda pointed.

And now the others were stirring, too.

Gill looked, saw the knolls, and scrambled to his feet for a better view. Since the rust eruptions had ceased, it was only natural he should conclude that these strange structures—like rearing great termite castles—were the sole source of Miranda's concern. And of course he knew immediately what they were: rust-worm hives, remembered from that previous visit. But here? How come he didn't recognize the landscape?

Angela got up, stood with Gill, knew what he was thinking. For she was thinking much the same thing. But while he searched for solutions in some trick of the synthesizer or a different program, she had already arrived at a far simpler conclusion. It was a question of orientation. "Spencer," she said, "correct me if I'm wrong, but the first time we were here . . . didn't the sun go down *between* the hives?"

And as quickly as that she had supplied the answer. "You're right!" he gasped. "It went down between them, set them glowing and made them visible. But this time it's going down way to one side. Ergo: this *is* a different train, and it's running on different tracks! There must be a network of tracks. Not only did we reenter the program at a different time but also in a different location."

"Hives?" Miranda grabbed Gill's elbow. "Do you mean rust-worm hives? And does that mean that those plumes I saw are . . . ?"

"Where?" Gill turned to her at once, followed her gaze as she pointed a shaky hand. Perfect timing: a geyser of rust jetted twenty feet high not a hundred yards from the train, which was now reaching the crest of the great dune. As it did so and the tracks leveled out again, so the weirdly intelligent engine cranked up a telescopic periscope from its flank to survey the terrain ahead.

And after several long moments (during which every member of the team believed that he or she could hear the train thinking, if not what it was thinking), then with a nerve-wrenching squeal of dry metal parts, the periscope quickly folded itself away again and the moat commenced issuing a glutinous gurgling. The oil was draining into a funnel at the rear end of the loading platform.

"Company!" George called out, pointing out and down at the oxidized surface of the rust desert, where some fifty yards to starboard something was creating a brand-new dune. Moving parallel with the tracks and keeping pace with the train, a mole run of rust was being *pushed up from below* in a ruler-straight line that built rapidly into a long barrow. Before their eyes (or as yet hidden from them) something was tunneling through the rust at fifteen to twenty miles per hour. And every fifty yards or so, like a sperm whale spouting, the unseen burrower would pause to emit a geyser of rust, fine particles of which drifted like spume before settling.

"Rust-worm!" said Gill. "And now you'll see the reason for the oil. Dual purpose: a lubricant for the engine and a repellent for the worms."

And as if the train had heard him, oil began to spray from a system of sprinklers down by the wheels; a fine stinking mist of the stuff that turned the rails and sleepers shiny black and soaked into the rust, darkening it for fifteen feet or more beyond the tracks and out into the desert.

Gathering speed along a slight decline, the train no longer strained. Gears changed up, and slowly but surely the rust-worm was left behind.

As they drew away from it, the thing quit its pursuit, thrust up its snout, and emerged. And:

"Good God Almighty!" George whispered the words like a prayer, his own nightmare temporarily forgotten in the face of the new threat. "And I thought your report was an exaggeration!"

"Me, too," said Miranda, sitting down with a jarring thump.

And Fred said, "When I think worms, they're small wet wriggly things that birds eat. But I wouldn't much care to see the bird that could eat that bastard!"

The worm was a telescopic snake of dull gray metal seventy-five feet long and five thick. The upper half of its head was a flat, tapering, bluntly thrusting snout, with eyes like inspection lamps set well back behind a hood with a protective grille. Under the snout there was a great hinged scoop, like the plankton-gathering mouth of a basking shark. Inside the scoop bright zigzags of electrical energy made a curtain of "teeth" between the jaws.

"But we're safe as long as the oil lasts out," Gill tried to reassure everyone, though no one had asked him. And a moment later:

"No," Angela contradicted him, "I'm not sure we are." They all looked where she was looking.

The track was curving now, beginning to turn away from the hives. But up ahead, where the metal ribbons wound between the mounds of taller, steeper than average dunes—

Rust had been heaped on the tracks!

A veritable wall of rust, a great bank of rust, and there was no way that the train was going to break through. And while it was apparently "sentient" in respect of certain other perils, this time the train didn't seem to recognize the threat. Indeed it was still gathering speed! And from a whistle on a pipe-stem flagstaff at one corner of the roof, it blew a series of shrill and perhaps desperate *toot!—toot!—toots!*

"We're not going to get any closer to the hives than this," Gill shouted. "It's time we got off."

"Are you crazy?" George Waite couldn't believe it. "We've got maybe fifteen seconds before we hit, and you're telling us to climb down from here?"

"No"—Gill shook his head—"I'm not crazy, just experienced. That rust is as fine as talc, and I don't remember saying anything about *climbing* down. Also, it's only ten seconds, not fifteen." Gathering Barney up, he licked tinder-dry lips, gave Angela a nod. "Here we go again."

And as she jumped, Angela yelled, "Five seconds!"

But it took less than that for the others to get airborne.

And then it was just as if they had landed here all over again; except Gill was right and the rust was dust, literally, so that landing and rolling down the embankment was far less than life threatening—but staying with the train would have been, most certainly.

Shaken, the six sprawled where they'd landed, watched the doomed engine gong-*banging* on along the tracks over the embankment. And with a sharp warning *toot!*—and a final, very exaggerated and definitely despairing *whoop! whoooop!*—it hit!

There was no cowcatcher on the train, nothing to dig in or slow however marginally its headlong rush to extinction. It hit the sloping pile of rust; its wheels cut through the soft stuff until the boxlike body plowed it up into a dense solid wall, and then the rear of the train rose up, slewed violently to one side—mercifully, the far side of the embankment—and toppled over. Its rear wheels and back end were the last they saw of it for the moment . . .

Until it blew.

That was perhaps a minute, or maybe ninety seconds; sufficient time, anyway, for the team to get their scattered senses together. And enough time for the rust-worms on the other side of the embankment to gather to the feast.

Plumes of rust geysered skyward on the unseen side of the embankment while a subdued, shuddering, gong-*bang* clanking continued to sound from the doomed train. And in a winded whisper, Gill voiced a freshly formed opinion:

"I think the trains are rigged to self-destruct. I've seen it twice now: the first time Angela and I, and Jack, were here, and also that spectacular suicide in the machine city. It seems to me that when they . . . well, when they come to the end of the line, they end it themselves. Which means that we really should be getting away from here."

He pointed in the direction of the rust-worm hives, across a wilderness of dunes that were steep-sided on this side, long-sloping on the other, like waves rolling on a beach. But pointing was all he had time for, for as he finished speaking there came a mighty explosion from the other side of the embankment.

Everyone ducked, shrank down into themselves, covered their heads. It was a natural reaction, and a wise one. Metallic debris of every size and shape, a cloud of rust, gouting fire and roiling black smoke at once leaped skyward as the wall of the embankment shook and brought down an avalanche of soft rust.

Bits of engine, pistons, a wheel, various entirely conjectural appendages that continued to twitch and convulse, rained down. But the train's suicide hadn't been entirely in vain; no, for it had taken some of the rust-worms with it. Several gently curved, gray-metal sections some five feet wide and eight long came fluttering down like leaves, bouncing and skittering where they hit: the outer shells or skins of a rust-worm or worms.

One of these landed close to Gill; he waited for the rest of the junk to stop falling, floundered through the rust to the curved section, and tugged at it. Light as aluminum, it skidded on the rust like a ski on ice! The ideal material for the skin of a rust-burrowing machine creature. Ideal for Gill's purpose, too.

"Is everyone okay?" he questioned as sounds of unleashed electrical energies sounded from beyond the embankment, and the geysers began to whoosh skyward as before. "Then let's go. And, Fred, George—grab yourselves one of these skins."

He and Angela hauled their skin to the crest of the first dune and along with Barney and Ki-no Sung rode it like a sled down the long slope on the other side. And Miranda, George, and Fred were right behind them.

As they dragged their skin sections up the steep side of the second dune, Miranda said, "Spencer, okay, I know I should have paid more attention to your report. But tell me anyway—how long before those rust-worms get through with the train?"

"Oh, there's a lot of metal there," Gill answered. "So no need to concern yourself with what's happening on *that* side of the embankment."

"But this side?" She just couldn't take a hint.

He wiped sweat and rust from his brow, and nodded. "Those hives are where these things breed—that is, where they build more worms—and we're heading for the hives. In fact, for the one that isn't a hive but a house, a House of Doors."

They had reached the crest of the rust dune; Gill pointed at the three great structures, the closest of which was maybe a half mile away. "That one," he said.

The scene was weird, otherworldly—naturally. The ball-bearing sun was halfway lost beyond the farthest horizon now, but its fading light still lit on the fantastic termite towers of the rust-worms. Beyond the House of Doors, the actual hives reared mountainous, two thousand or more feet high. Rust-worms came and went around their bases, which were enveloped in dust storms, rust eruptions. The towers or castles themselves were holed, tunneled, and fretted to their topmost spires like maggoty cheese, where worms were active on the outside as well as the insides of their nests. They to and froed between the myriad entrances like wasps around a pile of rotten apples.

But as for the third, the closest "hive" . . . it was roughly the same size and shape as the others, but its purpose was entirely different. Steep, red-rusted ramps fanned out like spokes from its base, and at the top of each ramp, set back in arched-over, cavernous recesses—

"Doors!" said Miranda, George, and Fred, almost in a single voice.

"Yes, and a whole houseful, at that," Gill answered, then experienced a moment of . . . what, déjà vu? But no, not really, for of course he had *in reality* said or thought the same thing once before. On that occasion, well things had managed to work out right. Now he must hope they would do the same again . . .

CHAPTER
37

SITH OF THE Ggyddn was laughing—or enjoying the alien equivalent of laughter—at the sight of an entirely computerized visual-effects Sith/ Bannerman having brutal sex with a willing, equally fictitious Miranda Marsh. And he was laughing, too, at Jack Turnbull who, from what evidence Sith had at his command, was entirely impotent to do anything about it.

But the fact was that alien or not, and despite that the picture on Sith's viewers was repulsive to him, the computer's sex show held by far the greater portion of his attention. The idea that if things had turned out differently he might *himself* have been in control of just such a construct as the fantastically equipped Bannerman, and that in different circumstances *he* might have been performing with the real female in a like fashion, making *him* the actual instrument of Turnbull's anticipated dementia . . . was fascinating to him. So much so that he was paying far less attention to what was happening in the synthesized 1970s Alt Deutscheshaus than he might otherwise have been. And for a fact what was happening there wasn't exactly as foreseen.

That was Sith's mood and situation. As for Turnbull's:

Until the porn show involving Sith/Bannerman and Miranda, the program of events had unfurled much as the big minder had anticipated. Right from the word go, he had more or less understood why he was here in the Charlottenburg district of a Berlin he'd previously known as a very young soldier: he was "only here for the beer." That is, in this his personal nightmare he had been given the "opportunity" to return to his addiction and renege once again on his oft-stated resolution. And what better place to do it than this? If proof of the minder's suspicion in this respect was required, then he could scarcely want for better proof than a barmaid who plied him with free beers—which certainly would not have been the case in the Berlin he'd once known. Not unless his feet were firmly under the table.

Also, the ease with which he'd been able to impersonate an officer (or rather the USMP corporal's gullibility and participation in that deception) simply didn't ring true. In his time Turnbull had had close contact with several military policemen; while none of them had done him any favors—and certainly not to the extent of offering him money—without exception they'd all given him a lot of trouble! Usually with good cause.

And finally there was the key to this business, the key he had used to open the door in Waite's loathsome brain. A chitin-plated key in the shape of a scorpion's claw fragment. Not the fragment or key itself but the fact that he'd been the one who turned it. *He*, Jack Turnbull, had "knocked" on that monstrous door—a merciful act, he had thought—which had pitched him headlong into this place, this synthesized Berlin with all its temptations and as yet unknown dangers, against which he must stand alone. Or fall.

Thus he'd guessed the truth of it: that this was his own personal nightmare, a place where he might so easily return to the sodden wreck he had been, and therefore one where his progress—indeed his honorable ambitions, with regard to Miranda Marsh—could be irreparably damaged and even reversed. And of course a place where he could die. For why else, if not to kill him, had Sith singled him out like this and separated him from his companions? Separated him, too, from Miranda.

But strong drink wouldn't be the only thing he would have to confront, Turnbull knew that. The booze was there to weaken him, unman him, and reduce his ability to fight during the *real* confrontation. So he had concluded, and so he had resisted . . .

At first it had been difficult. The beer looked so good, and Turnbull's trials had been so many; but those of his colleagues' had been just as many, yet to a man or a woman they'd proved themselves bigger, stronger than their worst fears and all the terrifying forces within themselves.

Armed in that knowledge and as time passed, the minder's will had strengthened. And despite that he lolled bleary-eyed at his table and the frothing beers came and the empty glasses went, still the drink did *not* go into him. And whatever it was that Sith had devised for him (whatever it was that was coming, that he knew *must* come if he sat here long enough without doing anything), from moment to moment Turnbull psyched himself up in preparation for it.

Which was why the sex show, however monstrous in its devising—and much more so in its obvious implications—came as something of an anticlimax. The minder had expected action, but not this kind of action. His revulsion, stupefaction, which had lasted only a matter of seconds for all that it had seemed like so many hours, had been annulled by the clatter of booted feet on the Alt Deutscheshaus's floorboards and the sight of three uniformed USMPs appearing from under the arch of the partition wall. And as the black corporal yelled: "Hold 'im, boys!" Turnbull was on his feet.

The wilting potted shrubs in their terra-cotta planters went over, pouring out large volumes of mud that consisted of dirt, cigarette ends, and spider debris . . . but mainly a gallon of beer! The slop hit the corporal's henchmen just as they reached the next to top step, and Turnbull hit them while they were still recoiling from it. One of them flew backward; his heels hit the bottom step; off balance, he slewed onto a table occupied by a big fat German who was engrossed in the sex show. And because this was Turnbull's Berlin, the big fat German hit the MP a second blow that drove him right through the shattering table. The other junior MP collided with the corporal and both of them went sprawling.

The minder jumped over them, his combat jacket flew open, and the folded-down machine pistol swept up into view. One big stride took him toward the bar, while the next launched him—one hand on the bar top, feetfirst—directly at the screen. Not valor but common sense; knowing now what the screen really was, he was firing as he vaulted, stitching it at close range. And his feet were passing through even as the screen, or door, dissolved into shards and tinkled in a crystal hailstorm down the wall . . . or what should have been a wall but wasn't.

As for Sith:

He had had three whole seconds for all of this to sink in, which wasn't long enough. With the greater part of his attention still riveted to the computerized porn, he hadn't realized what was going wrong until too late—or more correctly, until he felt the pain. *Pain!*

He was hit! In the upper part of one of his three stabilizers! Leaking fluids! Injured! Not fatally, no, but definitely infuriatingly! And Turnbull, the "Neanderthal" or Ggyddn equivalent, was hurtling through the screen toward him right now—was right here in the control room!

"Fucking thing!" the big minder snarled, bouncing upright off the oddly rubbery floor. "You ugly fucking thing!" Yet for all that he was mad, Turnbull was disoriented, too. And worse, his gun had jammed. Worse still, it might *not* have jammed but he could simply be out of ammo. Hell, and he could have sworn there were a couple of shots left! But that aside; what was it Gill had said about this bloody jellyfish? A low-gravity creature? So would that make the belt device he was wearing about his middle some kind of compensator?

The minder paced forward, and Sith, apparently floating, drifted back against the synthesizer's control bank, trying to focus his panicking mind on hitting the right "buttons." Turnbull was within easy reach of him now, his gun transferred to his left hand, while in his right . . .

The fragment of scorpion claw! Thone metal! And Turnbull was swinging it at Sith's gravity belt!

"This is for everybody," the big minder grunted. "Especially for Miranda. Consider yourself a stain, Sith!"

The claw swept in a swift arc, but not swift enough. Sith had found the buttons and pressed them, and however shakily he was back in command of the computer, the synthesizer. The claw met nothing but thin air and Turnbull was thrown right off balance as he spun uselessly, dizzily in a suddenly "changed" control room.

Sith was still floating there beside the weird controls—that bank of "formless" material that appeared to be more color than matter—but the room itself, Sith with it, and indeed the entire rainbow-hued control bank, seemed to have elongated, leaving the minder at one end of the room and the alien at the other . . . precisely the effect that Sith had achieved the first time Turnbull and his colleagues were here: a confusing space warp or expansion, as when the deenergized Castle on the lighthouse rock had swelled to enclose them. It was by no means illusory . . . and the minder's weapon remained jammed. But even if it wasn't, instinct told him that bullets couldn't get to Sith while his "fingers" were on the controls. Anything that forced its way between them would simply widen the gap. As it was widening even now!

The room became a tunnel with flowing, multicolored walls; Turnbull had seen this before; he grew dizzy from the apparent acceleration. Then, in a moment, everything contracted down to normal, and the minder lost his balance and sat down . . .

In night and mist and eight or nine inches of swamp!

Christ, that place again! And humpbacked shapes surfacing right under him, and maybe twenty-five yards away, a door rising up out of the slop. Turnbull knew what it would look like, and he was right.

Of iron-banded oak, arched and massive, ornate, Gothic, and forbidding, that door. But better by far than what was bulging up out of the mud and the ooze. Better *any* kind of escape route than the massively coiled snail shell—and its *occupant*, with its corrugated, blue-gray foot expanding and contracting, propelling the creature toward the momentarily paralyzed minder—and its luminous green eyes intent upon him, and its flickering tongue buzz-sawing eagerly in jaws that ground in anticipation under a sloping, hideously mobile face at the end of a straining, outstretched neck . . .

The minder was big, but not *that* big. He ran for the door in the House of Doors, his feet sinking in the muck, then his lower legs, and on up to his thighs, before he got there. And it was a question of who or what would get there first: him or the closest of the great snails. For even as he made a final, desperate effort and leaped for the knocker, a blurring, thrumming tongue was only inches behind him. And how he thanked his lucky stars that he was sober then, and a deal more sober than ever he'd been for as long as he could remember.

But knock he did—with the acid stench of snail slime rising all around, and the gliding beast-thing's tongue tearing at his tattered combat-suit trousers—one frantic smashing home of that great iron question mark upon the Gothic door . . .

That immediately cracked open and sucked him in.

The sun was almost down now on Gill's world of mad machines. A fan of metallic sheen rays stuck up from the dune horizon as if painted there, half-obscured by the farthest of the three rust-worm hives. But even here on this machine planet twilight was a strange time—or an even stranger time, but a bad time in any event—to judge distances or rely on eyesight alone. One mound of rust looked much like another. Until it moved.

"Look out!" from Stannersly, as the steeper wall of a dune collapsed almost under their feet. They were at the crest, positioning their worm-skin sleds for the very last run. The last, yes, because at least where distance was concerned the strange distortions of dusk had lied in their favor; they were a deal closer to the cone-shaped House of Doors than they'd imagined. There it stood, with its rusty ramps fanning outward, and its stem soaring upward as if reaching for identical ball-bearing stars like bullet holes in the banded ocher dome of the sky.

This last run down the gradual slope would carry them to what looked like a compacted rust circumference of maybe fifty feet, within or beyond which lay the splayed foot of the closest ramp. One last run, and a mad scramble across that crushed rust fringe . . . they would be there.

And now this: as they boarded their skins, the bank fell away behind them, resulting in Fred Stannersly's shout. The last to board, Fred was hanging on to the rear of the worm-skin section and looking back the way they'd come. Thus he was closer to the source of the collapse—or rather the eruption—and had seen its cause.

A rust-worm, the thing's head had come thrusting out of the dune maybe halfway down the steep slope, flinging a bomb burst of rust before it and causing the bank above it to crumble around its tubular neck and "flow" down the dune in a red avalanche. But if the whole worm should emerge, then the crest might cave in entirely.

Fred saw this, shouted, "Move!" gave the skin a shove, and jumped on behind George and Miranda. Slightly in the lead, Angela, Gill, and Ki-no Sung looked back fearfully as the hiss and sputter of weird energies sounded. But Barney was the wisest of them; he had been mobile from the first tremor and was already down on the level, heading for the foot of the ramp.

The rust-worm's head rose up above the dune, swaying and climbing higher as the "neck" and body elongated from the rust, then curved backward and began to turn like a corkscrew, drilling a swath through the crest of the quivering dune and pointing the worm in the direction of the fleeing humans. Stirred up by this incredible action, a dervish of rust was set in motion, obscuring for a moment the rest of what was taking place.

At the bottom of the wave where it leveled out, Gill and his party were off their skin, floundering through shallow rust and heading for the hard-packed perimeter. It seemed they must surely make it that far, but they also knew that that in itself wasn't going to guarantee their safety. A short distance behind them George and Miranda plowed in their wake, but bringing up the rear Fred panicked where he'd snagged his flying jacket in a tangle of buckled metal at the end of the worm skin. The rust-worm saw him; thrusting its head into the rust it blew a great plume, commenced a burrow that drove straight for Fred.

It was darker now, and the imitation hive—the House of Doors—stood silhouetted against a deepening burnt-red horizon. But in the genuine, more distant hives, lights had come on that, if they'd kept still, might easily be mistaken for interior illuminations. But in fact they moved, came and went over the surface of the hives in pairs, forming marvelously intricate patterns and making it at once apparent that they were the headlamp "eyes" of rust-worms.

Likewise the worm chasing Fred: as it "spouted" again right behind him and its spatulate head erupted from the softer rust, so its lamp eyes blinked on and trapped him in their twin beams. Moreover, the worm's electrical "teeth" were visible, zigzagging between its gaping upper and lower jaws.

Fred was free of hindrance now, but the worm was too close. Moving sinuously, its neck slid through the last of the softer rust and dragged its seventy-foot-long body free to lie on the surface. Swaying from side to side, the head lifted up, surged forward, lifted higher yet, and arched over Fred at the foot of the ramp. There he sensed its proximity, recognized the inevitable, paused, turned, and looked up at it.

"Run, Fred!" Miranda had stopped halfway up the ramp and was looking back at him. And George had even started back down again—Gill, too, and Ki-no Sung—shouting and waving their arms to attract the thing's attention, deliberately endangering themselves where they ran back down the ramp. And Fred standing there as if he were hypnotized, his hands held up before his face as if to ward off the thing that held him in its headlamp gaze.

When the worm struck it was with cobralike speed. The head snapped forward, retracted, Fred was gone . . . and the next moment was back again, as the thing spat him out. He landed in the last few inches of soft rust, bounced, lay still.

"Hey, fucking worm!" George skidded to a halt, stood over Fred's prone, smoking form. "Me next, you snake-eyed bastard!"

"Fred's jacket," Gill panted, joining George beneath that swaying head. "Get his jacket off. He drenched it in that oil; that's what saved him." But he qualified it with the thought: *If he was saved.*

They got him out of his jacket, and still the great head swayed over them. Then George twirled the jacket like a bolas, let it fly straight into the worm's face. And Gill was right: the rust-worm reared back. The oily leather and sheepskin hit like a slap, and the worm reacted the same way— as if it had been slapped, hard!

Fred's jacket came twirling down. Gill grabbed it, began dragging it behind with one hand, while helping George and Ki-no Sung haul Fred with the other. But the rust-worm followed, undulating between the spurs of the ramps where they narrowed inward to the great stem of the false hive, moving slowly but keeping abreast of the knot of humans. And always its head was level with them or rising above them as they climbed the ramp, and its headlamp eyes glaring at them as more and more of its concertina length pushed up to support it.

Soon they would be beyond its reach, higher than the worm was tall, but it knew that as well as they did. Blue and white lightning meshed between its electrode jaws; its entire outline began glowing with an eerie luminosity as the creature built up a massive electrical charge within itself. Then—with a reverberating *clang!*—its body fastened magnetically to the side of the ramp, began to snake upward and inward at an angle calculated to intercept the route of its prey.

And now the head of the beast came gliding into view over the rim of the ramp ahead of them, while above it, on a ledge surrounding the central mass of the House of Doors, Angela and Miranda found scabs of rust to throw at the thing. It looked up at them, headlamp eyes blinking, however briefly, then ignored them for the moment and returned its gaze to Gill's party where they were stalled. While out across the rust desert, other eyes were appearing now, and dark low humps forming in the ferrous-metal rubble and beginning to converge on the false hive.

But Gill still had Fred's jacket; holding it before him like a bullfighter's cloak, he inched up the ramp with George and Ki-no Sung behind him, half carrying, half dragging Fred.

"God, are we done for or what?" George rasped.

"Welcome back to the world of the still living," Gill told him, without looking back. "Isn't it better than the dead place you were in a few hours ago? Isn't it worth fighting for?"

"I'm still fighting, aren't I?" George answered. And Gill thought, *Well, that's one good thing*—and he hoped it wouldn't be the last.

But the rust-worm had a new trick, one that it had probably learned from Angela and Miranda. Fastening its jaws on the rim of the ramp, it tore off a chunk of compressed rust the size of a small car. And placing it central on the ramp, it pushed with its head until the mass started sliding. Gill's party scrambled to one side, let the rapidly disintegrating mass go smoking by them.

But already the rust-worm was repeating its trick. Taking a second bite out of the ramp, it lifted its head and . . .

Spang! One of its eyes blinked out in a shattering of crystal!

The worm jerked, recoiled, dropped its rust payload into the chasm, and shook its head violently this way and that. Then it held still, slowly and threateningly turned its head, focused its one remaining eye in a tight beam on the four men. And very deliberately, it bent its ugly head toward them. Except this time, instead of shying from Fred's jacket, it kept right on coming.

Spang! And the other eye went. And now Gill knew where it had gone, and who had sent it there.

He hadn't dared to hope, to recognize that first gunshot, but now he could do much more than hope. The worm commenced a frenzied, whipping dance—of agony? Gill wondered—broke free of the ramp, and collapsed upon itself, coiling and uncoiling, giving off arcs of leaping electrical fire, and clattering into the deeps between the ramp spurs. Down below, it threshed about like a crippled snake.

And there at the head of the ramp, with Angela and Miranda, there stood Jack Turnbull, shaking his weapon at the ocher sky and shouting like a madman: "Come on up, you blokes, quick as you like. You're not meat for the worms just yet!"

No, they weren't, but the crippled rust-worm was. For as Gill's party joined the others on the ledge, and they all drew back out of sight, so the worms from the desert came bursting through the red wave of the last dune, converging on the chasm between the spurs. All the clashing and spouting and sounds of savage destruction rising from the darkness then told dramatically of the blinded worm's fate, but that was something that could only last for so long.

"Time we weren't here," said the big minder.

Gill looked at him—at the grimy, slimy, haggard as hell minder, and Miranda with her arms around him—and said, "What? But you've only just arrived . . . thank God! Where in hell have you been, Jack?"

"Been to the movies," Turnbull answered. "Oh, and a couple of other places, too. Tell you about it later. But for now you tell me something. Which door are we going through, and who'll be doing the knocking?"

"Let's get Fred into one of these caves, see what we can do for him, take a moment to think it through," suggested Gill.

"Okay, but not that one," the minder said, leading them all away from the nearest entrance. "That's the one I just came out of. And brother, I'm not going back in there!"

CHAPTER
38

AMAZINGLY, FRED CAME to while they were carrying him into the back of one of the many shallow caves in the base of the imitation hive. In fact these caves, or more properly tunnels, were each the entrance to a door. As to which door to enter—or to escape through—that choice was always the prerogative of the control group, though in this case the "specimens" didn't much care. For they had already come to the conclusion that in this game the door itself wasn't as important as the one who knocked upon it.

"So what's going on?" said Fred, opening his eyes and looking up into Turnbull's face. And then he gasped. "Jack? You're back!"

"A poet, too," said the minder, grinning. "And I just love your crazy suntan."

The pilot's face and hands were crisscrossed with shallow burns: the "taste-bud" burns of a rust-worm, as if he'd walked into an electrified chicken-wire fence.

"Where's my jacket?" Fred shivered, struggling until they stood him on his own two feet. He staggered a little while they held him, then finally propped himself up against the congealed rust wall. "That rust-worm—?"

"Got your jacket." Gill nodded.

"But it didn't get you," George told him. "Or it wished it hadn't, anyway."

"Where are we?" Fred wanted to know. "A cave?"

"A cave with a door," the minder said. "Just a few minutes ago, I came through one just like it." He fished in his pockets for matches, found them, and struck one.

It was getting darker now, and true night coming down. The silver ball-bearing starlight lit the mouth of the tunnel a little, but back here it was the smoky dark of a mineshaft. By the light of Turnbull's match (from a book bearing the legend "Alt Deutscheshaus, Berlin") they examined the door: a plug of gray slag five to six feet across, filling the tunnel's end as snug as a cork in a bottle. No knocker and no number, but they knew it was a door all right. Angela, Gill, and Turnbull (of course), they had all seen its like before.

"That's a door?" Miranda sounded dubious. "But if so, then how do we knock?"

"We just push, or fall against it," Angela told her. "That was how it worked last time."

"And it's my turn, right?" said Fred. "Ouch!"

They looked at him. "It's my face," he said, gingerly fingering himself. "Stings like hell."

"But it'll heal quickly, too," Angela told him. "This is a House of Doors, remember?"

Fred nodded. "And I just slid down a snake—and a really *big* fucker at that!" Though he spat the words out with feeling, the ladies made no complaint.

The light died and Turnbull lit another match. "So, what's happening?" he said.

"We're waiting for Fred," Gill answered. "It's his turn, I think, and—"

"Wait," said Angela. "I've been thinking."

They looked at her, and the minder said, "Let's sit down. I mean, if we're going to deliberate let's be comfortable about it, right? Frankly, I'm dead knackered."

"Likewise," said Gill. "And that goes for all of us. Okay, we'll sit . . . but how many matches do you have? They're all the light we have left. In this place, anyway." Indeed light wasn't the only thing they were short of; they didn't have much of anything. The minder's machine pistol and scalloped claw weapon, a sausage bag containing a battered scorpion eye and severed antenna, their tattered clothing, and that was it.

"I picked up three or four books," the minder said. "Don't worry, we won't run out. Not for a few minutes. I'll be sparing with them. Okay, Angela, shoot. But keep it short. I've a feeling that when those worms are done chomping on their old buddy, then that they'll be looking for new playmates."

And there in that cramped conduit of a tunnel, in the fake rust-worm hive on Gill's mad machine world, the seven sat down to talk. The match flickered out; Turnbull didn't light another for the moment; they listened to each other breathing, and to distant sounds of metallic mayhem. And in a while Angela said:

"I've been working on our numbers."

"Our what?" That was Miranda's voice, her words, but with nothing of her former bite. Even in Jack Turnbull's arms she no longer felt safe.

"Just listen to Angela," said Gill. "The last time out, her numbers saved our lives."

"I've been working on our numbers," Angela said again, "and I've been thinking about a lot of the things that we've already worked out . . . like, how it's the one who knocks who determines what the next place will be like."

"Which is something I can't figure," said George. "I mean, this is a machine—a bloody big computer, a synthesizer—so how does it read our minds? How can a machine possibly know our worst fears?"

And Angela said, "Spencer?"

"Okay, I'll try," Gill answered. "See, it's the physiology of the Thone or the Ggyddn. It's the physical makeup or organic functions of these bloody aliens. Let me explain. We are human. We're pretty densely constructed; we work by fueling ourselves and by leeching energy from our food, and then by venting waste products to make room for more fuel. And of course we use oxygen in the process of burning our fuel, and water as a coolant, if you take my meaning. And we build our machines to imitate life, to perform the same functions. Take a motor car, for instance:

"It burns petrol, produces power, exhausts dead gases, and uses water and air for coolants. Ergo our engines work the same way we work. If we were plant intelligences we'd be using photosynthesis to drive chlorophyll-based engines—which is probably why we hit on the idea so late on in our evolution, because we *aren't* plants. So now we get to the Thone, or the Ggyddn.

"They are physical weaklings. Low-gravity types who aren't capable of pushing buttons. They simply don't have the tactile strength for it. Nor do they themselves have voices. Their constructs do, but that's to enable them to talk to 'lesser' life-forms like us. Therefore voice-activated machines or computers are out. So what *do* they have? Well, they have powerful minds! And thus *mind*-activated computers are in. Are you beginning to get the picture?"

"The House of Doors reads our minds?" From Miranda again.

"It's the only explanation," said Gill.

"And that's where my numbers come in," said Angela.

A match flared and the minder floated in its welcome light, while the others became disembodied faces against the darkness. And: "Make it quick, Angela," Turnbull warned. "I don't know if you've noticed, but it's gone just a little too quiet out there for my liking." And indeed there was an eerie silence from the weird world outside.

"Very well," she answered. And after a moment's thought she went on: "I've always been interested in numerology, that's the 'science' of working out a person's fate, destiny, and psychic profile by the use of numbers. The method I know is called the Hebrew system, where the letters of the alphabet stand for numbers from one to eight." She quickly listed the various values:

1.	2.	3.	4.	5.	6.	7.	8.
A	B	C	D	E	U	O	F
I	K	G	M	H	V	Z	P
Q	R	L	T	N	W		
J	S			X			
Y							

Then:

"Okay," she continued. "Now, we three 'old hands' have been through all this before, but you new people haven't. So I did a job on your numbers, too. Miranda, you add up like this:

"4, 1, 2, 1, 5, 4, 1, and 4, 1, 2, 3, 5. That adds up to thirty-three which adds up to six. So you're a six. But there's something very odd here. You see, *all* of you are sixes! Well, all of you with the exception of Ki-no Sung. But originally he was only planted here as Sith's spy, so I'm discounting him."

By the light of another of Turnbull's matches, George, Fred, and Miranda looked at one another. And Fred said, "So?"

But by now Gill had got the message. "666." He nodded, and: "I believe I know what you're getting at."

"Well get to it, for Christ's sake!" said the minder, urgently. "Unless I'm mistaken that was a headlamp beam just crossed the mouth of this bloody hole!"

"The world of the big crystal," said Gill. "Don't you remember, Jack? That's where I finally broke into the computer, and it's the one place we haven't visited yet, not this time around. Perhaps Sith was hoping we'd keep the hell out of there . . . and maybe he's deliberately *kept* us out. But now Angela might just have shown us how to break in!"

"What?" George wasn't with it, and neither was Miranda nor Fred.

"It's a supernatural world," Turnbull told them. "I mean a place where ghoulies and ghosties and ten-leggedy beasties are for real. And it's the worst possible place you could imagine! Spencer, do you really think we should . . . ?"

"I don't think we have any choice," Gill cut him off. "See, there goes your headlamp beam again!" And suddenly the mouth of the tunnel was ablaze with white light.

They were all on their feet now. "So what do we do?" Miranda shrilled, plainly on the edge of losing it.

"Picture your childhood spooks," Gill snapped. "Do it now, all of you: Miranda, George, and Fred. Fasten your minds on it: a place where the dead rise from their coffins, where vampires and werewolves roam at the full of the moon, and where zombies walk in the mists that crawl from graveyards. Have you got it? Good, then hang on to it. And be frightened, people, be absolutely *terrified,* be—"

"Be quick!" yelled the minder as the white light enveloped them all and a tangle of electrical energies, the "snarl" of a rust-worm, set the shadows strobing all around.

In another moment the three had leaped to the plug of gray slag and fallen against it in a tangle. Gill had barely enough time to snatch up Barney, and then—

Behind them, the roof of the tunnel caved in and came crashing down in massive chunks, completely blocking the entrance and crushing the thrusting head of the rust-worm. While ahead of them, the circular slab of fused slag simply disappeared, and in its place a whole new world stood waiting.

Except it wasn't new, and Gill and his two companions of old knew that it would only wait until nightfall . . .

There are deserts and there are deserts. But at least this one was of a kind that Gill's party could relate to. For it was of sand, not iron oxide. It was composed of the dust of worn-down mountains, not the rust of worn-out machinery. And if Gill and Angela and the minder hadn't known better, it could even be a desert of Earth. But they did know better.

"This is it," Turnbull corroborated what his companions of that earlier time were already thinking. Standing at the crest of a dune (but a *sand* dune this time) with one big hand shielding his eyes, he surveyed the terrain all around. "As far as I can tell," he continued, "we've ended up exactly

where we were the last time. If so, then just three or four miles thataway"—
he pointed—"is where we'll find the big crystal in the hills. Last time it
glinted; this time it doesn't. But then again, the shadows are longer, too.
The same place but a different time of day—evening, at a guess. See the
kites up there, or whatever they are? Well if they're anything like desert
birds back home, it's the cool of evening that brings them out. It was in
Afghanistan, anyway . . ."

High in the sky, birds of prey—or if not of prey, then of carrion, certainly—circled lazily, riding on the thermals that rose from the furnace
sands. And the bruised and battered seven could almost feel their bright
hungry eyes upon them.

They had arrived here (they'd materialized here) no more than ten to
fifteen minutes ago. Then a brief period of readjustment, of getting their
second wind, before any kind of activity. Typical of the big minder, he had
been the first to get it together. Despite all of his recent travails, Turnbull
was in fact in far better shape than the rest of them. This didn't in any way
surprise Gill; his past experience of the man spoke volumes. The minder's
stamina was legendary.

As Turnbull jumped, then tobogganed down the dune on his backside,
Miranda said, "Gentlemen, Angela and I have some business to attend to."
And when they looked at her, she very deliberately, very calmly continued:
"We need to go to the toilet. And frankly, if you men don't make yourselves
scarce I for one am going to do it anyway!"

The five moved off, Jack Turnbull in the lead, and waited up around
the bend of a sweeping dune. They, too, felt the need to answer the call of
nature, did so, buried the evidence under scuffed sand. Then, while they
were waiting for the women, Gill and the minder had a chance to talk.

Gill didn't need to say a lot; the minder had experienced Gill's machine
world before and had pretty much guessed how the rest of them had made
it to the false rust-worm hive, the House of Doors. The part that really did
focus his interest was about Miranda . . . how she'd been responsible for
galvanizing the rest of them, her determination with regard to himself, and
how she had set herself only one goal: to discover his whereabouts, go to
him, and be with him no matter what.

"Some woman," he said with a grin when Gill was done. "But will it
be the same when—or if—we get out of this? Will she still feel that way,
d'you think?"

Gill nodded. "If you want to place your bet now, I'll give hundred to
one odds that she will."

Then Turnbull stopped grinning and told Gill about the Alt Deutscheshaus, Berlin, 1970. He ended up showing him a book of matches to prove

it. "That alien bastard thing!" the big minder spat the words out like they were poison. "But I was sober as a judge. He must have spattered whatever he has for shit across a couple dozen light-years when I came through that screen at him! I'm pretty sure I hit the bastard, too. Damn shame it couldn't have been fatal."

The women came around the dune's sweeping curve. They had followed the plodding footprints of the men; they looked tired but undefeated, and Gill hoped his appearance gave the same impression. His appearance—*hah!* That was a laugh! But what the hell, they were all in the same boat.

The girls . . . well they were quite obviously girls. There could be no disguising that, despite the jobs of work they had done on each other to ensure that their feminine charms weren't too openly displayed. But their clothing was literally in tatters, and there was no couturier in all the wide world—in the old world they knew, that is—who could have arranged scraps of rag, ribboned trouser legs, and torn blouses any differently to provide a basic element of decency. Given a day or two more of this kind of wear and tear and they'd be down to denim bikinis!

As for the men:

They were dirty, oily, ragged, bearded, bleary-eyed, and generally at the end of their tether; but yet again the minder was holding up best. He had been trained in warfare, after all—trained to look after his "gear"—and this was his kind of business. Survival of the fittest, and Jack Turnbull was certainly that. He was *now*, anyway.

Gill's eyes took them all in. He looked at Ki-no Sung and wondered how much of this was registering, how much the Korean accepted. Or had he long since given up? It was a while since the little man had spoken. But then, what's beyond understanding is beyond talking about. Perhaps that's how it was.

Then there was George. Nothing wrong with his brain now, thanks to the healing powers of the House of Doors. But on the other hand his mind contained memories that had no right being there, which he wouldn't find easy to erase. George had fought through this far because he wasn't quite the Ministry flunkey that Gill had thought him. No, instead he was a man that Gill would gladly call his friend.

Which left only Fred Stannersly. But looking at Fred now, Gill saw something quite different from the man he'd grown to know. The rest of them had noticed it, too, and all eyes were on the pilot. *His* eyes, however, were everywhere!

Turnbull touched Gill's elbow. "Now what the hell . . . ?" he whispered. Fred heard him anyway; his head turned in the minder's direction, but he didn't quite look *at* him. And Stannersly's eyes were weirdly vacant, or not vacant but unfocused, and he kept blinking, staring, shaking his head, peering this way and that.

Gill went to him, reached out, and touched him—and Fred ducked, shrank back from him, flew backward as if he'd been struck, and was brought up short by the side of the dune. But it was more than that; during Fred's inexplicable reaction to Gill's approach, everything had seemed to blur, like an alien distortion of reality. And now he lay there panting, gasping, frightened, with his eyes screwed shut.

Finally Gill got it. "Fred?" he said. "Is this your spatial thing? Disorientation?"

"It was me," the other mumbled. "It had to be fucking me!" And he sprawled there against the side of the dune, twitching a little but, Gill somehow knew, not *daring* to move any more than that.

Gill sat beside him, said, "It's me, Fred. It's okay. But what do you mean, it was you? Are you saying you came through the door first?"

The other nodded, but it wasn't a nod. His head went up in a grotesque twist—an effeminate half twirl, an odd gyration—and came down to thump on his chest. A spastic's nod . . . or that of a man whose brain no longer had any sense of direction. "It's getting worse," he said. "Spencer!" He clutched at Gill, missed him at first, despite that he was right there, and said again, "Spencer, I think you'll have to leave me. Can't see me making it, not like this." His eyes were still screwed shut.

"No way," George said. He had come up to them, stood over them. "No one is leaving anyone. Listen, Fred: your burns are fading. Already, yes. And this will fade, too."

The big minder was also there. "We can't carry you, Fred," he said, "not all the way. But we can lead you, and we sure as hell aren't leaving you. What is this thing, anyway?"

"It's this place," Fred answered. "Okay, it's your supernatural world—but it's *my* world, too. My spatial thing, my worst nightmare. A place where all of the dimensions are wrong. When Spencer touched me, it was as if his hand came from a million miles away, came at the speed of light! It was like he was going to hit me. And you saw my reaction. I moved, backward—but it wasn't me that moved! *It was the place!* And it's getting worse. I can feel it. You know how the corridor, the tunnel, in the Castle stretched out like elastic? It's the same thing. And it's in *me!* Should I show you? I think I can. I *feel* I can."

"Fred, Fred!" said Angela. "It's all in the mind. You have to control it."

But Gill said, "It isn't in his mind. Or it is, but not in the way you mean.

When he moved away from me, that wasn't a natural movement. It was his thing working, but exaggerated out of all proportion by the House of Doors." And then, to Fred: "How do you mean, you can show us?"

Fred was silent, kept still for a moment, then said, "Are those kites still there?"

They looked, and they were. "Yes," said Turnbull. "They're still there."

"Then watch," Fred told them. And he opened his eyes; eyes that swiveled this way and that, then stared up, up, up at the sky. Up there, the birds were like disembodied eyebrows floating on the blue. But suddenly the air *rippled*—like a mirage, like the air over a tarmac road on a searing hot day—and just as suddenly the birds were gone.

"Jesus!" said George. "Gone!"

"No," said Fred, closing his eyes. "They're not gone. Look again. See those dots in the sky? That's them. They're a thousand feet higher, that's all. And I could do that to you, too. I could do it to the whole fucking place!" With which he suddenly let go of Gill's arm and drew back into himself. "So that's why you've got to leave me here—because I can't chance doing that to you."

"But doing what?" Angela sat beside him.

"Sending you away," Fred told her. "Shooting you the hell out of here, but accidentally, without wanting to. See, I don't understand this thing. I'm not in control of it."

They were all standing or seated around him now, not knowing what to do or say. Then Miranda wrapped her arms about herself and shivered. The shadows were almost visibly lengthening, and the dune's shadow had fallen over them.

"Nightfall," said Gill. "And soon."

"We can just make it to those hills if we leave now," said Turnbull. And more ominously: "Maybe."

But Gill, looking thoughtful, or desperate, or both, said, "Or maybe we can make it a damn sight faster than that. Seven league boots, by God!"

"What's that?" said Angela.

"Seven league boots," Gill said again. "Can't you see it? Fred's wearing seven league boots—or their equivalent. If he could only control this thing, why—it could be our way out!"

"Explain," said the minder.

"Wait." Gill held up a hand. And to the pilot: "Fred, will this thing of yours work in reverse? And do you think you could hold it while we move you?"

"In . . . in reverse?"

"Can you draw things closer, as well as push them away?"

"I don't know," said the other in a whimper. "I mean, it's like the whole fucking world is elastic, and I don't know which way it's stretching!"

"Just hang on to it, Fred," Gill told him. "We're going to move you." And they carried him like a baby to the crest of the dune. In the distance, the hills were like a pale blue frill on a white sand horizon. But to one side, the sun sat low over the desert. Much too low.

At Gill's direction they sat Fred down on the crest of the dune, balanced him—Turnbull on one side and Gill on the other—and pointed his face toward the hills. And:

"This is it, Fred," said Gill. "When I say go, open your eyes, your mind, and try to bring things closer. Okay?"

"Oh, God! Oh, Jesus!" said Fred. "You don't know what it's like. But I'll try." And Gill wasn't going to give him time to change his mind.

"Okay," he said. *"Go . . . !"*

CHAPTER
39

A ND FRED WENT, literally! Space warped—there was no other way to describe it. Things elongated. Fred elongated. Like the piece of elastic he had alluded to, he appeared to stretch out, to become immensely *deep* from front to rear. He was, for a moment of time, of normal height and normal width, but of incredible thickness! And when the elastic snapped back again, he was no longer there. But his colleagues had seen him go; they had seen the elastic draw him *from the other end!*

As for Gill and Turnbull, who had been holding Fred steady, they too had been part of it. Their arms had seemed to lengthen on his shoulders; they *had* lengthened, by virtue of their intrusion into hyperspace, and stretched halfway to infinity before the two men cried out and threw themselves backward, away from Fred's influence. And as they sprawled there on the sand mouthing like idiots and hugging their arms, so the others rushed to see what harm had befallen them. None, apparently, just shock.

When it got through to Angela that Gill was okay, finally she burst out, "Spencer Gill, you . . . you . . . you were right!" And her anger—mainly fear, for him—went out of her. "But Spencer, poor Fred! What happened to him?"

"Together," Gill gasped as the weird tingling went out of his arm. "Jack, Miranda, all of you. Stay together, in a bunch. I mean now! Barney . . . here, boy!"

Sensing Gill's urgency, the others crowded to him—even Ki-no Sung, though he could scarcely comprehend what was going on. But then, neither could the rest of them. Answering Gill's call, Barney came scampering and licked his face with a tongue like a rasp. And then they were all together.

"Spencer, what is it?" Angela hugged him anxiously.

"It's what I hope is *going* to be," he told her. "It's what I hope Fred will do." And George Waite got the idea.

"Tunnel time? Like in the Castle?"

"Right," Gill tried to say, but instead said, *"Rrrriiiggghhhttt"*

The desert flew beneath them, its miles contracting down to nothing in a single instant of time. And yet there was little or no sensation of movement or acceleration but merely the knowledge that "things" weren't right. Yet a moment later they were very right indeed.

Those members of the party who were standing stumbled and fell. The dog yipped, skittered, sat down hard on his rump, and stayed there. Gill and the minder, still seated following the initial experiment, swayed and put down their hands to steady themselves (and felt grit and pebbles, not sand), while Angela and Miranda collapsed beside them.

And out of the breathless silence, a small, very uncertain voice—Fred Stannersly's voice—said: "Did I . . . did I manage to get you? Did I get all of you?" But at first no one answered, because to a man and a woman they had closed their eyes.

When finally Gill dared look, they were at the foot of the low hills. Moreover, up there in the hazy blue crags, something glittered in the light that glanced from its crystal facets . . .

All of that was forty minutes ago. Now they were climbing into the hills, and Turnbull was carrying Fred slung over his shoulder in the fireman's lift position with his arms all adangle to the rear. "Do you think he'll be mad about it?" The minder was joking, of course. In the event of his survival, Fred wouldn't give a damn.

Gill said so in no uncertain manner. "He wouldn't care if you hit him twice as hard. Anyway, I'm as much to blame as you for giving you the nod. I mean, there was no way we could just let Fred run loose with that kind of power! Okay, so it worked out fine this time. But I don't much like the idea that there could have been a *next* time. And anyway, he was just as likely to lose himself as any of us. No, Fred is safest where and how he is right now. And by the way, it's my turn to carry him."

George, Gill, and the minder were sharing the load; Ki-no Sung, because of his disability, was helping the women. As for Barney the dog: he was doing point duty up front, and making a pretty good job of it. Gill was keeping a watchful eye on their route, and so far they were sticking to much the same path that they'd taken the last time.

"About an hour and a half to sundown," Angela called back. And: "Spencer, I'm glad for all that hiking we were doing. It's finally paying off."

"True enough," he grunted, taking Fred's weight. "But the way I remember it, I wasn't loaded down with—*uh!*—a hundred and sixty pounds of camping kit at the time!"

And so they struggled into the heights . . .

Until Miranda suddenly stopped short and said, "Water! I can hear it."

And Ki-no Sung nodded, cocked his head on one side, said, "I hear him. Is water, yes."

"Now that you mention it," said Turnbull, "I'm as thirsty as hell. Have been for a long time. I've stopped sweating, too. And when I think of all that booze in the Alt Deutscheshaus . . . So what's the next step, death by dehydration?"

They were climbing to one side of a spur; cresting it and scanning their surroundings, Miranda said, "No, not yet, Jack!" And she pointed. "There it is. A little spring!"

And in just a few minutes they were taking a break, drinking the life-giving water—but not before Barney had tried it out for them. "Useful little bugger." George patted the mongrel on the head. "What'll you do with him, Spencer, supposing we do get out of this?"

"Do with him? Anything he wants," Gill answered. "I'll fix him up with the biggest kennel in the world, feed him choicest rabbit all his days, miss him like hell when he's gone. Provided, that is, I don't go first."

"Are we on a ladder?" Turnbull mused, more to himself than to anyone else.

And Gill said, "I know what you mean. And I've been thinking the same thing. Things are still sticky but they are beginning to work out. I can't figure it. Sith told us he'd changed the program and this is his game. But if so—I mean if that were entirely true—then how come we're still alive? Or does the House of Doors compensate for his bad intentions? Is there a fail-safe that even he can't override?"

"Like this water," said Angela.

Miranda washed her face in the cool, clear liquid bubbling up from a crack in a cliff face of fine limestone, tossed back her wet hair, and said, "The water? What about it?"

"Why now?" said Angela. "We're all hungry as hell, but we could go without food awhile yet. Water, on the other hand, is an absolute necessity. Also, we weren't really as thirsty as we should have been." She frowned, shook her head. "It's like I'm asking myself: is the synthesizer trying to give back a little of what has been taken from us? And if so, is it because it was taken away illegally? Spencer's answer could be the right one: that Sith has gone too far. The Thone did have their own twisted sense of ethics, after all."

"Well, let's hope we're right," said Gill. "But one thing's for sure: we're on the right trail. That thing up there—that crystal, computer, House of Doors—it's the real thing. I can feel it from here. That great machine just working away, doing its alien thing. Another facet of the synthesizer, a different face of the same dice. We're on the one side and Sith's on the other. So is our world, and halfway to wrack and ruin by now. And the crystal stands smack in the middle . . ."

"A thought," said Turnbull.

"Shoot," said Gill. "But let's get under way first, talk as we go. The sun won't hold up forever, and this is a very weird place when darkness falls."

They got under way. And since they no longer had anything to carry—except the unconscious Fred, and Turnbull his gun, and Angela their sole surviving sausage bag—there was nothing to delay them. And then Turnbull said:

"Do you suppose it will remember you?"

"Eh? Remember?" Gill was right behind him, toiling in the minder's footsteps, lifting one plodding boot after the other. "Are you talking about the crystal?"

"That's exactly what I'm talking about," Turnbull answered. "Telepathy, you said. Well if it's a telepathic machine, won't it recognize a mind it's known once before?" And:

"You know," said Gill, "that's a thought that never dawned on me?"

Turnbull grunted, kept climbing, didn't look back. "Well, let's just hope *you* are a thought that *has* dawned on the machine!" he answered. "I mean, won't this super-duper alien computer wonder why we're being tested twice? It's a brain, right? It thinks, therefore it is . . . or something."

"Maybe," said Gill, with something of fresh hope glinting in his eyes. "Just maybe. And we also have the scorpion antenna which might make for a point of contact and help me get back in sync with the thing." Then, for a moment anxious, he glanced at Angela. "We do still have it, right?"

Climbing beside him, she patted the battered bag where it hung from her naked shoulder. "The stinger, and the broken eye, too," she answered. "Apart from Jack's machine pistol, they're about the only things we do have!"

"Little loaves and fishes," said Miranda. "That's what we need right now: a bloody miracle! We're scarcely well equipped to save a world."

"The world can wait a little while longer," Gill told her. "It will have to. First we have to save ourselves . . ."

Sith of the Ggyddn was furious. He was in "pain," too, and for the first time in a long time he was uncertain, rattled. Things weren't working out entirely to plan—nothing like it, in fact—and the Thone synthesizer was giving him problems. There were forces at work here that he didn't understand; there were rules that couldn't be broken; there was a lesson that he should have learned the first time around, which he had failed to learn. It was perhaps time to get out, or at least to check the accessibility of his bolt-hole.

Ggyddn telepathy over a distance wasn't impossible but it was considered gauche. Sith needed to speak to Gys U Kalk, the so-called "Grand" Ggyddn, and attempted to do so using the Castle's instrumentation . . . and couldn't. The pyramid node wasn't accepting calls. Or rather, and according to the instrumentation, it was, but not from Sith. Wherefore he was obliged to use long-distance telepathy after all. This meant, of course, that their discourse would be "overheard" by other Ggyddn operatives in the various nodes and in the mother ship. Well, that couldn't be helped; Sith *must* talk to Gys U Kalk.

The Kalk picked up his call at once, cut him short, opened channels through the instrumentation. Which in itself was a warning . . . that communications had been broken by Gys U Kalk, not because of some simple problem with instrumentation. And:

"Yes?" said the Kalk (icily, Sith thought).

"I have suffered several setbacks," Sith answered. "As you know, this is a Thone synthesizer, and it appears to be malfunctioning. I believe the transmat is down; it no longer registers on instrumentation, or rather registers as being in use. Quite obviously that is a fault, for who else would be using it? Also, the color codes are wont to change of their own accord, interfering with my control. Last but not least, I have been injured. It's a small thing and my colonies will of course replenish the damaged tissues. But recalling our initial conversation, I conclude that you were in fact correct and a vendetta against this Spencer Gill and his colleagues was an unnecessary adventure."

And after a while. "Is that all? Have you done?" (And the Grand Ggyddn's "tone" was still icy.)

"Do I need to say anything else?" Sith tried not to snap. "My requirements are self-explanatory. Since this synthesizer's instrumentation has a mind of its own, and the transmat is malfunctioning, yours or some other's will have to lock on, boost its efficiency, and pull me out!"

"You *have* done, then?" said Gys U Kalk. "Very well, now I have several things to say. First the reason you could not communicate with me: all sensor equipment, including all communication links except this one, are currently engaged in boosting our far-scanning capacity. This has become necessary since we detected incoming vessels; which is to say Thone ships in warp, approaching these coordinates."

"The Thone?" Sith felt something that a human being would describe as the first small inkling of a large impending problem. "But what business would they have here?"

"I think that I am the one who should ask that question," Gys U Kalk answered. "And you are the one who should answer it. Are you not in fact operating a Thone synthesizer?"

"What? But of course I am! What are you saying?"

"I am saying," (and now the Kalk's tone was utterly frigid), "that when you reactivated or allowed that synthesizer to be reactivated, it commenced sending out a signal. It has communicated with the Thone and they have found reason to answer in person! I am saying that they probably know it is you—Sith, whom they placed in isolation, imprisoning you on a cold, dead moon—who is operating their synthesizer. And if the complexity of these ongoing signals from *and to* your synthesizer's computer is any gauge of the information they carry, they likewise know not only all that you have done . . . *but everything that we are trying to do!*"

"But . . . they never before interfered with the Ggyddn!"

"True, and yet they are coming."

"They abandoned this world, considering its inhabitants a . . . a *worthy* species! Hah!"

"Even worthy of their interference, it would seem," said the Kalk. "These malfunctions you mentioned: are you sure that is all they are? Recently, Sith, you were Thone. Now say: just how many of the synthesizer's principles have you breached?"

"Its principles?" Sith "shouted." "Thone principles? I am Ggyddn! And the synthesizer is only a machine, a tool!"

"A tool you failed to use correctly. A machine whose programming you attempted to override, which has apparently taken exception to your interference."

And finally Sith panicked. "Gys U Kalk—*you have to get me out of here!*"

But now there was a long fraught silence before: "I think not," said the Kalk.

"What?" Sith couldn't believe it. "But I can't transmat on my own. And I am *injured,* and—"

"How were you injured?" said the Kalk.

"A weapon. One of these animals—"

"These . . . 'Neanderthals'?" Sarcasm, from the Grand Ggyddn! And much more than sarcasm still to come. "Sith, because of you our plans are in jeopardy. Because of your petty feud, we shall be drawn into conflict with the Thone. You were unworthy of the Thone, and you are unworthy of the Ggyddn. I recall that I once threatened you with a certain containment chamber I can cool to within half a degree of absolute zero. Believe me, if I were to transmat you out of there right now, you might face a far worse fate than my containment chamber! But I won't. You have trapped yourself in your synthesizer. Stay there, feud on, and fend for yourself . . . as it now appears we must fend for ourselves when the Thone arrive."

"You intend to engage them?" (Astonishment.)

"The ship is now rejoined, entire, and the nodes recalled. We are strong; if they want a fight we may have their measure."

"You'll fight, and abandon me?" Sith couldn't believe it.

"Would that we had never rescued you from that prison moon in the first place," said Gys U Kalk . . . and fell abruptly silent, his aura withdrawing into the communicator, which likewise closed down . . .

Thar she glows," said Turnbull wearily as he crested the last rocky spur and looked down into a scree-littered reentry remembered only too well from the last time he was here. And as Gill and the others joined the minder, there indeed she glowed: the great crystal, with the last of the sunlight slipping from its facets as the shadows began to settle.

Not that the sun was down yet, not quite, but the surrounding crags were cutting off its light as it curved ever closer to the horizon. And there on the ribs of the spur, silhouetted like so many scarecrows in the gloaming light, Spencer Gill and his companions looked down on the great crystal, the heart and soul of the House of Doors. If it had a soul.

It lay embedded in rubble and surrounded by loose scree in the shadows of the reentry between twin spurs. And despite that it appeared exactly the same as last time, still it was so obviously alien—so *strange* a thing—as to be a magnet to the eyes; once glimpsed, it was hard to look away from.

Now that the sun was off it, the crystal was a dull, slaty color, a gigantic many-faceted jewel with a heart of stone. It might have grown there, except it was far more perfect than Nature would have made it, and there were aspects she could never have incorporated. It was a strange crystal in a weird maze of worlds, but it was also, unmistakably, a House of Doors. Around its perimeter, its facets were oblongs, and set central in each oblong was an obsidian door. Even from the elevated position that Gill's party occcupied, still the grotesque knockers were visible. Shaped like gargoyles with rings through their noses, they were set in skull-shaped quartz inlays that were themselves set high in the otherwise blank obsidian slabs.

It was beautiful in its simplicity, ugly in its implications, frightening in its clear purpose—which was to frighten. Like warning hieroglyphs on some pharaoh's tomb, the skull and gargoyle motifs cried out: Stay away! Go back! Don't touch! *Or perhaps,* Gill thought, as he had thought in that earlier time: *Abandon hope all ye who enter here.*

George was carrying Fred. Lowering the unconscious man as gently as possible to a flat space, he panted, "Lord, just let me get my breath a minute." Gill looked at him, said:

"We can slide him the rest of the way. This loose scree and dirt won't hurt him." And to the minder, "Just how hard did you hit him, anyway? I mean, how long is he likely to be out?"

Turnbull shrugged but not uncaringly. "If you were to fall asleep right now," he said, "how long would you stay down? The full night? I'm pretty damn sure I would! Nine or ten hours at least. So it should be the same for Fred—with knobs on!"

Gill nodded. "Makes sense. But I'd rather be sure. So when we get him down there it might be a good idea to blindfold him and tie him up like Ki-no Sung that time . . ."

The climb down into the reentry was simplicity itself; sliding on their heels and ragged backsides, they made small avalanches of grit in front and smoky tracks behind down the scree slope. Gill and the minder looked after Fred, who never felt a thing. But once they were down in the hollow between the spurs, Gill warned them: "Keep well away from the crystal. From now on that's my province."

Then, looking at the sky, which was a darker blue now, he wondered when the first stars were due to appear. Time was rapidly narrowing down, and events beginning to focus themselves; focusing Gill's mind, too, as once again he contemplated the great crystal. The last time he'd fought this fight it had been hell—literally—and something told him that this time would be no different. Sith would have learned his lessons that time, surely? And now he'd be wanting to teach a few of his own.

Yet Gill was no longer afraid. And looking at the others, he didn't believe they were either. He knew that you can only push or threaten people to a point, beyond which threats have no meaning. His party had reached that point, and all that was left was the will to fight. Just so long as they had breath in them, that was exactly what they would do.

And one other thing Gill knew. That if the end were truly in sight—

and whatever that end would be—then just like the last time this was *where* it would be: here in these alien hills on this synthesized, supernatural world of the great crystal.

With that in mind he took the sausage bag from Angela and went to sit not too far from the enigmatic crystal. And as the shadows grew longer still, he tried to fight off his weariness and concentrate his machine mind upon this latest freakish facet of the House of Doors . . .

CHAPTER
40

T HE TRANSMAT WAS part of the system that powered Thone vessels. It was a spin-off from the sophisticated propulsion system that warped space and permitted Thone and Ggyddn alike to cross near infinite distances in finite time. If the transmat was faulty—an unheard of situation—then Gys U Kalk was correct and Sith was trapped here in the Castle on a hostile planet. Quite simply, he would not dare attempt to depart. This Earth was a cold, inhospitable world, it was true, but space was far colder, and in a vessel whose systems were gradually breaking down—

It didn't bear thinking about.

But stay here, and Sith had at least a chance. Gys U Kalk had known that when he said, "Stay, feud on, and fend for yourself." A chance to put the synthesizer back to rights, a chance to correct its malfunctions, and a final chance for life. But a slim chance by even the best estimate, and slimmer yet if Spencer Gill and his people were to escape from the House of Doors back into their rightful world. For he knew what they would do then: that they would call down the wrath of the entire planet upon him, and no way that Sith might fend them off.

One small "strategic" nuclear weapon . . . the Castle node was synthetic, true, but synthetic stone. The shock and disintegrative power of the blast would be such that Sith would not even know it had happened.

Thus his existence—and his continuing existence—was full of ifs and buts. Compared to his prison moon, this would seem a vastly superior environment, true . . . but for how long? If the Thone were on their way, and if the Ggyddn chose to desert this region of space, where did that leave Sith? Obviously the Thone would discover him here; homing in on this treacherous beacon of which the Kalk had spoken, they would doubtless deal with Sith according to their ridiculous "ethics."

And how long before they got here?

Or, if the Ggyddn chose to stay and defend their right to this world, what then? If the Thone won, Sith was done for! And if the Ggyddn won, they wouldn't want him here to perhaps interfere with their restructuring of this their most recent acquisition; and in Sith's mind there yet floated a picture of Gys U Kalk's containment chamber, where even metals would break down into crystals, and the crystals to elemental gases.

Thus Sith appeared to have but one recourse: to repair or reinstruct the synthesizer as quickly as possible, and fleeing Thone and Ggyddn both leave the Earth to its fate. Except—

An impossible, even ridiculous, thing: when Sith performed a diagnostic to trace the fault in the transmat's flux, he discovered it to lie . . . in the mind of a man? This allegedly "thinking" machine had done an unthinkable thing, rerouting its space-warping power through the mind and person of a human being—the one called Fred Stannersly. And thus while Stannersly lived, Sith no-longer-of-the-Ggyddn was immobilized and a good many of the synthesizer's functions compromised.

While Stannersly lived, yes.

But of course while *any* of them lived Sith knew he could never be at peace with himself, and that in his liquid dreams—in his *own* worst nightmares—his hatred and loathing would burn like acid forever. Unless he staunched it now . . .

Jack Turnbull stood over Gill where he sat propped up against a boulder, and said, "Spencer? Are you okay?"

Gill looked up at him, at the minder's upper body and face limned against a backdrop of space and bright, alien constellations, and gave a massive start. Night! It must have come down as quickly as that! And he had been asleep!

"You've been out for half an hour," Turnbull quietly grunted, leaning forward and putting a hand on his shoulder to hold him down. "Now don't go jumping about or you'll panic them half to death. I told them that we'd seen you like this before, that it's how you work things out. Angela backed me up. So now start acting like everything is just great, and whatever it is you're supposed to be doing . . . for fuck's sake do it! Oh, and another thing. While you're getting it together, you might want to tell me what it is you were smiling about."

Smiling? Gill settled back, licked dry lips, looked across the depression to where the others were seated with their backs to a rocky outcrop. "Jesus, I've let you down!" he said. "And I was smiling?"

Turnbull shook his head. "No, you haven't let us down, not yet. You're just human like the rest of us, and no harm done so far. But the sun went down about the same time you did, and now it's nervous-making time. So, Spencer my lad, if you have any of those little tricks you like to employ at times like this, well I'd be checking them out if I were you." He shivered (which was unusual for the big minder), then went on: "The night's starting to feel queer to me. Hell, but this is a queer place."

"I was smiling?" Gill mumbled again, no longer smiling but frowning now. And almost fully awake, he tried to remember what he'd been dreaming. He had a theory concerning sleep—or more properly dreams—about how they're the clearing houses for all the rubbish of the waking world. He knew the story of Friedrich August Kekule's benzine ring dream, and had heard of many authors whose tales seemed to have the odd habit of resolving themselves during sleep. Nor would it be the first time that Gill's problems had found their solutions in his subconscious mind.

"Smiling, yes," said the minder, "if that's the right description. A grim sort of smile, really, but a smile definitely. So?"

"Wait!" Gill cut him off, holding up a hand. And Turnbull waited . . . while Gill turned his head to look at the great crystal, and to listen to it. No one else in the world—no human being—would have heard a thing, but Spencer Gill was no other human being. And to him the multifaceted rock, that great crystal, was a living thing no less than any other machine. A living machine that tried to speak to him . . . even as it had tried to speak to him in his sleep!

"*Christ!*" he cried then, sitting up straighter. The others heard and came running. All of them except Fred, who lay unconscious, loosely bound and gagged where they'd put him for safekeeping.

"Spencer, what is it?" Angela fell to her knees beside him in the scree.

But Gill held her off—held up his hands to the others, too—and breathlessly said, "Go back . . . you, too, Jack. Leave this to me now." And to Turnbull especially: "I'm not the only one who woke up just now. This crystal, the House of Doors, is awake, too. It wasn't especially active before. But it is now, and I'd be much happier if you were all farther away from it."

Barney had arrived along with the others; plainly nervous, he licked Gill's face, whined in the back of his throat, skittered here and there in his fashion. But quick-stepping around Gill he accidentally collided with the sausage bag—and immediately shied away from it.

And Gill had sensed it at the same time as the dog: a vibration, a tingle, the same sensation he had known before in the clearing with the sacrificial slab, and again in George Waite's cancerous brain world. And: "People, you have to move back from here," he said. "And I do mean now!"

As they began to move away, Angela reluctantly, Gill tore open the sausage bag and took out the stinger antenna and damaged eye. The big minder was still with him and said, "Is there anything you need? Can I be of help? Hell, it seems wrong that you should be the only one in danger!"

Gill looked at him and said, "Stay if you insist, as long as the girls and the others are out of it. In any case, if anything happens to us it will likely happen to them, too."

"So what *is* happening?" said Turnbull, stepping closer.

Gill looked at the stinger in his left hand and the eye in his right. "These things are active," he said. "Rather, they're *reacting*—to the presence of the crystal. They're alien machines, Jack, and like little magnets they're under the influence of that big magnet, the House of Doors. And this one, the eye, is leeching power like crazy."

He put down the stinger, looked into the broken cup of the eye. In there, reflected in pale starlight from the inner lens, his own face looked back at him. Or it *should* have been his own face, but inverted as it was, he couldn't tell. Turnbull on the other hand was standing opposite, and he saw the face the right way up. Which was just as well for Gill, who had suddenly stiffened, his *own* face seeming to crumple in some unbearable agony as he fell to his knees!

But the minder had given a massive start, yelled, '*Bannerman!*' and snatched the eye clear of Gill's hands, by which time it was glowing with a radiant light.

Gill sprawled on the ground, his hands to his head, but now that Turnbull had taken the eye from him the sudden, agonizing pain was receding as quickly as it had come. He breathed deeply, felt his strength flowing back into him . . . and simultaneously sensed a rapid build-up of explosive energy from the eye. Lurching to his feet, he yelled, "Jack, get rid of it!"

His warning was hardly necessary, for guided by sheer instinct the minder had already acted.

Hurled away with every ounce of his strength, the "dead" eye—a screen in its own right—curved up and out into the night, and down beyond the sheer cliffs at the foot of the reentry. And the dazzling webs of energy that traced its plummeting flight, and finally the thunderous bombburst that played a drumroll across the hills and bathed them in a brilliant white light, told all too graphically of the fate of everyone concerned if Turnbull hadn't taken the initiative.

"Sith's last throw," said Gill, blinking the dazzle out of his eyes as the rumble of several small avalanches subsided.

"Mine, surely," said Turnbull, watching the glow over the reentry fading and blinking out. Then he nodded, said, "I know what you mean . . . but not how you mean it. His last throw?"

"The screens," said Gill. "He could have used a screen at any time, just as he did on my machine world. Don't you remember—when he warned me not to cheat? After that, he could have blasted us whenever we came face-to-face with a scorpion, could have used their eyes as targeting devices, or simply overloaded them to the point of destruction. But he did neither. He wanted to prolong the agony, give us hell; which he has done, and very successfully. So what's changed now, eh? Sith *had* me just now, paralyzed with the pain of whatever it is he can do to me. But you'll have noticed, he can only do it when he has me in view, on a viewscreen. The moment you snatched the eye from me, when he couldn't see me, I quickly recovered. And, by God, he intended to kill us all out of hand! I mean, this time he was *really* trying!"

The minder shrugged, looked puzzled. "So suddenly he's in a hurry. He wants us dead by whatever means and as soon as possible."

"Right," said Gill. "Maybe because things are going wrong for him. You asked me if the telepathic computer, the synthesizer, would know me, if it would recognize me from that previous time. And you know something, Jack? I think you were right and it does!"

Turnbull slapped his thigh. "It's maintaining the balance?"

Gill nodded. "I think so. And Sith knows it. God, let me be right, but it's not just skill or blind fortune that's kept us alive, Jack. It's the House of Doors!"

"That explains the look on Sith/Bannerman's face," the minder said. "Staring at me from that eye, he looked about as mad as hell. But why does he keep wearing that bloody human suit?"

"So that we'll *know* he's mad as hell," Gill answered. "You must admit, you can't read much emotion in the look on a jellyfish's face! And since you're the one who injured him, he probably likes you about the same as he likes me—not a lot." He stooped and picked up the stinger, but gingerly.

"But it's not just the bullet hole I put in his liquid guts that he's worried about, right?" Turnbull said. "I mean, he can heal himself in no time, grow a new colony or something."

"That's right," Gill answered. "Unless you hit a vital organ or really cut him up, he'll be okay. No, I'm sure I'm right and Sith's losing control. And I'm sure that you're right, too, and the synthesizer knows or recognizes me. So now I've got to find a way to get back on good terms with it."

While they talked, their colleagues had moved closer again. Gill waved them back and said, "Look, all of you, I'm still not a hundred percent sure of what I'm doing. I'm not even ten percent sure! So give me a chance, okay? Meanwhile, if you want to help, just keep your eyes open. One of you might like to climb back up to the spur and keep a lookout. And Jack will stay here with me, act as my backup. Okay?" And once again they followed his instructions.

"Like herding sheep?" Turnbull lifted an inquiring eyebrow.

But Gill shook his head . . . then nodded. "Well, maybe. But as long as I'm not driving them to the slaughter I don't mind."

He looked at the stinger. "Sith knows exactly where we are now. It seems to me your shot put him off, maybe caused him to lose track of us. The scorpion eye was the obvious way to find us again, but he couldn't use it, couldn't see out of it while it was in the sausage bag. And now . . . now I'm wondering about this stinger. When I use it, will Sith know it? I mean, can he overload it, like he did with the eye?"

"You'll use it to contact the synthesizer?" Turnbull looked dubious. "Despite what just happened with the eye?"

Gill nodded. "And right away," he said. "This is the world of the beast, it's night, and we're running short of time."

"Let's do it," the minder was resigned now, "and we'll see what we'll see. Or if things blow up in our faces, we won't . . ."

Gill pointed the stinger, the alien antenna, at the great crystal and concentrated his mind on feeling for the machine locked in its heart of synthesized stone. Then he reeled, and Turnbull took hold of his shoulders to steady him. "Hey, are you okay?"

"Yes," Gill said with a nod. "I'm okay. I felt some kind of contact, that's all. Jack, do me a favor and keep quiet now. I can't do this and talk, too."

He concentrated again, and felt his mind gripped, examined . . . and recognized, yes! And: *I'm in! I'm in!* he thought. *I've got through to the House of Doors!*

"I'm in," the great crystal answered him like an echo. "I'm in to the House of Doors!" (Gill could almost hear its analytical brain working, examining his thoughts.)

Synthesizer, computer, said Gill. *I am worthy. We—my companions and I—are worthy. Don't you remember?*

"I remember," said the voice that wasn't a voice, in Gill's machine mind. "There are conflicting instructions. You are worthy, you are not worthy. The issue will be resolved."

But you have been reprogrammed to kill, or to permit death by inaction. Is it your usual function, to kill? Or is it your true function to analyze, test, verify?

"You are worthy . . . it would seem. Therefore programming is at fault. The issue will be resolved. One final test."

A test? What kind of test? But it's unfair! We've been tested, and we were found worthy!

"I am a tool. Use me. Prove yourself. Prove yourselves . . ." And the voice that wasn't a voice faded from Gill's mind.

*   *   *

Spencer!" Turnbull's gritty voice—his hand on Gill's shoulder—drew him back to earth. "Spencer, things are happening!"

"I know," Gill said. And then he saw where the minder was pointing: straight up into the sky, where all of the constellations were changing.

Changing, flowing, forming patterns—pictures far clearer than the ancient Greeks ever imagined the mythical creatures of the zodiac. The stars flowed together, became scenes on a backdrop as wide as space itself. But such scenes!

Disembodied, cancer-pitted brains trailed writhing spinal columns across the sky. "Surgeons" in white gowns and surgical masks marched in line, bearing claw hammers in their hands and staring down on Miranda through eyes that burned. Naked, dead, and rotting Rod Denholms crumbled down the sky, far more lustful and loathsome in death than ever he was in life . . . all of them beckoning to Angela, and thrusting lewdly with bony hips. Ki-no Sung's Lotus knelt in agony, with her hands around her huge, split-open belly, which spewed a horde of malformed midgets, all with Sung's face, that crawled on her like slugs and bit at her bleeding breasts. And all the time she pointed accusingly at Sung, cursing him from writhing lips.

They each of them saw their own worst nightmare written in the sky; even Jack Turnbull and Spencer Gill, standing close to the great crystal.

For Gill it was a sky full of mad Heath-Robinson mobiles, more menacing to him than an army of Frankenstein monsters, or the crazed robots of fanciful science fiction novels. For these were machines that his imagination simply couldn't grasp; they were beyond his machine empathy to comprehend, even to contemplate. But he knew their real purpose was more than that: they were there to distract, to lure his mind from the truth, from its all-important contact with the crystal.

And for Turnbull: it was a repeat performance of what he had witnessed in the Alt Deutscheshaus in a 1970s Berlin. And despite his enormous strength of will and physical strength, it was almost too much to bear. His grip tightened on the machine pistol . . .

And a short, savage burst of bullets stitched the sky, shattered the illusion, brought everyone to his or her senses; momentarily, at least.

"On our side?" the minder's words grated from between his clenched teeth. "The synthesizer? You could have fooled me!" He checked his magazine, cursed, and hurled his empty weapon clattering into the rocks. "And that's me just run dry."

"One final test," said Gill. "That's what it told me: that we're to prove ourselves."

Turnbull looked hopeful. "One last test? And that was it?"

Gill shook his head. "No, it's still coming. I can feel it building."

At which precise moment George Waite shouted down from the ridge of the spur: "There's movement down below. Something—a lot of somethings—are coming up the hillside!"

"Better come back down," Gill called up to him. And to the rest of them: "All of you, come to me now, and bring Fred. Put him over there with his back to that rock." Then he turned to the minder. "Whatever this is, we may as well face it together. Fred, too, where we can keep an eye on him."

Miranda was the first to get to the crystal; throwing herself into Turnbull's arms, she said, "Oh, Jack!"

He hushed her and said, "It isn't over yet. We aren't finished yet."

Angela looked at Gill, saw the way his face was set, knew that this was it. "What do you want us to do?" she said.

"We wait," said Gill. And because he couldn't help it, he pointed the stinger at the crystal where it loomed as big as a blackly shining house, and said or thought: *So here we all are. And now what are you waiting for? You bloody, black-hearted . . . machine!*

Not a good idea, but not such a bad one, either. Defiance is the last stand of the undefeated, the indefatigable.

And the crystal blurred into life, into soundless motion! Like some giant child's humming top without the hum, it twirled until its facets—its doors—were indistinct; whirled until they sharpened up again, like a roulette or wagon wheel, as the rotation slowed. And yet its motion failed to disturb a single pebble in the surrounding scree jumble. And as it slowed . . .

The six ragged human beings who staggered there saw that its doors now bore names, and one number.

From left to right, widdershins, the names read: GILL, DENHOLM, TURN-BULL, MARSH, SUNG, and WAITE. The lone number was 13.

The House of Doors stopped spinning, came to a halt. And:

"Our names," said Miranda.

"All except Fred's," Turnbull said, nodding. "And the number?"

"Sith's," said Angela at once. "3, 1, 4, and 5. They add up to thirteen."

"But don't we add them together to get four?" said Miranda.

"Not in my book," said Angela. "Not this time. 13 will do nicely, thank you. Unlucky for some . . . for Sith, I hope!"

Barney was skittering, yipping again. And out of the near-distant dark came slow footfalls, an eerie slithering, and the clatter of disturbed rocks. Up on the ridge, strange figures—or perhaps not so strange, perhaps familiar—were silhouetted against the darkling sky.

"Oh, my God!" Miranda gasped.

But Turnbull reached inside his combat jacket and took out his claw fragment. "Uh-uh." He shook his head. "God had nothing to do with this, Miranda. No, this was started by an ugly alien little bastard who never even heard of Him."

"That's right," Gill said. "He started it, and now it's up to us to finish it."

And where before the night had been merely fearful, now it was alive with terror . . .

CHAPTER
41

A COMMAND—IN SHARP, Stacatto Chinese—rang out! And Ki-no Sung hissed like a snake, cursed in the same tongue, and said, "They come . . . for me!"

A dozen figures, hard to make out in the pale starlight but plainly uniformed, came sliding down the steep scree slope from the spur. And Jack Turnbull yelled, "Down!" as he saw the glint of blued steel. The six crouched, fell behind a shallow outcropping shelf, watched the uniformed soldiers taking up firing positions. Then another sharp command, and again Ki-no Sung's hiss of warning.

The night came alive with stuttering gunfire! Bullets spanged against the rocky ridge, sending sparks, rock splinters, and plumes of dust flying. And in the flashes of hot light from the muzzles, Gill and his friends could see who their enemies were: the Red Chinese army types from Ki-no Sung's synthesized China! Their red-star insignia and the flapping-ear defenders of their headgear were unmistakable.

"Shit, we're dead!" the big minder said in Gill's ear, not loud enough for the others to hear over the snarl of lead. "We have nothing to fight back with."

Gill glanced at him, saw movement out of the corner of his eye. It was the House of Doors: a blur of motion, bringing the door bearing Sung's name to a central position facing directly across the depression . . . toward the kneeling soldiers. And:

"I am a tool—use me." The synthesizer's "words" floated to the surface of Gill's memory. And now he understood.

"Ki-no Sung's nightmare . . . and his door!" he muttered.

"Eh?" Turnbull picked up a rock and hurled it at the soldiers, who were now advancing line abreast.

"Ki-no Sung!" Gill yelled. "Your door, that one . . ." and he pointed. "You knock, now. Do it now!"

Wild-eyed, Sung shook his head, didn't understand. But the way Gill pointed, gestured, there could be but one meaning. And Sung had learned to trust these people, and this man, above all others. For after all and since the beginning of this nightmarish adventure, there had been no one else to trust.

He went, kept low, crept, reached the door, knocked on the gargoyle knocker above his name, SUNG. And as the soldiers came at the run, firing from the hip, the Korean threw himself flat, rolled away from the door, and hugged the earth. Which was just as well.

Gill and the minder were watching; their jaws fell open as Ki-no Sung's door cracked down the middle and opened outward, and twin-mounted cannons thrust their ugly 30mm reinforced muzzles into view.

"Russian," Turnbull shouted. "I saw the likes in Afghanistan mounted on APCs. Even had the chance to fire one, when the mujahideen captured it." And:

Good job you did, thought Gill, because it was too late to speak and hope to be heard over the blast of the suddenly pounding guns. *A very good job you did. For the synthesizer has snatched the design right out of your head!*

Screams, and a gouting of ruptured earth and red, ravaged flesh (synthesized Red Army flesh) and the narrow reentry shuddering to the thunder and less so to its echoes, as the cannons fell silent and smoked from their hot muzzles. And soundlessly the guns withdrew, and the obsidian panels closed on them.

Where a line of Red soldiers had advanced abreast, nothing was left standing. But small craters put up a veil of drifting smoke . . .

To cover the advance of something far worse!

The *things* came on like snakes; they came slithering like snakes or monstrous tadpoles, but they were neither. They were diseased brains, the brains of George Waite's worst nightmares. Bone-white and whipping behind them, their tails were tapering, knuckled spinal columns; like flensed flagellates pushing them forward.

"Jesus *God!*" George cried his horror.

"Those ugly things!" Miranda was beside herself, bobbing up and down, and clutching at the minder's shoulder. "But what harm can they do?"

"Let's not wait to find out," Gill answered. "You women, stay here. The rest of you . . . let's see what these things are made of."

They took up rocks; Turnbull had his scorpion-claw weapon; with nothing more than these primitive tools, they went out to meet the stuff of nightmares.

There were more than a dozen of the things, and they were fast-moving; Gill himself was the first to find out "what they were made of." Slamming a rock down hard on the brain head of a tadpole, he saw the pulp tear and heard it squelch, but that didn't stop it. The hideous thing *attached* itself to his right leg, clinging like a leech! And as Gill stamped and yelped his horror, a second living brain reared up on its spine, fastened to his thigh, and commenced climbing.

Beside him, the minder stooped to sever a white-gleaming spinal column . . . only to have the "head" leap to his face! He gurgled as the thing covered his mouth, tried to tear it loose, succeeded only after a great deal of frenzied effort. And Turnbull's face was red from the incredible suction of the thing.

But George was the preferred target. As the brains brought the others to their knees one by one, they left them and transferred to George. He was literally covered in the things. Which was when Angela yelled: "George, your door. You have to knock!"

Under a suffocating blanket of diseased rottenness, Waite heard her. Staggering, stumbling, he somehow fought his way to the great crystal.

The doors had changed position again, and the one with the name WAITE stood central. With Gill and the others fighting to rip the leechlike brains from him, George reached out a clutching claw hand to the gargoyle knocker, lifted it, and let it fall. The night-black obsidian panel slid open with a sigh, to reveal an even blacker space beyond. And indeed it was the *jet*-black of deepest space. Space, but purer than the skies above. Deep space, airless, cold, glittering with far stars: it sucked at the people in the reentry, and especially at Waite where he tottered in front of the open door.

A wind gathered, roared in through the door, took dust and dirt and twisted them into spiral streams that buffeted George and threatened to bowl him over. Gill and Turnbull threw themselves flat, grabbed his ankles, dragged him backward even as he fell. And the wind took his nightmare brains and ripped them from him. One by one they went tumbling into the icy void, stiffening as they flew, turning end over end and finally freezing, shivering into shards. Their fragments twinkled glassily, icily, as they drifted from view.

And Waite's door slid shut . . .

But Gill and the others had got the message now. The synthesizer was maintaining the balance, fighting fire with its own—with *their* own—fire. "It can't override its programming," Gill gasped, "but it can give us the means to fight back. When we avail ourselves, so we prove ourselves worthy." And at last they knew what to do.

When the "doctors" with their surgical gowns, masks, and hammers came, Miranda asked no questions but watched the spinning crystal until the door marked MARSH clicked into the central position. And then without a word she knocked. The minder was right behind her, picking her up and lifting her bodily to one side even as the door reversed itself on central pivots.

Fight fire with fire, yes. And projected on beams of living energy, surgical saws came buzzing, ripping into view from the darkness beyond the door—ripping into Miranda's would-be tormentors, too. Which was something that none of Gill's group could watch. But it was over quickly.

Angela's stumbling, crumbling Rods fared no better; their rotting bodies melted in lances of rampant heat from her door.

Then it was Gill's turn. *Fight fire with fire,* he thought as his mad machines came drifting, clanking, trundling up over the ridge and down into the place of the crystal. They were of every crazy shape and lunatic design that a man could imagine, and some that Heath-Robinson himself could never have imagined. They were intent on crushing Gill, mangling him in their weird gears, but he knew exactly how to deal with them.

It came as no surprise to him when he knocked on his door to witness the eruption of a rust-worm. But this worm was interested in only one thing: the destruction of his mad machines. And that, too, was over very quickly.

"Which leaves only me," said the minder. "And surely Sith has something special worked out for me."

But Gill said, "Maybe not. Maybe the synthesizer has something special worked out for him."

Turnbull held his claw weapon tightly in a great fist and looked suspiciously, nervously all about in the night. "There's nothing happening," he said, disbelievingly.

Gill was equally nervous. "Just because we can't see anything doesn't mean it isn't happening. You'd better knock anyway."

And so the minder knocked upon his door . . . which simply vanished, revealing a web of energies that pulsed, crawled, and crackled within the obsidian frame. Turnbull began to back off—and an arc of brilliant blue fire leaped free of the web and struck at the scalloped scorpion-claw fragment clutched in his hand! Held fast by the writhing, sputtering arc of energy, the fragment glowed; likewise the big minder's hand and arm, glowing with a shimmering radiance. But in another moment the arc was switched off, the web died, snapped out of existence, and the obsidian door reappeared in its place.

"Now what the hell . . . ?" Turnbull was on his knees, nursing his hand and arm.

"You've been armed," said Gill, simply. "The claw has been your weapon no less than your machine pistol. Well you've lost the use of the one, so the synthesizer has made up the deficiency."

"You know that for a certainty?" Turnbull picked up the claw, but gingerly.

"Yes," Gill answered in a faraway voice that his friends hadn't heard before, and his eyes were equally strange gazing at the great crystal. He staggered a little then, and his hand went to his brow, but Angela was there to hold the others back from him.

"I think he's done it," she said in a whisper. "He understands the crystal, the synthesizer, and it understands him."

Gill snapped out of it, waved them back from the crystal, said, "Sith . . . he's coming! Just like the last time—when it all went wrong for him, when things didn't work for him—he's coming to do his own dirty work. Coming anytime now. Anytime at all."

Gill was right in one way, wrong in another. Sith was coming, yes, but it wouldn't be at all like the last time . . .

While they waited they tended to Fred. He was still out but he mumbled now and then and seemed restless where he lay with his back to the flat, sloping surface of a rock.

"He doesn't have a door," Angela pointed out.

"Maybe Spencer can explain that," said the minder. "Well, when he's done whatever it is that he's doing." For Gill stood a little way apart, and his attention was rapt on the House of Doors. Having established rapport, he no longer used the scorpion stinger-antenna to communicate with it but simply looked and listened. And he was certain that the crystal was likewise looking at and listening to him. But it was easier now, and he didn't have to concentrate so hard.

He had heard Angela's comment and the minder's answer, and now said, "Fred doesn't need a door. He is a door! He's acting as part of the synthesizer, or rather it is acting through him. But he's only human and can't control it. And while he's unconscious it can't control him."

"Makes sense," said the minder, looking blank. He shrugged, shook his head, turned to Angela, and said, "I wish you'd never asked!"

Suddenly Gill stiffened, took two paces backward away from the crystal. "Sith's been busy," he said. "He's built himself a new construct. One of the few remaining facilities the synthesizer has allowed him."

"Built a construct?" The minder repeated as they backed away from the crystal, which was spinning again. "What the hell for? He has Bannerman, doesn't he?"

"But the Bannerman construct failed him the last time out," Gill answered tightly. "So this time he"—the door with the number 13 clicked into its central slot. There was no knocker, no need for a knocker: this door only opened from Sith's side, the synthesizer's control room—"*this time he won't be taking any chances!*"

The door stood still a moment, then *widened* until the obsidian facet was as wide as three doors. And finally it shattered, came bursting outward onto the scree in shards of black stone, as Sith's new construct crashed through.

At first they thought it was a scorpion; it *was* a scorpion, but with several embellishments. More pincer claws; more eyes, set in the scalloped rim of its chitin-plated carapace; and the stinger . . . was more than just a stinger.

It was in fact Sith/Bannerman, or the upper half of him at least. Rising up, curving forward from the scorpion's rear end, the stinger swayed as before. For two-thirds of its length, it was quite simply a stinger. But the final third was Sith/Bannerman from the waist up. He had arms but no legs . . . but then, what did he need with legs when he had the scorpion? And like some weird, hybrid centaur he surveyed the landscape, not only with the eyes in Bannerman's head but also with the scorpion's eyes, taking in the entire scene at a glance.

The six backed off, they turned and ran, with George Waite shouting, "And how do we fight this, Spencer? Christ, we've no weapons to fight this! And no doors we can use, either."

Gill grabbed up Fred Stannersly, and the minder was there to give him a hand. Ki-no Sung danced and gibbered, urging the others on, while Barney put his tail between his legs and made straight for the steep side of the spur. And indeed he had the right idea, for all of Gill's party were following him.

But while Barney might make it, Gill knew that the rest of the group wouldn't. They didn't have the time, had no strength for the climb. Fred was showing signs of waking when they all fetched a halt at the foot of the scree slope. There, unceremoniously, Gill and Turnbull let Fred slump to the loose scree and the dirt, and turned to face the monstrous hybrid.

And the Sith/Bannerman/scorpion came scuttling, and Bannerman's synthetic eyes burned a deep crimson while his voice *whooshed!* as he called ahead: "The game is over, Spencer Gill. It could have lasted a little longer but no, you had to cheat. Well you can't say I didn't warn you about that. Anyway, since you can't play by my rules, I shall simply take the ball away. The ball and everything else. But basically your lives."

Fred was awake, twitching and mumbling where they'd dropped him to the soft dirt. "Gill!" he gasped. "Spencer . . . the blindfold!"

The Sith-thing had paused; it edged a little closer, with its pincers held open, spread wide to enclose them. "And you," Sith's voice roared like a fire under the bellows and his eyes burned more redly yet, "Jack Turnbull, you damned Neanderthal! Ah, how you gave of your best! But as you see your best wasn't good enough. I shall nip you oh-so-slowly. Nip you men . . . and rip you women . . ." Menacingly, the crab legs scuttled, the scorpion edged closer yet.

But as Gill saw where most of its crystal eyes were focused, and sensed Sith's most immediate desire; his own words returned to mind: *Fred doesn't need a door . . . He is acting as a part of the synthesizer . . . The synthesizer is acting* through *him!*

So why not let it? And Gill went to his knees, tore Fred's blindfold loose from his eyes and forehead, propped him up, and let him see what was happening.

Sith saw what he'd done. He whooshed his alarm, said, "Ah, no!" and came crushing forward. But too late. And:

"Fuck you!" said Fred, and emphasized his words with a forward jerk of his head.

The air shimmered. The scorpion elongated, stretched forty paces deep until Fred released the elastic. And the Sith construct went crashing against the crystal, smacking into it at that same incredible velocity. "The application of an old principle," said Fred then, "that two objects can't occupy the same space at the same time. That's what every pilot thinks whenever he spots another aircraft in his airspace."

The scorpion's carapace was shattered; it seemed to be melted, welded half in and half out of the crystal amid the wreckage of the door that Sith had used. And the Sith stinger swayed helplessly this way and that, while crackling skeins of energy buzzed and sputtered over the entire area of damage.

Gill could scarcely believe it. Until finally, "We got the bastard!" he said. "Fred got—"

The entire alien world blinked out . . . darkness swirled . . . daylight came blindingly. And Gill sat down along with the rest of them, and finished what he'd started to say:

"—the bastard!"

"Wasn't he just," said the minder, hugging Miranda tightly in his arms.

But Angela cried, "It isn't over yet!" And she pointed.

They were on the lighthouse rock, and the Castle stood on the same flat surface where Gill had placed it when first they came here. Moreover, it was the same *size* as when first they'd come here. A very small castle now.

"Deactivated," said Gill. "Yet that bastard survives." His gaze followed Angela's pointing finger.

It was Sith, or the upper half of the Bannerman construct, rising slowly into the air with an antigravity belt around his chest. "The belt," said Gill. "It must double as a shock absorber. That's how he survived that crash. And we're going to lose him."

"Maybe not," said the minder grimly. He still had the claw fragment in his hand, and now he hurled it like a boomerang and with deadly aim. The thing was still energized; lightning arced between it and the floating construct, and it followed the bolt home to Bannerman's chest and sank half of its length into him.

Thone metal cuts Thone metal. Outside, the construct was synthetic flesh; inside, it was a thin envelope of Thone metal. And inside that it was Sith. The claw section had found a vital part of him: the central ganglion itself.

There sounded a whooshing cry, a grating screech, a high-pitched gurgle, and the construct went limp. It lost altitude, drifted a little to one side, fell the last six feet, and clattered down onto the hard lighthouse rock.

When the seven went to it they found it facedown, motionless, dead. And when they turned it on its back a vile mixture of blood and a thin, evil-smelling liquid spilled from the jagged root of the claw where it protruded from Bannerman's chest. The strange, jellylike liquid was Sith, flattening to a stain on the lighthouse rock and rapidly evaporating in the alien atmosphere and unforgiving gravity of Earth . . .

Gill picked up the House of Doors and said, "Fred, about that principle of yours? How does it go? That two solid objects may not occupy the same space at the same time?"

"Right," said Fred.

Gill held up the tiny House of Doors to the sky and said, "They've left. The Ggyddn have left the Earth, but they haven't gone far. They're out there somewhere, waiting for the Thone."

"How can you know that?" Miranda, hugged tight in the big minder's arms, no longer doubted but was merely puzzled.

Gill looked at her, and his eyes were strange and distant again. "I can sense them," he said. "I can talk to their synthesizer. It's the heart of their mother ship, and all the various nodes are now concentrated in her. They are at battle stations, waiting for the Thone. But I think it's time we showed them all something, Thone and Ggyddn alike."

Gill concentrated on the miniature castle in his hand, and slowly turned to face the southeast. "There," he said. "That's where they are." And: "Fred, do you think we can do it one last time, you and I together? For after all, you're the transmat."

"Was," said the other. "But maybe just one last time . . . ?"

They concentrated, and the tiny castle elongated into the sky, curved over the horizon, and disappeared. "Into the heart of the Ggyddn mother ship," said Gill. "Why, a thing as small as that was easily assimilated."

"But not for long," said Fred. "Not if you reactivate it!"

"That's right," Gill answered. "Not if it was a full-sized Castle. For two objects can't occupy the same space at the same time, right, Fred? Two birds with one stone."

And again he concentrated his unearthly will, his machine empathy, in the sky to the southeast.

It was night over the Indian Ocean, a night bright with stars—but for a few brief moments a brighter star shone in the firmament. It pulsed into being like a nova, lasted only a fraction of the time, then died and was gone.

While on the lighthouse rock, Gill said, "Done. It's all over." Then, as Barney came romping and barking from the direction of the lighthouse, the battle-weary group linked arms and headed for Fred's helicopter . . .

EPILOGUE

W HEN STANNERSLY'S HELICOPTER crossed the coast near Plymouth, it had already been flying over weed for half an hour. But the weed was dark brown, in places black, and quite obviously dead. Instead of tossing and churning, it rose and fell on the sluggish swell, and it was plain that the action of the sea was rapidly breaking it down. Seagulls wheeled over it, made rafts of its rotting, scablike masses, pecked at it suspiciously. And cutting through it with comparative ease, fishing vessels were making for the cleaner, deeper waters again.

"We can refuel at Exeter," said Fred, turning to check on his passengers. He looked terrible, but then they all did. "We can eat, too," he went on, "and maybe sleep for an hour or two before going on to London."

But the big minder was already asleep; he lolled against Miranda, who cradled his head. "I'll call London from the airport," she said. "Fill them in on a few more details."

Via his cockpit radio, Fred had already reported the situation, attempted to forestall any desperate last-minute action that might have been going down. Mercifully, there hadn't been any. Common sense, Spencer Gill's kind of common sense, had prevailed worldwide; no one, no government, had resorted to the use of nuclear weapons. In a world of alien-engendered ecological decline—in a world that already had been dying—that would have been the ultimate disaster. And after Fred received the all-clear and passed it on, no one could have been happier with the outcome than Miranda Marsh.

Angela snuggled close to Gill, held him as if she'd never again let go, and said, "What about that one?" She meant Ki-no Sung, who was also slumped in his seat, fast asleep. "He's suffered an awful lot, and with that hand of his . . . he can never be the same again."

Gill said, "He won't have to be. He's a hero. When he gets back to China—I mean the real China—he'll be feted like no one before him. One hell of a comrade, our Ki-no Sung! That's a job for Miranda: to make sure he gets all the fanfare he's due, and that his people back home know all about it."

"I'll see to it," Miranda readily agreed. Following which there was one last thing that Gill had to see to.

As Angela nodded off, and all the rest sat drowsing, Gill settled back in his seat and let his mutant machine mind wander out, out to where there were no machines. Or to where the only machines were alien. But no longer alien to Spencer Gill . . .

Aboard the Thone vessel, the communication system's color code changed and screens throughout the ship began to display a message that was readable to the Thone in the flux and flow of the ever-active walls. This was not a captain-to-crew transmission; it had no onboard origin, and it wasn't a ship-to-ship communication. For which reason it was of enormous and extraordinary interest to the various Thone controllers in their nodes.

They read the message, and sent back: "Who are you?"

"Ask your synthesizer," the answer came back at the speed of thought. "The computer knows me."

"And you say the Ggyddn are no more?"

"The ones you were coming to investigate are no more, that is true. If there are others, they are not my concern."

"And you are responsible for their . . . not being?"

"No, *they* were responsible. I—we—found them unworthy."

"And now you warn us off, too?"

"You have no business in our space, with our world or system of worlds. Check with the Grand Thone. Tell him what I have told you: that the next time we meet, we shall be visiting you. In peace, I hope."

"We will tell him, certainly." And:

"Good!" said Spencer Gill. "Earth out . . ."

BRIAN LUMLEY
ON THE WORLD WIDE WEB
Stop by and visit us on the WWW:
http://www.bright.net/ stryker/dm   lumley.html
(an official USA site)

Also on:
http://www.itv.se/ al090/necroscope/
(an official European site)

And you can reach us at:
<necrotec@globalnet.co.uk>

Barbara Ann Lumley

E-MAIL FAN MAIL WELCOME

Brian would be pleased to answer your E-mail
provided your questions are kept brief.

You can visit these three great sites on the
World Wide Web:

http://www.bright.net/~stryker/dm_lumley.html
(An Official USA Site)

http://www.itv.se/~a1090/necroscope/lumley.html
(An Official European Site)

http://www.vvm.com/~kcorley/deadspeak.html

You can reach us at:

<necrotec@globalnet.co.uk>

Barbara Ann (Silky) Lumley